NO MERCY

MARTINA COLE
NO MERCY

HEADLINE

First published in 2019 by
HEADLINE PUBLISHING GROUP

Cataloguing in Publication Data is available from the British Library

Hardback ISBN 978 1 4722 4940 1
Trade paperback ISBN 978 1 4722 4941 8

Typeset in 12/16 pt ITC Galliard Std by Jouve (UK), Milton Keynes
Printed and bound in Great Britain by Clays Ltd, Elcograf S.p.A.

HEADLINE PUBLISHING GROUP
An Hachette UK Company
Carmelite House
50 Victoria Embankment
London EC4Y 0DZ

www.headline.co.uk
www.hachette.co.uk

For my beautiful new granddaughter Loretta, another wonderful addition to my family.

Also thanks and much love to Darley Anderson, Jane Morpeth and Tim Hely Hutchinson CBE, for over twenty-five years as a great team!

Prologue

2011

Blessed are the merciful, for they will be shown mercy.

Matthew 5:7

Eilish wondered why the fuck she bothered with any of it, but she knew that the feeling wouldn't last. It never did.

Sometimes it was brought home to her that the businesses were all she really had now – and this outcome was something she couldn't have done anything to avoid. Life certainly seemed to throw her more than her fair share of shit-storms, and she could do nothing but sort them out as best she knew how.

She looked down at the photographs. It didn't seem possible that she was here, in her flat, looking at the smiling faces of the people she loved and wondering how – or even if – she should address the catastrophe that had befallen them.

It had all happened so fast, and with such precise planning and foresight, she couldn't help but be impressed. One thing she had been taught in her family was to respect anyone who had a bit of nous about them. You might not like them – and you might want to kill them – but you had to admire their acumen. It was only fair and honest to give credit where it was due.

She poured herself another large Scotch and took a deep gulp. She glanced at one of the photos scattered around her on her bed; it was of her and her brothers as kids. They looked so happy and carefree. But that was another lie, this time for the camera. She wondered how many other families had the same snapshots in their albums – of gap-toothed, smiling kids with their expensive clothes, playing against beautiful backdrops – when in reality they were slowly dying inside.

She was the youngest, the only girl, and they'd treated her as such.

She couldn't get the earlier phone call with her mother out of her head – it was like a worm eating away at her.

She rubbed her belly and wondered if she had really done the right thing, but she had to believe that she had. She had kept her pregnancy secret from everyone around her – and that was all to the good now. As her mother had said, the children in this family were cursed, brought into the world with pain and without mercy.

That was something the Davis family were good at, as anyone would tell you. There was no mercy for anyone – least of all their own flesh and blood.

Finally, she cried.

Book One

1980

Whatever women do they must do twice as well as men to be thought half as good.

Charlotte Whitton (1896–1975)

Chapter One

'For fuck's sake, Mum, anyone would think I was a fucking moron the way you carry on.'

Diana Davis sighed and held on to her temper as best she could under the circumstances. She loved this boy of hers, but she was well aware that he had a lot to learn where the game was concerned. Angus thought that the sword was mightier than the pen. What he needed to understand was that anyone could pick a fight and earn a reputation for violence – that was the easy part. A knife, a hammer or a gun would quickly make a body known to those who didn't matter! The real deal was making sure you got a rep with people who actually *did* matter.

'Well, Angus, you *are* a fucking moron on occasion, that's the bottom line.' She lit herself a cigarette, taking a deep pull on it to calm her anger, as she said candidly, 'You do *not* take anything on yourself until you run it by me. That's the law! For your information, son, you picked a fight with the one man I am currently relying on to bring serious money into my business. *My* business, not yours, incidentally!' She shook her head in frustration. 'Like I need this in my life! I'm fighting against men all the time. I don't want to be fighting you too, son. And if you don't wind your neck in then I will.'

Angus Davis knew that his mother spoke the truth. At nineteen, he was still too young to be taken seriously, and sometimes he was fool enough to try and interfere with things that were, frankly, way over his head. But he did these things for the right reasons – he was trying to look out for his mum. Not that Diana Davis needed looking out for. She could piss all over most of the men she dealt with. And she dealt with a lot of men. Hard men. Men who respected his mother and were more than willing to work with her and for her.

He recognised he had inadvertently undermined her here. It was food for thought. But what bothered him was that the men on their payroll saw him as an extension of her and not as a man in his own right.

'And it doesn't help that you and his son aren't exactly bosom fucking buddies, does it?'

Angus knew when to shut up, and this was one of those times. He had royally clumped Danny Cave while they were both incarcerated in a young offenders' prison awaiting their bail hearings. No one questioned his mother's morals, especially not a piece of shite like Danny Cave. Angus guessed that his mother knew exactly what had been said and why the incident had occurred – after all, there was fuck-all that escaped her attention. His dad used to say she was always up before everyone else had set their alarm clocks!

Unlike his mother, Angus didn't have it in him to turn the other cheek. One of Diana's great strengths was the ability to ignore whatever interfered with her ultimate goals. She could swallow anything if circumstances played to her favour, plus she knew the people involved were usually relieved that they had been given a swerve and that was something to file away for later. He knew that she was right, that often the best way was the hard way; wipe your mouth and keep your eye on the big picture.

8

Angus didn't work that way. Diana expected it from him, but her son had what she referred to as a 'loser's temperament', meaning his temper would be his downfall. As she pointed out frequently though, not on her fucking dime. His lack of control was something she couldn't afford, and his reaction to Danny Cave had really yanked her chain.

He could see that, on one level, he had been out of order. But deep inside he still felt he had done the right thing. After all, she was his *mother*. It wasn't like he had had a tear-up over nothing. It didn't matter that she could more than look after herself. This was different. It was family. It was about blood. And Danny Cave had been out of fucking order – even his old man had agreed with that. Clumped his son in the visiting room, in full view of everyone. He was making a point, and Angus understood that: Danny Cave the elder was telling Diana Davis that he had it all under control. He wasn't going to let his son get away with being a lairy ponce.

Not that Diana Davis gave a flying fuck what people said. She never had. As she had told Angus repeatedly, 'You can't educate haddock.' It was only ignorant fuckers who cared about what other people thought. You had to rise above it, as she had. Who gave a shit in the grand scheme of things? You had to ignore the no-marks, or the fact you were bothered showed you were no better than them.

Diana inspired loyalty in those around her and that was because she would move heaven and earth to help a friend in need. That was why people were so enamoured of her. She would also always listen to reason – provided that reasoning was in her favour. If it went against her interests in any way, it never augured well for those on the other side of the bargaining table. If you crossed her she would hunt you down like a rabid dog.

Angus had a lot of his mum in him, but also a good dose of his father. Big Angus had been a renowned bank robber – he was remembered as the main man. He had been huge, well mannered and a prime mover throughout his illustrious career. Most importantly, he could have a row when the need arose. He was excellent at his chosen profession, and that was because he had a reputation for knowing how to plan, how to recruit and how to execute the perfect blag.

People had travelled far and wide for his opinion and for his take on a rob. And he would give his honest opinion – for a price, of course. He could get in and out in nanoseconds, and always made sure that no one was harmed and no one was too frightened during the event. His calm voice was enough to make the people involved do as he requested. The sawn-off shotgun helped too. But, as his mum always said, it was a prop, nothing more.

His father was a hard man but never towards civilians, and that was very important for his son to know. You never harmed anyone who wasn't in the game, and you never brought in anyone who you couldn't trust implicitly.

His mum was a good teacher, and he appreciated that, but Angus was getting older and he was champing at the bit to get himself fully immersed in the world in which he had been brought up. As young as he was, he believed he was destined for great things – that was a given, considering his parentage – but he felt like it was taking too long to get anywhere.

Angus wanted everything immediately. He wanted to be straight in at the top, not still learning the trade like a fucking plumber or a gas fitter. But he was also aware that his mum, as lovely as she was, would take him out without a second's thought if he pushed her too hard. She would not countenance what she saw as insubordination. She was hard, as hard as fucking nails, when she needed to be.

His granddad had once described her as the only woman he had ever met who not only thought like a man, but could fight like one too. Angus knew the truth of that statement, as did many people who had tried to thwart her over the years. She had fought hammer and tongs to get where she was today. She was at the top of her game, in a predominantly man's world, and that took guts. It also took brains and, more importantly, it took respect. And that was something she had earned in spades.

Unlike his mother, he didn't have her knack for patience, or indeed her knack for thinking things through. That was something that was going to be proved to him very soon.

It would change his life for ever.

Chapter Two

Diana Davis was her son's biggest advocate in public, and also his biggest critic in private.

He was a bit too like his father for comfort. She had loved the man but, just like her son, he had had no Off button. He had relied on her to make sure that everything ran smoothly, which she had done – through trial and error to begin with. Big Angus was a clever man, no one could ever dispute that, but it was she who actually took him in hand and made sure that he used his talents for their good.

She was the one who recruited for him and who made sure that he didn't make a mug of himself. He had a dangerous tendency to rely on his mates, as opposed to looking for more skilled men, who were more inclined to go on the rob with a modicum of sense. Her old man could rob anywhere – it was a knack he had. His problem was he would recruit complete and utter morons because he liked them! Or because he felt he owed them. That was just not good business sense. She had had to explain that to him, over and over again, and finally he had listened to her.

In reality, he had not had any choice; he had come to realise she was far more savvy than he would ever be. They were a good team, and that was something he had cherished in the end, because she had a real business brain and he didn't.

During his biggest lump, she had taken over and not only planned the blags but also recruited whoever she felt was the best candidate for the job in hand. She had done her homework, and he couldn't fault her. When he got out he had relied on her opinions because, after serving that big sentence, he had been determined never to be banged up again.

Big Angus was a natural thief, but he wasn't a natural when it came to picking appropriate cohorts. He would happily take on men who couldn't rob a fucking Wendy house without detailed information. Diana had ensured that she mined the best there was to accompany him on his regular jaunts into post offices and banks and, of course, building societies. Big Angus could always be taken in by a sob story or his misguided loyalty to an old mate who needed a hand to get back on his feet. He was a fucking soft touch.

Diana had taken his natural talent and she had enhanced it. Most of his cronies were well aware that she was the real brains of the outfit. That had suited her, because she wasn't a fool and she knew that she needed to be able to look out for herself should the worst happen. Well, the worst *had* happened – the cancer, that had taken him before his time – and, after his death, she had fought for her place in their world and stayed there.

Now she had to turn this boy of hers into something resembling a Brainiac. And that, she feared, would be the hardest task she had ever undertaken. So far he wasn't exactly the brightest bulb on the Christmas tree, but she felt he had promise. At least that's what she told herself – Christ Himself knew she had her work cut out.

Smiling now, she looked at her son and said, 'Right then, let's put this behind us and go and see your granny. She's cooked dinner for us.'

Angus followed her out, deciding that if she was willing to offer the olive branch he would be a fool not to accept it. Plus his granny was a blinding cook, and he couldn't do any wrong in her eyes. So all in all, he felt that today, at least, he'd had a result.

Chapter Three

'Leave him alone, for fuck's sake, Di. He's still only young, he will learn.'

Jane O'Leary was loud in defence of her grandson, as Diana knew she would be. She couldn't see anything wrong with him – he was perfection personified. Diana got it, he was her flesh and blood. But the woman couldn't see anything that he did as remotely wrong. Jane would defend him to the death – and so she should – but not to her, his own mother. Especially not when Diana was trying to teach him a very valuable lesson about the economics of villainy. It really grated on her sometimes.

'You need to give him some responsibility. That would be the making of him.'

Diana rolled her eyes in consternation. She lit a cigarette and pulled on it deeply before saying in a tired voice, 'For fuck's sake, Mum, he still watches *The Banana Splits*. And you should try getting him out of his pit before pissing lunchtime.'

Jane sighed as she basted the roast potatoes her grandson loved.

'Well, he's his father's son then. We all know Angus, God rest his soul, wasn't nine-to-five material.'

She blessed herself reverently and Diana felt the urge to laugh; her mother was such a hypocrite. This was a woman who would lie under oath without the blink of an eye, yet she saw herself as well up there at the right hand of the Father when it suited her. God, she loved this woman, as much as she aggravated her at times. 'He battered that boy senseless, Mum.'

Jane shrugged casually. 'From what I hear, he was questioning your morals. Young Angus reacted as any man would, especially that big galoot you married. Big Angus would have throttled him too, as well you know.'

Diana was clearly wasting her time.

'Anyway, I heard that young Danny's father was as incensed as your man there. He isn't a fucking fool by anyone's standards.'

The trouble was, her mother was absolutely right. Danny Senior *was* fucking fuming, but only because he was worried that his little ray of sunshine would be taken out by someone close to her. She had a loyal workforce, and some of them were a bit *too* loyal at times, but she wasn't going to knock that. It had stood her in good stead over the years, and she was proud of it. She stood by them as well, and that was how it should be. It was mutual respect.

She and Danny Senior had always got on well together. He must know that she would make sure no one would cross the line. But a rogue fucker? That wasn't unheard of, in their line of business: a new Face trying to make their mark; an old Face who might think they were being sidelined and looking for an in.

The old guard were shitting themselves and she didn't blame them. They really were dinosaurs, and she was more interested in a younger fan base – which she had, because she wasn't a bullshitter. She was still regarded as a force to be reckoned with, her reputation was without stain. She was someone who people dreamed of working for and eventually with. It was well known that if you were a part of her crew, you could only go on to

16

bigger and better things. She basically guaranteed that, because she was respected and she cherry-picked the best.

The problem was that her son and heir was a loose cannon. He needed a wake-up call, and she was going to make sure that he had one. You had to be cruel to be kind sometimes. She would give him something to think about, and she would wait and observe how he dealt with it. Diana was quite capable of being a slippery bastard when the need arose.

She watched as her mother gave her son his dinner on a tray on his lap while he stared at the telly. She saw how her mother smiled at her grandson and stroked his hair and treated him like visiting royalty – which he was considered to be in this house.

Diana had deliberately never had another child because she realised that the more kids she had, the less chance she would have of a life of her own. Her old man had been banged up for a lot of her son's life and she had not relished visiting him with her child in tow. But she had done it, because he had deserved to know his son, and her son had deserved to know his father. It had galled her all the same. She had hated every second she had spent with her son in those prison visiting rooms, even though her husband had been seen as one of the good guys, had been respected by the cons and POs alike. Her little boy had been treated like he was something special because of his father's reputation and he had come to believe it.

She wasn't a fool, she knew that her son wasn't ever going to be an academic, but he wasn't cut out for the norm either. He was bright enough but he had sussed out his father's place in the world at a young age and he wanted to emulate him. He had been brought up on stories about his dad. Stories that had been stretched in the telling and had glamorised his way

17

of life. No one had explained to young Angus the loneliness of waiting for a man you loved and who couldn't parent the child he had produced because he was locked away.

Her son had been fed endless tales of derring-do, and told funny anecdotes of his father's wit and cunning. No one had ever told him that it was she who had kept it all going, even after his death, that it was she who had fought not only to claim what they were owed but also to make sure that it was invested so they could have a good life.

Sometimes, like today, it really did rankle with her, because she had been as guilty as everyone else of turning her husband into a martyr. No one had ever explained to her son that, without her behind him, Big Angus would not have got as far as he had. She made sure that the hangers-on – and there were plenty of them to go around – weren't given fucking house room. And, after her husband's death, she had used the insurance, along with her natural intelligence for earning a coin, to get where she was today.

She sat at the kitchen table with her mum and chatted about nothing of any relevance. But inside she was tired, and she was angry. It grieved her that her son was still filling his head with stories from days gone by and missing the big picture.

No matter how anyone dressed it up to please her, Angus, her darling son, was a spoiled little cunt.

Chapter Four

Jimmy Fernandez was shattered. He had been out most of the night with his brother, Christos, and they were making their last call before dawn.

They were both relieved to see the back of a difficult shift. It was only a Wednesday and it had been fraught with aggravation from the off. What was wrong with these people? Why did they want to shoot the fucking messengers?

They were only delivering what was ordered – and explaining that the prices were going up. It wasn't fucking rocket science. It wasn't as if it was the first time they had delivered bad news. Coke was like gold these days – it fluctuated with the market.

The Filth had managed to cut them off from the docks – Tilbury and Harwich – that's without what had happened up north. It was now an expensive product, which the hoorays in London didn't seem to care about. But the clubbers in London and the home counties were not too thrilled. That was to be expected, but why blame them? They had no say in any of it, and they read the fucking papers surely? The Filth were crowing about cutting off the cocaine trail.

Well, dream on, imbeciles. Everyone knew that was just a piss in the ocean and within weeks things would be back to normal.

It was laughable, but the abuse in the meantime was fucking outrageous.

The price of coke was judged by who was buying it. If it was in certain West End clubs then it was three times as much as anywhere else. It was easier to rinse the punters there because they were such fools. It was also cut to fuck once it went past Whitechapel. There was hardly any gear in the stuff that hit the clubs in Soho anyway. Couldn't get a cat high, but at least they paid without a row. They wouldn't know a decent bit of gear if they were granted it with a royal charter.

As the boys got into their car they were both hacked off with the night's events. Who needed that shit? They were only doing their job. They didn't earn any extra, for fuck's sake.

When the guy in the motorcycle helmet walked up to the driver's window, they both looked at him with genuine interest. The guy lifted his visor. Smiling, he gestured for them to open the window.

Jimmy had a sudden feeling that this wasn't kosher. They were down a back alley in Ilford, and the sun was just coming up.

He took the first shot in the eye.

His brother took three shots: two to the head and one in the back.

He had tried to escape.

Chapter Five

Diana was woken up by the shrill ringing of the telephone beside her bed.

It was six in the morning and she looked at it with trepidation; there was nothing good to be told at that time of the day. She pulled away from the man beside her. He was awake too now, and he leaned up on his elbow as she answered the phone. Like her, he guessed it wasn't going to be good news.

'What?'

Her usual answer to any phone call was uttered with severe indignation. It had served her well over the years. It had always stopped the caller from trying to get their excuses in first. The last thing she wanted was someone's bullshit, especially if they had fucked up and wanted to get their alibi in first. She was only interested in facts.

She was fully awake within seconds, and her voice was shrill as she screamed, 'You are fucking kidding me!' She listened for a few more moments and, when she replaced the receiver, she looked at Gabriel Riley and said angrily, 'Bring the car round, we have an event.'

Gabriel looked at her without moving before he started to roll a joint. Diana watched him while she tried to take in what she had just heard. It was totally unbelievable.

Gabe lit the joint and took a deep pull on it, then offered it to Diana. She accepted it gratefully and took a toke while she tried to comprehend what the hell had happened.

Gabriel looked at her troubled face and said seriously, 'What is it, Di?'

She loved looking at this man. He was a lot younger than her, but they had a connection, they had really great sex and they could talk about anything.

Gabriel was a Jamaican from Kingston, in his thirties. He was a handsome man, a real Rastaman. They had met in a blues club that she had financed, and they had hit it off immediately. In more ways than one. He had supplied her with top-grade grass and she had basically cornered his market.

It had suited him, because she was everything he had ever wanted in a female. Gabriel had never really been attracted to the girls who orbited his world. They were pretty and they were young but they were looking to him to teach them about life. He didn't want that burden – he wanted a real woman, like Diana Davis. She was strong, she was good-looking, but more importantly for him, she was interesting. She always had something to say and it was relevant and it was educational.

He didn't care about the age difference. She had that extra something that a certain type of man could recognise and appreciate. He had been attracted to her from the first time he had clapped eyes on her.

It had taken a while to get her into his life properly. But he had persevered and proved to her that this wasn't just about the sex for him. Though he wasn't complaining, of course – the sex was pretty good – but Gabriel genuinely loved her, and even though she was older and far more successful than him, he didn't mind, because he would have her on any terms. He knew marriage would never be on the cards – she'd made it clear to him from the start she never wanted that aggravation again. But Gabriel wasn't going anywhere.

'Before I get dressed and get the car, tell me what the fuck has happened, Di!'

She tugged once more on the joint before she answered him.

'It seems, Gabe, that someone has seen fit to murder Jimmy and Christos Fernandez. Two lovely young lads who have no clout whatsoever in my business dealings.'

Gabriel looked at her shocked face, taking in the enormity of what she had said.

'Listen, Di, this can't have anything to do with you, darling. They must have done something on the outside. I mean they were fucking harmless. Without you behind them, they wouldn't have stood a chance in the real world.'

Diana didn't reply. She had her own thoughts on what had taken place, but she wasn't going to share them with anyone – even Gabe – until she knew more. That was one of her strengths: she never ever let anyone else know what she was thinking. She certainly wasn't going to break the habit of a lifetime now.

'Get dressed, Gabe, I need to be somewhere.'

She got out of bed and pulled on a dressing gown, and as she walked into her dressing room she could feel Gabriel's eyes burning into her back. Like she cared right now. He was a great fuck and she loved him, but where her work was concerned he wasn't a part of it, no matter how much he might want to be. One thing she had learned the hard way was to never let anyone think they had a say in her life and especially her business. That was wholly her domain.

She had always liked the Fernandez lads; she couldn't understand why they had been singled out for such harsh treatment. But she would find out. And, when she did, God help whoever was responsible.

Chapter Six

Diana looked at the two dead bodies and closed her eyes in distress. There was so much blood in and around the car.

She noticed that their money bag and drugs had been removed before the police arrived. But that was what she paid her lot for.

The young policemen stayed at a decent distance away from her, and the plain-clothes, DI Carter, was already giving the OK for the forensic team to go in. She turned to him and smiled her gratitude.

He opened his arms wide and said grimly, 'Look, Di, this was a hit. It's going to cause fucking murders. You need to sort this quick sharp, darling.'

She rolled her eyes dramatically and said sarcastically, 'Oh, you fucking think? Is that a professional opinion or something you picked up reading the *Sun*?'

DI Carter took a deep breath, aware that he was being observed by his workforce – who already didn't have the greatest respect for him. 'Come on, Di, play fair, for crying out loud,' he whispered angrily.

Diana looked again at the two dead men in the car before turning back to Carter as she said seriously, 'You are right. This does look like a professional hit. But why? Who would come after this pair of ice creams? They are just grunts. Lovely lads, but they don't have any clout. They delivered and they picked up, they weren't important enough to be targeted.'

Carter nodded his agreement. 'So you have to ask yourself, who could these lads have annoyed? Or, more to the point, who could be sending you a message?'

Diana didn't answer him. She couldn't take her eyes off the two young lads whose heads were blown away but who were so low down on her radar she couldn't imagine who would even dream of doing something so heinous and for what gain.

'It has to be something else they were involved in. There was nothing they were doing for me that could warrant this kind of reaction. They were nothing, just basic drones. They had to be doing a Dolly on the side.' She closed her eyes and sighed heavily. 'I'll go with you to tell their mum as she is a mate. Fucking hell, they had the easiest job in the Smoke. How did this happen?'

DI Carter didn't reply. He liked Diana Davis – he always had – but she needed to have a good long look around her. Because if this wasn't an outside job then it had come from within. Like her, he couldn't see why these two young guys had been targeted. She paid enough to make sure they carried out their jobs without aggravation, even though they were well down on the food chain.

This had to be a professional hit, and that was always a worry, not just for the police but for everyone concerned. This was not a little contretemps, this was a well-planned murder of two young men.

No matter what Diana wanted to believe, DI Carter couldn't shake the suspicion that this was the start of something big. So he told her as much, because he respected her and because he wanted a heads-up himself when it all went fucking Pete Tong.

Chapter Seven

Rosina Fernandez was devastated. She looked first at the policemen on her doorstep and then when she saw Diana she knew immediately what had happened.

She crumpled to the floor in utter distress. She was a small woman with thick dark hair and large brown eyes. Her sons had looked like her, but they had inherited their father's height and his physique. She had four sons and two daughters altogether and she had brought them up alone after her husband had disappeared one day and never returned. She had accepted her lot, as she had always accepted whatever life had thrown at her.

Diana watched as her friend was lifted up and laid on to her sofa, and then she waited as one of the policemen explained to her the circumstances of her sons' deaths. She watched Rosina pull herself together, swallowing down her hurt and her anger. She was clearly not going to say a word until she knew exactly what her sons were being accused of.

Rosina knew the benefit of keeping quiet until you knew the score. She wouldn't risk incriminating her sons. She would fight for them and their reputations, dead or alive. She had other sons to think of too, and she knew the score as well as anyone.

Diana watched as the other policeman poured out a couple

of large Scotches. She gave one to her friend as she said firmly, 'You can all fuck off now.'

She waited until they had cleared the room, then, taking her friend's hand, she said sincerely, 'I'm so sorry, Rosina, but I don't think this has anything to do with me or their job.'

Rosina swallowed the whisky down in a gulp. She nodded her agreement.

'They weren't doing anything for me that could warrant this kind of problem. I have to ask you, Rose, were they caught up in any other work that I didn't know about? Maybe with their older brothers?' Diana guessed she was wasting her time, but she had to ask. 'Or any outside agency?'

She looked into her friend's face for something that might tell her that this woman knew more than she was letting on. Normally Rosina was straighter than an arrow, she couldn't lie if her life depended on it. Unless it was for her sons, of course, then she would lie like a professional.

'Come on, Rose, this is important, you need to tell me anything that you might think was even a bit suspect.' There was the hint of a threat in Diana's tone.

But Rosina shook her head in anguish. 'Really, Diana, they loved working for you. They wouldn't dream of working for anyone else. And the older boys are still working for Marcus Green. I swear that they never spoke to me about a different job.'

'Are you sure they weren't doing a Dolly? Honestly, at this time, why would I even care, darling? Like you, I just want to know what happened.'

Rosina shook her head again in despair. 'There was nothing that I can remember, Diana, and they loved you. You've always been my good friend, and they knew that.'

She finally broke down and started to cry. Diana held her

tightly as she sobbed. She whispered kind words and hugged her friend close, all the time wondering who was trying to fuck with her head, and planning what she would do to them when she found out.

She stayed until Rosina's family were all around her and then she left.

She was on a mission now.

Chapter Eight

Gabriel smiled at Diana as she got into her car.

'Fucking hell, you still here, Gabe?'

'Of course I'm still here, darling. You think I wouldn't wait for you, see you're all right?'

Diana arched a brow at him.

'Look, Gabe, I really don't need a fucking minder. I have more than enough men working for me. I appreciate your zealousness but I have never needed looking after, and that isn't going to change any time soon, darling.'

Gabriel looked at her as if he had never seen her before. Her tone of voice and her attitude was something he knew she could unleash on other people but rarely on him.

Diana saw the effect her words were having on Gabriel. He had been in her life for over two years and for the first time he was angry.

Gabriel nodded eventually. He was holding back his fury and his hurt; he had to get out of there as soon as possible before he retaliated. If he didn't go, he would fucking lose it with her and that is exactly what she wanted. She wanted someone to take out her frustration with tonight's events on. He knew her better than she knew herself.

'Do you know what, Di? You go for it. I'm going home.' He

got out of the car and then, bending down, he looked in the window at her and he said quietly, 'I'm warning you, lady, one day you will push me away and I will finally take the hint. You need someone beside you tonight. It's not a weakness, Di. But what do you do? You treat me like one of your workers. Well, fuck you.'

He walked away from her, and she watched him go. He was wrong. She didn't need anyone and that suited her. It always had. She didn't care about him going, it was exactly what she wanted. She had to remind him that he wasn't important to her in any way.

But, deep down, she knew it wasn't true.

Chapter Nine

Diana was in Barking Police Station, drinking brandy with a policeman she had been dealing with for years. He was a Filth who was known as a friend of the criminal fraternity and who could be relied on to liaise in certain circumstances. He was also a personal friend of Diana's – though they didn't advertise that fact, naturally.

Derek Jones was an old warrior who had been around in the sixties as a PC, and he had earned his reputation as a good guy while he simultaneously climbed the ladder in the force. His success came from knowing everyone's secrets, and he was not averse to trading them for a price. Never for money though – only for the common good. He would trade one scam to find out about another, bigger scam. He didn't always use the information he garnered – he was far too shrewd for that – but he did barter it.

He was liked and respected, a perfect go-between, especially for the people higher up the food chain who valued not only his expertise but also his sense of fair play. He had been the reason there had not been a turf war for a long time.

Derek looked at Diana and said honestly, 'I haven't heard a dicky bird, Di. That's the truth of it. Neither have any of my lads. They would have mentioned it.'

Diana nodded; she had expected this. But she was well aware that Derek would likely be in the know sooner rather than later, so she said as much.

'Well, Del Boy, I'm just reminding you that if and when you do hear, I hope I will be the first to know.'

He rolled his eyes theatrically. 'Well, what do you think, Di, eh?'

She finished her brandy. 'I know, Del, but this is a fucking melon scratcher all right. I can't imagine who would want to out that pair. They are of no interest to anyone other than their mother.'

Derek Jones shrugged. 'It's a different world now, Di. There's no decency any more, we are dealing with complete fucking lunatics. It's the new generation, they want everything overnight.'

Diana didn't answer him. He was as out of the game as she was.

And that was not a place she wanted to be.

Chapter Ten

Silas Warner was worried, and he wasn't a man who worried without cause. He was well aware he was going to get a visit, and he wasn't exactly looking forward to it. He had made a big Rick, and he wasn't sure how he could walk away from it.

He had known deep in his guts that he should never have agreed to deal with the Coleman brothers. They were on the way up, but they were unpredictable little fuckers. And, now that he had heard the bad news about the shooting in Ilford, he was getting anxious.

Christos and Jimmy had been introduced by him as a new avenue to sell drugs – no more and no less – he just thought he was opening up a new way for them to sell their product. That he had been given a sweetener had just seemed a fair exchange at the time. He couldn't have foreseen what might happen – he wasn't Doris fucking Stokes.

Now he was at panic stations because he would have to tell Diana and she did not suffer fools gladly. But he had genuinely believed that he was doing what he was paid to do.

He had tried to open up a new revenue stream that would benefit everyone concerned – true, mainly for him and his sons. Only they were now worried for their lives.

Diana wasn't exactly an easy woman, even when she wasn't

pushed. She made a vicious man look like a pussycat when she was affronted.

What had possessed him? He wondered if he had a death wish.

He wiped his hand across his big moon face and knew that he would have a hard time convincing Diana that there had not been an ulterior motive.

He ran to the toilet again; his bowels were looser than a trophy wife's credit card. He had fucked up big time. His only hope was to confess. Diana Davis would appreciate hearing the truth from him directly. She was a lot of things, but she was fair. No one would argue about that.

He took a deep breath and picked up the phone. She would much rather meet him on neutral ground, especially if she was about to off him. If only he could help his boys.

All he could do was hope that he could talk her round in some way.

Chapter Eleven

'Mum, listen to me, will you, for once? Let me put my ear to the ground and see what I can come up with, yeah?'

Diana looked at her son, who she loved with all her heart, but who was about as useful as the fucking Old Bill that she was paying a fortune to at this particular moment in time. She stopped herself from saying that though. She had to let Angus think that she did actually listen to him and – more importantly – that she genuinely was interested in his opinions, however off the wall they might turn out to be.

'Look, son, if you can find out anything I will be only too pleased, believe me.'

Angus was thrilled to hear that answer; she was finally giving him a chance. Until he proved himself, he knew she wouldn't take him seriously, and that was something he needed to do as soon as possible.

He was determined to sort this out before she did. He wasn't completely sure how to bring that miracle about.

But he had an idea.

Chapter Twelve

Angus was extremely irritated because, as far as he was concerned, anyone on the Davis payroll should automatically agree with him. That came with the territory.

Royston Rogers was not best pleased. He worked with Angus, and he liked him, but he wasn't happy about doing anything that Diana wasn't in on. He might not be feminist of the year, but he knew who paid his fucking wages. Plus he respected her; she was a Face in her own right. It didn't sit right with him to go behind her back, no matter how innocuous this fucking upstart might try to make it out.

Royston Rogers, nicknamed Trigger, was caught between two fences. At the end of the day he worked with Angus and, as much as he could be annoyed by him, he knew that he meant well. He was young, he was impulsive but he was loyal. There was no getting away from the fact that young Angus would defend him to the death. Roy felt the urge to do exactly the same for him but he didn't want to put himself in the line of fire for no good reason. Angus wanted to meet up with that muppet Warner! He was about as trustworthy as he was honest.

It stood to reason that he was involved somehow, and that

could not be a good thing – especially as he was a known consort of the Coleman brothers. But he kept his own counsel and followed Angus out to the motor.

Roy had annoyed him enough as it was.

Chapter Thirteen

Davie and Peter Coleman were laughing as they walked out of the back of their cousin's betting shop in East Ham.

Davie Coleman was known as a bit of a wag, and was generally seen as a comedian by his peers. He was also the more ruthless of the brothers and the quicker to take offence. He had a natural arrogance that set people's teeth on edge, especially when he was taking the piss out of them. Both the brothers were on the up, but it was the general consensus that Davie was the one in charge, and that suited Davie Coleman down to the ground. Peter was bigger and heavier, but he wasn't exactly sharp as a tack. The relationship worked well for them, and they were both happy with their stations in life.

As they went to their BMW, neither saw the two men with the sawn-off shotguns stepping out of the shadows of the small car park and aiming them at their chests.

It was Davie who caught sight of them first, and he opened his mouth to speak. But before he could utter a word, he was felled alongside his brother. Lying on the ground he watched in shocked amazement as the two men in balaclavas calmly walked away, without a second glance.

Then there was pandemonium as the boys' cousin discovered

them lying on the filthy concrete with their life's blood seeping away. They were twenty and twenty-one respectively.

By the time the authorities arrived, the rain had started and the sound of distant thunder could be heard over the traffic noise.

There was blood and mud everywhere – as one of the constables remarked drily, 'They picked a good night for it anyway.'

The laughter was subdued, but it was there nevertheless.

The Coleman brothers wouldn't be too sad a loss for the police, there was no denying that.

Chapter Fourteen

'Are you trying to be fucking funny, Silas?'

Silas Warner knew just how unpredictable Angus Davis could be. Even without Diana as his mother, he would still have been an intimidating enemy. He had a lot of his father in him. His sheer size alone, coupled with his rugged features that seemed to be permanently in frown mode, was worrying enough, but it was his voice – rich, deep and with an edge of menace in even his most mundane statements – that confirmed Angus had what it took to be an enforcer, and that was something you were born with. You couldn't acquire that, it had to come naturally.

He had old-school masculinity, and he had it in spades. He wasn't fully grown yet, so Christ Himself only knew what the finished article would be like!

Silas wasn't exactly easily scared. But there was a deeply dangerous streak inside this lad that would one day make him a very formidable opponent.

The fight he'd had in the nick was already earning legendary status. He'd striped that boy up bad. Now Angus was giving him a dressing down, and he was quite willing to stand there and take it. But he believed that all was not lost. If Silas could get a word in edgeways, he could salvage something out of this abortion.

Silas took a deep breath and looked Angus in the eye. 'Would I try to be humorous in a situation of this magnitude? I just want to see if you are interested in a business proposition, that's all.'

Angus looked at Roy, and they both shook their heads in disbelief.

Angus took his time lighting a cigarette and he pulled on it a few times before saying to Roy, 'He's got some fucking gall, I'll give him that.'

Both Roy and Silas were watching his cigarette carefully. Angus was known to use them as a weapon. As he pointed out, they were cheap and effective and, if used properly, left a scar so the person involved would have a lifetime reminder not to be a cunt in the future.

The small lock-up was cold and dark. Silas was sitting on the only chair, a rickety affair that looked and felt like it would collapse at any moment. There were what looked suspiciously like bloodstains on the floor and the walls, and evidence of rats was everywhere.

Psychologically, Silas couldn't fault the lad. He knew how to instil fear – and he had to admit, he was doing just that!

Angus smiled suddenly, a bright smile that lit up his handsome face.

'Don't tell me – you want to offer me the drug deals in London and Spain that were to be the Coleman brothers'? I assume you will be wanting a taste, as it was your connections that set this up in the first place? And you would like me to forget about this diabolical liberty you said the Coleman brothers committed – namely outing two of my very good friends, the Fernandez brothers. Thus, your thinking is two wrongs really can make a right.'

Silas closed his eyes. He was weary, he was terrified, wondering if and when he would find out his ultimate fate – and if he could negotiate for his sons' safe passage. 'If you talk to the Colemans' cousin, Jonny, he will tell you all you need to know about the set-up. He was in on it too. But I swear I didn't know they would be stupid enough to out those two lads – there was no need for that, it was utter madness. But these are the Colemans we are talking about. Jonny is a good lad, he has a bit of nous about him, which is more than I could say for his cousins.'

Angus stared at the frightened man in front of him and toyed with the idea of beating him to death to put an end to this charade.

'I think you can safely assume I know just about all there is to know about the deal. But please feel free to enlighten me, in case I missed something.'

So Silas Warner talked.

He talked as if his life depended on it – which, of course, it did.

Chapter Fifteen

Diana Davis wasn't sure what to think when her son sat her down and relayed his antics of the last thirty-six hours to her in minute detail. One half of her was impressed, she had to be honest about that much. But the other half was mortified that he didn't understand the actual economics of what might have happened had he failed.

He had managed this feat of derring-do because he was her son, and she wondered if he had any inkling that might be the case. But, in the interests of fairness, what he had achieved was pretty impressive. He had done sterling work – albeit with a taste for the dramatic – and she had to commend that.

She poured them each a coffee and they sat in silence for a few minutes, each occupied with their own thoughts.

Finally, Angus said determinedly, 'I had to sort it, Mum. The Fernandez brothers were my mates, and it was my business that had been affected. If I had let you square it, where would that have left me? I know you think I'm still a kid, but I'm not. I have given that old tosser Silas a pass because I know he's a decent broker, and he knows the people in Spain well. He won't try any antics now, not after the carnage he's caused for everyone. I own him now, and he knows that. I am flying out to Marbella with Roy on Thursday to meet with the people concerned. We will go through the options, get everything in place, and that will basically be it.'

Diana half-smiled and nodded. 'You did well, considering, I will grant you that. But in future you must run things past me first, OK? I need to be in the loop, son. More importantly, we need to work together – and I promise from now on that I will listen to what you have to say.'

Angus reached for her hand. 'That's all I want, Mum. I don't want to go behind your back, but I ain't as stupid as you think. How could I be, with you and my dad as role models? All my life I have heard the stories about you two. Well, now I need to make my own stories.'

Diana couldn't argue with that. And it would not augur well for the future if she pushed him away. This son of hers was a ticking time bomb. She could keep a closer eye on him if she let him have some leeway. She was prepared to keep him within her sights and if he fucked up, she would be there to sort it, no matter how bad.

She honestly didn't have a choice. He was champing at the bit. He had proven himself today, and he knew it. She had to accept that.

She sighed and then she said honestly, 'Be careful of Willy Mc-Cormack, he's a wily old cunt. On the plus side he was good friends with your father – did a few blags together in their younger days. I will talk to some old Faces who have retired out there, so you have contacts of your own. It's full of opportunity – but then it always was, being so close to Morocco. We know a fair few on the run out there.' She gave him an assessing look. 'But, knowing you, it will be the nightlife you'll be more interested in.'

Angus grinned and gulped his coffee. 'Don't worry, Mum, I will sort the business end first.'

Diana could hear the relief in his voice. She wondered if she was just too close to him and, as his mother, couldn't see his potential. That was a definite probability, as her old man used to say. If Angus naused this up, she would know – one way or the other – and she had plenty of people on her payroll who could smooth the way for him, if needs be. She decided to change the subject and get on to firmer ground.

'How is Lorna?'

Angus groaned. 'She's well upset. One of her mates, Maggie Simmonds, jumped in front of a train at Upney station a few days ago. Fucking mental, ain't it? Only fifteen. What could be so terrible you would want to top yourself at that age?'

Diana was genuinely shocked. 'What, little Maggie? I heard there had been a suicide, but I never dreamed it was anyone we knew. Her poor fucking parents.'

'Lorna reckons she was suffering from depression but she kept it quiet. All her mates are in shock so I don't think I will be missed too much this weekend. To be honest, I'll be glad to get away from it all.'

It didn't strike either of them that they themselves had both been the cause of more than a few deaths over the last few days. It was a knack they both had – the ability to separate their criminal life from what they termed their real lives. Neither of them saw anything even remotely ironic in the conversation they were having.

That was why they could do what they did, and do it so well.

Chapter Sixteen

Jonny Coleman was absolutely fit to be tied, not because his cousins had been murdered but because they had brought on him untold fucking aggravation in the form of the Davis family. The last thing he needed was a tear-up with that lot. He didn't stand a chance.

Unlike his cousins, he was well aware of his limitations. He had to make a name for himself as a person of integrity and a person of trust – not someone who knocked off people like the Fernandez brothers on a stoned and drunken whim. If Davie and Peter weren't already dead he would cheerfully have killed them himself.

Now he was waiting for the knock on the door at any time. When it came, he needed to be ready.

He sipped his brandy and looked nostalgically around the small drinking club in Ilford – the only thing his old man had ever achieved. Jonny had inherited it when his father had been shot in a betting incident in Leeds prison a few years before. He had taken it over and kept it going and made a success of it. His clientele might not be exactly kosher, but they were good people, in their own way, and they respected him and his father because he ran a tidy club where people could talk business without fear. He also slung a few strippers on often enough to keep the wives and girlfriends out.

Now everything he had worked for was at risk of being ruined over that pair of fuckers' stupidity. He looked around him at the shining bar, and the newly painted walls; it wasn't the fucking Ritz, but it was a decent little earner. He hoped his mum got a few quid for it, if and when the worst happened.

Jonny was twenty-seven years old, and the chances were he would not see twenty-eight – and all because he had loyalty to his family. If only his cousins had shown that same sense of loyalty. He was sorry they were dead, and he would miss them, but they had caused so much upset. He still felt a burning anger towards them.

When the door opened and Angus Davis walked in with his side-kick, Roy Rogers, it took all Jonny's nerve not to make a run for it.

Angus stood there for a few moments, taking in his surroundings. He liked this place, it had a nice atmosphere. He had supplied the strippers on a few occasions – and he had appreciated that Jonny had always insisted on them being of a certain age, not schoolgirl material.

The three men looked at each other eventually, long and hard.

Then Angus said jovially, 'That brandy looks the business. Pour a couple out for me and Trigger, and we can go through the Spanish deal. What do you say?'

Jonny felt the ice water retreat from his bowels and, smiling weakly, he said hoarsely, 'Pick a table and I'll bring them over.'

The funny thing was, he liked Angus. You couldn't help it – he was charming, and he could be fun. Jonny also knew that what Angus had done to his cousins was necessary for the equilibrium of their society. And, in all honesty, they had brought it on themselves.

Jonny would forgive, even if he wouldn't forget. After all, what choice did he have really if he wanted to survive?

They settled down to business.

Chapter Seventeen

Gabriel and Diana were sitting in her office in her house in Epping.

She was sipping a glass of Chardonnay and he was watching her, as he so often did. There was something about her that really affected him. She had a lovely face, even if it was a little battered round the edges these days. She had a good body, she kept herself fit, and she knew how to dress. Her eyes were a light blue that looked grey when she was angry, and her hair – expensively cut and conditioned – was a deep shade of blonde that was too perfect to be natural.

He felt the usual stirring within him as he looked at her. She was graceful, feminine – the way she moved had always drawn him in. She was argumentative and arrogant at times, and she could be scathing, but that was only a part of her persona. When they were alone together, especially in bed, he saw a softer, more vulnerable side to her that no one else knew about.

'Will you stop staring at me, Gabe? You're giving me the heebie-jeebies.'

They both laughed.

It was her way of breaking the ice. Since she had basically dismissed him on the street, they had been strained. She genuinely wondered what brought him back. If he'd treated her like she did him, she would have left him – or stabbed him, depending on her mood at the time. But he put up with her, and a big part of her was pleased that he did – though another piece of her couldn't understand how he could allow her to treat him like she did.

'I don't think anything could scare you, Di.'

She laughed and finished off her wine, then she held out the glass for him to refill it for her. She was a bit pissed, and she was enjoying the sensation; it felt good to lose control of her emotions sometimes.

'Oh, I do get scared occasionally – everybody does, I suppose. But it's whether or not you let other people know how you're feeling that counts. After I lost Big Angus, I was scared, deep inside, but I swallowed it down and I got on with it. My old man used to say, "People only know what you tell them." It's true – same with emotions, people only know what you show them.'

Gabe sat back down in the easy chair and nodded his agreement. 'You worried about young Angus going out to Spain?'

'Wouldn't you be, in my shoes?'

Gabe lit a joint and pulled on it deeply. 'He's going to be all right. He's a bit more on the ball than any of us give him credit for. Plus you have a few people to keep an eye on him out there. And Royston is as loyal as fuck, he will be there beside him.'

Diana sighed heavily. 'What's wrong with me? It doesn't matter how old he gets, he will always be my little boy. Until this week, I wouldn't trust him to tie his own shoelaces without me looking over his shoulder. Now look at him! He's the new kid on the block.' She laughed. 'I feel fucking old!'

Gabe knew there was a grain of truth in what she was saying, and didn't laugh with her. He knew her too well to risk that – especially after she had had a few glasses of the old vino. She could turn on a coin, and he didn't want a repeat of the other night.

Instead, he knelt down in front of her and handed her the joint. 'Remember the old saying, a woman's only as old as the man she feels!'

They laughed comfortably together then, and he sat by her feet as they finished the joint. He loved her far more than she would ever realise – and he believed that, in her own way, she loved him too.

Angus was young and he still needed to learn the finer points of negotiating, but Gabe had a few contacts out there too and, with them and Diana's, the boy should be in good company. All they could hope was that he had the sense to keep his alcohol intake down and not let his natural belligerence shine through. The people in Spain were hard fuckers. But, if he played his cards right, Angus would be a good match for them. Diana had long tentacles, and she had bankrolled more than a few of the people who were now the movers and shakers out there. She had always played the long game and invested wisely, not only with money but with the people she had loaned it to. You didn't get to her stage in life without having a sense of who you could trust – and what to do with anyone who broke that trust. Diana was ruthless, but she was also funny, approachable and stagger-ingly intelligent.

He felt her squeeze his shoulder, and he placed his hand over hers. She had beautiful hands, always well manicured. She was all things to him, and that made him vulnerable. But he pushed those thoughts away, because they were finally back on an even keel and he didn't want to ruin that.

'The Fernandez brothers' funeral is next week, Gabe. I don't know how Rosina will cope, God love her.' The sadness in her voice was evident.

He pushed back his head, so he was nestled between her legs. 'She's a strong lady, Di. She will get over it eventually. But she will need her family and friends around her.'

Diana nodded and sighed. 'The Colemans' funeral will be without mourners, because I've put the word out. What a pair of little fuckers! And the Fernandez funeral is going to be packed, I've made sure of that. It's a help to the family to see their loved ones so well thought of. It's not much, I know, but it's all I can do.'

Gabe stood up and refilled both their glasses, without answering her. In all truthfulness, he didn't know what to say. This was the part of Diana that he would always fear: her vindictiveness.

She knew the Coleman brothers' family well too, especially the mum. They had also been friends for years. But Diana could turn on anyone, without a backward glance. It was like she deleted them from her brain somehow.

Once she decided they were persona non grata, it was as if they had never existed. Not in her world anyway.

Chapter Eighteen

'I'll only be gone a few days, darling, a week at the most. If I can get the business out of the way sooner then I will.'

Lorna Connolly was nearly sixteen years old and she knew bullshit when she heard it. She was a good-looking girl, and while her looks had attracted Angus Davis from the moment he clapped eyes on her at Mass, it was her intelligence that had won the day – that, and the fact she wouldn't sleep with him, no matter what.

She wasn't stupid, and she certainly wasn't going to waste her virginity on just anyone. She would save it for her wedding night, like God intended. Once it was gone, she couldn't get it back, and that meant it wasn't going cheap. It was a mistake too many girls made these days; men didn't want someone else's leftovers, they wanted to know they had been there first. She wanted the full package – the dress, the house, the kids, the lifestyle – and she wouldn't settle for less. Lorna knew her worth.

She plastered on a sweet smile. 'Honestly, Angus, you go and have a lovely time. It's been a tough week all round. I need to knuckle down for my exams anyway. I intend to do well, you know that.'

He smiled back at her. She was a fucking Brahma, this girl of his. She was young – not that he was old – but she had the right mindset for the life she would be leading. He had found his life's partner, young as they were. He had known, the first time he had seen her, that she was special – and that had been proved to him, time and again, since.

Even at fifteen, she looked and acted much older; she drank the occasional glass of wine but didn't smoke anything, legal or otherwise. She was on the ball, she knew what she wanted to do in her life, and she was willing to work for it.

He would have more chance of breaking into the Bank of England than her drawers – and even that pleased him, if he was honest. Not that it stopped him trying, but he was quite happy to be naused off, because he knew the wait would be worth it. Plus there were plenty of girls out there only too willing to drop their drawers without a fight as and when he felt the urge – which he did on a regular basis. He had a feeling that Lorna knew and turned a blind eye. She was fifteen going on thirty. He actually loved her – not a word he would ever have used lightly.

But he was looking forward to a bit of suntanned skirt out in Spain. Everyone knew the sun loosened the inhibitions. Lot of blondes went out to Marbella hoping to snare a Face – and he was, after all, a Face. When he was finished, he was determined to be *the* Face. The Face of Faces, as he told himself. That was what he was working towards anyway. Like Lorna, he was a determined personality. And, like Lorna, he would stop at nothing to get exactly what he wanted.

'It's Maggie's funeral on Monday, Angus. I don't know how I can bear it.'

She looked totally woebegone, and he instinctively put his arm around her and hugged her close.

'What a thing to do, eh? Step in front of a fucking train! I mean, why would she do something like that?'

Lorna shook her head and, pulling away from Angus, she

whispered, 'It was terrible, I couldn't believe it. One minute we were there, waiting for the train, and the next she just threw herself in front of it. Just jumped! I couldn't believe what I was seeing. I tried to grab her, but I was too late. I see it every time I close my eyes!'

'Oh, darling, it must have been horrific! Did she say anything to you? I know you were good friends. Did she confide in you about what was bothering her?'

Lorna shook her head again, and Angus could see she was near to tears.

'No, Angus. She said nothing about what was bothering her.'

He knew that she had had a big argument with Maggie a few days before the suicide, but he was too shrewd to mention that fact. Lorna must be feeling so guilty over it, and he wasn't going to start that conversation tonight. There was no way he was going to postpone Spain to accompany her to Maggie's funeral – and if he wasn't careful, that would be the upshot. He knew it was selfish, but it was what it was. He'd never been a fucking romantic hero, and he wasn't starting now.

What Maggie had done was an abomination, especially for Catholics. Worst sin you could commit, killing yourself! Life was a gift from God, for fuck's sake! You shouldn't mock God. Oh no, Angus had it all planned. Like his old man had told him: enjoy your life, sin yourself stupid. And, when you get to a certain age, you repent your arse off. It was how it worked – cover all your bases.

'Listen, darling, you know that you were a good friend to her and you did all you could. She was obviously a bit fucking Radio Rental, that's nothing to do with you. Go to the funeral and pay your respects, my lovely. But remember, she wasn't the whole five quid, and that's nothing you could have changed.'

Lorna looked at him and smiled again; she looked happier this time.

'That's just what I needed to hear, Angus. You always say the right thing. Her mum wants me to speak at her funeral, and I will. I will honour her and her life, because we were great mates.'

He held her close again, feeling the outline of her rather pert and firm breasts. He had a bet with himself that they were a D cup. He hoped that he was right.

'Life is for the living, darling, especially at our age. Whatever demons she was battling, I honestly don't believe anyone could have helped her with them.'

'I know you are right, Angus. I feel so much better now.'

He hugged her tightly again, trying to cop another quick feel. He had dodged a bullet there. He loved this girl, but not enough to cancel what he knew was going to be a blinding week in Spain.

He was sorry for poor Maggie and all that, but she was the instigator of a lot of grief. He didn't want any part of that circus, because that is what it would be – a load of hormonal teenagers with something to be neurotic about. He would send an outrageous wreath, his mum would go with Gabe, and he could lie back in Spain with a large joint and a compact little bird.

He remembered the priest at his father's funeral saying that his old man was in a better place where he had thrown off worldly things and worries. Something like that anyway – he couldn't remember the exact terminology. What he did understand, though, was that once you were gone then that was basically it. Nothing could hurt you any more. No, life was definitely for the living. The dead were to be remembered and loved. Or not, depending who the dead person was, of course.

Sinead Connolly, Lorna's mother, came bustling into the room, making a big production of it as usual, causing Angus and Lorna to jump apart – as if they'd been caught in bed together naked.

Angus smiled at her amiably. She had missed her vocation in life, she should have been a nun. She watched her daughter like the proverbial hawk. She didn't fucking need to. Lorna might as well have had barbed-wire knickers for all the chance he had of getting in there.

Silly old bat. But he smiled and said yes to the cup of tea, and then counted down the time till he could leave without a fight. Lorna's mother made Nosferatu look like an amateur. He sipped his tea and made small talk with the potential mother-in-law. What else could he do but get the old bat onside? And even though they had a sort of stand-off, this was one war he was going to win. Her daughter would be his, by hook or by fucking crook. So she could keep her face that looked like a well-slapped arse, and suck it up. No one stopped him doing what he wanted.

Bring on Espania! He needed a bit of the old currant bun on his skin. And he wanted to get out of London and get this new business venture off the ground. He wanted to prove to his mum and everyone else just what he was actually capable of. He felt that this was his time and he wanted to cash in on that feeling, because he was determined to make himself the number one.

He had planned a quick night out before his flight tomorrow, with Tommy Becks, a mate who had just been released from Pentonville. He was a great guy who had been treated abominably by the judicial system. Angus was looking forward to it – the perfect evening before he went on his Spanish adventure. Tommy was home, and that was something to celebrate. He also felt that his own elevation into the criminal fraternity was worth a few chugs of vodka.

Life was finally looking up, and Angus Davis was going to enjoy every second of it.

Chapter Nineteen

Tommy Becks wasn't a big lad, but he looked like he could handle himself, which he could. He was capable of causing serious violence at the drop of a hat.

Like Angus, he knew that the majority of the population would only fight if they needed to. Like Angus, he could harm someone badly without any real reason for it. Getting paid to hurt someone wasn't beyond his remit, and everyone knew that – especially the police.

Since he was a schoolboy he had been repeatedly arrested for violence. He was what the psychologist at the young offenders' unit referred to as 'prone to violence', to which he had answered aggressively, and with a large dose of sarcasm, 'Gee, you fucking think?'

But this time he had been on remand for attacking a man who had tried to sexually assault one of the dancers at the club he minded. Imelda was eighteen – well stacked and with the face of a virgin – earning her crust for her little boy as best she could. Tommy had heard her scream and found a forty-year-old money broker trying to get her into his Mercedes. Her top was ripped and her eye was already closing up.

He had smashed the man around the car park, and then smashed him again, explaining that he was out of order and she was a dancer, not a fucking escort. You pay to look, but don't you dare touch, because that is one of the things that will get you hammered. No matter what you might do, legally or otherwise, women and girls were off the agenda. You didn't ever hurt a female, even if you felt like it. Mouthy, argumentative birds were a part of their world. The women they dealt with were very vocal, especially if they caught you out with a bit of strange. It was their prerogative – after all, they were the number one bird, and they had the right. Even if they were so incensed they attacked you first, even with a weapon that could be anything from a stiletto heel to a glass or a bottle, it was still a big no to retaliate.

Tommy was now in the pub, being fêted by his friends as a hero. But three months on remand had not done wonders for his demeanour. The money broker had finally dropped the charges when he had been battered to fuck by a group of teenagers on skateboards outside his rather nice house in Sidcup. The leader had reminded him that this was just the start of a war campaign that would make Monty look like an amateur.

You had to look after your own: Tommy had with Imelda, and Angus Davis had with him. They had always been mates, but now Tommy owed Angus. He owed him big time, but that suited Angus down to the ground. They were birds of the proverbial feather.

Angus came into the pub like the champion he was. He had made a name for himself, literally overnight. He was finally someone in his own right, and not because of his parents. That alone was making him buzz. He could already sense the difference in the people around him – the respect – along with a new attitude that told him he had finally made his own name that had nothing to do with his heritage. He knew the value of getting the people who mattered onside. His mother had taught him that.

Angus stood in front of Tommy with his arms open wide, and the two young men hugged tightly. This was observed by everyone in the room.

'Great to see you home, Tom, and not before time.'

It was dramatic, just what everyone wanted to see. These were two men who had earned respect and who were both dangerous as fuck.

The atmosphere in the pub was electric. Angus had put two grand behind the bar, and Roy had brought in a top DJ. It was packed out with young people determined to have a good time, and the free drink and the notable DJ guaranteed that.

The Oaks was owned by Diana and had been recently refurbished. It now attracted a much younger clientele, and that was why Angus had decided to hold the party there. It was ten minutes away from some decent clubs, and it was also off the main road. If any trouble occurred, it could be taken care of quickly and efficiently, without too many witnesses. That was the great thing about East London: everyone knew the score and they were more than happy to keep out of what wasn't their business.

Angus looked at his friend with pride. Tommy was a handsome fuck, and no mistake. He had that extra something that guaranteed him an in to the world they inhabited. Like Angus, he had the likeability factor that was so important to success in their game.

He had been nicked for a crime that should never have been a crime in the first place. It was laughable to think that he had been banged up because a fucking middle-aged man couldn't distinguish between fact and his fantasy. Well, that ponce was now in traction and would think twice before he hassled another young girl. Angus remembered his mum had always drummed

into his head that sex offences against women – rape or assault –
were the only crimes where the victim had to prove it had
happened. She used to say, 'No one asks a burglary victim if
they wanted it to happen. Or a mugging victim. No one questions a bank when it gets robbed.'

She was right and all. Why should a girl have to prove she
was attacked?

Tommy passed him a large tequila and, taking it, Angus shouted
above the noise, 'Come through to the back with me, Tom, and
we can get away from the noise. We've got a lot to catch up on!'

Tommy followed him through the packed-out pub. He could
smell sweat, Blue Grass perfume and Paco Rabanne aftershave.

After Pentonville, it smelt like heaven.

Chapter Twenty

Jonny Coleman walked into The Oaks pub with his head held high and his shoulders back. He knew that he had to front this all out if he was going to redeem himself and his family. And the only way he could do that was to make sure that Angus Davis and his mother knew that he wasn't going to lose any sleep over his cousins' demise. Truthfully, he could happily have whacked them himself for the trouble they had caused him.

He felt sure he could work with Angus and he hoped that Angus was willing to give him a chance. His cousins' stupidity would always be there between them – that was human nature. He would just have to put the work in proving himself for years.

He looked around the pub and was impressed. It was expensively decorated and full of young people who were all either high or looking to get high at some point during the evening. There was a huge customer base in this place alone. Like Angus, he knew that the police were still unaware of the new wave of drugs. The plods were still going after the poor heroin addicts. They didn't see cocaine as too dangerous because they were all on it themselves. It was taking over from speed – it wasn't the drug of fucking rich people any more. It was within any clubber's reach, along with MDMA.

It was a market that was desperate to be regulated – and with the foreign gangs involved, it needed to be regulated pronto. That was where he could come in, because he could sew it all up mathematically – he knew that Angus was as aware of that as he was.

They were young and they were hungry, and they recognised that in each other. They both needed to be that little bit more on the ball than their counterparts, and he would make sure that they were.

Angus Davis was becoming known as someone who was willing to listen to reason. Rumour had it he'd taken that on board from his mother – it was something people always said about her. The Davises weren't like the old guard who were set in their ways and unwilling to change – which was why *they* were all either banged up or living on their past reputations. It was a different world now, and it was changing by the day.

Jonny was given a large gin and tonic at the bar by Roy, who everyone knew was Angus's minder. He was expertly walked through the crowd to the end of the bar, where Angus would be holding court. He observed Angus and Tommy Becks walking out of the back office together, and he knew he was witnessing a match made in criminal heaven. He couldn't fault either of them – he would have done exactly the same in their positions. He sipped his drink and looked around him at the strange that was congregating at the bar.

Angus greeted him like a long-lost brother, which told everyone there that he was an accepted part of the firm, that his cousins' rash actions were forgiven, and that he was a welcome addition to the new order.

By the end of the night, Jonny Coleman was drunk – content in the knowledge that he was walking a brand-new road – and he couldn't have been happier.

Chapter Twenty-one

Angus woke up at the Marbella Beach Hotel and stretched happily. He walked through his suite and opened the patio doors to step out on to his large terrace. He stood there for a few moments, scratching his nuts and taking in the blue waters of the Mediterranean Sea. It was a beautiful vista all right, and he loved it.

He had been out to Spain many times as a kid, but now he was here as a businessman. He could feel the heat of the sun on his skin, and he closed his eyes in ecstasy.

Through his mum, he had an interest in quite a few clubs and wine bars. She had got in on the ground floor, with his dad. Puerto Banús didn't even exist until 1970, when it had been built by a Spanish property developer – called Banús, of all things! Since then, it had become the playground of the rich and famous, and also the rich and not-exactly-kosher.

Marbella was the perfect place for anyone who needed to launder money or start a new life, because it was getting a bit difficult in the UK. Morocco was a short boat ride away, so for anyone interested in purchasing guns, drugs – or even going on the run for a while – it was the perfect destination. It had everything that a body could want or, indeed, need. Spain was where people retired to live in the sun, and where business deals could be done in relative peace. As long as you dealt with a like-minded Spaniard, you were rocking in more ways than one!

Spain was like the old Wild West, just waiting to be conquered by the right people. The seventies had been populated by people like his parents, and the eighties were when Spain's non-existent extradition laws were being used to their utmost. There was a legal system in place that practically guaranteed that anything you felt like doing could, in time, be done.

It was a con man's dream destination, and now that included the timeshare shysters and the people selling off Spanish land that they didn't actually own to naive Brits looking for the dream home in the sun. The con men were starting to irritate the real criminals because they were giving the place a bad name, and that was not good for anyone. But, for all that, the place was still where people wanted to go to relax, drink and make merry.

It was only a couple of hours' flight from the UK but, unlike Benidorm and Calpe, Marbella was still considered upmarket and had a certain cachet to it. It had everything, from wine bars to nightclubs, and no expense had been spared on these establishments. Angus had been well impressed, but he wondered what his mum would think about scantily clad young girls dancing in cages. She could be a bit funny about things like that. But, as the manager of the club explained, you didn't have a dog and bark yourself. They brought in the punters – along with the named DJs, who were a breed apart already.

Not that he was complaining, of course. And as he was now going to be one of the main drug suppliers, he knew that it would be like printing money. Clubs, drink, girls and drugs went hand in hand for this generation, and that suited him right down to the ground.

He was meeting with Willy McCormack that evening. Angus

knew him from the days when he used to come out here on holiday as a kid with his mum and dad. He had not known till recently that his mum had invested heavily out here and was considered one of the old guard by everyone.

She was a shrewdie all right. If it had been left to his old man, he would have just treated this place as a massive piss-up. Angus knew that he had a lot of his father in him – he could be a flake. But he also knew that he had his mother in him too and he was determined to make sure that, as much as he liked to play, he got the work sorted first.

He heard the bedroom door open and watched as a tall redhead with lightly tanned skin, wearing his soiled shirt, walked towards him. In the clear light of day she wasn't as nifty as she had seemed the night before, but she was still what he would class a sort. She went into the small kitchen and started to make coffee. He assumed she had been here before, and that didn't surprise him in the least.

She wasn't exactly a wilting violet, which was a relief. He didn't want aggravation of any kind – especially not from a professional virgin, and there were plenty of them out here, looking for a fucking mark, though he was a bit young to be hustled like that. He assumed that she had been designated to him, along with the other girl who he had actually fancied. Such was the life of a young man on the cusp of greatness.

He laughed to himself as he called out to her gaily, 'Morning!'

She smiled again and yawned. She didn't have the greatest railings. He knew she was a cokehead, but he wasn't going to say a word. She was a one-night stand; he wasn't interested in marrying her. He just wished he could remember her name. He was sure it started with a J, but he couldn't swear to it. Fucking tequila shots were a bastard.

He had lost the girl he had met earlier in the evening – she had made this one look like a dog in comparison – but it had been a wild night and, as far as he could remember, he had had a blinding time. He didn't have swollen knuckles or any bruises, so there definitely hadn't been a tear-up of any kind. He was glad about that. But he was also a bit annoyed with himself, because he knew that this was not the time to get too out of it. This wasn't a jolly boys' outing, this was a serious work event – and his mother would be monitoring him, because she wasn't a mug and she knew him well.

People would be reporting back to her and, even though it irritated him, he understood her reasoning. He was still only a boy in her eyes – in most people's eyes – which was why he had Roy watching over him like a fucking Norland Nanny. He had to swallow, because whatever he 'decided' would have already been decided by his mum first. She would just be waiting to see if he agreed with her, because that was how she rolled. He had accepted that now: she knew her onions, and she had the final word. It did annoy him, he was only human, but without her he wouldn't even be here.

His old mum had surrounded herself with a big and loyal team. She really didn't need him, but she had given him a chance. He couldn't let her down.

He sipped his coffee, and then he said seriously, 'What's your name, sweetheart?'

She grinned lazily and, walking towards him, she placed her well-manicured hands on his chest. 'It's Leona.'

He pushed her hands away roughly, and said genially, 'Fuck me, I could have sworn it started with a J. Get dressed, darling, and fuck off. I'm a busy boy.'

He admired the way she did as she was asked, without a word. He wondered who was paying for her time.

Because it wasn't going to be him.

Chapter Twenty-two

Willy McCormack was a big man in all ways. He was well over six feet, overweight, and loud like a foghorn. He shouted as a matter of course, and he loved a good joke – especially at his own expense.

Willy was still in receipt of a thick head of hair, an expensive set of teeth and the gift of the proverbial gab. He could charm the birds out of the trees, and the drawers off almost any woman he set his mind on. His name and reputation helped, of course, and the younger women he romanced were always given a lovely gift and the sob story that he was married and he loved his wife. The point was, he did love his wife, with all his considerable heart, and she loved him back. But she turned a blind eye, because she knew that these girls were just an occupational hazard.

Katherine McCormack was a lot of things but she wasn't a fool. They were living in Spain, where the ugliest man on the planet could pull – if he had a few quid and a good rep. She knew these girls saw themselves as being able to usurp her, the mother of his children, and, if possible, give him a baby – which was the real prize, of course, as it meant they would be taken care of permanently. But she knew her Willy, fucker that he was, loved her with every ounce of his being. Didn't stop her wanting to stab him in the heart though. And it didn't stop her knowing that his misdemeanours were the talk of the Costas. But she prided herself on being a realist. She wouldn't cause World War Three because he was shagging a young girl who couldn't ever keep him interested long term.

They not only had children together but they had built their empire together, and she was not about to throw that away in a hissy fit. He had been enamoured of strange since day one – that would never change. She was intelligent enough to realise, early on, that it was part of the lifestyle and nothing personal. They had strip clubs, hostess clubs and now they had the lap-dancing clubs; he was surrounded by good-looking girls constantly.

She had no intention of going the way of her friends, forcing a divorce from a man they still loved and who they knew better than anyone else ever would. Who they knew would destroy them, because he had no choice. The men they were married to didn't have any intention of divorcing them until they were caught out. Then they turned vindictive, because deep down they didn't want to divorce their children's mother – and worse, they didn't like being shown up for the pieces of shit they really were.

It was laughable really, because if she had even looked at another man – or another man had come after her – Willy would have murdered him without a second's thought, and he would have been patted on the back for his actions by his peers. But, even knowing all that, Katherine loved her husband. And, come what may, she made sure that his girls were removed from his eyeline within weeks. In fairness, he did usually get rid of them first, and she appreciated that he did that for her. He didn't allow them to get a foothold or to publicly humiliate her.

That had only ever happened once; a young North London girl with big tits, and even bigger hair, had thought she had pussy-whipped him over two nights. Katherine had actually felt sorry for her. She had arrived at one of their restaurants with her little friends in their skimpy clothes and cheap shoes. Willy had nearly passed out with annoyance, and she had observed from a distance as they were removed from her presence – and removed from Marbella. They couldn't have got a dose of clap, let alone another job. Willy had made sure of that, and his anger had been astronomical.

He had apologised to her repeatedly, until she had finally told him to let it fucking go. She was over it, and the sooner he was, the better it would be for them. But it had shown everyone that she was not to be ignored. Overnight, she was suddenly flavour of the month, especially when it concerned the girlfriends of those men whose weddings she had attended and whose wives she was still good friends with.

She was also on the lookout for her old friend Diana Davis: Diana was, like her, a survivor. Diana could also out-think and out-manoeuvre the men she dealt with. That was why she had the creds and she had the respect of men who only saw women as wives, mothers or strange.

Katherine also knew that her husband was on the road to destruction. Well, she wasn't surprised. But she was not going to see her sons done out of what they were entitled to. She was a loyal wife, but she was a much more loyal mother. She might have swallowed her knob where her husband's little sluts were concerned, but when it came to her kids, she would take out anyone who stood in her way.

If only Willy listened occasionally. Diana was a good friend to her, and she owed her a lot. She also recognised the fact that, if anything happened to her old man, without Diana she would be fucked. She was aware that Willy was considering tucking young

Angus up, and she just couldn't comprehend why her old man would even dream he could get away with such skulduggery. It was another bad decision that was caused by the white stuff.

When anyone selling a certain product started to snort said product, it never ended well. Willy should have known that better than anyone – after all, it was how he had become king of the hill. So she was digging, and she would find out what she needed to know. Like her sons, who saw their father for the lairy cunt he was, she wasn't going to let him ruin everything because he had got a taste for the snort. After all these years, Willy had become a fucking cliché. She didn't know what was worse: the way he had carried on in the past, or the way he was carrying on now. Either was embarrassing for her, whatever way she looked at it.

All she could do now was minimise the scale of destruction for her family, and she was determined to do just that.

Because she hadn't lived with Willy McCormack for years without learning something.

Chapter Twenty-three

Roy Rogers was tired, but he was enjoying this sojourn in Marbella with young Angus. And he was impressed, despite himself, at how well the young man was acquitting himself.

Roy was not there just as an observer – he had to report in to Diana, and Angus was aware of that. He had told her that the boy was handling himself well, but he was also having a bit of a good time into the bargain. That was par for the course, especially where Angus was concerned. That boy could have a night out in a morgue. It was a part of his considerable charm unfortunately. But, all in all, Roy was well pleased with how things were turning out – better than he had ever expected.

His only real worry was he didn't trust Willy McCormack, and that was because he sensed the animosity coming off him in waves. He clearly resented what he saw as Diana sending a young pup in to take over his business, even though he knew as well as everyone else that it was actually *Diana's* business – always had been and always would be. She had made sure of that from the first investment – and she had put a lot of dosh into said investments. There was no one on the Bella who didn't know the truth of that, especially anyone who dealt with Willy; they would all be waiting with bated breath to see how things panned out. As always, Roy's money was on Diana.

She would be all over this, if he knew her as well as he thought he did.

He willed his phone to ring so he could find out what Diana wanted him to do next. He had been hearing some disquieting things about Willy McCormack, and he had reported back to Diana. The general consensus was that he was snorting his own blow, and that was never a good situation.

Cocaine made people think they were being had over, made them paranoid and, in extreme cases, it could get them killed. Should be a government health warning on those little plastic baggies – 'Don't snort whilst being a cunt' – it was detrimental to the people around you. What Roy had found the most inter-esting, though, was the amount of people willing to tell him about Willy's stupidity – on the quiet, of course. That told Roy two things. One, that people had had enough of the Scottish wanker. And two, that the problem really was out of hand if he was making enemies of the people who relied on him for an earn.

He sat patiently nursing a large rum and Diet Coke, while he waited for Diana to tell him what his state of play was to be.

One thing with this job was there was never a dull moment.

Chapter Twenty-four

Abad Said liked to think of himself as an entrepreneur. He had been born in Marrakesh and spent his childhood between Morocco and East London, as his father was a travelling man.

His mother, Amina, had died when he was a baby and he had been cared for by his maternal grandmother, a woman he still couldn't bring himself to like, let alone love. His father, Abad Senior, said it was because she blamed him for her daughter's demise – and that even though she knew that was a load of old shite, it kept her happy, so who cared?

When he was old enough to look after himself, he travelled with his father, a drug dealer with long hair, a handsome face and an eye for the ladies. It had been an education all right, and he had loved every second of it. Consequently, he spoke perfect Moroccan and perfect cockney – a lethal combination, because he had inherited his father's good looks as well as his appetite for chasing women. He also enjoyed the occasional male bed companion, and it fitted perfectly into his lifestyle. He was a hedonist in every way, and even at the Mosque he didn't feel that he was doing anything wrong.

He and his father had a good relationship. Abad Senior was now a wealthy man, bringing up a new family with a Moroccan girl he had fallen in love with while setting up a drugs run in Tangiers. These days young Abad was the main man, and he loved it. He worked under his father's jurisdiction, and that suited him too. He had no problem fitting in with whoever he was around at the time and, in the drugs game, that went a long way to securing trust and, more importantly, friendships. A strong friendship was paramount to good negotiations and earning goodwill.

He was looking forward to meeting up with young Angus Davis. They had a great rapport and genuinely liked each other's company. They had a lot in common, and they were more or less of an age, though Abad was a few years older. They particularly shared having a parent who pulled all the strings, and they both accepted that with outward good grace, no matter what they might feel inwardly.

Abad's father and Angus's mother went back years and anyone would think they were in a mutual appreciation society. Nevertheless, their boys were under no illusions that they would also take the other out on a whim, if the situation warranted it. Such were the vagaries of the drugs kingdoms.

Abad Senior was the undisputed king of the hashish and cocaine deals that happened in Marbella. It was just a short trip across the water, and it was a well-planned and well-executed business. All the correct people were bought off generously, and the men involved were discreet and blended in with either environment, wearing the djellaba on the Moroccan side, and changing into smart, bespoke clothes before hitting Spain.

They had it basically all sewn up and, though it wasn't devoid of problems, so far there had been none that couldn't be sorted quickly and easily. Usually, the person who had transgressed did a disappearing act – another great use for the regular sea journeys.

All in all, Abad was content with his lot, and as he walked into the offices of the Magico Club he was looking forward to seeing Angus again.

Chapter Twenty-five

The offices were on the sixth floor of a large Spanish-built block. It was innocuous enough, with the club itself spreading across the whole of the ground floor. The offices were spartan and without the glitz and glamour of the rest of the place.

The club was done out in a mix of chrome, glass and elaborate tiling and mirrors, designed to show off the girls who danced in the nightclub and the private rooms where punters could enjoy a quiet evening away from the prying eyes of wives and girlfriends. It was a lucrative business, and Magico was a club that was sought after by anyone who was anyone on the Banús.

In the office Abad was given a large whisky – Chivas Regal, the real stuff, not the shit they served the customers – and he sat on a low black leather sofa and lit himself a Camel cigarette happily.

Big Willy McCormack was his usual larger-than-life self, and although he looked a bit the worse for wear, with eyes that were red-rimmed and manic, he was exuding his usual charisma. There had always been an underlying danger about Willy that was a part of his charm but would also remind people exactly who they were dealing with. He was unpredictable, and that worked to his advantage, obviously.

Abad remembered a story his father had told him about a

wild night in Tangiers when Willy had been mortally offended by a Moroccan guy who had inadvertently knocked his drink all over his white linen shirt. Willy had cut his throat and left him behind the restaurant, gone back to the boat, changed his clothes and come back to the dinner as happy as the proverbial pig in shit. Another night, he would have bought the bloke a drink and not said a dicky bird; he was unpredictable all right. He was also snorting coke like it was about to be rationed, and that didn't help with his temperament.

Willy poured a large vodka down his throat and immediately got himself another. He had his two usual goons with him, Larry Pike and Petey Webster. They had been friends since they were kids, and they were like the Three Amigos. Imposing men, and dangerous in their chosen fields – they were a winning act.

'How's your old man? Still knocking out kids with that young bird?'

Abad laughed. 'Regularly! He's trying to get me to settle down now!'

They laughed at the absurdity of the situation. Abad Senior was a model husband and father these days.

'The price we pay for getting old, boy!'

Abad swallowed his drink and his glass was immediately refilled by Petey Webster.

'Where's Angus? He taking the fucking piss or what? I hate waiting for people.'

Abad just shrugged. He had no intention of getting into this kind of conversation, especially not with Willy.

Petey was now cutting up lines of coke on the glass surface of the coffee table, big fat white lines that were glistening in the late-evening sunshine. Abad didn't mind a blast now and again, once his working day was over. He used it to prolong the night, he had never seen the sense in using it to think. The whole deal with coke was you didn't fucking think, your brain started racing like a train all over the place, and your attention span was limited.

He watched as Willy snorted two huge lines, one after the other. Abad was aware that the other two didn't follow suit. Then the door crashed open and in walked Angus and Roy, all light-coloured clothes and bonhomie.

Angus rubbed his hands together and said jovially, 'Right, I'm here! Let's get this party started!'

Chapter Twenty-six

Willy could hardly contain his annoyance, and everyone in the room was aware of that – especially Angus, who seemed to find it amusing.

Willy's addled mind wondered if the boy's youth and arrogance were the real reasons he disliked him so much. He had a good earner with Diana, but to send this child out and expect him to treat him like visiting royalty really rankled. They all watched as Petey poured Angus a Jameson's and Roy a rum and Coke.

Angus sipped his drink daintily, holding the glass so his pinkie was poking out like Lady Bracknell, and he said in a thick Cork accent, 'Irish whiskey and guns, the Irish way of life.'

Abad laughed, but Willy didn't. It annoyed him that the boy didn't drink Scotch whisky, that he made a point of refusing it to deliberately annoy him. At least, that is what he believed at this moment in time. In all honesty, he preferred Jameson's himself, but he couldn't really broadcast that fact to the nation. He was being paranoid, and they could all see it. He was so out of it, he was capable of discovering what he saw as an intended slight in an ashtray.

Willy was once a man of presence and refinement, who was respected by his peers, and whose name could instil fear into the hearts of the hardest men in Europe. Looking at him now, anyone who knew him then would be embarrassed to see the caricature he had become.

Somewhere inside, Willy was thinking all this, he just couldn't find the words to say any of it out loud. He felt the familiar tightening in his chest that told him he needed to slow down and clear his head. He wasn't a complete fool; he still had moments of stunning clarity. Unfortunately, they were becoming few and far between.

Looking around him at the young men who he knew intended to mug him off, he felt a pang of sorrow. They were nice lads in their own ways, and he would kill them humanely. A bullet to the head, quick and clean. After all, as he had explained to his partners, he wasn't a cruel man, this was just business.

Diana would see the sense of it; she knew the danger that young fucker would one day be to her. He had too much of his old man in him for Willy's liking. He was a natural-born thief. But unlike his old man, he didn't rob banks – he wanted to rob the hands that were feeding him.

Willy knelt down and snorted another couple of lines of near pure cocaine. He snorted with real zeal, throwing his head back and sniffing loudly. He felt the rush as it hit his brain, and wondered why he had never bothered with this before. He was like a born-again teenager, and he could feel the stench of treachery all around him. Even his wife was beginning to seem a bit off with him. What was her problem? He worked hard and he played hard – she'd known that from day one.

'Any of that left to sell to the punters, Willy?'

Willy grinned and said sarcastically, 'Plenty more where that comes from.'

Angus smiled that amiable, friendly smile he had that made people like him. 'I'm only asking because you are snorting it like it's an Olympic fucking sport. I haven't seen someone snort so fast since the barrister at my dad's trial!'

Now they did all laugh – even Willy, who was experiencing one of his lightning mood changes.

'You're a cheeky little sod!'

He stood up unsteadily and pulled Angus into a tight bear hug that lasted long moments. Everyone in the room knew it had to hurt, but Angus didn't make a sound. He just allowed it to happen and smiled that easy smile that aggravated Willy so much.

Eventually, exhausted, Willy let him go. He looked deranged – even his magnificent hair suddenly looked electrified. He felt that he was somehow letting himself down, there was a part of him that knew he was too out of it again. Angus just patted him on the shoulder gently and went across to the sofa, where he sat down.

Abad had moved over so Angus could join him. Willy observed them for a few seconds and realised that they really were the new generation, and there was nothing anyone could do to stop the march of time. He envied them their youth and the times they lived in; he hated that they were both only there because of the people who had created them. Neither of these fuckers had ever really known the streets. Never had to do a day's real collar in their lives. It had all been handed to them on plates.

He would enjoy getting rid of Angus especially, because he was an irritating little twat who had an arrogance that really got his goat. The jury was out on Abad at the moment, but he wasn't ruling it out. Abad's old man was pussy-whipped these days, but Willy could see it for the fucking liberty it was. If Abad decided to play the hero when his playmate was being removed from the premises, he would have signed his own death warrant.

Chapter Twenty-seven

Willy knelt on the floor once more and sat back on his hunkers. Larry Pike pushed another large vodka into his hands, and he took a deep draught before he settled his gaze on the two young lads. He was aware of Roy being there, but that was par for the course. Diana wasn't letting this ponce out without a minder, and he completely understood that. Roy Rogers had his creds, there was no doubting that.

He watched Angus and Abad in fascination. They looked what they were: friends, old mates, two vibrant young men who had led a charmed life. Angus sipped his whiskey and smiled. As the two men began chatting, it was as if nothing that had just gone on had been noteworthy. Willy had squeezed that skinny little fucker like an orange and – he had to give credit where it was due – the lad hadn't batted an eyelid. He knew men who would have been destroyed by his actions, because they would have understood it was a precursor to something *much* more serious.

He watched them intently; his brain was in overdrive and his heart was beating loudly in his ears. 'You look immaculate, Abad. Is that Armani?'

Abad nodded. 'Got it in London last time I was over, bought myself some blinding gear, and stopped off at Browns for me shoes, thanks to your tip, Angus!'

The two men laughed jovially. Willy shook his head in mock despair. Was this really the next generation of Faces? His brain couldn't take it in.

'You sound like a right pair of tarts, going on about clothes and shoes like a pair of fucking women.'

Angus laughed ostensibly good-naturedly. 'Oi, you! Being well turned out isn't a crime these days, is it?'

There was a hint of underlying menace in the question but Willy was too far gone to pick up on it.

'Seriously, can you two hear yourselves?'

Abad took his lead from Angus; he knew when to keep his trap shut

Angus laughed out loud – a real laugh, deep and rich – and, looking at Willy, he said, 'I hear you were a bit of a gent in your day, Willy, all bespoke suits from Savile Row and monogrammed shirts! Eddie Richardson said they used to call you the dog's gonads.'

Now all the men were laughing, even Roy, because that was true: he had been a dandy in his day had Willy McCormack.

Willy swallowed down the rest of his vodka. Once again, his glass was immediately replenished. He pulled himself to his feet and wiped his nose vigorously. He was well aware that he was getting a reputation, but he didn't give a shit. He was Big Willy McCormack, he could do what the fuck he liked. Especially on the Port.

He looked at Angus and wondered how Diana, who had a shrewd business brain, and who could coax a guinea out of a ten-pence piece, could have got this kid of hers so wrong. His boys were like him: shrewd to a fault. He had made sure of that. He laughed suddenly, a genuine laugh.

'Here, Angus, you still doing that word-a-day thing with the dictionary?'

Angus stood up and, laughing along with Willy, he said, 'Funny you should say that, Willy. My new word yesterday was "miscreant". It's another word for traitor. It's a great one, it rolls off the tongue. Miscreant: it means immoral, evil, unprincipled.'

Abad felt the danger in the air and wondered where this was all leading. He could feel the tension coming off Angus in waves.

'Miscreant. A posh word for a cunt, if you like, Willy.'

Willy was completely and utterly drunk now, as well as coked out of his box. He was aware that something was occurring; he just couldn't quite work out what that might be.

Angus walked to where Willy was standing by the huge glass windows, and he said smoothly, 'Now today's word is a fucking belter. It's "defenestrated".'

Willy was nonplussed for a moment. But he was willing to get into the craic – he had forgotten that he was going to kill this boy, and that it had all been planned to the last detail.

'De fucking what?'

Roy stood up and joined Petey and Larry. The atmosphere was charged. Even Willy was aware that there was something not quite right.

'It means to die by being chucked through a fucking window. Who would have thought there was a word for that?' Angus was genuinely amused that such a word could be in the English language.

Willy was looking at him with absolute amazement. And he had to agree that was a showstopper, in all fairness. A word for such a criminal act didn't seem possible, but one thing he knew was that Angus took his words very seriously. Somewhere in Willy's head he wondered if it was a legal term.

'It could happen to anyone, Willy, especially to someone who was foolish enough to think they could get one over on me or mine.'

Once the words had finally penetrated his brain, Willy looked around him with abject disbelief. He saw his two oldest friends and Roy Rogers, a man he admired and had always liked, surrounding him. Angus was still smiling that fucking annoying smile he had; he was clearly enjoying himself. And why wouldn't he? Willy would have been smiling like that himself if the boot had been on the other foot.

He had been well and truly outfoxed, tucked up, and the treachery of his oldest mates was not lost on him. He was absolutely devastated. He looked at Larry Pike and Petey Webster, who he had brought up the ranks and given a good living to. He was a dead man – there was no way out of this – and somewhere in his drink- and drug-addled brain he knew he had brought it all on himself.

'Fucking come on then, you treacherous bastards. I ain't going down without a tear-up.'

Abad watched as Willy put up a good fight, but he was no match for the four men who systematically beat him to a pulp and, once they had subdued him, picked him up and threw him unceremoniously through the large glass windows that over-looked the Mediterranean and the beautiful beach.

When it was over, Angus poured himself another large Jameson's and, looking at Abad, he said conversationally, 'I've booked us a table at my mate's restaurant. They do beautiful sea bass, but good steak too if that's what takes your fancy.'

Abad smiled, as was expected of him. This wasn't his circus, and these certainly weren't his monkeys. He had no intention of getting involved in any way.

'Sounds good to me, mate.'

Angus shook hands with Larry and Petey. Leaving them to sort out the mess, he walked out with Abad and Roy, his step light and his laughter hanging on the air.

When they had gone, Larry shook his head sagely and said to Petey, 'I'll ring his old woman. She made a deal with Diana, she knew this had to go down.'

Petey shrugged. 'Didn't we all! I tell you now, Larry, he wouldn't listen to reason. We both tried to tell him, to warn him. It's a fucking shame. I loved him like a brother.'

Larry shrugged dispassionately. 'Listen to me, Petey, he became a liability and a potential laughing stock. If that man was in his right mind, and it was one of us in his position, we would have been outed a lot sooner.'

Petey Webster looked at the devastation around him and, picking up a bottle of whiskey, he said sadly, 'True.'

Chapter Twenty-eight

Diana hung up the phone. 'It's done, Gabe, he slung him through a window at Magico. Apparently he landed in the car park. So that's that. But I do wish sometimes that my Angus wasn't such a showman.'

Gabriel shrugged. 'In fairness, Di, this was a warning that was being sent out to everyone we deal with, so it had to be a bit spectacular. This wasn't just a disappear-off-the-face-of-the-earth job, leaving everyone wondering what the truth was. This was a fucking lesson for everyone concerned. Willy had asked for it – he was going to kill your son, remember – so this needed to be dramatic.'

Diana nodded, because Gabriel had a point. It was his intention of harming her son that had really sealed Willy's fate.

'It was certainly that, by all accounts. His head split like a fucking pistachio nut. Once I heard he was snorting his own gear, I should have stepped in.'

Gabriel just shrugged again. 'Shoulda, woulda, coulda – the old story, girl. He was a fool to himself, and even his old woman knew that.'

Diana sighed. She sipped at her wine.

'He was great, back in the day – he could make a cat laugh. He was good to me after my old man died too. It's a shame that he ended up a pathetic cliché – his family deserved better than that. *He* deserved better than that.'

Gabriel didn't answer. As far as he was concerned, it was over.

Big Willy McCormack had a special place in her heart, but Diana knew this was no time for sentiment. She changed the subject and poured herself another large wine. She was secretly proud of her Angus. She was beginning to understand that in this new world showmanship was a necessary evil – unlike the days of old, when everything was kept under the radar. She consoled herself with the fact that she could walk away in another few years, as long as her Angus kept on doing the good deeds.

He was the new breed, as Gabriel kept pointing out. She would sit back and observe, but that wouldn't stop her from putting in her ten pence, should she feel the need. Obviously. But if she was honest, totally honest with herself, she was pleased with Angus and his night's work.

His father would have been over the moon. He had proved himself a formidable opponent: he had arranged for the police presence, for the witnesses who saw Willy 'jump', and for the negotiations with the people closest to Willy, bringing them on board. Her boy had an innate cunning which he had inherited from her. Now she was willing to give him his head for a while; she was interested to see how he coped with the life.

So far, he was doing pretty well. But she still had a few people watching out for him, not just Roy. She knew this could get nasty, and Angus had to understand the need to cover all bases.

If he couldn't, he was in the wrong profession.

Chapter Twenty-nine

Angus was in the Electric nightclub – VIP bar of course – and was being treated like the King of the Banús.

Tonight he had made his mark. He knew that it was with his mother's permission, but even that couldn't piss on his firework. As Roy had pointed out, she was the main Face on the Costa and basically everyone worked for her in one way or another. He had also pointed out that his dad's reputation, along with his mother's, was an asset if he would only embrace his name and his family connections.

Angus saw that he talked a lot of sense, especially as he had told him what to do and what to say to get Big Willy McCormack's people on board. Roy had told him in such a way that he had had no choice but to listen and learn. That was his mother's influence. He had really had a learning curve with this trip. He had always liked and respected Roy, because he had his creds – and Angus also knew that he would die for him, if the situation warranted it. Now he could see he could learn a lot from him too.

His mum could generate real loyalty, and it wasn't just because she paid a good whack. His mum knew the name of everyone who worked for her, no matter how lowly, and she also knew the names of her workers' spouses and kids. Diana was loved and respected because she made a point of remembering the details of her people's lives, and he had heard that from Roy.

Roy had been determined to make him listen, for once in his life, and to also understand that he was still a young gun, and nothing came easily to anyone. Angus had no problem with killing Willy; he had no qualms about murder. He had no conscience, as such – though he had always liked Willy's kids, and he hoped they could all still be friends. He was aware that his mum had struck a deal with Willy's wife, an old friend of hers from way back.

It had finally hit him out here in Marbella, the truth of the life he was a part of. He would always remember what Roy had explained to him, and how he had made sure that he understood exactly what the score was in the criminal world. He looked around him; he could feel the admiration and the excitement that being in his company was causing. He was finally on his way, and he believed that he had acquitted himself as well as he could.

He saw Abad smooching two blondes, and he grinned as he saw him grab both their arses at once. They had a lot in common – like him, Abad had a lot to live up to. Angus saw a girl with white-blonde hair and the bluest eyes he had ever encountered looking at him hungrily. She was dressed just enough to interest him, and she had good legs. He motioned for the bouncer to let her into the VIP area, and she smiled at him seductively as she sashayed towards him.

He was disappointed at how easily she was tempted in, because he would have preferred to have worked for her attention. It was the girls that didn't care who he was that really attracted him. Like his Lorna. She would have died before she would have lowered herself to frequent a place like this.

The girl was in front of him now, and she said huskily, 'Hi, Angus, my name's Diana.'

Angus looked at her beautiful face and her stunning body, and he started to laugh. He called Abad and his girls over and, as they sipped champagne at the bar, he said to Diana, 'Nothing personal, but I'm going to have to swap you, darling.' He pushed her into Abad's arms and pulled one of Abad's girls into his.

She was a tiny thing, with a beautiful smile and a neat little body – Abad's cup of tea all right. She smelt of Chanel N° 5 and Max Factor lipstick. He was well pleased with her; she was like a doll, and she was also very amenable.

As he stood by the bar, he accepted the accolades and the faux friendships offered to him from all and sundry. He saw Abad watching him closely, and he knew that Abad had experienced the same treatment at some point. He saw that Roy was always nearby, without being obtrusive. He also noticed three new guys who were obviously there in Roy's employ. He admired the way the man had arranged everything, with the minimum of fuss. He would need the extra muscle after this night's work. After tonight, he would have to watch his back. He was in the real world now.

Roy caught his attention and winked at him. The music was starting to get louder, and the VIP bar was filling up. He pushed past Abad and stood in front of Roy.

'You OK, boy?'

He could see the worry on the older man's face, and he felt the tug of love that told him he was with family.

Angus hugged him tightly, and kissing him on his forehead he whispered loudly in his ear, 'What can I say, Roy? Thank you for everything.'

Roy understood that, at last, Angus Davis had learned the magic formula. He was finally learning that to be anyone in their world you had to know when to trust, when to share, and most importantly when to make that judgement. No matter who you were dealing with, you couldn't always trust people, even those closest to you. You had to learn to read situations. Suss them out. Use your instincts, even with people you had known all your life. It was a hard lesson, but a lesson well learned.

Hugging him back, he said seriously, 'I love you like my own blood.'

Angus knew that was true. He also knew that, until this trip to Marbella, he had not understood exactly how fucking lucky he was. This had been what his mum called a red-letter day. He felt like he could conquer the world.

This was in his blood, this was what he was born for. This was everything he had ever wanted.

Book Two

1983

Cruel he looks, but calm and strong,
Like one who does, not suffers wrong.

Prometheus Unbound,
Percy Bysshe Shelley (1792–1822)

Chapter Thirty

'Oh come on, Angus, stop being a cunt.'

Angus was laughing, along with everyone else; he could take a joke at times. The trouble with Angus was, it depended on who was making the joke – and how funny it actually was.

Roy had noticed that, as the lad had grown into his role in the business, he had also grown into his role as a man. He was very like his father in looks, but he had the natural cunning of his mother. That was what made him so dangerous and so unpredictable. In their world, though, that made for a winning combination. Roy was proud of the man Angus had become, and he liked to think it was, in part, down to his influence. He was close to the lad, and he had seen him come into his own. One way in which Angus had matured was that he was willing to listen to advice. He might not take it, but he was open to other people's opinions, and that showed he was growing up.

Diana still had some reservations, and Roy understood that. Overall, she was pleased with the way Angus was acquitting himself, but she was also a bit wary because he could be very unpredictable with people he didn't like. That was something he needed to work on – and he was trying – but Angus didn't suffer fools gladly, even if they could give him an earn. The arrogance of youth – and the fact that he was treated like the second coming everywhere he went because of his familial connections – didn't help. Plus he was well liked by a lot of people because he wasn't above a good night out with his workforce, and he was known for his generosity to the people who surrounded him – if they did an exemplary job.

Angus was sensible enough to reward the people who worked for him if they went that extra mile. He encouraged that and, consequently, loyalty towards him was a given. He kept himself busy, but he encouraged his workers to approach him, giving the impression that he was the all-round 'nice guy'. He saw the value in being approachable; it guaranteed that the people in his orbit could talk to him should they feel the need.

Diana didn't like that. She saw the value in being benevolent but also inspiring awe from a distance, but she missed the point. It was a different world now. Angus not only attended the raves, he made a point of being seen around and about. He was a visible presence in their world *and* the regular one. It was the new order, and Angus Davis was rewriting the rules.

Angus laughed once more, and looking at Roy he said teasingly, 'If anyone else called me a cunt . . .'

The two men hugged tightly. They were closer than ever. Angus had learned just what a great asset Roy was to him. He was his surrogate father really, and they both understood that – even if it was never said out loud. But they were comfortable together and rarely apart.

Roy laughed. 'Well, what can I say, mate? If the cap fits!'

They laughed together again before Angus said soberly, 'I'm dreading this meeting, if I'm honest, Roy. This geezer gets on my fucking tits.'

They sighed in unison. Geoffrey Pole was a new Face on the scene, and he left a bad taste in Angus's mouth. There was something really off about him, although there was no reason anyone could find to corroborate that feeling. It was deep in his gut, and he just couldn't take to him.

Roy poured them both a drink. He understood exactly what Angus meant – he felt the same. But like Diana and every other business person in London, he knew they had to deal with him. Geoffrey Pole was a fucking serious earn.

His main problem was he was a flash geezer and a poser, and that didn't sit well with a lot of the people he dealt with. He was a piss-taker, but he had a knack of seeing an earn before anyone else did, working out the next big thing – and in the clubs that was invaluable. He knew exactly which DJs to promote and the right people they needed to frequent the clubs. He made sure they got column inches, because they had soap stars and now footballers in the VIP areas, as well as up-and-coming singers and bands. They were given a free night out, and they guaranteed photos in the tabloids; it worked well for everyone.

Geoffrey saw the value of the minor celebrities. These people encouraged every wannabe to frequent their premises. Girls came from far and wide in the hope of catching the eye of the latest heart-throb, and they dressed to impress. If the girls were particularly lovely they were offered access to the VIP lounge, and they lapped it up.

In truth, Angus loved being in there with West Ham players – he was a Boleyn Boy, after all. But he still couldn't bring himself to trust Geoffrey Pole, even if the man was bringing in a fortune.

He looked around the bar. Even in the afternoon this place looked classy. The carpets were cleaned regularly, he made sure of that, and the bar itself was always shining brightly. This place was like all his premises: spotlessly clean, and with books that the taxman couldn't fault. No matter how hard they tried!

This was the VIP bar in Celebrities, one of their clubs in East London. It was on three floors, and it was a storming success. They didn't need to con, they were coining it in. They had to turn people away from the doors. Thanks to this Geoffrey Pole, they were getting the exposure they needed. So why couldn't Angus take to the fucker?

He sipped his drink and looked around him once more. He had asked the chef to come in early to make some canapés. He watched as one of the waiters placed the platters on the bar. They looked like something from a top restaurant and that pleased him – he wanted to make an impression. He knew that Geoffrey Pole only drank Bollinger champagne, so there was a bottle on ice and another in the chiller. He hoped the second one wouldn't be needed.

'You ready for this?'

Angus shrugged and smiled wryly. ''Course. Let's get it over with.'

Chapter Thirty-one

Diana was with Lorna, who was heavily pregnant and not in the best of moods.

Lorna was a beautiful girl, but she was what Diana classed as 'high maintenance'. Ever since the wedding, she had been asserting herself in more ways than one. Diana didn't appreciate the girl's belief that she had any kind of say in her business. What did she know about any of it? It was *her* business, until she said otherwise, meaning she passed the yoke permanently to her son. Even then, she would make sure that this girl only ever got the benefits, never a share. She was intelligent, but she didn't have the street smarts needed for their world.

Lorna was also a natural-born killjoy. She didn't know how to just let go and enjoy herself; everything in her life was a trial in some way. She had a beautiful home, a prestige car, she had money, and she had carte blanche where the house was concerned. But if you listened to her talk, life was one big, terrible drama, from the minute she got up till the moment she went to bed.

Lorna was her mother's daughter all right, they could both squeeze the joy out of a sock. Consequently, that meant neither Angus nor anyone within his circle, including Diana, could enjoy their lives either. Lorna seemed to wallow in her morning sickness, her backache, her swollen ankles – she was making pregnancy seem like a terminal illness. Gabriel called her a 'born-again moaner'. Even at the house in Marbella, she found fault with everything, from the swimming pool to the way the kitchen had been laid out. Considering she came from a council house, it took all of Diana's willpower not to point that fact out. But Angus was obsessed with her – that was the only way she could describe her son's feelings for this girl.

At first she had thought Lorna would be a steadying influence on her son. But in the year since the marriage, it had been hard to keep her mouth shut at times. Lorna had shown herself to be so controlling and so self-righteous that Diana had begun to question her son's choice. She just knew she had to keep her opinions to herself though because if she ever voiced them, there would be more fights than Rocky. Since the wedding, Lorna had become like an old woman in her fussy ways.

Diana saw that this didn't faze her Angus. He kowtowed to her, because he thought that was how she should be acting. She was the ultimate good girl, and that was what had attracted him from the outset. He didn't see that it was because she was the antithesis of all the other women in his life – strong women who worked and did their whack. He thought that she needed looking after, and Lorna needed a lot of things – especially materially – but being looked after wasn't one of them.

Lorna Davis got what she wanted through a mixture of making people feel guilty and acting like the big bad world was her enemy. When Lorna went off the deep end it was not a pretty sight.

Diana knew her son was already being unfaithful to her. She didn't like it but what could she do? He had begun sniffing out strange within weeks of the honeymoon. He wasn't inter-ested in them romantically, they were simply a means to an end.

She could only assume he was getting off them what he wasn't getting at home. God help them if and when Lorna found out. But she didn't like to dwell on that. What she did know was that when all was said and done he worshipped this girl, and more so now that they had a child on the way.

Today they were at a private clinic in London to see the doctor who, according to Lorna, delivered the babies of royalty and the rich and famous. It wasn't cheap and, even though Diana wasn't short of a few quid, she resented paying out this kind of money to a doctor who was as bent as a two-bob clock, as her mother would say.

'Come on, Lorna, let me help you up the stairs, darling.'

She knew the girl was more than capable of walking up the stairs on her own. Even at eight months pregnant, she was still as thin as a rake. She was on a special diet that she had heard was used by people like Madonna to keep them slim and attractive. But Lorna liked the attention, and Diana would make whatever fuss was needed for her daughter-in-law to keep the peace.

They walked into the foyer and the receptionist in her faux nurse-type uniform smiled widely and walked them through to the doctor immediately, leaving everyone else waiting for their turn.

As they walked into his surgery, Lorna put on a tragic expression and said plaintively, 'I'm still suffering from morning sickness.'

Diana rolled her eyes and plastered a smile on her face.

Chapter Thirty-two

Geoffrey Pole wasn't a man who inspired friendship, but that didn't bother him. He didn't need friends.

He was invaluable, whatever people thought of him, and he genuinely didn't care about being popular. The Angus Davises of this world needed him; he knew his worth, and he also knew the people he needed to get behind him so he could achieve his goals.

Agents paid him a fortune to get their clients in the papers. It was what he was good at, and it was also something he actually enjoyed. The tabloids relied on him to give them gossip, and Angus Davis – with his family connections – was a gift, in more ways than one. He gave the stories the element of danger that had been sadly lacking since the days of the Krays and the Richardsons.

Geoffrey actually liked Angus, even though he was aware the feeling wasn't mutual, and Geoffrey knew that it wasn't because he was gayer than a Mexican tablecloth. He had understood from day one that his sexuality didn't bother Angus Davis. It had amazed him, if he was honest. Normally, the criminal elements were terrified of people like him; he was out, he was proud, and more flamboyant than Danny La Rue on amphetamines. No, Angus just didn't like him as a person, and he could live with that.

Geoffrey deliberately held his hand out dramatically. And Angus, because he had had a few drinks, held Geoffrey's hand in his and kissed it, as if the man was a princess. Geoffrey was so taken aback that he laughed delightedly, and Angus, who had followed the drinks with a couple of lines of coke, laughed with him. Roy Rogers smiled – he knew that Angus was determined to find something to like in this man.

'Champagne all round.'

Geoffrey was aware that he was making headway, so he said generously, 'That sounds good to me, A.' He always called Angus 'A' – and, for some reason, Angus allowed it.

Geoffrey's entourage were all gay, but they were also hard men if the situation warranted it. Angus acknowledged that, and even though he didn't like Geoffrey, he did respect him and what he had achieved. It was why he dealt with him; Geoffrey knew his job, and he did it well.

They were standing in the bar with glasses of champagne, and Angus smiled that easy smile of his that secretly made Geoffrey go weak at the knees. Raising his glass, he said, 'To you, Geoff, and a big thank-you for the sterling work you do.'

Geoffrey knew that it had not been easy for Angus to do what he had just done, and he appreciated that he had bothered to do it. He understood far more than the men he worked with would ever even guess.

He put on his best camp voice as he cried, 'I never thought I would see the day! We will be on a date next!'

Angus laughed heartily and, taking a big draught of his champagne, he held it aloft once more. 'Oh come on now, Geoffrey, I'm a married man!'

Geoffrey grinned. 'I've heard that before, darling!' Everyone was laughing, some more than others, when Geoffrey waved his people away, saying, 'My priest is as bad. He said to me on Sunday, I prayed for you last night! I said, you should have fucking rung me. I'd have been straight round!'

Angus had always appreciated a good joke. He spat his champagne all over the place and laughed so much he had to wipe his eyes.

'Get yourselves a seat, I need to talk business.'

Angus was reminded that Geoffrey had a lot more going for him than anyone might think. He would be a fool to underestimate this man. He might be as camp as Christmas, but he could also have a row, should the situation warrant it. As he'd said to Angus, in the early days, 'I'm queer but I'm not a fucking cissy. You get my drift?' Angus had respected that, and it had stood both of them in good stead since.

When it was just the three of them at the bar, Geoffrey smiled at Roy and said quietly, 'I know you will stay, and I want you to. What I have to say needs a witness, because you two aren't going to be impressed.'

Angus filled up their glasses and raised his eyebrows expectantly. '*News of the World* again?'

Geoffrey sighed theatrically and sipped his champagne before saying seriously, 'I'm here to do you a big favour.'

Angus didn't answer. He just waited for him to say whatever was on his mind.

'You never heard this from me, right? But it's come to my attention, through an old associate of mine, that Joey Barbossa is looking to move in on your clubs in Spain.' Angus made as if to speak, and Geoffrey held his hand up to stop him. 'Joey is a penny-ante dealer, we all know that. But I don't like disloyalty, and I know you are giving him a wage. He's been seen with the Juarez family, and you and I know what that means.

106

I'm warning you because you played fair with me. And as I said earlier, I don't like disloyalty. What you do with this information is your business, but I got this on very good authority. Whatever happens, it never came from me.'

Angus and Roy were both pole-axed by his words. Joey Barbossa was dependent on them for his daily bread. It didn't make any sense that someone who was no more than a drone could even dream of doing them such potential damage.

Geoffrey smiled and sipped his champagne once more. 'He's been a busy boy, and the Juarez brothers giving him credibility really hasn't helped. Talk to Colin Bates – he deals in Magico on a Sunday night. His family are the Bateses from Liverpool. Good people, as you know. They are making a mark there, but they wouldn't tread on your toes to do it. They are very sensible. But this needs to be nipped in the bud – your manager is not keeping his eye on the ball.'

Angus could feel the anger growing inside him. That this had been happening under his nose! He prided himself on knowing what was occurring with everyone he dealt with.

Geoffrey put his well-manicured hand on his arm and held him tightly. 'I am giving you a heads-up, Angus, because I like you. You need to show your face in Marbs on a regular basis. It's basically bandit country, these days. Everyone wants a fucking slice.'

Angus nodded his agreement.

'And, remember, you never heard this from me.'

Angus was well aware that he had just had the touch of touches. He also realised that Geoffrey had a network that was obviously far superior to his own. What he couldn't understand was why none of his own people knew about this. What was his manager, Dennis White, playing at? He was spreading money all over the fucking Port, and for what?

Spain was being looked at by everyone, these days; money laundering was the big incentive. Buy huge villas for cash, and then mortgage them. It was happening in London too; pay two million in cash and then mortgage it, and you had clean money to use as you wished. It was taking over from the drugs, if he was honest. There were more Russians and Croatians investing out there, but he had never thought for one minute that they could impinge on his businesses.

This was a complete piss-take, especially if the Juarez brothers were trying to tuck him up on the say-so of fucking Barbossa. Geoffrey was right, he had taken his eye off the fucking ball. Or so it seemed.

'I really appreciate this, Geoffrey.'

He grinned, and Angus had to admit he had a wonderful set of railings.

'Well, what can I say? You would be surprised what I hear.'

Angus nodded. 'Obviously.'

Chapter Thirty-three

Lorna was back home and lying on her sofa watching *EastEnders*.

She liked being pregnant, it suited her. She knew that Angus was thrilled about the baby. Like her, he understood the importance of having a child.

She knew his mum was like hers; they just thought it was something that happened to everyone: 'Get on with it, it's the most natural thing in the world. Women are giving birth all over the world all the time.' Well, she wasn't just anyone. Her having a baby was not going to be denigrated because most women were capable of giving birth. That really angered her. Any woman could give birth, but it was whether or not they did the absolute best for their baby that really mattered.

Lorna believed that any child they created deserved every advantage, and she would make sure her children got exactly that. This baby was wanted, loved and already cherished. There was a lot more to having a child than people realised – especially people who came from where they did. She would make sure that her children were given the best of everything.

No matter what.

Chapter Thirty-four

'Get the plane fuelled, we need to go to Spain.'

Roy Rogers nodded. He was ahead of Angus and had already put things in motion.

'It's done, Angus. We're flying into a private airfield so we don't announce our arrival.'

Angus was fuming, but he was also planning his next steps in his head.

'You know the worst of it, Roy? All that wedge we are weighing out in Spain, and fucking Geoffrey had to give us a heads-up! It's bandit country all right, and I will fucking remind them all *exactly* who they are dealing with.'

Roy nodded.

There wasn't anything he could say. He would do the same in Angus's position.

Roy had taught him well.

Chapter Thirty-five

Alejandro and Matias Juarez were pretty sure they had cornered their little market in Puerto Banús.

They were basically no more than Spanish thugs, but they had a few friends who thought they might be worth backing, if they could produce what they claimed they could. Joey Barbossa was promising them the earth and seemed sure that he had the insider knowledge needed to see this deal through. It was their chance to enter the big time. Everyone knew that Angus was letting the Banús slide – or at least that was the talk on the street. Since he had become a married man, with a baby on the way, his visits had been few and far between.

It was the perfect time for a coup. While everyone was concentrating on something else, the Juarez brothers believed they could just slip into the role that had been established by Angus Davis. Of course, they hadn't broadcast this. They had flown under the radar, trusting that Joey Barbossa was leading them in the right direction and would uphold his end of the bargain. After all, he worked for Angus Davis – so if anyone knew the score, it had to be him. Plus they were talking to a lot of the dealers at the clubs, and if they were offering a better arrangement then they would be quids in.

This was a cut-throat game, as Joey was always saying. As

long as you could deliver on your promises, you were in for the long haul. It was about building trust and a rapport with the people you were selling to. Once you had established a good relationship, the rest would come naturally.

Everyone liked a deal – that was a given – and once they knew they had a good one, they would readily change their allegiance.

It was simple economics.

Chapter Thirty-six

Dennis White was in a bar in Marbella when he noticed a drug deal going on before his very eyes.

He was shocked to the core, mainly because he had a big stake in this bar, and as easy-going as the Spanish police might be, they certainly wouldn't appreciate a piss-take like this. He gestured to his minder, Leonard O'Brien, and alerted him to what was occurring. They both watched in wonder as a scruffy little ponce, who should never have been given houseroom, did a deal right in front of them.

The man looked like a tramp. He should have been refused entry to the bar, let alone be allowed to get to the upper floors. It was a complete liberty, especially considering they were in the VIP bar trying to close a deal of their own.

Lenny knew his job, and he removed the offending article with the minimum of fuss. He walked the man swiftly through the bar and into the lift that would take them to the upstairs offices. He also took the opportunity while in the lift to give the man a quick but serious clump. Lenny was irritated that he'd had to leave a good-looking girl wearing hot pants and very high-heeled designer shoes that he had purchased for her that afternoon. He had been promised the night of his life, and he intended to keep that promise – come hell or fucking high water.

He was not a happy bunny.

He threw the man unceremoniously on to the office floor and pushed his foot down on the man's neck so he couldn't get up off the floor – and couldn't breathe that well either. Not that it would have mattered. Lenny and the man both knew there would never be a fight – well, not a fair one anyway.

Lenny frisked him for a weapon, but his gut instinct told him there wouldn't be one.

Dennis White came into the room and glanced around him with distaste. He looked at the man on the floor with a size-twelve foot on his neck, and he said conversationally, 'Are you on your own fucking drugs, you mug?'

The man was staring at Lenny in fear, and when Dennis's rather expensive shoe hit him in the face he knew he was fucked. Dennis White kicked him four times, breaking his nose, several teeth and a cheekbone. Dennis White was a great believer in doing your own dirty work, should the occasion merit it.

It certainly did today.

'So, first question. Who the fuck let you in?'

Chapter Thirty-seven

Dennis White was terrified. He couldn't believe that a scum-bag like this was dealing in his club – a club he ran for Angus Davis, whose mother made Baby Jane Hudson look like a fucking Girl Guide.

It was like his worst nightmare had come true. He was on the verge of having a heart attack with the worry of it all. Someone he trusted, who worked for him, had allowed this shit-bag access. Now he had to find out who that was, because this could cause fucking murders. Literally.

It was just un-fucking-believable, as he kept repeating to Lenny. How in God's name had this happened?

'Right, geezer. What is your name, you lunatic?'

The man was only too pleased to spill, as Lenny knew he would be; there was nothing like a foot on the windpipe to get people talking. If this fucker had infiltrated the club, it meant that he personally had taken his eye off the ball. Which of course he had – for a twenty-two-year-old built like Marilyn Monroe who could blow him like a train – hence the expensive shoes.

Dennis was not too thrilled about any of this, and Lenny couldn't blame him. It was about making up the difference now, and talking his way out of real trouble. Lenny spent half his life at the club on a good wedge so Dennis White didn't have to. Lenny had a lot of explaining to do.

Arif, his head bouncer, was fucked left, right and sideways, because he had to be in on this. This low-life would not have had houseroom without his say-so. He had been given an in all right, the treacherous sod. That told Lenny that Arif was not doing his job, and that it would soon be common knowledge. But it also told him that the old adage 'there's no fool like an old fool' was truer than ever. He couldn't believe he had been so fucking stupid and no one had given him a heads-up. He was determined to clean this place up – providing he survived the night, of course.

That was the trouble with Spain – it was like being on an extended holiday. The sun, the beach, the clubs, daytime drinking, seeing your mates everywhere. It was dangerous, because it just wasn't like actual work.

Dennis smiled nastily and said sarcastically, 'So, Leonard, from what I understand from dead boy here, the Juarez brothers are apparently taking us all for complete mugs. And that ponce Joey Barbossa is in the mix. Now my question to you is, how the fucking hell didn't you know? I was under the impression you were my main man. I trusted you, and I pay you a wedge of Olympian standards to ensure this kind of mayhem doesn't occur on my watch.'

Lenny wished the floor would open up and swallow him, but he knew that wasn't going to happen. So when Dennis went to the cupboard and brought out the baseball bat, he had no choice but to accept what was coming to him. He could easily take his boss in a fight. They both knew that – it was why Dennis had the baseball bat – but he wasn't about to make that mistake. He had to take what was dished out and pray he survived it.

Lenny could only hope that he could salvage something from his years of loyal service. Though, in all honesty, he wouldn't forgive or forget, if the boot was on the other foot. Lenny was known to bear a grudge. It was part of his persona, why they paid him so much to look after the businesses. When Dennis passed the bat to him, he felt a rush of adrenalin. He understood that he wasn't dead in the water yet, that he was still useful.

'Batter him, and batter him good.'

Lenny did as requested.

He had never been so relieved in his life. But he still had to face Angus Davis, and that was not going to be what he would call pleasant. Like Dennis, it was his biggest fear. They were both aware that they had fucked up. They were also both aware that neither of them had heard even a whisper of what was about to go down. That, in itself, was enough for Angus Davis to wipe them off the face of the earth. They understood his position – after all, they were being paid to prevent lunacy like this.

And lunacy it was.

Angus would skin them alive and laugh while he was doing it. He really didn't suffer fools gladly. And why would he? He paid everyone's wages, and he paid well to make sure that this kind of shit didn't happen.

Chapter Thirty-eight

Angus was furious because his wife was ready to drop their baby and he had to fly out to Marbella and leave her on a whim. He was going to nip this in the bud and be on his way within hours.

He was angry because he felt that it was somehow his fault that the Juarez brothers and Joey Barbossa felt they could take him for a complete cunt. It was unbelievable and insulting. Just thinking about it made him feel so provoked and so indignant that he could cheerfully murder someone.

It was a complete piss-take, and he was not a man who could overlook such an insult. A crowd of morons thinking they could mug him off without a second's thought! It was just without any kind of merit. Anyone who knew him, and knew him well, would not even consider such a stupid concept. They had to know that he wouldn't allow such brainlessness to flourish in his organisation. After all, he was nothing if not a hands-on employer.

Roy Rogers was every bit as angry, but he was also thinking seriously about who could really be behind this lunacy. Joey Barbossa couldn't work out a clue in the *Sun* crossword, let alone think he could pull something like this, without a few big guns. He was what would be regarded as 'cranially challenged', if you wanted to be politically correct about it. Otherwise, he was as thick as the proverbial shit, and couldn't be trusted to work out his wages without an abacus and his mum on the end of a phone.

It was laughable, outrageous. Whoever was bankrolling this was either on the ball, and up for the war this was going to cause on the ground, or they were on a fucking death wish. Those were the only two scenarios that were even remotely believable.

So who had the front, the nerve and the firepower?

Chapter Thirty-nine

Joey Barbossa was in a restaurant on the marina.

It had a wonderful chef and a very expensive menu – the cheapest starter was over a tenner. It went against the grain in a lot of ways, but he knew that he had to start living it large now he was a man of substance.

When it was all over, this would be his new life; he would be dealing with people who thought this was the norm. He needed to remember that he was now a player, and he would have to embrace this lifestyle with gusto.

He couldn't believe how easy it had been so far. But there was a long way to go before this was all on the definite. The Juarez brothers had known they couldn't do this on their own. So they'd wanted to bring some firepower from Manchester, which had been Joey's job. He knew he could do it – that was why they'd needed him.

They had to take Angus out, of course, but that was just business, nothing personal. Everyone liked Angus, but he didn't spend enough time on the Banús to keep his house in order.

To think about it, even Dennis White had to have the ache. He was left here like the poor relation to sort everything out, while Angus reaped the rewards. Even Dennis must have worked that one out, surely!

It was simple economics. Once Angus was out of the way, there would be a big hole, and Joey was determined to fill it.

Chapter Forty

'Where the fuck are we?'

Angus wasn't impressed. He was tired, and he was aggravated. They had landed in what amounted to a field.

Roy held his hand up and said vehemently, 'Listen to yourself, will you? You're so angry and so fucking sure of yourself, it never even occurred to you that you might be flying into a death trap, did it? I am not saying we are, but what I am saying is, better safe than fucking sorry, yeah?'

Angus looked at Roy for long moments. He could hear the fear in his voice, and he was well aware that he should have been thinking along those same lines. But he was too angry, and that would always be his downfall. Roy was right; he was too fucking sure of himself at times. He was thinking about his wife and baby. He wasn't thinking about the actual reason he was even coming out here. It had not even occurred to him that he might be in danger in any way, shape or form.

He was Angus Davis. He felt he was invincible. But he needed to be reminded that, in his position, he could never, ever believe he was one hundred per cent safe, because that was the price he paid to live the life that he did.

'You remember that we are in bandit country here, Angus. We have our creds, but we are dealing with every piece of shit that decides to take a stake out here. Since you married Lorna, and now with the baby on the way, you are like a fucking joke. Even your mum is worried, and she loves the bones of you. You've been taking your eyes off the prize, son, and this should be a warning to you. This load of old fanny should never have happened. You should have been involved in everything that went on here – you should never trust someone else to do your fucking work.'

Angus had not been creamed like this since he was a teenager, and he knew that Roy had to think that it was needed, or he would never have said a word.

'I told you, over and over again, to keep a wary eye on the clubs. I have, and even I didn't see this shit-storm coming, and that's because it's being run by a load of fucking muppets. But those muppets could have got a foothold, because you and I know that there are plenty of people waiting to step into our shoes. Fucking grow up, will you, Angus?'

Angus knew that he had drunk too much brandy, and that he had no answer to Roy's argument, so he said nothing. There wasn't anything he could say. He had fucked up, that was the long and the short of it.

They disembarked from the plane quietly, each lost in their own thoughts.

When the guns went off, they hit the ground.

As anyone with half a brain would.

Chapter Forty-one

Joey Barbossa was drunk and happy as he walked into the private club with the Juarez brothers.

He had arranged this days before, knowing that they would want to celebrate. This was a really upmarket lap-dancing club: just footballers, soap stars and the general rich and famous. He knew that it was a touch just to be invited in, let alone be given a private room for a party.

They were waiting for the call that would tell them that they had carte blanche – because that was what they had planned for, and planned for well. Once Angus was out of the way, there was nothing to stop them from taking what they wanted. It was a hard line, 'us or them' situation. As they walked into the private room, they all felt a rush of excitement – this was their future. This was the beginning of the life they had paid a fortune – in money and blood – to live.

Joey took the call at 11.50 p.m.

Smiling widely, he said with mock sadness, while rubbing his hands together like a pantomime villain, 'It's done. Angus Davis and Roy Rogers are no more. They thought that flying into a different airport would be enough. Luckily, we had previous know-ledge aforethought and we could adjust our plans as needed.'

Even the Juarez brothers thought that Joey was a bit of a

cunt; they knew that they spoke much better English than him. They were both surprised that he had managed to arrange what he had promised. They would have been more than happy to sort out the details themselves, but if Joey could make it happen then they were quite pleased to let him take the fallout.

Joey was just a means to an end – but, of course, he wasn't aware of that fact. He wouldn't be around for much longer. After all, who wanted a grass on the firm?

This had worked out well all around really.

What they had wanted was Angus Davis gone. Because once he was out of the way, it would be easy to get a hold in the clubs. It would be fair game.

That was how it worked.

This was the Costas, and anything fucking went here.

Chapter Forty-two

Diana was worried. There was something not right about this latest drama in Spain.

The fact that she couldn't get Dennis White or the illustrious Leonard on the phone didn't help. Gabriel wasn't bothered in the least; he said that she should let her boy sort it himself. But there was still something bothering her and she didn't know what it was.

Her son knew his job; he was proving himself to be a natural, in all fairness. Still her instincts were telling her that there was something wrong with this latest debacle.

Something sinister.

She wondered if it was because she was about to become a grandmother and that her son was becoming a father. She wished she could ask her old mum about it – ask how she felt when young Angus had been born. She'd loved the bones of her grandson that was for sure. But Jane had had a sudden heart attack not long after the wedding – it was as though she was content once she saw her Angus happy. She'd never been overly affectionate with her daughter but Diana missed her all the same.

She poured herself a large Scotch and took a swig, relishing the warmth. She knew how life shifted when you suddenly had something precious to lose. Something that was real. Something that was tangible. She looked at Gabriel and saw him watching her. She knew that she was lucky, because he did genuinely love her; that was something that couldn't be manufactured. But she couldn't let that affect her, because she had to make sure that nothing interfered with her life or her work.

If she was a man, she could have done what she liked – shag for England, spend her time in hostess clubs, whatever. It would be expected. But as a woman, she wasn't afforded that kind of leeway. People were shocked enough by her lifestyle with Gabriel; she had fought to be treated like the men she dealt with. And yet she also knew that she would be judged by any man she slept with.

Gabriel poured her another whisky and, shaking his handsome head, he said gently, 'Stop worrying, Di, it's being sorted.'

For the first time ever, she didn't say anything, and Gabriel could see the fear in her eyes.

'If anything happens to my boy, I swear I will decimate Spain and every fucker out there.'

Gabriel sighed heavily. 'I think that's a given, don't you? But I promise you, nothing is going to happen to your boy tonight.'

He hoped that he was right. No one could guarantee anything in their game, that was the trouble. There was many a man buried well before his time because of a business deal that someone else wanted. The secret was to keep one step ahead of the game.

It was the way of the world.

Chapter Forty-three

Joey Barbossa was drunk, happy and giddy with power.

He had arranged the demise of Angus Davis! It would cause murders, but if no one knew it was him, he was confident that he could ride out this storm and go on to bigger and better things. Working with the Juarez brothers was just the beginning. He had lined up a veritable who's who of the criminal under-world to help him in his quest to take over the dealing in the clubs, the bars and even the Mugs pubs, where the tourists went and believed they were rubbing shoulders with the criminal elite. Dream on! Joey was so impressed with the private room – the place was just fucking outrageous. They not only had a full bar but there were leather sofas like something from a Channel 4 programme. He only had to nod and he was offered every drink under the sun, and that told him that he was being treated with respect. He was seen as a man of means. He was a man to be reckoned with.

This had been his dream all his life. It was why he had thrown his lot in with the Juarez brothers and sold his mates down the river. But it had been worth it, because he would now be a main player, someone of note.

When the girls came in to give them a private dance, he thought he had died and gone to heaven. These were young women who were beautiful and sexy, and available for a price. When he was known to be a part of this world, these girls would fight each other to get to him. That is what money and prestige did for men like him. It guaranteed strange that was not only young and beautiful but also open to opportunities. The ugliest fuck in Christendom could bag a good-looking bird, marry it and produce beautiful kids, if they were a Face.

He knew how this worked, and he was all for it.

This was the world of commerce – the world of business – and he was finally going to be a part of it.

Chapter Forty-four

Roy and Angus were in a restaurant in Marbella, right on the waterfront.

They were sitting with a huge tableful of people, most of whom they only knew by sight. But Abad was there, with a young dancer who had caught his eye. He was smiling but he clearly wasn't happy, and Angus appreciated that. Abad knew what was really going down tonight.

There was champagne on the table, and everyone was determined to have a great time – so great, in fact, that no one would forget them. This was the best alibi ever, yet it didn't sit well with Angus, because he liked to sort out his problems personally. But he was willing to swallow his knob. He didn't really have a choice – though he wondered why he had even travelled all this way if he wasn't to be allowed to sort this out himself.

He had left a pregnant wife, and he was raring to get his hands on the culprits concerned! He picked up his glass of champagne and swallowed it down irritably.

Abad refilled his glass and, grinning at the room, he said under his breath, 'Relax, for fuck's sake, Angus. The Juarez brothers have dragged a lot of people into this shit. You can't be anywhere near them, but the fact you are here speaks volumes.'

Angus nodded. 'Fucking try and shoot me? What a piss-take, what a diabolical fucking liberty!'

Abad shrugged. 'But they didn't succeed, did they? I made sure of that. So relax and make a night of it. I have a photographer taking photos with the time on. Try to look happy, will you?'

Angus knew he had a touch with this friend of his. He owed Roy and Abad his life, but what had happened still rankled.

Abad leaned in to him and, as they clinked glasses, Abad whispered in his ear, 'Don't worry, I have saved the best till last. You will get your revenge, mate. But not yet. We need to get through this charade first.'

Angus finally smiled, his first real one of the night.

This was more like it.

He was nothing in his business if not hands-on.

Chapter Forty-five

Leonard and Dennis were waiting at the club for Angus and Roy to arrive.

They were pleased with themselves, because they had taken things in hand before Angus had even stepped off the plane. That had to count for something. They had fucked up, but they had sorted it as soon as. They had to believe that Angus would appreciate that.

They were sure that they had headed off any trouble before it could cause real problems.

But when Angus finally walked into the offices, they were both as frightened as they were relieved.

Chapter Forty-six

Joey Barbossa knew that it was all over for him, and he was gutted.

He had no doubt that he was going to die. It was how that was bothering him. He could only hope it was quick, he was already resigned to his fate.

He had had what was generally referred to as a 'capture'. He had been fucked over, that was obvious, and he was sensible enough to know that there wasn't anything he could do or say to prevent his demise.

He was lying on the floor of a warehouse in a small industrial estate outside of La Conception. It was quiet, late at night, and it was deserted. He could smell oil and sweat, which was basically all this shithole was good for. It was supposed to be a car repair shop. It was a perfect front for the business they were really in, though. Everyone was aware that it was easy enough to carry out any kind of business here, providing you knew the right people. That was why this place was so competitive – there was so much to earn, and so many different businesses to earn from.

All he had wanted was a taste. He had wanted to be somebody. That was natural, surely?

He was crying intermittently, and he could hear the Juarez brothers cursing and trying to break free of their bonds. He admired their optimism, but he knew they didn't have a chance in hell. They were all dead.

For fuck's sake, they had tried to murder Angus Davis! If they had managed it, they might have been in with a chance. Angus Davis was a real adversary, he wasn't a mug, and that was why he had to die. But on reflection, he knew that the Juarez brothers had not allowed for Angus Davis being not only well liked but also his mother's son. Joey had finally seen that he had involved himself in the biggest fuck-up, because he had not researched his opponents.

Hindsight was, apparently, a wonderful thing. He sighed sadly.

It was over twenty-four hours since they had been brought here, and no one had been near or by. He was hot and thirsty, he was in pain from his bonds, and he had already defecated in his trousers. He regretted eating all that fucking rich food in that posh restaurant, though his fear could have something to do with it too.

He could feel the heat overwhelming him. He was sweating like a pig, and he wondered if they were going to let them die of thirst. He wouldn't put that past Angus Davis. He was known for his viciousness – that was part of his persona. He wondered how long it would be before Angus turned up.

Like the avenging angel.

At this point Joey was hoping he would to put them all out of their misery.

Sooner rather than later.

Chapter Forty-seven

'It's been long enough. I think it's time we went and did the dirty, don't you?'

Angus was getting antsy. He wanted to get in there and teach them a lesson they wouldn't forget.

Roy shook his head. 'You ain't going nowhere, Angus, except home.'

Angus was standing in his beautiful suite with a large Jacky D in his hand and the determination to cause havoc coursing through his veins.

He laughed loudly. 'Are you fucking joking? I won't rest until I see these fuckers face to face . . .'

Roy shook his head slowly. 'You are not going anywhere near them, you hear me? They are in a unit in La Conception.'

Angus was not impressed, and it showed.

'Excuse me? I have been totally fucking mugged off, and you think I should do nothing? Seriously, Roy?'

He was up for a fight, and Roy sighed heavily.

Running his hands over his cropped hair, he shouted, 'Yes, Angus, that's exactly what I think you should do. Go home to your wife and wait for your baby. Joey and the Juarez brothers are going to be miraculously found in a month's time. They will have died of hunger and thirst. There's a big heatwave at the moment, so their bodies will be in a terrible condition. That will hit the papers, and everyone will know that it was down to you. I think it is a much better lesson than a bullet in the back of the head. It's evil and it's nasty, and it takes time.

'Trust me on this, Angus, OK? I do not want you anywhere near those fuckers, because we would have to get rid of the bodies. As it stands, there is nothing to put any of us there. But when they are found, it will send a message all over Spain, and that is exactly what we need to do.'

Angus knew that Roy was making sense, but there was still a part of him that wanted to sort these fuckers out personally.

Roy understood that so he said reasonably, 'Listen to me. They are going to die a terrible death, Angus. It will take days – and everyone will know that, because I will make sure they know. This is Spain, and this needs a different way of dealing with things. Trust me, you will thank me for this one day. We aren't going out shooting and maiming – that's for the fucking plastic gangsters – we are going to sort this subtly. Show that we have a bit more nous than to start blood wars. Believe me, everyone will thank us for it. Especially the Filth.'

Angus shrugged, calmer now, but then he was always ready to listen to reason when it was explained to him by Roy. He trusted him with his life.

'How long will it take?'

Roy opened his arms, because he only knew what he had been told.

'Well, with this heat, probably another few days. It won't be pleasant, I can promise you that. It will be a slow and painful death. And that will make every fucking newspaper, I guarantee it. Everyone will know exactly how these cunts died. I have a few journalists who will kill for this story. Just go home and leave me to sort this out, will you?'

Angus nodded. He could live with that, especially if it added to his credibility – which, of course, this would. It was the 1980s, not the old days of murder in the streets and bloodbaths to prove a point, and he understood that. He actually liked this death, it pleased him. Dying of thirst had a certain panache to it. It appealed to his sense of fair play.

They had tried to kill him, so these fuckers dying slowly, but surely, was actually a fitting revenge. He was only sorry he had not thought of it himself.

'Do you know something, Roy? You are absolutely right. Fuck them! Let them starve. I had a wonderful word the other day from my dictionary: "marasmus". Basically, it means under-nourishment or starvation – could even be used to describe anorexia. It really encompasses what we are going to achieve here. How wonderful is that? I was wondering when and how I could use it in conversation, you know. It's a powerful word. We just don't appreciate the English language at all.'

Roy didn't answer him. He didn't know what to say. Angus and his fucking words could really get on his nerves sometimes.

Then Angus changed the subject completely, saying, 'But what about Dennis White? We need to keep an eye on him now surely? He took his eye off the ball.'

Roy nodded in agreement. 'In fairness, Angus, I don't think that will happen again, do you?'

Angus swallowed down the last of his drink before answering sociably, 'You have a point there, Roy. I think he has learned a valuable lesson. You can't trust any sod out here.'

Chapter Forty-eight

Lorna was tired out but she was pleased she had not put on too much weight – in fact, she still looked slim and sexy from behind – she had made sure of that. She wasn't going to let herself get half the size of a house, so she made sure she ate properly and healthily. She wasn't going to let her body be ruined beyond repair. She had seen that happen to too many of her contemporaries – they were like Man Mountain Dean after giving birth and she was too shrewd for that. She was going to pop straight back into shape and Angus would be thrilled.

She looked around her; she loved this house. They were living in a four-bedroom detached farmhouse on nine acres. She had viewed it and wanted it. Thanks to her Angus, they now owned it. That it irritated Diana, she knew, but Lorna didn't care. Diana had to be sensible enough to recognise that what Lorna wanted, she got. That was how it worked, how it would *always* work.

Lorna had used her pregnancy as a means to get what she wanted, because she knew what was best for them all. They were settled in Essex, not too far from London, and they had a home for life. That is what had sold it to Angus really – her telling him that they would have access to perfect schools, wonderful shops and, even better, there were nine acres of land fenced off that could guarantee them privacy. She knew that would eventually be what they needed. Her attitude was, why not buy into that now? And, of course, Angus agreed with her.

The house was beautiful, like something from *Emmerdale Farm*. It had just been renovated; the kitchen alone was a dream – it even had an AGA. She had read in *House & Garden* that an AGA was a must for the perfect home, and it kept it so warm all the time. Angus had had to talk his mother into helping them buy the place, but that was not Lorna's problem. She was producing the grandchild, and so she should get what she wanted surely? She loved Angus with all her heart, and he did her – they were a perfect couple – so Diana should make sure they had what they wanted. Diana's grandchild would be born into a world that suited its station in life: a beautiful home that would be worthy of her children and the life they would be living, the schools they would attend, the friends they would make. And, last but not least, it would provide the privacy needed when married to a man like Angus.

After all, as much as she loved him, Lorna wasn't unaware of his lifestyle and his businesses. She had thought everything through and convinced Angus that she was right. She had hinted at the off chance of a police raid, and the fact they would have plenty of warning given the distance from the gates to the front door. She had obviously tempered that with visions of the children having a wonderland to explore in complete safety.

Angus had loved the idea of a tennis court and swimming pool. There were outbuildings too, even a barn; they had a lot of land, and they could build on to it, as and when they needed to. It could grow over the years, as they would grow together as a family. They would soon be the proud parents of their very own baby. She had never seen her Angus so excited about anything before – this child was everything to him.

She could hear her mother coming through with the tea and toast she had requested, and she smiled. Angus was due home soon. She was aware that it had not been exactly the greatest trip to Marbella he had ever experienced. She could hear the disappointment in his voice when he'd spoken to her. She would find out what had happened, of course. She had to know the score, and that was only natural. She wasn't going to be one of those wives who weren't savvy enough to keep their eye on the old man's business.

Angus accepted that she needed to know what was going down; she needed to be prepared. She knew that he respected her for it. Because no matter what he might do, she never questioned it. And she didn't offer an opinion either way. She just wanted to be in the know. Knowledge was power. She had read that somewhere, many years ago, and it had struck a chord in her mind.

She bit into her toast and savoured the richness of the butter on her tongue. 'Oh, Mum, this is just what the doctor ordered!'

Sinead Connolly looked at her beautiful daughter and forced a smile. This one had fallen on her feet all right, and the usual guilt she felt rose to the surface once more. She loved this girl but, deep down, she didn't like her. Truth be told, she had not liked her for a long time. Her Lorna had always been self-contained, even as a child, emotionally closed off and determined to get her own way, no matter what.

Sinead was looking forward to this grandchild. She wanted an outlet for her love, because her daughter had never really needed it.

Chapter Forty-nine

Angus was still smarting from the attempted shooting, even though he knew the culprits had been dealt with.

The actual experience had rattled him more than he would ever admit. He had not been impressed about being so close to the receiving end of death at its most raw and visceral. Without Roy and his natural nous, this trip could have had a completely different outcome. That was what was bothering him. He wasn't frightened of dying, per se – he knew the pitfalls of his chosen profession – but he had never really understood the value of life. Until now.

He had never before felt so close to death. Now it was all over, and he was out of danger, his brief contact with it had thrown him. Suddenly it was all he could think about, it was filling his mind. He had believed that he was invincible, and now – for the first time – he understood that wasn't actually the case.

He had been lucky that his mum and Roy had always given him protection. He appreciated that. But he also knew now that nothing was guaranteed. Facing his own mortality gave him food for thought. He could finally see his mother's point of view. She was always going on about him watching his back, not putting himself in harm's way. He had laughed at her, even mugged her off at times. He realised now that this was the arrogance of youth.

His mum was an old hand. Not that he would ever use the epithet 'old' to her face, of course. He felt a rush of love for her. While, at times, she irritated him because she held all the cards, he couldn't deny that she deserved to hold said cards. Until this debacle he had not really appreciated that fact. Now, though, he had actually experienced what could happen when you least expected it. He wanted to hug her to him and apologise to her for every time he had rolled his eyes, or sighed with boredom, when she was trying to give him her advice.

How could he have been so crass and so obtuse? She was only looking out for him and trying to educate him in the finer points of their world. Roy had always been angry with him for his attitude towards his mum, and now he finally got it. He had been mollycoddled really. His mum had done it to protect him, as he would her – and as he would his new wife and baby.

It had also made him realise that when you did decide to remove someone from your orbit, it had to be done properly, with aplomb. Not just with excellent foresight, but also with a pretty good plan B. He wondered how he had never truly understood anything, until these last few days, and he was able to admit that he had not been clever enough to work out that he had actually been looked out for. It had just been the norm to him.

Roy had ensured that the people around him had been trustworthy and loyal, and until this had all happened he had just accepted it. He owed that man a debt that he could never repay. Because of his mum and Roy Rogers he had never had to worry about his personal safety. But now he had to start thinking long and hard about that himself. He needed to start taking responsibility for his own life.

He had been given a big wake-up call. He had to prove to everyone that he could look after himself, and his family.

And that included his mother and Roy Rogers.

Chapter Fifty

When Lorna picked up the phone she was half asleep.

Through half-closed eyes, she saw that it was after two in the morning, and she assumed it was Angus, telling her he had landed safely and was on his way home.

'Is that you, Angus?'

No one answered her. There was just silence and the hiss of a landline.

'Angus?'

She was wide awake now, and she pulled herself up into a sitting position, her belly feeling heavy and cumbersome. She listened eagerly, hoping to hear his voice.

Then she heard a woman's voice say huskily, 'Is Angus there?'

Lorna stared at the phone for a few seconds before speaking. 'Who shall I say is calling?'

The woman laughed lightly. She sounded full of fun and life as she said, 'Would you tell him it's Mandy?'

Lorna didn't answer her for long moments. She just sat there in abject disbelief. That this *person* could ring her house, ring her home! That this *person* actually had her phone number – her private phone number – was a shock in itself.

'Mandy fucking who?'

Lorna's voice was harder than a concrete bollard, and the girl on the other end of the phone seemed to pick that up.

'I said Mandy fucking who?'

Lorna was so agitated, she could feel the child quickening inside her. She felt as if she had been stabbed through the heart.

She took a deep breath to calm herself and then she said airily, 'Listen, darling, I assume you are one of the dancers in one of the clubs or whatever. They are *my* clubs too, you stupid cow, and he's my fucking husband, darling. You crossed a line when you rang our home. You really need to understand that when I find you, I will fucking kill you, and that is not an idle threat. But that's nothing to the wrath of my Angus when he finds out what you've done.'

She replaced the receiver as gently as she could. She was not going to slam it down, because that is what this girl wanted. She lay back on her pillows and made herself take more deep breaths until her anger had passed.

Sometimes she could cheerfully knock Angus out, he was so fucking predictable. Another no-brain with plastic tits and a make-up overdose no doubt. The girl was probably regretting her impulsive action already, she had sounded very young and very drunk. Lorna was really more interested in where this Mandy had got their home phone number, because she knew that she had not been given it by Angus – of that much she was sure. He could be a cunt of Olympian standards, but even he wasn't that big a cunt.

She would box clever with this latest escapade. The one thing she believed was that her Angus loved her above all others, and that was what really mattered. You couldn't hold a man like her Angus to his marital vows; there would always be other women.

She just had to make sure they didn't last.

Chapter Fifty-one

Angus was caught bang to rights, and he knew it.

That young Mandy had not seemed the type to cause murders, but he was obviously wrong. She had seemed like a little mouse, but he had really underestimated her. He couldn't believe it – what had possessed her? The dozy bitch. He had fucked her a few times, he had never declared undying love.

He knew he would have to tread carefully after this latest scandal. Lorna wouldn't let this slip by her. He had made it home, safe and sound, and got into bed as quietly as possible. He had pulled Lorna and his baby into his arms, caressing her belly, loving the feel of them so close to him, because they were the most important things in his life. After what had happened in Spain, he felt an even greater need for this woman he had married and the child they had created.

He had been just about to drop off when Lorna had said sleepily, 'Oh, you are home, darling.'

He hugged her even closer and kissed her hair. 'I've missed you, darling, I'm so glad to be home.'

Lorna kissed his hands and pulled him closer to her. 'I missed you too, Angus. And oh, before I forget, Mandy rang you at about two this morning.'

He had not said a word. He had just waited with trepidation for the ball to drop.

But – nothing. Lorna had just gone straight back to sleep.

That alone was a worry. She could keep an argument going for days if the fancy took her – and it frequently did if she felt she was within her rights. It was strange because she was the only woman he would take that kind of treatment off. He supposed it was because he respected her as well as loved her. He had been looking out for strange since day one. But if he thought she had slept with another man, he would have no worry about killing her and the culprit involved.

She wasn't like that though. He knew that he would always be enough for her. She wasn't looking for anything other than him; he had taken her virginity and she had given herself to him one hundred per cent. Even if he got twenty-five years in prison, she would wait for him without a second's thought. She was that loyal and that good.

Unfortunately, he couldn't say the same. He loved her with every ounce of his being but he just couldn't be faithful. He had tried, God knows he had tried. But he just couldn't do it. He loved being romantic with her – he showered her with flowers, chocolates and jewellery. She blossomed when they were alone together, and only he saw that side of her.

But she wasn't as sexual as he was, she wasn't as adventurous, and he appreciated that about her. He had found himself a decent and good woman, and these days they were few and far between. He loved his life with her, that they were going to have a family together, and he enjoyed being with her. But he also needed a plain, good old-fashioned fuck on a regular basis, with no strings, no dramas and no romance. He couldn't be faithful to one woman, it just wasn't in him.

147

It didn't make him love Lorna less. In fact, it made him love her more, if that was possible. He didn't want her to satisfy the needs that his outside women filled. She was going to be the mother of his children; her mouth would kiss his baby. He didn't expect her to be as earthy as the women he pursued, and he knew that Lorna wouldn't countenance it anyway. She was a lady.

But he didn't like being caught out like this. That fucking Mandy was going to be launched into outer space tomorrow. The stupid bloody bitch had committed the cardinal sin: she had made the mistake of thinking that she was important to him. Important enough to think that she could interfere with his home life. That he would not swallow. She had the shock of her life coming to her tomorrow, and she would rue the day she had crossed him and upset his wife.

That was something he would never allow from anyone, let alone a fucking lap dancer who had been round the turf more times than a prize-winning greyhound.

Chapter Fifty-two

Gabriel and Angus were in their new wine bar and club in Old Compton Street.

It looked fantastic, and they were both confident that it would be a good earner. It would also be legitimate, and that was its main asset. They were looking for mainstream legit businesses that could explain away their lifestyles. The big mistake that a lot of Faces made was that they lived beyond their means, and it was a red flag to the Filth.

Angus even knew a bloke who was bringing in a fortune and still signing on the fucking dole. It was ludicrous and, worse than that, it put everyone they dealt with in jeopardy too. He wanted to be off the radar, not putting himself on it. Now the moron was doing a lump and a half, and that could all have been avoided with a little forward planning.

Gabriel went behind the bar and poured them each a large brandy.

'Cheers, Angus. This is a right touch, mate, it looks fantastic.'

Angus grinned happily. 'I think it will be a little goldmine. I've found us a brilliant chef. He's a terrific guy – gayer than a maypole – and let's face it, this will probably be a gay club because of where it's situated. I don't care. You know me: live and let live. Anyway, Geoffrey Pole is going to give it his seal of approval, and that will guarantee the punters.'

Gabriel nodded. He knew the score as well as Angus did – though, unlike Angus, he wasn't that comfortable around the gays. They still spooked him. Angus guessed that Gabriel wouldn't be frequenting this place very often, but that didn't bother him in the least. Each to their own, was his attitude. Personally, he didn't really care about what people did in their own homes.

Gabriel drank his brandy quickly and then poured himself another.

'You're on it early, Gabe! My mother giving you a hard time, mate?'

Gabriel grinned. 'She always gives me a hard time, you know what she's like.'

They laughed together companionably. They got on well and genuinely liked each other. Gabriel appreciated that Angus didn't judge his mother or him. He had always just accepted the relationship, and that meant the world to him.

'I need a favour, Gabe, but it has to be between us.'

Gabriel was intrigued, because Angus rarely asked anyone for anything.

'If I can help, mate, I will.'

Angus smiled, pleased that Gabriel hadn't even had to think over his request for a second.

'I want you to keep my mum away from here for a few days, if you can, until the official opening night. I want to arrange a surprise for her.'

Gabriel was visibly taken aback at his request. Angus understood then that Gabriel thought he had wanted him to help him in the business in some way, and he made a mental note to do just that – get him involved in more than just this club.

He was one of the good people and Angus needed good people around him, Marbella had proved that. The events in Spain had really given him food for thought, as his old granny would say.

So he smiled and said genially, 'And once this place is up and running, I have a couple of other business propositions I want to run past you. We can have a nice lunch somewhere and talk things through.'

Gabriel looked made up. 'That sounds good to me, mate.'

He would like to work properly with Angus. And he knew it would please Diana, because it would be another person watching over her son, whether he liked it or not.

Angus checked his watch, a large and expensive TAG Heuer. He had always had a penchant for the outlandish, and the watch suited his personality. He believed that you should look the business at all times, and he made sure that he did.

'I need to get to the club in King's Cross, I have a bit of business that needs sorting.'

Gabriel knew exactly what that business was, but he didn't say anything. He didn't need to rock that particular boat.

Chapter Fifty-three

Mandy Downs was sober and of sound mind when she walked into the BB Club.

She was also very subdued and she didn't look her usual made-up and dressed-up self. In fact, she was in tracksuit bottoms and a baggy T-shirt with Duran Duran on the front; she just hadn't been up for anything since she had opened her eyes that morning. Truth be told, she was terrified of the fallout from her stupid fucking antics of the night before.

She couldn't believe she had been so reckless. But there was something about Angus that really appealed to her, and she had fallen for him hard. One thing she knew, though, was that she had to face the music, no matter what, because the last thing she wanted was Angus looking for her. As her best friend, Angel, had remarked on the phone earlier, 'Girl, you better find him first because believe me, Angus is not going to be a happy bunny.' Talk about stating the fucking obvious!

She had to get this over with. And she would apologise, because she knew she was well out of order. His wife was pregnant. What had possessed her? But she knew exactly what had possessed her. Too much champagne – or what passed for champagne in this shithole – and too much cocaine.

She went through to the dressing rooms quietly. She was

aware that Big Bobby Talbot didn't hail her as he usually did, and that alone told her all she needed to know. As she entered the club itself from the foyer, she saw Angus sitting at the bar with a glass of beer. He held his arms out, as if he was pleased to see her, and she walked towards him with trepidation.

'Hello, Mandy, I understand you had a word with my lovely wife at two o'clock this morning. Now my wife is usually a chatty person. But being heavily pregnant and asleep, she wasn't exactly, as I understand from her, what you might call friendly.' When she didn't answer, he bellowed angrily, 'Are you for real, you stupid bitch? You rang my home? Where my wife sleeps and where my child will soon be ensconced! Are you off your fucking head, woman?'

Mandy had heard tales about Angus when he was angry, but she had never experienced it herself, and his shouting terrified her. She felt the tears come, but she couldn't say a word; she was too scared, and too worried about saying the wrong thing. One thing she had learned, growing up with a violent alcoholic for a father, was to keep her mouth shut and just let the storm pass. If only her mother had learned that lesson, how different all their lives could have been.

Angus could feel the fear coming off Mandy and knew that he had done his job. Truth be told, he actually felt sorry for her. She was a nice girl, caught up in a shit world. He couldn't hold that against her. But he had to make sure that she knew she had fucked up, and fucked up big time. He also had to make her understand that they were never going to be an item in any way, shape or form.

He looked at her forlorn face. She was a good-looking sort – and she was all natural, he couldn't take that away from her. Even her hair was naturally blonde, collar and cuffs. She would be a real little touch for the right man, but that man wasn't him. She had a lovely personality, didn't have much to say for herself – but then he wanted a fuck, not a thesis on Third World poverty.

He opened his arms wide and she ran into them gratefully. She needed to be treated nicely now – after all, he wasn't a bully – plus he still had to find out how she got his phone number.

'I'm so sorry, Angus, I knew as soon as I made the call I had done wrong. But I was drunk, out of it. And I missed you.'

Angus hugged her to him and stroked her beautiful hair. He would miss that hair; it was so long and thick, and when she was splayed on the bed it was like a silken halo. She was a real looker, there was no disputing that.

'Look, Mandy, you have caused me a lot of upset and aggravation with my wife. Darling, I would never leave her – you know that. She is the only woman who will ever bear my name. You're a nice girl, but she is my actual *wife*, and I can't have people upsetting her – ever.'

Mandy was really crying now. She felt so guilty – and so relieved that he wasn't still balling her out.

'Come on, calm yourself down, Mandy. Now I need to ask you something, and I want a truthful answer, OK?' He tilted her face up so he could look into her eyes. 'Who gave you my home number?'

Mandy shook her head and smiled tearfully. 'No one gave it to me. I just saw you dial it.'

Angus raised an eyebrow. 'You are telling me that you saw me dial a number, and you remembered it?'

She nodded, and then repeated the number back to him. 'I have always had that knack, Angus. I only have to see something once and I can remember it.'

Angus wasn't sure if she was taking the piss.

Mandy saw the disbelief on his face, and she said quickly, 'I can prove it. Write something down and show it to me, and I will tell you exactly what you wrote.'

Angus got off the stool and walked behind the bar. He poured out two glasses of brandy, then he picked up a pad and a pencil and went back to his seat.

He handed her a drink, saying, 'Have a sip of that, and wipe your nose, darling.'

He wrote on the pad four phone numbers and the address of a man he'd had reason to visit a few weeks earlier. He handed the pad to Mandy. She glanced over it, and handed it back.

'Come on then, clever bollocks, show me what you can do.'

No one was more surprised than Angus when she did just that. She repeated it all back to him verbatim.

'I am a bit nervous, Angus, so you have to allow for that.'

He was blown away, and he immediately wrote down another set of numbers, random this time, and a verse from a poem he had always loved.

Once again, she repeated it all back to him, number perfect, and word for word.

'You know what you have, don't you, Mandy? I was reading about this a while ago. You have an eidetic memory. Mostly kids have it, I think, then lose it. But a small percentage of the population keep it. It's also called a photographic memory. It's a fucking wonderful gift to possess.'

Mandy was just pleased she had made him happy. She had always had that gift; it just came naturally to her.

Angus rubbed his hands together gleefully. 'You and me are going to use that gift of yours, Mandy, and it is going to make you a wealthy woman, providing you do what I say. Now do you think you could do that for me?'

Mandy Downs nodded happily, thankful that she had dodged a bullet, because she had been sure she would be out of work from today and, even worse, barred from any of the other clubs. But it seemed that she was still in with a chance, and anything that kept her near this man would always be a good thing to her.

'Let me make a few phone calls, darling, while you finish your drink.'

She finished her brandy in one gulp and smiled tremulously as Angus refilled her glass.

He winked at her saucily. He had not even dreamed that someone like her could actually be of any real value. She was just a good-looking girl, a lap-dancing slag who he had used to scratch an itch, because that was all these girls were, could ever be. But she had a gift that, in the right hands, could be utilised in so many ways.

She was a dream come true. Who would have thought that today would have ended up giving him so much pleasure? It just went to prove that you never knew what was around the fucking corner.

The first person he rang was his mother.

Chapter Fifty-four

Angus had stayed close to home for a few days. He knew what he had to do to convince Lorna that he was suitably contrite.

He was genuinely devastated that she had been subjected to that kind of humiliation; he would never have wished that on her. He was in the wrong in every way, and he was quite content to show Lorna that. He had also boxed clever because he had asked for her input in making the first night of the new club a thank-you to his mum, and listened to her ideas for planning it all.

If there was one thing his Lorna loved, it was planning things, and being in charge. His mother had helped them buy this place, and Lorna was going to make sure that his mum knew that they were grateful for that. She might not love his mum, but she was savvy enough not to bite the hand that fed them. She was full of ideas and, in fairness, some of them were excellent.

Lorna had a natural talent for what was tasteful, and that was something he knew was instinctive. Even the way she dressed was perfect; she looked amazing and sexy, without revealing anything, and she didn't overload the make-up. That was a big part of her charm, as far as he was concerned.

Angus lay in bed beside her, listening to her breathing. She slept so quietly and she looked so exquisite, with her high cheekbones and her lustrous hair, that he could happily watch her for hours.

He felt the sudden dampness and wondered for a few moments what it could be. He thought for a split second that she had wet the bed. When she sat up and groaned, he felt panic rising inside him.

'My waters have broken, Angus. Ring the hospital and get my bag. We need to get going!'

She doubled over in pain, and he heard her shouting for her mother, who was staying with them in preparation for the baby.

Sinead came into the bedroom, half asleep, but she took one look at her daughter and said quickly, 'Oh, darling, you're definitely on your time.' She looked at Angus and shouted, 'Well, get dressed and get the fucking car! This baby is on its way.'

Angus obeyed. As he was getting his trousers on, he was struck by the excitement of a man about to meet his first child. It was suddenly real, and he felt the rush of adrenalin.

As he ran back into the bedroom, Sinead shouted, 'Phone an ambulance, Angus! This baby ain't hanging around for no fucker, it's already well on its way.'

He did as he was told. This was women's work, he wasn't about to question any of it. Then he went back into the bedroom, and he knelt by the bed and held Lorna's hand as she grunted in pain.

'The ambulance will be here in a minute, darling, don't worry.'

Lorna looked magnificent. She was in control, and he could see her concentrating on every movement of their child. Every time she had a contraction, she squeezed his hand tightly and he watched her face, amazed at how she stopped herself from crying out from what was obviously such incredible pain. Then she kicked off the blankets, and he saw her back arching as she pushed down while swallowing another scream.

'Fucking hell, Angus, this is too quick. You jammy cow, Lorna.'

Lorna and her mother started to laugh, and Angus watched in amazement as they giggled together.

'Oh, Mum, it hurts.'

'Of course it hurts – look at the size of Angus's head. If it takes after him, it will be like birthing Frankenstein's monster.'

Now Lorna and her mother were laughing and crying at the same time.

Angus couldn't believe that his Lorna could find humour among all this blood and gore. He put his hands to his head, because he just didn't know what he was supposed to do. His wife was in agony on the bed. She was bleeding, and he could see her belly tightening with every pain, and yet she was laughing. It was just outside of anything he had ever seen or experienced in his whole life.

His mother had gone through this pain to bring him into the world. And from what he had heard, his dad was in the pub being patted on the back for his part in this miracle.

Then Lorna seemed to change, and he felt it, as did his mother-in-law.

'Oh, Mum, Angus . . . the pain, the fucking pain!'

Sinead smiled at her daughter and said, 'You are crowning, darling, the baby's head is coming out. You're nearly there, Lorna.'

Lorna put her head on her chest and she pushed, and as she pushed, she let out a howl like an animal. Angus watched in shock and awe as his child's head came out of his wife's body. He had never seen anything so vicious or so violent or so beautiful in his whole life.

'You're nearly there, Lorna, one more push, darling. Oh, where the fuck is the ambulance!'

Angus watched in utter astonishment as his child emerged, and he watched as his Lorna pulled herself up, crying, 'Is it OK, Mum, is it OK?'

Then he heard the ambulance, and he ran down to open the gates and let them in so they could tell him that his wife was going to be all right. Because after what he had just witnessed, he couldn't believe that women could go through that more than once in their lives.

It was visceral, it was bloody, and it was miraculous. His beautiful Lorna had not only grown but she had even birthed a human being, all by herself. She had expelled that child from her body in pain, and she had still been laughing. It was just the most perfect thing he had ever been witness to. And he didn't care how many times this same thing happened in the world, every second of the day, to him it had been a revelation, and he loved and respected his wife – and his own mother – even more than he had before.

The ambulance men were fantastic, and he watched as they looked over his wife and child, cut the cord and declared them both hale and hearty. When they put them in the ambulance to take them to the hospital, he hugged his wife so tightly she had to prise his arms away from her.

'It's a boy, Angus, in case you were wondering.'

He was crying with emotion as he kissed them both tenderly. 'You were a warrior tonight, Lorna, you were just magnificent, darling.'

Sinead laughed then. 'What she was, Angus, was bloody lucky. It was all over in no time.'

Angus went to the hospital with his wife and son in the ambulance. He had never felt such a rush in his life. He couldn't stop staring at his wife and his son, this lad he had seen entering the world. He had heard all the talk from the other men about their wives, and their kids being born, but nothing had prepared him for the drama and the reality of it. He knew that he would never forget this night as long as he lived, and he didn't ever want to.

Lorna smiled at him happily as she cradled their son in her arms. 'We will call him Angus, like you.'

Angus just nodded. He couldn't take his eyes off his son who, if he was being honest, looked like a wrinkly, miserable old man. He was already deeply in love. This was the start of a whole new chapter in his life, and he knew that never again would he ever feel completely safe, because he now had an Achilles heel.

He now had someone he would happily die for.

Book Three

1988

What ought a man to be? Well, my short answer is himself.

Peer Gynt,
Henrik Ibsen (1828–1906)

Chapter Fifty-five

The music was heavy and loud, and the whole place was absolutely banging – it was exactly what Angus wanted.

He could smell the sweat, which equalled success, and that was all he was interested in. There was a vibe that ran through certain clubs. He always felt it when he walked in – and not just because he owned them. If they didn't have that feeling within three months of opening then he was quite happy to let them go, sell them on, and let the new owners trade on his name for a while.

It was a competitive market, and no one understood that better than he did. He made sure that they had the most in-demand DJs, the very newest music and also the best people working the floors. That meant employing good-looking boys and girls who were an attraction in themselves. They were also there to guide the punters to not only the top-priced alcoholic beverages but also the best drugs that could be purchased, with an unspoken guarantee that they were the safest they could hope for. Angus had seen the sense in that, and he had made it his mission to ensure that the drugs supplied in his venues were not fucking home-made and liable to kill the very people he was catering for. That kind of business would be pointless.

He wasn't running a one-off rave; he had clubs that were

open regularly and were known as *the* places to be. This generation had mobile phones, and word travelled fast, sourcing the places they wanted to go.

What kept him on top was that he offered a service that was not only quality but was also appreciated by the punters and brought them back time and time again. All this lot wanted was a few good Es, decent music and a good drink; it wasn't exactly rocket science. He was basically printing his own dosh.

Supply and demand was the great British anti-work ethic for criminals since World War Two. The black economy had kept this country afloat since time began, and even though past governments had tried their hardest to destroy it, everyone knew that would never happen. This country couldn't exist without it. That was the beauty of a consumer society, and Maggie Thatcher was its biggest advocate. They were mugs, and they were too fucking blinkered by their policies to even give it a whirl.

If they just legalised cannabis, they could pay for everything – from the NHS to the OAPs – without batting a fucking eyelid. But no, it cost the taxpayers a fortune to bankroll court cases for an eighth of home grown, clogging up the judicial system and the prisons. The sentences were fucking outrageous, considering that cannabis was organic.

It was scandalous really, because these people who were governing the laws were so set in their ways, they should have been pensioned off years ago. They weren't really aware enough to make laws for the emerging generations, they didn't understand that times had changed drastically since their youth. Give old Maggie her due, at least she encouraged free enterprise. She was a bit of a battleaxe, but you couldn't fault her when it came to earning a good crust.

As usual, Angus was being walked through the club with his

minders all around him. Even that was just for show. Angus knew that the people who frequented his clubs loved that he was mentioned in the tabloids. There was a lot of talk about him, of course, but no one could ever prove anything, he made sure of that. But he was a Face, and he knew that for his clubs to work he had to be seen, and he was. It all added to his reputation – a reputation that stood up quite well on its own. The talk about him just enhanced his business and his clubs, and that was what it was all about these days.

It was a great time to be a villain because, basically, they were once again flavour of the fucking month. It was like the fifties and sixties, when the Faces were seen as glamorous and someone to aspire to be. And if you had a good idea for an earn, you would be listened to.

As he moved through the club, people tried to get his attention and act like they knew him. Every now and then he would wave to someone, or acknowledge a greeting. As the *Sun* had said recently, move over Peter Stringfellow, there was a new king of the clubs.

He had a certain public persona, and that was useful because it guaranteed him an alibi as and when he needed it. He knew how to play the game, and he played it with aplomb. He was a showman, and that was a big part of his attraction for the women and the men around him.

As he stepped into the private lift that would take him up to his offices, he winked and smiled at two girls who were standing nearby and watching him in awe. He sighed regretfully. If he didn't have a serious meeting, he would have invited the two of them up to his offices and done them, one after the other. It would not have been the first time. He made sure to use a condom on the strangers; after all, you couldn't be too careful – the last thing he needed in his life was to give his wife a round of applause. The fucking clap.

He might be a family man but, as he often said, he wasn't a fucking eunuch. There was too much strange and too little time. He was surrounded by it – it was basically an occupational hazard.

His Lorna enjoyed him making love to her, and he felt the same. But once every six weeks wasn't exactly his idea of a lively fucking sex life. She could do without it for months and not bat a fucking eyelid. That was her prerogative – she was the mother of two boys now, and his wife; she deserved his utmost respect. They had different body clocks, different outlooks, and completely different ideas when it came to the boudoir. Lorna accepted that and, after that palaver with Mandy, he made sure that his dalliances never, *ever* encroached on their relationship. Consequently, they had a truly wonderful life. They were happy and contented when they were together, and that was all that mattered to him.

Once the lift arrived at the offices, he started to laugh, and Roy laughed with him, even though he didn't know quite what the joke was. But Angus did have an infectious laugh.

'Did you see him and all, Roy?'

Roy shook his head but was still laughing. Desmond Mabele and Jonathan Heartland, his minders, just stood there watching. Both had faces like a well-slapped arse. They knew they were not paid to give opinions.

'See who?'

Angus wasn't laughing any more. 'Dicky Matthews was at the main bar with that little queen. What's his name? He was with Geoffrey for a while. Star? Starina? One of them fucking drag names.'

Roy wasn't laughing now either. He stared at Angus for long moments before saying quietly, 'Sharina, is that who you mean?'

Angus nodded, relieved to have got the right person. It would have driven him mad otherwise. 'That's it, him. He's got some fucking front, showing his boat-race here.'

Roy shrugged nonchalantly – he wasn't sure what Angus was getting at. 'Why would you think that, Angus? He ain't done nothing to us. He is always in those circles – you know that as well as I do.'

Angus looked at Roy and said seriously, 'He was with that treacherous bastard Jackie Saunders when we took him out. I didn't like him then, and I like him even less now.'

Roy tried to brush his concerns aside. 'Come on, Angus, think about it. He is a tart! He is like our girls – they are with whoever has the money. He is no threat to us.'

Angus shook his head. 'I just don't trust him, Roy, there's something off about him. I warned Geoffrey Pole about him, and he will tell you that himself. That boy has a slipperiness about him, something not fucking kosher. And now he's here with Dicky? He's a pretty boy, I get that. But he ain't *that* pretty.'

Roy thought about it; he could understand where Angus was coming from. He was amazed at how Angus had even noticed him – particularly in a club that could comfortably hold a thousand people. But Angus had that edge, and he had to admire him for it.

'I will keep an eye on him, Angus, OK?'

Angus nodded. 'You do that. And remember, he was the last person to see Jackie Saunders alive.'

The implication was there, and Roy was sensible enough to take what he was hearing seriously. 'Of course I do, Angus.'

Angus rubbed his hands together and said to his minders

169

jovially, 'Well, come on, lads, throw a couple of lines and I will pour the Jameson's. This is going to be a night to remember.'

They all laughed, but Roy was distracted. Angus had undoubtedly picked up on something. He had a strange knack of sniffing out not just traitors but outright skulduggery. He could smell a con from a thousand feet away, and he was always right. He had inherited that from his mother.

It was a skill that had kept Diana's old man in the driving seat for so long, and her at the top of her game. It made the people they worked with trust her judgement and respect it. Both Diana and Angus could smell a bullshitter within nanoseconds, and that was a real bonus in their game.

Roy would look into this little queen, and he would find out the score with him.

As Angus always opined, you could never be too cautious. That had been proved on more than one occasion.

Chapter Fifty-six

Lorna stopped to catch her breath for a moment, and stretched happily.

She loved the early mornings, and she liked to run. That had become her thing over the last few years. She had really got into running; it was weird because she had never been what could be called the energetic type. But she had taken up jogging after her second son, Sean, was born, and it had eventually turned into actual running.

She had joined a gym, and it had been good at first, but it had not been right for her. She didn't like that there were so many people there. Then she had started running with her personal trainer, and she had found that she actually enjoyed it – no one had been more surprised than her. She still had the personal trainer, twice a week, but now he came to the house and they did a workout here. She was in fantastic shape even after two kids.

She ran every day, and she felt so much healthier for it, but it also afforded her time to think. She did her best thinking while she was running, and that had just added to the attraction. She ran across their land, and that was a real treat, because she loved running in the darkness, just her and her thoughts. It was when she finally felt free. She ran in the dark until the sun came up. That was something she really treasured; it was just a fantastic feeling to chase the sunrise.

As much as she loved her children, there was something about the time to herself in the really early morning that appealed to her. There was the quiet and the knowledge that she was completely alone.

More or less anyway.

She knew that there were armed men around the property; that was a given, considering the life they lived. But Angus had ensured that she didn't see them, so she could have the illusion of solitude. She regretted that they had to have people around them night and day, but a part of her recognised that it was the price they had to pay for the life they lived. It was a very privileged life that she loved, and she wouldn't give it up for anything. Angus told her just enough of what he was doing so that if he ever had a capture – God forbid – and the Old Bill ever questioned her, she would know exactly what she needed to say. He didn't want her to worry about anything else.

As she ran back towards her house, she stopped under the silver birch trees that they couldn't touch, because they were under a protection order. That was something she loved too – that these trees had been there for hundreds of years. She could hear Angus's car coming down the drive and she sighed sadly. Her peace was broken. She took a deep breath and started to run again towards her beautiful home.

It was much bigger these days, and it looked stunning in the morning light. They had added to it, but made sure the newer parts looked as old as the rest of it, and she never tired of admiring what she had achieved with it.

Angus got out of the Bentley and he waited patiently until

she ran into his open arms, then he kissed her heartily and hugged her to him.

'You and your bleeding running, girl. But you do look good on it, lady.'

She grinned with pleasure, because that was exactly what she wanted to hear.

'You look like shit, Angus. Another all-nighter?'

Angus opened his arms in a gesture of supplication.

'You know my work starts when everyone else is going to bed, darling.'

Lorna kissed him once again on the lips.

'Come on, Angus, I'll cook you a good breakfast before you go to bed. The boys will be up soon and we can all eat together.'

On days like this, Angus just couldn't fault her. She knew exactly what he needed, and she gave it to him. He was the luckiest man on the planet.

'That sounds absolutely perfect, my lovely.'

They walked into the house together, wrapped in each other's arms, and his driver shook his head sagely and wished his wife had been so easy-going. She could cause a fight in an empty house.

There was no denying it, Angus Davis was one fucking jammy bastard, in more ways than one.

Chapter Fifty-seven

Diana was listening to Roy as he explained her son's reservations about Sharina, the little queen who kept on popping up where he wasn't wanted.

'He was with Roger Matthews' boy? Dicky?' Diana was interested now.

Roy laughed. 'Well, he is the gay one, isn't he? So yeah. But I think your Angus might have a point. That lad seems to be around a lot of people we have dealt with, in one way or another. There's no telling what he knows or who he might spill to.'

Diana nodded. 'I get what you're saying, but it could just be a coincidence. I mean, let's face it, they are always together. They are all gay guys – friends – it's no different to us lot out and about, is it?'

Roy knew she was speaking sense, but he also felt that her son had an excellent radar for traitors.

'Look, Di, I will lay my cards on the table. Over the years, there's one thing I have had to accept, and that is your boy is a lot like you. He can sniff out a fucking romancer from a hundred paces. If he says this bastard needs looking at then I am right behind him.'

Diana was willing to agree that he had a point. She had a

sixth sense, and she had always hoped that her son had inherited it, because in their game it was a real bonus.

'OK, if you are so adamant then you make sure someone keeps an eye on him. After all, Trigger, like you say, he does seem to keep some interesting company. I will bankroll whatever you think is necessary.'

Roy nodded. She had called him Trigger, and that was a term of endearment between them. And she had also said she would give him carte blanche, and pay for it, so her son didn't know the extent of their digging. He could understand that too. Angus didn't need to know, unless there was something worth knowing.

Roy Rogers was well pleased. He would be all over that little fucker like a rash. Now Sharina was on his radar, he'd decided he didn't trust him for a moment.

Chapter Fifty-eight

Angus was in his offices in Old Compton Street. He felt right at home here, and he loved this particular club.

It was the venue that he felt had really put him on the map. He had a nostalgia for it, because he had opened it with a huge party for his mum. That had been an absolute blinder of a night. Anyone who was anyone was there and Angus had never felt more the Big I Am until that moment, everyone praising his beautiful wife and baby and marvelling at what a benevolent son he was to Diana to throw her such a spectacular celebration.

The club had just grown bigger and more famous as the years had gone on. It was becoming an institution, and so it should. He had a wonderful staff too – loyal and honest. From this place alone he could now prove his lifestyle to the taxman, should that ever become necessary. This place, like all his others, was straighter than the majority of the clientele. That was the fucking best thing about it; they were doing so well with the legitimate clubs that everything else was basically bunce.

He was looking forward to seeing Geoffrey Pole. After their rocky start, they had become very good friends over the years, and now he genuinely liked the guy. It was one of the rare times Angus's gut instinct had been off – he could admit that now. Geoffrey had proven his loyalty and his worth. He was on the ball in certain circles, and that was always worth knowing. Geoffrey had the knack of being able to find out anything, if the price was right.

He heard Geoffrey before he saw him, and he smiled at the man's determination to make himself known to all and sundry. He was just so loud, and camper than a row of tents. That was the Geoffrey he knew and loved.

When he walked into the room, Angus hugged him like a brother and said seriously, 'This was supposed to be a private meeting, remember.'

Geoffrey laughed loudly as he said, 'For me, darling, this is!'

Angus Davis laughed with him because, in reality, he knew he couldn't have expected anything else. 'You are a funny fucker, Geoffrey.'

Geoffrey Pole put his hands under his chin, as if he was praying, and rolled his eyes like an ingénue as he said, 'I love it when you talk dirty to me, Angus.'

They both laughed again. They had developed a good friendship, and that was important to them both.

They needed each other, and they were both more than aware of that.

Chapter Fifty-nine

Diana and Gabriel were in a private club in Brixton.

Gabriel had inherited this place, many years before, from a win while playing poker. He had kept it, although few people knew that he actually owned it. He had let the original owner and his wife and kids stay there, as if nothing untoward had happened. They paid him a peppercorn rent, and life went on as usual. But occasionally, like today, he requested the use of the rooms for his private business. It was a deal that worked well for all involved.

Janelle, the landlord's wife, brought through a tray of drinks, and Diana smiled her thanks. On the tray was a bottle of Jameson's and six glasses.

'How are the boys, Janelle? Bloody hell, the spit of their father I hear!'

Janelle laughed. 'Oh, they're their father's sons all right. But what can I do, Di?'

The two women laughed together, both comfortable in each other's company.

'I hear you, darling.'

They chatted for another few minutes, and then Janelle left them to it.

They were in the back of the club and waiting for the knock

on the door. When it came, they looked at one another for a few seconds and then Gabriel let their guests inside.

Dicky Matthews was already on his dignity; he was under the mistaken impression that he was important in some way. Diana was looking forward to disabusing him of that notion, but she knew how to play the game – especially with ice creams like him. He was an embarrassment to himself and his family – a bully, no more and no less. He was everything that was wrong with the new wave of Faces.

Smiling widely, she said, 'Oh my goodness, just look at you, all grown-up.'

Dicky visibly relaxed at her tone and remembered that this woman was a good friend of his mum and his dad. 'So what's with the cloak and dagger then?' He could hear the nervousness in his own voice and he didn't like it. But Diana Davis was a legend in her own lunchtime and he was suddenly acutely aware that he was here in the middle of Brixton, alone and vulnerable, and being interrogated by a woman who the hardest of men spoke of with respect.

Diana poured them all a large whiskey and said, 'That is exactly what I was going to ask you! Great minds, eh?'

Gabriel held out a chair and said quietly, 'I'd sit down, if I was you.'

Dicky Matthews did exactly as he had been told. He really didn't know what else to do.

Chapter Sixty

'Do you know what, Angus? Sometimes you really fucking annoy me.'

Angus was genuinely taken aback. He could hear the anger in Geoffrey's voice, and that was something he had not expected. He had a lot of respect for this man, and he assumed that Geoffrey knew that. He stood up suddenly; he was not only annoyed himself now, he was really offended.

He looked at Geoffrey and said seriously, 'How the fuck can you say something like that to me?'

Geoffrey sighed heavily and, waving his hands, he said, 'Oh, for fuck's sake, sit down and get off your high horse for five minutes! Just have a day off, will you? Honestly, Angus, how long have we been mates? And I mean mates, real friends.'

Angus shook his head in bewilderment. 'Years, Geoff, fucking years.'

Geoffrey Pole nodded his head pointedly at the answer. 'Precisely, and yet you bring me here to ask me about some kind of skulduggery, without thinking that if I had heard anything about it, I would have come and told you anyway. Because I have in the past, remember?'

Angus knew that what the man said was true, and he had to hold his hand up. But, in all honesty, today wasn't really the day for heart-searching and breathtaking honesty. He just wanted answers, and he wanted them quick.

'Geoff, listen to me, I know that if you had heard anything credible, you would have shared it with me before now. But I also know that there is something going on with Dicky Matthews and that queen, fucking Sharina, or whatever she calls herself. She was with Jackie before he was outed permanently. Now I called you here to ask you, as a friend, if you think that cunt is on a mission. Only she seems to be in a lot of company that has – shall we say? – fucked me and other people I know right off.'

Geoffrey swallowed down his drink, and then he said saucily, 'OK, I can see where you are coming from. But, honestly, all I ever knew him as was a bum chum – no more and no less – and let's face it, he ain't getting any younger. I will ask around and see what I can find out, but seriously I have never heard his name mentioned outside of a bedroom. He isn't what us gays would call "in the first flush of youth" – and, in fairness to him, he was a beautiful boy in his day. But you know us lot, fucking dog years, over the hill by twenty-five.

'I can't see it myself. He is just with whoever is paying for his drinks. He isn't capable of thinking anything through logically, and he certainly couldn't work a con. More fool him! If he had used his brain when he was younger, he would be sitting pretty now, with his own drum and a bit of a pension. Believe me, Angus, an original thought in his head would die of fucking loneliness.'

Angus shrugged genially. 'I hope I'm wrong, Geoffrey, but by the same token he seems to keep strange bedfellows, from my point of view. I just need to know if he might become a problem to me in the future, and I am sure you can understand my reasoning.'

Geoffrey nodded and smiled. There was another underlying threat, and that was as it should be, because Geoffrey would have done the same thing had he been in Angus's position.

'Well, when you put it like that . . .'

The two men laughed together, but they both knew they now had an understanding.

Chapter Sixty-one

Dicky Matthews was frightened. He wasn't sure why he was being interrogated in a backstreet boozer off the Railton Road in Brixton, but it felt like Diana and her entourage expected him to provide the answers they were looking for. He could only hope that he had them. What the fuck could they possibly want from him that warranted this kind of private meeting?

His family connections had always ensured he could carry on pretty much how he wanted, and that suited him. But he was more than aware that it didn't extend as far as the Davis family. Diana smiled, and Dicky had to admit that, even at her advanced age, she still looked fucking good for it. He wouldn't kick her out of bed, if he was that way inclined, which – thank the Lord – he wasn't. But he adored women, especially strong ones. And strength was in the way Diana carried herself.

His mother was much younger, but she had given up on her figure years ago. He had tried to help her, but it was a pointless exercise. She had no interest whatsoever in keeping herself smart and well groomed. Her life was all about fried food and fucking soaps. He loved her – she was his mum – but he wished she had a bit of nous about her. Still she was what she was and he couldn't change that – God knows, he had tried.

When he looked at Diana, he couldn't help but be impressed.

She really did take care of herself, always dressed well, had a good figure, and her legs were still worth a second look. She wore heels, and that impressed him. She was everything that he would love his old mum to be.

'Earth to fucking Dicky!'

Diana's voice was loud, and he realised that he had been off in his own world; that was one of the after-effects of the MDMA. It always got him thinking deeply about everything when he was coming down.

'Sorry, I was miles away. I was just thinking . . . well, to be honest, I was admiring your outfit. You are always so well turned out.'

Diana knew that the boy was actually telling the truth. He was coming down hard, and that worked in her favour, so she topped up his whiskey.

'Well, thank you, I will take that as a compliment. Now let's have a drink and a chat, and then you can be on your merry way.'

They clinked glasses and both took a deep mouthful of the Jameson's. Dicky was feeling more relaxed now, and it was evident.

Diana went for the kill: 'So who's the little queen you are often with? What's her name? Sharina?'

Dicky was suddenly enlightened. Oh, this was going to be easy! He couldn't understand why he had ever been worried. He could clear this up in no time.

'Actually her real name is not Sharina, believe it or not.'

Diana rolled her eyes in an exaggerated fashion and said jokingly, 'Fucking hell, Dicky, you think?'

Dicky chose to ignore the sarcasm, and instead he said seriously, 'His real name is Michael Greenberg and his family are right proper Jews. You can imagine what they must think of him, can't you? But I can tell you, until today, I have never had

184

any reason to think he is anything other than a pretty boy. He isn't what you would call a candidate for MENSA, if you know what I'm saying. He is a fuck buddy and, believe me, having a serious conversation with him would be like pulling teeth.'

Diana had a feeling that Dicky was telling the truth. Or at least he thought it was the truth anyway. So the only other scenario was that this little love was working for somebody else. Maybe they needed to talk to him themselves – especially as he was apparently related to the Greenberg family. Now that was a revelation. It was something she needed to think about, and she also needed to talk to her son about it.

She'd had her dealings with Solly Greenberg over the years, but she had never even heard a whisper about this son of his, and that in itself bothered her. It was what her old man would have called a melon scratcher all right. Like her son, Diana had a sense there was something going on that needed to be investigated.

It just didn't feel right.

Chapter Sixty-two

'Oh, would you just let it go, Angus, and see this for what it is? We are on the same page, for fuck's sake. I think that is a compliment to both of us.'

Angus wasn't in the least impressed with his mother's interference. More so because he knew she could only have been told about the situation by Roy.

Diana poured three large Scotches and, passing a glass each to Gabriel and Angus, she said earnestly, 'All right, son, I hold my hand up. I keep an eye on you, because that is what mothers do. I always have. You have two boys of your own now, and believe me, Angus, you will be as bad as I am, if not fucking worse. The thought of anyone hurting them, even with words, feels like you are personally harmed yourself. That need to protect never leaves you, and that is how it should be.'

As much as she had annoyed him, Angus understood what his mother was saying to him. He would murder for his sons – and he would do it joyfully, to make sure they were taken care of – but her actions still irked him.

'For fuck's sake, Mum, I run all these businesses – not just here, but in Spain too. You stepping in like this makes me look like a fucking amateur, like I need my mum to do my fighting for me. What am I, seven?'

Diana sighed. She knew what he was saying was right – she should have brought him in on her plan – but, in fairness, they still didn't know if there even was a situation to deal with yet.

She said as much. 'Look, there's nothing to say that this is even viable. We are both relying on our shit-detectors. I wanted to have a nose and see what the score is. I promise if there had been anything to tell you then you would have been the first to know.'

Angus shook his head angrily. 'I know that Roy reports to you, and I get that, I do. But he should have left me to sort this out. I'm angry with him because I feel like I am being policed – and that's not something I am comfortable with, Mother. I mean, correct me if I'm wrong, but I do believe that avoiding surveillance is the whole object of our chosen business.'

The irony of his words wasn't lost on any of them. Neither was the sarcasm, of course. The worst thing with her Angus was that, when the fancy took him, he could talk such absolute bollocks because of his love of words.

Diana had the grace to look at least a little chastised. She walked to her son and, putting her arms on his shoulders, she forced him to look into her eyes as she said, 'Roy loves you like a son. He was just looking out for you, Angus, and that is something that you should be grateful for.'

Angus knew that he should fight her. But he couldn't, because what she was saying was true. That didn't make it better though. She had still mugged him off, even if she had done it for what she thought were the right reasons.

'That is not the point. You have to stop fucking pre-empting me, Mum. I am doing a sterling job, and I really don't need a babysitter, OK?'

Diana nodded reluctantly. He was still governed by his

emotions, especially when he was angry. That was what he had inherited from his father. Her Angus had had a taste for the dramatic and the theatrical, and that was all well and good, but it could quite easily come back and bite him on the arse when he least expected it.

She kept her peace this time. Instead she said humbly, 'What can I say except I'm sorry, son?'

Gabriel had to turn away. He couldn't watch her, but he had to admire her; she knew exactly how to manipulate a situation for her own ends.

'Listen, I am meeting with Solly Greenberg later. And I think you should be a part of that meet.'

Chapter Sixty-three

Angus was impressed that his mother had sorted a meeting with the man himself so quickly. But, then again, she had been dealing with Solomon Greenberg for a long time and, without her, he would never have known that the man even existed.

Solomon Greenberg kept himself very much to himself, and rarely mixed with anyone outside of his own circle. Angus had never seen the man in the flesh; he had always dealt with his sons, or other family members. So this would be an education of sorts, and that alone piqued his interest.

It was always the same with his mum, she never ceased to amaze; just when you thought you had her bang to rights, she would pull off a stunt that would leave you panting in antici-pation. He couldn't deny that, as much as she annoyed him, he was impressed with her. He remembered once, as a kid, hearing her talk to Albie Marks, a real old fucking Face, who had come to her for a handout when he had got out of nick. He was an old-school gentleman, with the air of a dangerous man who felt he was entitled to a wage. Angus had come in on the tail end of the conversation, and he had listened with respect – after all, everyone had heard of Albie Marks.

'You and your old man owe me, Diana, and you know that. What you giving me – a poxy two grand?'

He had heard the threat and the menace in the man's voice, seen the way he was standing there with his prison haircut and his cheap suit, expecting to have a fight for what he deemed his rights.

His mum had looked at the man for long moments before she had said viciously, 'I will overlook your attitude today and put it down to overexcitement about being out of nick, Albie. You were a good friend of my old man, and that is the only reason you got a fucking halfpenny off me. You've been away a very long time and, as I am of a pleasant disposition, I will not have the fuck hammered out of you, for old times' sake. Now take your money and fuck off before I change my mind.'

Only she could have pulled that off – and Angus had known that, even then, as a young child. That she had finally decided to bring him into the fold and was taking him with her today as an equal meant the world to him.

Roy had explained, over and over again, that if he didn't act the goat so much, his mother would have brought him in a lot sooner. Today he understood that. But if this was what it took for her to finally admit that he was a grown-up then he was more than happy to swallow his knob and go along with it.

In all honesty, what choice did he really have? Like Albie Marks, he had learned that his mother was a law unto herself. She was a hard act to follow.

He had really had the best of teachers, he could never deny that. She was at the top of her profession, and she was still someone to be reckoned with.

Chapter Sixty-four

Solomon Greenberg and his wife had retired to Leigh-on-Sea a few years earlier. They had bought a beautiful detached house that overlooked the estuary, and they had settled there quite happily. Both were glad to leave North London behind, although they still had all their businesses, of course.

Solomon and his wife, Rachel, had a large family: four sons and two daughters. All were adults now, and most of them lived within a ten-minute drive. They didn't count their son Michael in the family, as he had been dead to them for many a year. His lifestyle had guaranteed that.

Solomon was aware that his wife and daughters still kept in contact with his errant son sporadically, and he had decided not to stop that or even mention it to them. They were women, and they didn't understand the world of men. Plus he knew that it gave his wife a measure of comfort to see her son, because it proved to her that his father had not had him murdered. He loved his wife with all his considerable heart, so he was more than willing to be magnanimous.

He couldn't even imagine what it must be like to grow a child inside of you and then deliver it into the world. Every time it happened, it was a miracle. But he also believed it gave women a weakness, and that had been proved to him on more

191

than one occasion. How his wife could even countenance having any kind of contact with that aberration she had produced, he just couldn't understand. But women were weak, and that was something he had to accept.

Now this son of his had brought him to the wrong kind of attention of the people he dealt with – who he had dealt with for many years – and he felt the shame that his son's lifestyle had brought upon him. He wished he had listened to his eldest brother, all those years ago: 'You cut out a cancer, Sol, and that is exactly what you have to do with Michael.'

It was his weakness; he had loved the boy. He had believed he would become a rabbi, or a scholar – someone he could be proud of – instead he was a *fagele*. It had broken his heart to know that he had harboured him in his home and had not seen him for what he really was.

It was a very difficult time for him, and he could feel the anger building inside him as the minutes passed. He had a reputation as a hard man, if need be; you didn't get to where he was in life by being weak.

As he waited for Diana Davis to arrive, he felt the weight of his shame as if it was an actual burden. His shoulders were stooped and his back was aching from the years of having to keep it all inside of him. He straightened himself up and looked around his beautiful home. No matter what, he had nothing to berate himself for. His son was nothing more than a kink of nature.

Anyway, it would all be over today, and that would be the end of it.

Chapter Sixty-five

Dicky Matthews was laughing his head off. He was completely stoned and, as he walked into his flat off West End Lane in West Hampstead, he couldn't stop himself from bursting out laughing again.

He looked at his friend Sharina. Until he had found out that he was so in demand, he had not really been that interested in him. He was funny, and he was available. Plus he was experienced, and so good at what he did! His tongue alone was worth its weight in gold – he could do things with it that even Dicky had never known were possible.

He was cheap too, and that had to be taken into consideration, because Dicky had always had a penchant for trade – it was what floated his boat. He cottaged in the most unlikely of places! But that was part of the thrill as far as he was concerned. Though he had minders – in case it all fell out of bed, of course – he wasn't that brave. But he did like to walk on the wild side occasionally, as Lou Reed so succinctly put it.

As they entered the large lounge area, Dicky was stopped in his tracks. There were two men in black tracksuits, standing there smiling amiably at him.

'All right, Dicky boy?'

He was so stoned, it took him a few seconds to take what

was happening on board. He turned around, expecting to see his minders, but they were nowhere to be seen. For the first time, he felt real fear. He had never, ever been without someone to look after him, to make sure he was safe.

He looked at Sharina, who was just standing there staring at the two men. Then Sharina looked at him sadly, before turning to the two men and saying, 'So, Daniel, long time no see.'

The bigger of the two men gave a small nod. He did look genuinely sorry to be there, and that was what Dicky Matthews would never forget as long as he lived.

'It is a long time, Michael. I have come to take you away.'

Sharina nodded acceptingly. He was wearing his straight gear: black trousers and a beautiful pink shirt. His make-up was subdued and he had on a pair of Marks & Spencer's sling-backs that didn't have a high heel but he loved them anyway.

'There's nothing I can say, is there?'

Daniel Greenberg shook his head sadly.

Dicky watched in abject horror as Sharina left the flat with the two men, quite willingly. In fact, he almost looked relieved. It occurred to Dicky that he had been a witness to this little tableau to make sure that it was documented, so that someone would be able to tell any relevant parties what had gone down.

He also knew that it was a threat of sorts, and that he was now involved in shit that he really would rather have swerved.

Chapter Sixty-six

Solomon Greenberg made sure that Diana and Angus were welcomed. These were people who needed that kind of respect, and they deserved it. He had a bottle of Jameson's on hand for them too – he was partial to a glass of that himself.

He had to stop a war before it started. He was a part of the criminal underworld and had been since he was a boy. He wasn't a fucking Jack the lad, as he thought of these new up-and-coming fuckers, who didn't have the brains to be part of his world long term. They were too greedy and they were too open; they didn't understand that the less people knew the safer they would be.

His businesses could be affected if he wasn't careful. That was his trump card – he always sorted out any kind of trouble before it got out of hand. He was old school, he still believed 'spare the rod and spoil the child', and that had been brought home to him during these last few days.

He settled Diana and Angus into his home, poured them both large whiskeys, and smiled at them amicably as he called to his wife to bring in the food. He was always the best of hosts, known for his largesse whenever he entertained.

Diana smiled back and kissed him on both his cheeks. 'Beautiful property, Sol, you must be very happy here.'

He laughed loudly. 'I always knew we would retire here, Di. We have family here, and the sea. Who doesn't love the sea?'

Diana smiled in agreement, but she knew that his congeniality was for show. She knew that he would have something up his sleeve. He was a slippery fucker – and she respected that.

Still, she laughed with him, and said jovially, 'Well, I can understand that, Solly, I always loved the sound of the sea too.' Then she took a large sip of her drink, before saying nostalgically, 'Remember, years ago, when we used to be on the beaches here, waiting for the drugs to be slung off the boats? Pulling the packages in from the tide? We earned a fucking fortune, didn't we?'

Solomon Greenberg was a big drug dealer, Angus knew that – well, everyone in the game did. But his mum had obviously been there with him at the start. And why didn't that surprise him?

Solomon smiled in a friendly way, but his eyes were pure malice. 'Those were the days, Di. We paved the way. We were the first to understand the real economics of it all. Remember when me and you got our first few keys of coke?'

Now Diana let out a real laugh, throaty and deep. Angus knew that laugh.

'Oh my God, I'd forgotten about that! And my Angus was in nick, and he had arranged the delivery. Oh fucking hell, what were we like?'

They laughed together again, and Solomon once more filled up the glasses. But both Angus and Diana noticed that it was Solomon who was drinking the most, and Diana knew that was unusual for him.

'We go back a long way, Diana, and we have always been straight with each other. So now I will be completely straight with you.'

Diana sipped her drink. She had a feeling that she knew what this man was going to say.

'My son Michael was a terrible disappointment to me, my brothers and my sons . . . but his mother and his sisters . . .' He shrugged sadly. 'They loved him and he loved them. What can I say? I couldn't do it to his mother. But today, I can promise you that he is gone, it's over for him. My Daniel is seeing to that as we speak. But what I will tell you is that, whatever he was, he wasn't the person that you are looking for. You need to look at Dicky Matthews and his latest associates.'

Diana didn't say a word.

Solomon took a deep sip of his drink, before continuing, 'No disrespect, Diana, but I didn't want my youngest son found like a paper chase all around London – his mother would never have coped with that. He is her baby. It's why I have never done anything about him until today.'

Diana Davis looked at this man who she had known and who she had worked with for many, many years, and she felt a stab of shame.

'Solly, all we wanted was to find out what he knew.'

Solomon smiled sadly and, filling their glasses once more, he said, '*Who* he knew, you mean. My son Daniel will give you everything you need to know, you have my word.'

That was enough for Diana.

'Come on, it's over. It's all in the past.' He held up his glass in a toast. '*L'chaim!* That is Hebrew for "to life". How ironic is that?'

Diana held up her glass, but she wondered how Solly could ever get over what he had done. His wife had served the food and left the room, and Diana knew that he would have told her what was happening. She would take some comfort from knowing that her sons would give her baby boy a good death. They would ensure that, at least, he would have a decent burial.

Such was life.

Chapter Sixty-seven

Roger Matthews was worried because he had heard the whispers about Solly's boy, and he had also heard that his own son was somehow involved.

He didn't have anything to do with his Dicky unless he really had to, because the lad irritated him beyond measure. It wasn't because he was gay either; Roger had known that from when Dicky was three and insisted that his mother paint his toenails along with hers. He was a queen from the day he could walk, and that had never bothered Roger. Dicky was his son, and he had loved him. He still did.

He had never had a problem with all that – he had never cared. He had three strapping sons and a daughter and he loved them all, and always would, but his Dicky could try the patience of a saint. He had a knack of getting himself into situations that needed his father's expertise to extract him from. He finally had to tell him, none too gently, that he was on his own and he had to start sorting his own fucking problems. After all, you could only do so much for your children, and if they didn't get with the programme then they had to learn about the big bad world the hard way.

Now, though, he knew that he couldn't stick to that resolution, because his son had got himself into shit that was deeper than the Atlantic Ocean and twice as bastard dangerous. He could cheerfully fucking chin him, and he had a feeling that he might just do that, if the occasion should present itself.

He also had to sort it out personally to ensure that the rest of his family wouldn't be tainted by his son's blatant stupidity. He was so angry he could almost taste it. That one of his sons could be this fucking impervious to what his actions could cause for his family was just beyond Roger's comprehension.

Angus Davis was not a lad to cross – everyone knew that these days. He had made a name for himself outside of his family business. He had a reputation as fair but cruel if crossed and, like everyone else in their world, Roger Matthews had heard the rumours about him.

Angus Davis was the new breed of villain. It couldn't be denied that anyone who crossed him seemed to disappear. And if they ever turned up, it seemed they didn't die of natural causes. That was not unusual in their world. But when it was rumoured that he had left people to starve to death, or removed body parts and left them to bleed out, it put a completely different complexion on things, naturally. Angus had a nasty streak in him, and anyone who didn't understand that before doing any kind of business with him, shouldn't be allowed out on their own.

He had his creds, did Angus. But then he also had his mother and her fucking weight behind him, should he need it, and that wasn't something to be dismissed either. Even though Roger Matthews knew that he had his own creds, he was also sensible enough to recognise that his were nowhere near the Davis clan's, especially when it came to the matriarch. She was as hard as nails. Everyone knew that she could be cruel if the fancy took her, and that fucking son of hers had obviously inherited that trait.

What Roger needed to find out was what had *actually* gone down, and then try to work from there. But he couldn't seem to locate his errant son, and that was a worry in itself. He smiled as best he could as his eldest son pulled up outside their main betting office. He could rely on Marcus to sort things out with the minimum of fuss. But he didn't feel his usual sense of comfort at that thought. This was where he did most of his serious business, and this was where he should feel fucking safe – except he didn't feel it now. In fact, he felt as if he was waiting for a bomb to drop. It had been years since he had felt this vulnerable, and he didn't like it, he didn't like it at all. He knew that the proverbial shit was about to hit the fan.

This was a situation that needed to be handled with tact and diplomacy; it would be pointless starting any kind of war.

He couldn't take the Davis family on. All he could do was swallow his knob and sort this out as best he could, with the minimum of aggravation.

Chapter Sixty-eight

Angus and Roy were eating lunch at The Ivy restaurant. Angus kept a table there – booked regularly for three days a week – and that wasn't cheap, by anyone's standards. It was one of his favourite places to eat, and his presence added to his persona of being a minor celebrity.

He often dined with soap stars and, occasionally, with credible actors who he would be introduced to by mutual friends. It never ceased to amaze him how certain people were drawn towards the criminal world. And he was an intelligent boy; they could only add to his credibility. He knew the value of being in the tabloids better than the agents who were always ringing his team and begging for him to give their latest munter a few column inches. It was all grist to his mill, because having such a high profile guaranteed that he was never 'seen' where certain incidences might occur.

He smiled at Roy as he watched him drink his beer. 'Only you would drink beer in here, when I have ordered us a lovely bottle of Chablis.'

Roy grinned. 'I'll have one glass, but wine gives me terrible indigestion. I'm a Red Stripe boy – always have been, always will be. Unless I am here, of course, and then I drink a Peroni.'

Angus began to laugh. 'I think we should get up a petition

and make them stock Red Stripe.' He poured Roy a glass of wine anyway.

Roy picked it up and, toasting him, he sipped it before grimacing and pretending to shudder in disgust. 'Angus, as your mum always says, you can't educate haddock.'

They laughed together, and then both set about their food.

'You ready for this meeting? I tell you, Roy, I have a bad feeling about it, you know? There's still something off, but I can't fucking work it out.'

Roy swallowed his food down and, burping loudly, he put a hand to his mouth quickly. 'If we have missed something, I am fucked if I know what it is. But, like you, I do feel uneasy.'

Angus looked at his friend seriously because he knew that if they both felt like this, something wasn't right. They were both experienced enough to know that it generally paid to listen to their instincts. They were quiet again for long moments, until a wannabe actor who had appeared in a couple of episodes of *EastEnders* recognised them and descended on them like they were the second coming.

Angus was going to give him the bum's rush but there were a couple of girls with him, and one of them appealed to him. Standing up, all smiles, and acting like he had just found his long-lost brother, Angus shook the man's hand and then invited them all to join him. Roy shook his head as he watched them settle at the table and start ordering champagne cocktails.

The skinny blonde with the expensive new tits, the bleached hair and shoes from Peacocks was pulled into the booth next to Angus and, as he turned the full force of his personality on her, Roy Rogers knew that she didn't stand a chance. But they had a meeting – and even Angus wouldn't dare to miss that.

It was what they would call a real wonderer, because it had been requested without any reason by someone who they had no interest in.

Though, of course, now that person was suddenly at the very top of their agenda.

Chapter Sixty-nine

Diana was the first to arrive in Bethnal Green and she came in via the back entrance of Roger Matthews' betting shop, with Gabriel by her side.

She was confident enough not to bring her minders inside with her. They waited outside and looked exactly like what they were being paid to look: menacing. They didn't like her going into situations alone, and she appreciated that, but she also knew that, if push ever came to shove, she could look after herself.

Roger Matthews was nervous and that was evident. Diana could find it in her heart to feel sorrow for him; his son had brought a great worry down on his head, and she believed that Roger didn't know what any of this was actually about. She admired him for trying to sort it though. Requesting this meeting had taken a lot of guts on his part. Roger was a decent man and that went a long way to explaining why she was gracing this fucker with her presence.

She had always been of the opinion that, if you used your loaf, you could find out what you needed to know without violence or force. It was always her last resort. If she was pushed, she would make sure that the people concerned didn't forget that they had brought it on themselves.

Diana smiled her huge smile that made people think they

were important to her, and she said genially, 'Always lovely to see you, Roger. I hope you have a drink here for me.'

Roger relaxed visibly at her kind words and said quickly, 'Of course, Diana, I have a bottle of Jameson's, and some information you need to know.'

As he poured them all a glass, his hands were visibly shaking. Gabriel looked at Diana and, shrugging gently, he raised his eyebrows because, like her, he wondered what this was all going to lead to.

When his eldest son, Marcus, came into the room, Roger turned to Diana and Gabriel and smiled. He was already feeling better with his son beside him.

If he had found out one thing with all this latest shite, it was that he was getting too old for any kind of skulduggery.

Chapter Seventy

Angus was in his element. The girl was called Destiny and, even though he had thought that might be a piss-take, he had eventually accepted that was her real name. She had finally shown him her library card, and he couldn't decide what he found the more outrageous: that she was really called Destiny, or that she *had* a fucking library card.

Both were incongruous and required him to suspend his disbelief. But once she had stripped off in his office in Old Compton Street, he had stopped caring. It was only when Roy had finally hammered on his door in anger, reminding him that they should already be in Bethnal Green, that he thanked her profusely and hurried her out into the bar.

He left her with her friends and an open tab, and he whistled cheerily as he finally made his way to his car and threw away her phone number. He certainly wouldn't be riding *that* again. She was all right, but not exactly a keeper. Roy was fuming and, even though Angus knew he had been out of order, he really thought that what had held him up had been tantamount to an emergency.

'Come on, Roy, you saw her, she was ripe for the picking! And, in her favour, she had a library card. I swear to God! I know I can exaggerate the charms of my amours at times but – I mean, come on – a fucking library card! That's a one-up to Blockbuster Video.'

Eventually, Roy had to laugh at him, because he was so earnest.

Only Angus could argue that an emergency fuck was an excuse to be late for a meeting like this one.

Chapter Seventy-one

'Is Angus coming?'

Diana had to admit she was as annoyed as young Marcus. She was very impressed with this lad. He had a presence about him, and that wasn't just because he was so good-looking – though that helped, obviously. He was well built, he clearly worked out and, even though he was showing due deference to his visitors, he wasn't being subservient. She had seen bigger men than him fold when she had interviewed them.

She sensed that Gabriel felt the same, because he was chatting to Marcus and his father while they waited for her son to finally arrive. She could quite happily smack her Angus at times, and this was one of them. She knew that it had to be a female – that would always be her son's weakness. As much as he loved Lorna, her son couldn't resist his attraction to strange.

Lorna was utterly self-contained, and Diana had sussed out early on that Lorna wasn't that enamoured of the sexual side of her marriage. But that was her prerogative; it didn't appeal to every woman. Lorna was the wife, the mother; she was the girl that Angus had loved from the moment he met her and who he saw as his soulmate. She was everything that he wanted in a life partner; her whole life revolved around his home and his kids, and that suited them both. But Lorna had to know that her husband wasn't faithful, and Diana wondered what she thought about it deep down.

When she had tried to broach the subject with Lorna, she had shut down. Lorna was like a closed book – a cold, distant look came into her eyes when anyone tried to talk to her about things she didn't want to acknowledge. Diana had taken the hint and never again tried to discuss anything remotely personal with her son's wife.

On the surface, Lorna was a wonderful wife and mother, but no one seemed able to get close to her to know what she was really thinking. Diana worried what would happen when the perfect surface cracked. It always did. Her main concern was her grandsons, who she adored. Not that she got to spend much time with them. Even at five and three, Lorna kept them on a strict timetable which didn't allow much time for freedom.

Angus let Lorna have her way – Diana knew he would do anything to keep his wife happy. And he would even ban his mother from their house if Lorna felt she wasn't toeing the line. Lorna was more than capable of insisting on that if she felt threatened in any way, shape or form.

Diana walked a fine line with that girl, and she did it for her grandchildren, not her son. If only Lorna could understand that she was on her side. Diana would be the best friend she could ever have asked for if she let her in; she would defend her to the death.

She snuck another look at her watch and decided that, when this was all over, she was going to launch that son of hers into outer fucking space.

Chapter Seventy-two

Lorna had been running for two hours, and she felt the energy suffusing her body.

It was such a rush – now she ran in the afternoons and evenings as well as the mornings – whenever she felt the need to relax. She felt almost high whenever she finished a long run – not that she would know what that was like, of course. She only drank occasionally, and she had never touched a drug in her life. She was very against anything like that, though she didn't count wine. She felt that wine was harmless – after all, everyone did it. It was even in the Bible. Didn't Jesus change the water into wine for a wedding? His endorsement was good enough for her.

As she walked into her kitchen, she could smell the aroma of the casserole that she had prepared earlier. She made sure that her boys had a good diet, and she also made sure that they ate whatever food she put in front of them. There was none of this 'I don't eat vegetables' crap in her home; her children ate what she cooked for them, and that was that. When she heard the way some of the mothers carried on about their children! Her sons had never had a McDonald's, ever – and if it was left to her, they never would.

She loved them, but she wasn't easy on them. That was something she had decided on from day one, and she had kept to it.

Angus was quite happy to back her up, and that was important, because he was not often around, due to the hours he had to work. They had a long weekend together every five weeks, and that was when they could be a proper family. That suited her too, if she was honest. They had a wonderful few days of making love, and just enjoying time with each other.

Her Angus would never be a nine-to-five man, but she relished being in charge of the house and the children, without Angus being there constantly. She actually liked her own company and she enjoyed being alone. That was why their marriage worked so well; they were compatible, even though they were worlds apart in many ways.

Chapter Seventy-three

Roy Rogers took the call on his car phone and sighed in annoyance.

Angus guessed he was getting a bollocking, and he knew that it was his fault. He had put himself and his needs before business, and that was something his mother couldn't and wouldn't accept. Angus could just imagine what was being said and had the sense to look contrite.

'Change of plan. The meet with Roger Matthews is over. Your mum and Gabriel want us to join them at Mohammad's scrapyard in North London. She sounds well pissed off.'

Angus didn't even bother to answer. As usual, there wasn't really anything he could say. But he was intrigued as to why they were meeting there, because his old school friend's yard wasn't somewhere she would normally frequent.

Roy answered his unspoken question. 'If we are meeting her there then it's serious, so get your fucking head around that.'

They were both quiet for the rest of the journey.

Chapter Seventy-four

Mohammad Baqri was a handsome lad, and he knew it.

He was tall, well dressed, and he liked to spend money. He was also shrewd and had a degree in Engineering from Bristol University. His father had made sure of that; he was a believer in education for education's sake. Not something that his sons felt particularly excited about – but he knew better than them how they felt about his plans for them, and it grieved him more than his sons actually realised.

Mohammad thought the world of Diana Davis. After all, without this woman, he wouldn't have the life he lived. His father was a good man, but he was also steeped in the old ways. It had taken him a long time to understand that his sons were not going to toe the company line and do what he said, without question.

They were Londoners, born and bred, and they had no intention of dressing like fucking peasants and bowing and scraping for the rest of their lives. They were grown men and they had not been brought up as assiduously as their father. It didn't help that their father had the family contacts in Afghanistan that guaranteed the purest drugs in Europe, which Mohammad now supplied. They all loved him, but they had fought him, and eventually they had won.

Diana Davis owned half of this scrapyard, and they had a good business partnership in as much as Mohammad gave her money on a regular basis and she left him to get on with it. If she wanted a meeting here then he was more than happy to oblige. After all, it was her investment that had made his father come around. His father wanted to buy her out but she had always refused, and he would love her to his dying day for that alone. He worked with his father, but not *for* him, and that suited him right down to the ground.

He heard a car pull into his yard, and he smiled as he went to open the door of the Portakabin. He was looking forward to seeing Diana; she was always so interesting and a lot of fun. He had been great friends with Angus since they were kids, but he couldn't help wondering what was bringing them here this night. He wasn't a fool – it had to be something serious, and something that they wanted to keep private. Well, that was fine by him, as he was more than willing to keep out of it all.

He was standing in the doorway of the Portakabin, waiting to greet Diana, when he saw the first man get out of the Range Rover. He noticed the sawn-off shotgun in the man's hands just as two other men descended from the car, one of whom he recognised as his old friend Mehmet Aksoy.

All he could think was fuck, fuck, *fuck!*

Chapter Seventy-five

Angus and Roy pulled up to the scrapyard, both annoyed to see that the gates were closed.

Angus got out of the BMW angrily. 'Really? What the actual fuck!'

He was not in the mood for aggravation, and this was a red rag to a bull. He saw Mohammad wave at them and, when he opened the gates by hand, Angus walked into the yard rather than get back into the car.

'You having a fucking laugh, mate? What's with the closed gates? We were expected.'

It was a large premises, and Angus walked up to the Porta-kabins on his dignity as Roy parked the car up. He saw that his mother's car was already there, and he sighed in annoyance. As he turned, he was astonished to see his mother standing there with a face like thunder – and what looked suspiciously like blood all over her rather expensive outfit.

'I fucking blame you for this, you lazy little sod!'

Angus took a few seconds to assimilate exactly what he was seeing. There was a large man with a seriously battered face sitting hunched in an office chair; another body was on the floor with its head blown off; and a third man was smoking a Turkish cigarette and drinking a large whiskey. He recognised the whiskey drinker as Mehmet Aksoy, a boy he and Mohammad had gone to school with, and who was part of the Turkish criminal system. He often had a drink with him if he came to one of the clubs; he was a decent bloke. Angus looked around him – he had no idea what had happened.

'What was it, Angus? Another brainless blonde with pretend tits and cheap shoes?'

That his mother had hit the nail on the head wasn't lost on either Angus or Roy.

Roy just hoped Angus didn't try and justify his actions by bringing up the library card. That really would put the icing on this particular fucking cake! Trouble was, he wouldn't put that past him – Angus could be crass at times.

Gabriel stepped in then, much to the relief of Mohammad and Mehmet.

'These fuckers came here to take out you and your mother! If it wasn't for young Mehmet here, and Mohammad's quick thinking, they would have managed it, because we walked into a fucking trap.'

Angus didn't say anything. He judged, at this time, he was better off keeping his own counsel until he had all the facts. But he could feel the anger welling up inside him, as the enormity of what he was hearing was finally hitting home. It didn't help that his mother was rattled – that wasn't something you saw every day. He could suddenly see the lines around her eyes and mouth; she was white underneath her carefully applied make-up, and he felt a sudden rush of love for her.

He roared in anger then. 'I hold my hand up, I was being a cunt. But I tell you this now, Mother, I will hunt these bastards down like fucking dogs. Planning to shoot my mother, were they? I'll rip their fucking nuts off and watch them eat them—'

Diana held her hand up for silence and, for once, her son complied. She could see that he was finally getting the seriousness of the situation, but she wasn't in the mood for these dramatics. Next thing, he would be pontificating on his word of the fucking day.

'Mohammad, tell him what happened.'

Mohammad was also drinking a large whiskey. Looking at Angus, he said angrily, 'I had left the gates open. I should have known better, of course. The Range Rover came in, and three men got out. I had assumed it was you or your mum, but then I saw the sawn-off fucking shotgun too. Nothing like maximum damage! Anyway, I shut the office door and went out to the back where, as luck would have it, I have a Kalashnikov I won off a Russian bloke at poker.

'Anyway, I heard a shot and then I heard Mehmet here shout, "Get your arse out here, I need help!" Though, in fairness, he didn't. He had already taken out gunman number one with his own piece, smashed the fuck out of gunman number two, and was smiling as I opened the door. Tell them what you said, it did make me laugh.'

Mehmet grinned. 'I said, "Fuck me, Mohammad, what a fucking day!"'

Now they all laughed. It broke the ice, and levelled out the atmosphere.

Angus looked at him and said quietly, 'Who are these wankers, and how were you roped in?'

Mehmet shrugged. 'I was told this morning to go with these two. The dead one is Iqbal Erdogan, a complete fucking wannabe, and him sitting there is my cousin Kamal. He isn't to be harmed, bless him, he just did what he was told. This was all paid for by a Turkish geezer who thinks that he's some kind of fucking

217

gangster, Yusuf Yildiz. I went along with it, for obvious reasons, but I tell you all now, Yildiz is a mad fucker, and that has got him as far as it has. He thinks he's some kind of criminal mastermind – and then he had the gall to recruit my lot to do his dirty work.'

Diana listened intently once more to what was being said; that was her speciality: listening. She was aware that he had not deviated from his earlier story.

'And where can we find this paragon of virtue?'

Mohammad grinned. 'That's the funny thing. He is, as we speak, in bed with his unofficial boyfriend at a flat he owns not ten minutes from here. Thanks to Mehmet, he thinks the job's done and life is good.' He swallowed down the last of his whiskey as he added, 'And I'm coming with you, OK? What a fucking liberty! They were going to fucking shoot me and all. Look at the aggravation they have caused me. I've got to get rid of the dead boy and torch my own fucking Portakabin. Then I have the aggravation of replacing everything. Oh, I want first fucking stab at this ponce.'

Diana laughed then at his absolute outrage, and she said cheerfully, 'And that you shall have, darling.'

Chapter Seventy-six

Yusuf Yildiz was pleased with himself; he felt that he had really brought off a coup. He was determined to prove to the world that he had the makings of a great man. His mother had drummed into him since birth that he was special, and he believed that, with every ounce of his being.

He wasn't cut out for the everyday life that afflicted so many of his friends. He did Friday Mosque, of course. That was a given, especially where his father and mother were concerned, but that was as far as it went. He had embraced a hedonistic lifestyle; if you wanted something, you went out and you took it. Well, he was certainly doing that – even his preference for handsome young men with blond hair and blue eyes had ceased to worry him.

His mother had found out and she had not said a word, except that he had to marry a good Turkish girl and keep his pastimes private. As she had explained, he wasn't the first, and he certainly wouldn't be the last. That actually made a lot of sense to him.

He wasn't sure about his father. But then he knew as long as he was earning, his father didn't give a shit. He had the impression that his father didn't really like him. He saw him as a deviant, he called him a *kibar* – and he didn't mean it in the polite sense either. He saw his son as less than human, but he couldn't change the fact that he was his fucking son. And, because of that, he was what the English called lumbered.

Well, that suited Yusuf. He couldn't stand the old fart anyway. He treated his mother abominably – he had tarts coming out of his ears, and he didn't even bother to hide them from her. He knew it broke her heart, and he could understand that. From an early age, she had cried as she told him about loving a man who treated her so badly. Her husband and her children were all she cared about, and that was why he revered her so much; she was everything to him.

He looked at his latest beau, a seventeen-year-old boy from Hackney called Alan, who had everything he required. He was small, thin and he had copious amounts of curly hair, and beautiful azure eyes. He was very effeminate, but that was what Yusuf liked; he wanted a boy to know who was the actual man in this relationship. And once he was finished with him, he would pay him handsomely and go on to the next one.

It was a business arrangement, nothing more. He liked this Alan though – he was a fun guy, and he had a quick brain. He just might last longer than the others. Only time would tell.

When the door to the flat opened, he assumed it was his minder, Raoul, coming in for a marathon piss. So when his bedroom door was slammed open and he saw the angry face of Angus Davis and his henchmen, he knew that his life was about to take a definite turn for the worse.

Little Alan's petrified shriek didn't help matters either.

Chapter Seventy-seven

Angus Junior and Sean were happy and relaxed, swimming in their pool, while their mother watched them closely from her lounge chair

Because they had done everything required – schoolwork for Angus and reading for Sean – she was quite happy to let them have this time in the pool. She explained even at this early age that they had to earn treats like this. As she was forever telling them: no one got anything for nothing.

Lorna watched her sons contentedly. She loved to see them laughing and smiling, it made her feel that she was doing a good job. That was really the difficult part of raising children: the constant fear that you were doing something wrong. She hoped fervently that they would not join the family business, and she would do everything in her power to try and make sure that didn't happen. She was determined to give her boys an alternative. Educate them, and show them that there was a different way of earning a crust, if they knuckled down and grafted for it.

She was pregnant again, and she couldn't wait to tell Angus. She hoped for a girl this time, because she really wanted a daughter, especially after two sons. She already had a name picked out. She could see her now – a girl to dress up and take shopping.

She allowed herself these little fantasies because they cheered her up, and she hoped they were the precursor to her dreams actually happening. She knew that Angus secretly wanted a girl too. A smaller version of her, he said, another perfect lady for his perfect home. She loved it when he said things like that; it made her feel special and wanted and needed. Considering his track record with other women, she thought he owed her that much at least.

She felt the black cloud begin to settle on her, the heaviness when the idea of Angus with other women came into her brain, and the anger began to rise. She pushed the negative thoughts away. She didn't want them ruining an otherwise perfect afternoon. She reached for her pills, sipped her iced tea and carried on listening to the boys as they splashed around, and eventually their laughter soothed her once more and all was right with her world again.

Chapter Seventy-eight

Yusuf Yildiz knew that he was fucked. Big time.

He was absolutely gutted. But there wasn't a lot that he could do about any of it. He assumed his minder was either dead or incapacitated. So much for that fucker and his bragging that he was harder than a wrestler's jockstrap!

He couldn't believe that he had been rumbled. That really fucking stung! He had been convinced that in one fell swoop he could take out that piece of shit Angus Davis and his mother, and not only gain a reputation overnight but also take over the numerous business opportunities that his actions would leave open to him. He could kick himself now, of course, but then hindsight was a fucking wonderful thing.

He watched as Alan scrambled from the bed, naked, and in tears. The boy knew that this wasn't a social call obviously. He felt a fleeting sorrow for Alan, because he knew that there was no way he was going to be allowed to walk away from this, and he was genuinely sorry for that.

When Angus shot the boy in the face, the blood sprayed all around the room. Yusuf could feel the fine droplets that hit his face and could taste the boy's blood on his lips. He felt sick. The fear was taking over now, but he was determined to die a good death.

Diana was watching him silently, with that fucking Rasta who seemed permanently glued to her hip. He saw Roy watching nonplussed too. When he saw Mohammad holding a large machete, he knew that Alan had been given a merciful death, which was something that was obviously not on the cards for him.

It took a lot to hold him down, because fear can really give added strength, and he wasn't a weakling by any stretch of the imagination. It was a long and dirty job, but it got much easier once Yusuf had bled out.

Angus knew that it wasn't easy to decapitate someone, but it had to be done. His head would be delivered to his family home as a warning to anyone in his tribe who might even think about retaliation.

Diana had a feeling Yusuf's father would be silently thanking them; they weren't exactly close by all accounts. It was his mother she felt sorry for. Everyone knew she thought the sun, the moon and the stars emerged from Yusuf's arsehole on a daily basis. She sighed, then looked distastefully at Angus, who was covered in blood.

Sometimes, she thought, he enjoyed this part of the game a little bit too much.

Chapter Seventy-nine

Although Angus had changed his clothes and showered at the offices in Soho, he still stood under the hot shower at home for a good ten minutes. The smell of blood lingered in his nostrils and he breathed the hot water in so he could get rid of any residue.

Blood was a fucker – a little went a long way – and there had been lots of it. He wasn't unduly bothered about what had happened. As far as he was concerned, the fucker had asked for it and he had been given it. End of. You didn't fight a Tonka truck with a Matchbox mini, that was the point.

He dried himself off, and nearly went through to the bedroom in a towel, before he remembered how funny Lorna could be about things like that. He quickly put the towel into the washing basket, and pulled on the dressing gown the boys at one of the clubs had given him for Christmas. It was deep blue and had 'Rocky the Italian Stallion' written across the back. *Italian Stallion* was a porn film that Sylvester Stallone had made in his youth, but of course his wife didn't know that – otherwise, nothing to do with him would be allowed on the premises. She had her standards all right.

He sat on the bed beside her. He loved this room; it was all subdued colours, and really calming. She had poured him a large

225

brandy and she smiled coyly as she handed it to him. She was drinking sparkling water, but that didn't surprise him. She wasn't a drinker – another one of her virtues, as far as he was concerned.

'I have some news for you, Angus.'

He looked deep into her beautiful eyes, and he just knew what she was going to tell him, and they both laughed delightedly.

'Oh, darling, another baby? Oh, I'm so made up! It has to be a girl, this time, I just know it.'

He kissed her, long and hard. She could feel the love emanating from him, and she knew that she was a lucky woman in so many ways. Whatever he was, whatever he did, she believed that he loved her with every ounce of his being. She felt enveloped in his adoration and that feeling was worth the world to her.

They talked about the future for a while, wrapped in each other's arms.

Eventually, Lorna said happily, 'How was your day, darling?'

Laughing gaily, Angus kissed the tip of her nose, before saying cheekily, 'It was fucking murder, darling.'

Lorna grinned contentedly as they lay together and discussed her chosen girl's name, because, like her husband, she was convinced that was what she was carrying.

That would be the icing on her already fabulous cake.

Book Four

2000

Husbands, love your wives, and be not bitter against them

Colossians 3:19

Chapter Eighty

'You were out of control, Angus, and that is not acceptable.'

Angus shrugged off the criticism in his usual angry way. 'Just shut the fuck up, will you, Roy? You can be like an old woman at times.'

Roy could feel the swell of anger inside him, and swallowed it down. When Angus was out of it like this he was wasting his time. The trouble was, Angus was out of it a lot recently, and it was becoming a real problem – not just for Angus but for everyone around him. He was losing control but couldn't see that there was anything even remotely wrong with his behaviour.

He had been steadily going downhill for the last few months and Roy, for the life of him, couldn't pinpoint why. It was like he woke up one morning and decided to become a grade-A cunt and wreck everything he had ever worked for. Everything they had *all* worked for. There were more than a few people who were complaining about him and his actions, and a lot of them worked with them or for them – that was the real worry.

If Diana didn't take the fucker in hand, they would have a mutiny to deal with. But she was leaving more and more to Gabriel lately, and that in itself wasn't a problem – he was trustworthy, one of the genuine good guys really. However, Gabriel had no say over Angus. Only his mother had that, and even her influence wasn't as great as it once was.

There was definitely something going on, but Roy couldn't seem to get to the bottom of it. Maybe Angus was having a mid-life crisis. Who fucking knew anything about what was ailing him? Maybe that wife of his had an inkling. But then, if she knew, she wouldn't say anything anyway. She wasn't exactly the friendliest of people at the best of times, and having a conversation with her was like extracting blood from the proverbial stone. She made her feelings quite plain about what she thought of anyone who worked with her husband.

He had no choice. He had to try and talk to Diana again, and hope that this time she listened to him.

Chapter Eighty-one

Jenny Marshal was pretty enough but her real assets were her hair, which was long, thick and lustrous, and her perfectly shaped legs.

She had something about her that spoke to a certain type of man, and she had accepted that from when she was fourteen years old. She attracted the Faces: the violent men, the ones who seemed to stand out from the crowd, like she did. She enjoyed the notoriety and she loved the unpredictability that surrounded them. Luckily for them, she was as attracted to them as they were enamoured of her. It was a perfect storm.

But now, at twenty years old, she had claimed herself a prize – and she wasn't going to let this one go. Angus Davis was not only her type of man but he was good-looking to boot – and that did make a change, she had to admit.

Most of the men she wanted weren't exactly the answer to a maiden's prayer. He was older than her – not that that was unusual – but he had a great youthfulness about him, and he was lots of fun. He was good in bed too – and that alone was a touch, as far as she was concerned – he had a bit of staying power. Her last one was abominable, she had been vaccinated slower! But oh, she had loved being seen with him and travelling to Spain and Portugal on holidays. He had been generous as well, and that always went a long way with her.

She couldn't abide mean men – well, men who were mean with money anyway. She liked a bit of a temper, and she enjoyed making them jealous to see how they reacted. She equated jealousy with love and, if they were rough with her, she found it strangely exciting as well as frightening. She loved to elicit that response from them; it gave her a feeling of power, of being in charge somehow. That it was the only power she had didn't occur to her. She didn't think about the future. Like most of her ilk, she just wanted a child and a guaranteed earn for the duration.

She was aware, though, that Angus wasn't exactly stable these days, and that did give her food for thought. But she was sure enough of her charms to believe that she was still on top. Which, after all, was Angus Davis's preferred position!

Like many others before her, Jenny Marshal believed that she had the magic touch to get Angus away from that boring wife of his.

Chapter Eighty-two

Diana was feeling tired again. She had planned to spend the day on her large, comfortable couch watching crap and eating toasted sandwiches, which she would wash down with endless cups of hot, sweet tea.

Her priorities had changed drastically over the last few years. She wasn't interested in anything new business-wise any more and, far from letting it bother her, she had decided to embrace the feeling. She wasn't exactly a spring chicken – she was getting more aware of that fact by the day. But she would never admit to her real age, even if her life depended on it, and she felt she still looked good, considering she wasn't a girl any more.

The one thing she loved about Gabriel was that he never saw her as any different to how she looked when they first met. Oh, she knew he took the occasional flier, but that behaviour had never particularly bothered her. If he was to see them on a regular basis then it would be cause for aggravation. But the odd lapse she could cope with – after all, she had been guilty of that behaviour herself over the years. It was just sex, and that had nothing to do with the life they shared.

She had seen too many relationships go down the pan because of infidelity, and she believed it was a natural part of human nature to seek out the occasional strange. Survival of the fittest and all that. But these days she was happy to leave the businesses in Gabriel's capable hands. It was something she'd sworn she'd never do but, over the years, with Gabe beside her constantly, she came to realise he was good at what he did, and she trusted him with her life. He was on his way now with Roy – who was not himself at the moment because of Angus and his latest escapades.

She knew what he was going to say and how she was going to answer him. She was going to go to the root of the problem, and sort it from there – not that she would tell any of them that, of course.

It paid to keep your own counsel at times like this. Knowledge was power, as the old saying went.

It was trite but fucking true.

Chapter Eighty-three

Lorna Davis was miserable, and that meant so was everyone else around her.

When she was unhappy, it was serious, and it meant that they all walked on eggshells around her until she was ready to once more bring them into her embrace. She was a woman who wouldn't take any shit off anyone – and that included her husband and family.

Lorna Davis had made a point of being a law unto herself, and that was something she took great pride in. She ran her household with precision and she made sure that her perfect family – her two handsome sons, gorgeous daughter and her beloved husband – had everything that they needed, provided they didn't go against her and what she deemed as acceptable behaviour. They all knew to toe the line, because it wasn't worth the aggravation she was capable of causing if they happened to upset her.

She prided herself on doing what was necessary for her family's well-being. Because that was all she really cared about: her family and her children having the best that life could offer them. Her Angus wasn't exactly a fucking saint, but he had always known how far he could push her. He had given her food for thought over the years, and she knew that he was always sorry for his actions, but now he had truly fucked up.

This time she was angry, really angry. She wasn't a fool – there was a line that could not be crossed. Her husband and his latest trollop had more than crossed that Maginot Line.

She was so furious with him that she couldn't breathe or think straight; it was like she was in the grip of a fever. She grasped for her pills and swallowed a handful. She had given her husband a lot of leeway over the years, and she had tried to understand that he needed other women. She had turned a blind eye over and over again, so she was within her rights to read him the riot act for this latest debacle and she would dare him to argue with her.

He was dead in the fucking water. She wasn't scared of him, she never had been. All that shit in the papers about him being dangerous and a big criminal, and the speculation surrounding him? None of it bothered her because she knew that she was the only person – after his mother – who he really cared for.

He was scared of losing her respect. That had always been her trump card. She had never once put a foot wrong, she knew her own worth, and she wasn't about to see that drop in his estimation, let alone hers.

Angus knew exactly what she was capable of, if pushed, and she was relying on that to make Angus do what was right. Because he wasn't in his right mind lately; the coke had taken him over, and she was more than aware of that fact.

She was a lot of things but a mug wasn't one of them. She was so offended by his behaviour, she wasn't sure herself if she could forgive him. Until now, nothing he had done had ever given her reason to doubt him – murder, torture, that went on in a different world as far as she was concerned. It was his work, his job. Her life was blameless, and she knew that, as did Angus and the Filth.

But this latest escapade, with a tart who thought she could

actually remove him from his family and home – and who was telling that to anyone who would listen – was beyond the pale. Lorna wasn't about to let her reputation be sullied by anyone.

This was war, and it was a war Lorna Davis was going to win.

Chapter Eighty-four

Angus was still sobering up, and he wasn't impressed that his mother and Gabriel were determined to talk with him.

He was well aware of what she was going to say to him – he wasn't a fucking moron. Deep down, he knew that she had every right to say it too. The fact that his old mum was bothering to travel all the way out to Brentwood was enough to warn him that it was serious. She wouldn't move out of her drum these days unless there was a dangerous gas leak. She had finally taken a step back from the businesses – and good luck to her.

She deserved to have her own time. Christ knew, she had worked hard enough all her life! Angus thought the world of Gabriel, and he trusted that he would look out for his mother's interests, as he always had done. He was thrilled to see her finally taking some time for herself. He knew that she was tired of it all.

She kept her hand in, and her name was still synonymous with villainy, even though no one could actually prove it. She had taught him well, and that was why he was so successful in his own businesses.

He had just opened this new nightclub called Wraps, in Brentwood, and it was already a big success. He had a great DJ and an A-list clientele. The VIP bar was open to actors, footballers

238

and the best-looking girls and boys. His spaces were sought after because of his reputation, and the fact that the papers were all over him like a rash.

His clubs were *the* places to be, and people came in droves from all over to say they had experienced them. He made sure that they were given a very warm welcome. To come to one of his venues was the stuff dreams were made of. He was already in talks to open a club in Manchester, and it was sure to be another huge Angus Davis success.

He made sure that he showed his face often enough for people to feel like they knew him – that was part of the experience and what made it special. The red-top papers were always on hand to photograph him and his guests. He had an innate skill for how to market his products for the maximum benefit.

Angus could live off his clubs quite easily, but he was happier chasing the real dollars, and they didn't come from strobe lighting and leather sofas. But he loved the kudos of the clubs, and the level of safety they afforded him when he was questioned about his lifestyle.

He'd put Mandy's talent to good use in his back offices years ago – kept on the down low from Lorna, of course – and she hadn't let him down yet. Her bookkeeping was immaculate, and she never forgot an earn. He kept every receipt for everything he owned – from TVs to his antiques to his cars – he was completely legitimate. He loved that the Filth and the Inland Revenue couldn't prove any different, no matter how hard they tried. He was basically putting up two fingers to the powers-that-be, and the more they tried to catch him out, the more he was determined to prove them wrong.

It was a game that he enjoyed playing, because he knew that he was going to win. He paid his VAT and his taxes at the very last minute, because that was also part of the game now. He made a big song and dance about it, and he queried everything with his accountants, who knew that their job was to give the taxman as much aggravation and provocation as possible – and they did that for him with gusto and a sneaky smile.

He had always made sure that he covered every angle and, until now, he had succeeded. But the last few months, he had pretty much dropped the ball, and he knew that he had to hold his hand up and admit his foolishness. He *might* have made a certain female think that she was of more importance than she was.

It all started when Angus began to feel that his life, which he had thought was blessed, wasn't as great as he might have believed. He was pushing forty, and he felt that there was something missing – something that he wanted that was just out of his reach. He only wished he knew what the fuck it was. Because it certainly wasn't Jenny fucking Marshal. She was a slapper with hopes of the big time. Well, good luck with that, darling.

He sat in the offices that were as luxurious as the rest of the club, sipping his usual Jameson's and wondering what the fuck was wrong with him and why he wasn't content with his life any more. He still loved Lorna with all his heart – she would always be the only woman for him, that was a definite. But there was undeniably something missing, and he couldn't shake that feeling off.

It bothered him. For the first time in his life, he didn't know what the next day would bring.

That was perfectly OK in his work life – in fact, it was a big part of the excitement, of the buzz – but where his personal life was concerned, this was a first.

Chapter Eighty-five

Jenny was in the toilets of Wraps nightclub. She was looking at herself, as usual, with a smug but critical eye.

She had dressed carefully for this evening's entertainment, making sure she looked spectacular. She had seen in the eyes of the bouncers as she had walked in the door that she had pulled it off. The club wasn't open for a few hours, and the fact they had let her in without a word told her that she had already made her mark. Well, that was what she had worked for, so she was pleased with the treatment she had received. They had not allowed her up to the offices, though, and that rankled, but she had asked them to tell Angus that she was here.

She put another layer of Pomegranate Crush on her lips and then ran a natural lip gloss over the top to maximise the look. She was still admiring herself when she heard the door open. She didn't take much notice, because she was too busy making sure that her make-up was perfect. She had huge eyes that were a deep blue, and she emphasised them with a kohl pencil that really made them stand out.

She understood make-up – it had been her hobby since she had been twelve years old – and she loved to experiment with it. She could actually have worked in the beauty industry, if she had been that way inclined; it was as natural to her as breathing. But working for a living wasn't on her agenda. She was quite happy to be kept and cosseted – and used, if she was completely honest. Her idea of working was keeping a man interested so that he paid her bills and made sure she was taken care of. She saw men as a wage, as a means to an end; she had what they wanted, and she would make sure that they paid for it. Quid pro quo, as her mother used to say, whatever the fuck that meant.

She stood back from the mirror and pulled down the tight black dress that only just covered her modesty, and she was smiling at herself when the pint glass hit her in the face. She couldn't understand for a few moments what was happening. Then she felt the glass hit her again, and she saw blood everywhere.

She dropped to her knees and instinctively covered her face and head as the glass hit her again and again. She could feel a flap of skin hanging down and touching her neck, and knew that it was her cheek. That's when the screaming started. She passed out on the floor as the toilets were suddenly filled with huge men in black suits.

The bouncers were in absolute shock but they grabbed Lorna Davis and held her down on the floor until Angus arrived on the scene. It was fucking bedlam, and no one knew what the fuck they were supposed to do for the best.

They were there to prevent fights, not deal with the boss's wife on a murder spree.

Lorna was still fighting them when Angus knocked her out with one punch.

Chapter Eighty-six

Diana looked at her son sadly. She honestly couldn't understand how he hadn't seen this coming.

Diana had never kidded herself about Lorna's obsession – and that obsession was her husband. She was dangerous where he was concerned; she didn't even like his relationship with her, his own mother.

Lorna had allowed him his little peccadilloes here and there, because she had understood that those girls didn't matter to him, only *she* mattered. He loved her, and he revered her as the mother of his children.

Lorna was a good girl. But, God forgive her, Diana had never trusted the good girls – not when they married men like her Angus. It was a recipe for disaster, because he would never change.

Now look what had happened. Now they had to try and sort out a mess that should never have been allowed to occur.

Chapter Eighty-seven

'You could have avoided all this, Angus, and you know it.'

Angus didn't answer. He didn't know what he could say – after all, it was the truth. His mother was absolutely right, he should have nipped this in the bud.

Diana knew that Angus was about to go into one of his 'Yes, you are right, I have been a cunt' modes. Except she wasn't Lorna, and that shit didn't wash with her. She said as much.

'Oh no you don't, Angus, you are not wriggling out of this by agreeing with me. I'm not Lorna – and the sooner you remember that, the better. You should never have let that Jenny get so close. What were you thinking? I know that Lorna has been good, but no woman is so good that she would allow a trollop to threaten her life and her children's lives. She was humiliated and that is down to you and your fucking drug-taking.

'You are like a child lately – and that child that you were fucking proves it. She's just a kid, for crying out loud. I have her in a private hospital, getting specialist treatment and plastic surgery, because your wife did a real number on her. I have promised her the fucking earth to keep this out of the courts. She picked my fucking pocket, and she had every right to. Even with forty stitches in her boat, she was still after the main chance. Oh, you certainly know how to pick them.'

Angus stayed silent. When his mum was like this it was pointless to argue. And what could he argue about? He had been a fool, and he had let the drugs and the excitement of being with young Jenny get the better of him.

Oh, he loved Lorna, but sometimes she bored him rigid. After a few days at home, he had to get away from her. But that had been the way since day one. Her sex drive was basically non-existent, and it always had been. She enjoyed him holding her, telling her how much he loved her, more than the actual physical side of marriage.

His problem was that he had allowed himself to get far too comfortable in the clubbing scene, and he should have taken himself in hand. He had enjoyed his dealings with the Cali Cartel – perhaps too much – but it had been a big fucking step forward as far as the drugs trade was concerned.

He had been a fool, because he had forgotten everything that had made his life so easy – forgotten that his Lorna was everything that he had ever aspired to have – and now he had caused her to attack Jenny. He had always known that Lorna wasn't a woman who took anything she saw as an insult lying down. She had the same quirk as him; she wasn't about to take shit off anyone without a fight.

He had felt like his life was boring because he had been home a lot more than usual. Lorna hadn't been happy about that either. She didn't like him interfering in the kids' lives unless she asked him expressly. The kids were her territory, her domain, and that had suited him when they were young. But they were older now, and they interested him. He could converse with them, and they were all clever and on the ball. They were nice kids, and they were *his* kids. They were the Davis dynasty, after all – and one day he wanted them to follow in his footsteps. He had two strapping lads to bring into the business – and maybe even little Eilish one day; she was the spit of her grandmother already. But even if he intimated as much to Lorna she would launch him into outer space. And that did not make for a happy home life.

Jenny, as big a mug as she was, had shown him that there was more to life than just work and family. She genuinely enjoyed every single day, she laughed at everything and nothing, and just waited to see what the world might bring to her.

Lorna's dedication to the house, the marriage and the family had become stale. He wanted to laugh with her, but it occurred to him that they had rarely laughed – unless it was about his mum, or someone close to them. His Lorna was a lot of things, but fun wasn't one of them.

His three children rarely spent time with his mother, because Lorna made sure of that. Diana saw them in what could only be called a Lorna-controlled environment. *She* cooked the meal, *she* picked the times and *she* decided when it was all going to end. She regulated everything, and always had done.

Until lately that had never bothered him – it wasn't something he had even thought about. Then his mum had asked him about Angus Junior's birthday, and he had not known what to say to her. He knew that he would have to ask his wife what was happening, and suddenly that had irked him. His mum adored her grandchildren and yet she only saw them sporadically, and at his wife's whim. She was just grateful to see them at all when she was allowed, and that knowledge had suddenly been like a red rag to a bull.

His mum was lovely, and his kids loved her as much as she loved them, especially Eilish, but he had allowed Lorna to dictate when, and if, they could see their grandmother. He had felt like this revelation gave him permission to do what he liked – because, in reality, he had swallowed that behaviour for years, rather than rock the boat, where his wife was concerned.

He wondered how he had ignored everything for so long. But deep down he knew why – it had made his life easier. This wasn't his finest hour, but he was determined to change everything from now on.

'Where's Lorna, Mum?'

'She's been sectioned. The consultant reckons it's best, in case this ever ends up in court.'

Angus nodded. He had guessed as much. She wasn't the full shilling at the moment, and it was best if she was taken out of the ball game for a while.

Diana squeezed her son's shoulder. 'Don't worry, son, Alexa is happy to stay with the kids – they are all right.'

He nodded. Alexa was their housekeeper, and the kids secretly loved her. Another one of Lorna's foibles was that she didn't like anyone around the kids – especially if the kids liked them more than her. It had taken a lot of persuasion to get her to agree to a housekeeper and God knew they'd been through more than their fair share over the years. But Angus felt better knowing there was someone there to keep an eye on things – namely Lorna. He sighed with tiredness. He really needed to sort his head out; he only wished he had done it sooner rather than later.

He saw Gabriel and his mother exchange the same look, and he knew it meant that they thought he couldn't cope with what had happened. Well, only time would tell, he supposed.

He had to go and see Ramiro, and that was something he couldn't cancel. This was a meeting that had to take place. It was the last thing he fucking needed, but work had to take precedence. That went without saying.

Work always came first in this family.

Chapter Eighty-eight

Sinead Connolly looked at her beautiful daughter and felt the sting of tears.

She believed that Lorna had been goaded into her actions, and she blamed Angus. It was his fault – it was always his fault, as far as she was concerned. Her daughter was besotted with that man, but that didn't stop him fucking anything with a pulse, even though he knew that it broke her daughter's heart.

She was holding her daughter's hand in hers. They might have what the shrinks would term a 'complicated relationship' but seeing her daughter looking so bad had really affected her. Lorna was still covered in blood, and it was obvious it wasn't hers. She didn't have a mark on her, but she looked like a woman with problems. Her appearance was old and haggard, and that wasn't her Lorna. Her Lorna had always taken good care of herself. This was what a man could do to you, if you weren't careful.

Lorna opened her eyes, and Sinead smiled gently at her. 'You're OK, darling, you're safe.'

Lorna looked around her at the hospital room and closed her eyes in distress as she realised where she was. She pulled her hand away from her mother's aggressively, and Sinead had to use all her willpower not to lose her temper. She knew what Lorna was capable of when she was like this, so she held her tongue. Instead, she said brightly, 'Shall we get you into the shower, lovely?'

Lorna was staring at her hands, and Sinead could see she was piecing together what had happened.

'Am I being nicked?'

Sinead shook her head quickly. 'Of course not, sweetheart, why would anyone want to nick you?'

Lorna closed her eyes in distress and, pulling herself up with difficulty, she looked at her mother and said seriously, 'I'm drugged out of my box, Mum, but even I know I crossed the line again.'

Sinead forced herself to smile once more. She always pretended that there wasn't really anything wrong. She expected the much-cursed Angus to sort it all out as usual.

'Don't be silly, darling, it's nothing. It was all a misunderstanding.'

Lorna could feel the effects of the psychotropic drugs they had pumped into her. She wondered how long they would keep her, this time, before she was deemed ready to go back to her home once more. She wished her mother would leave her in peace, but she knew she needed her for the next few hours. She couldn't wait to shower and get this blood off her. Every time she closed her eyes, she relived her anger at that fucking girl once more.

She wasn't sorry for what she had done, far from it. She just hoped that Angus could buy them out of it, and she had a feeling that, as usual, he would do just that. What choice did he have? One thing was for sure, he wouldn't be wanting that little whore in his bed any more. No one would. She had messed that bitch up to teach her a fucking lesson: leave other women's men alone. That bitch had asked for all she got. It was the way of the world. Well, her world anyway. Once she had become a threat to Lorna and her kids, that girl had been living on borrowed time.

She allowed her mother to help her into the shower and she stood under the hot spray, enjoying the feel of the water running down her body. As she washed away the blood, she felt her mood lifting.

It had happened. It was over. And they would go on from here.

Angus would sort it, as he had before, and her actions would keep him close to home for a while, until she was back on her feet.

Guilt was a powerful emotion, and she knew that better than anyone.

Chapter Eighty-nine

Ramiro Rodriguez was impressed, and he wasn't afraid to show it. As he looked around the Soho offices, he was smiling widely with absolute pleasure

He had a wonderful set of teeth – they were brilliant white in his suntanned face, and he was proud of them. He had bought them in Miami, and they had not been cheap. He had fantastic bone structure, which he had inherited from his mother. She was a Colombian but her father had been a Brazilian, so Ramiro also had thick black hair. Coupled with his Irish grandfather's blue eyes, he knew he was a one-off, and that suited him. Altogether, he was a very handsome man. He stood out from the crowd, and that had opened many doors for him. Men liked him, and women loved him.

He was built like the proverbial brick shithouse, and he stood head and shoulders above most of the men he dealt with. He looked intimidating enough, so he didn't have to use his muscle. Consequently, he was always smiling and ready to see the good in any situation. It was a big part of his charm. As long as everything was going his way, he was a happy bunny, and he made a point of being friendly and amenable. It cost him nothing, and it brought him genuine friendships.

He liked Angus Davis, he respected and trusted him. He

believed that Angus was a man who would never betray anyone. Angus was innately decent and Ramiro understood that, because he was the same. They were both cut from the same cloth, as his mother would have said.

But he had heard the whispers about Angus's personal troubles, and he needed to know if they were going to affect him. One thing he had learned, over the years, was that troubles on the home front could cause a man to take his eye off the ball. Women and sex were the reason most men ended up in prison. It was a sad fact of life.

He had to find out what was going on, so he could decide where he needed to go from here. But he was willing to give Angus the benefit of the doubt, because this deal had been a year in the making, and he didn't like to think what might happen if it turned out that he had been wasting his valuable time.

He poured himself a large whiskey and sat back down in the very comfortable chair. Either way, he would know the score this evening.

He glanced at his watch and sighed. He was early, as always, so that meant that Angus and his people weren't yet late. He couldn't abide lateness; he felt that it was rude and showed a lack of respect for the people you were dealing with. It was tantamount to saying that their time was far more precious than yours, and that was a mistake that others had made in the past – a mistake they never repeated. That was his only foible and, as foibles went, he thought it was a pretty good one.

Disrespect was something that he couldn't, and wouldn't, countenance from anyone, no matter who they were.

Chapter Ninety

Angus Davis arrived with time to spare because he knew that the Colombians were easily offended.

Angus smiled like a man who had just won the lottery and did exactly what was expected of him. Truth be told, he was pleased to have something to take his mind off his troubles. Plus he liked Ramiro – they always had a good time together. They were kindred spirits in many ways, and they always ended up in one of the clubs with a couple of birds and a few lines to open up the night.

He would see his wife tomorrow and make peace. But for the moment, he had other things to think about.

He had fucked up, and he was aware of that, but it wasn't anything he couldn't sort out, and that was what he had to concentrate on.

Nevertheless, Jenny's destroyed face was not something he would forget in a hurry.

Or who was responsible for it.

Chapter Ninety-one

Sinead was with Diana and Gabriel as they waited for the consultant to join them.

The hospital was private, very expensive, and known for its discretion where certain patients were concerned. That was why they had used it over the years. Everyone knew that Lorna needed a 'break' sometimes – at least, that was how they explained it to themselves. But this latest episode had given them food for thought.

Mr Jeffrey Collins was a small man with a loud voice and a bad case of dandruff. He had an easy smile and a great bedside manner. He was also not frightened to say what he thought, and that was why Angus and Diana respected him so much.

He knew what he was talking about, and he didn't sugar-coat anything. He understood that, where the mentally unbalanced were concerned, the people around them needed to know the truth. They relied on him to take care of any situation that might occur, and deal with it in the best way he could.

He came into the office with his usual swagger. He was a man who knew his worth and expected the people he dealt with to understand that he wouldn't take any nonsense from anyone, least of all the patients he was dealing with. He charged the earth and he did what was needed for the family concerned; his price was high but worth it, because he kept his patients out of the system. They weren't on any databases, and their privacy was guaranteed.

That he used the money to fund his gambling was accepted by everyone concerned. In fact, that was how Diana had found him – through a mutual friend who owned a casino and who was owed a fortune by the unlucky Jeffrey. She had bailed him out, and they had been good friends ever since.

Jeffrey Collins smiled at everyone and, pouring himself a port, he offered, 'Anyone?'

He gave Diana and Gabriel large Scotches, but he ignored Sinead. She wasn't of any importance where her daughter was concerned.

He lit a Marlboro Light and, sitting in his captain's chair, he said curiously, 'No Angus tonight?'

Diana shook her head. 'He's working, but he will be here as soon as. How is she?'

Jeffrey steepled his fingers. 'She's calmed down now. We put her on anti-psychotics again. I think she will be back to normal in a few days, but this time you have to make sure that she takes the medication prescribed. She's bipolar, and nothing is going to change that. If she kept taking her medication then these episodes wouldn't happen. I've explained this to Angus over and over again. She thinks she's OK and she stops taking her tablets, but that isn't an option for her. When she tried to stab Sean, I told Angus—'

Diana almost leapt from her chair as she shouted, 'What did you just say? She threatened Sean with a fucking blade? When the fuck did that happen?'

Jeffrey Collins sipped his port before answering her. 'Calm down, it was a few weeks ago, and Angus was there to sort the situation. But I explained in great detail to him, once more, the importance of keeping her on her drug regime. She can go for months, years even, before she has an episode. But if she kept to her medication, these events wouldn't happen at all.'

Diana was looking at Sinead. She had her head down, which was how Diana knew that she had been aware of her daughter's actions.

She knew now what had been bothering her son these last few weeks. She understood that he had been under enormous pressure.

Gabriel pushed Diana back into her chair with gentle force, before saying sensibly, 'I think we all now fully understand the importance of keeping Lorna on her medication, and we will ensure that happens, no matter what.'

Jeffrey gave a satisfied smile. He hoped they would keep to their promise, because Lorna was a loose cannon. He knew that Angus had made sure there was a housekeeper with a nursing degree on hand – but this latest escapade proved that she needed proper supervision and proper medication.

He only hoped that, this time, they actually listened to him and implemented his recommendations about Lorna's mental well-being.

Chapter Ninety-two

Lorna was feeling a lot better, and she was well aware that it was due to the medication she was on.

She wasn't a fool, and she knew when she had gone too far – that was something she had always sussed *after* the fact. Unfortunately, before the fact she wasn't always thinking straight. It was when she was overwhelmed, when she couldn't distinguish what was real in her own life any more, when she would feel that everything was getting away from her. That was the worst of this really, when she couldn't understand anything except her own anger or her own thoughts.

Angus had to have known that she wasn't the full ten bob, because he had taken precautions. This time, though, he seemed to have abandoned her, and that rankled. It hurt.

She depended on him to take care of her, as he always had – that was why they were such a great couple. She had warned him that she knew about that girl and that should have been enough to rein him in.

She remembered attacking Jenny, and she still didn't feel bad about it. She was well within her rights. That girl had humiliated her, because she was getting a name as her husband's fucking mistress. As if she would ever allow that! She would not be made out to be a mug by anyone. She had her pride, and that pride was worth everything to her.

Yes, she had been out of order, but she had been the victim of another psychotic episode, and she put the blame for that squarely on Angus's shoulders.

She was happy putting everything that had happened down to Angus and his need to look for enjoyment outside of his family. He knew that she would do anything to keep her family safe from harm – after all, she had learned from the best, and that was her husband. When it came to violence, he couldn't really criticise her. He wasn't what you would call without sin himself.

She carefully applied her make-up and fixed her hair because she knew that Angus was coming to see her. She had always made sure that he saw her looking good whatever was going on between them. She didn't need him using the excuse that she'd let herself go as a free pass to pursue other women. This was all his fault. She swallowed his girls but she wouldn't ever swallow a regular one. That was a pact between them, and he had broken it.

She could feel the anger rising up inside her, once again, and she forced herself to calm down. This was the time for being humble, for looking vulnerable and shocked, and in need of his help. Oh, she knew just what was needed at a time like this. She was a fucking expert.

Angus popped his head around the door with a huge smile, and she couldn't help but smile back at him.

'Oh, darling, you look beautiful. How are you feeling?'

She could hear the worry in his voice, and that bothered her, because she knew it meant he was still unsure of her state of mind.

'I'm fine, Angus, I promise you that.'

He came into the room and shut the door behind him. He went to the bed and sat beside her, taking her hands in his. She smiled once more. He knew that she didn't like too big a display of affection, that wasn't her style.

She squeezed his hands, and said sadly, 'I'm so sorry, Angus, I promise I will take the tablets religiously this time.'

Angus sighed gently. She knew this was the Lorna he loved – the quiet, ladylike Lorna who had her head together and who he trusted with his life.

'Jeffrey says you must this time, darling. Once they are in your system, they can do their job. It's dangerous to just stop taking them. Honestly, Lorna, you have to swear to me on the kids' lives that you will keep taking them this time.'

Lorna wasn't impressed at being asked to swear her children's lives away but she knew she was not in a position to bargain, so she smiled widely and said, 'I swear, Angus. This time I will do what I am told. I know that my temper can sometimes get the better of me, and that is something I have had to face up to. But in my defence, you didn't exactly help the situation, did you, darling?'

Angus didn't answer her. Instead, he kissed her hands gently, over and over again, as he knew she liked that. Then, with an underlying warning that wasn't lost on either of them, he said, 'Look, Lorna, whatever I might have done with that Jenny, nothing can excuse what you did to her. You have to understand that, darling. You destroyed her face, her whole life – she's only twenty. I was the one you should have taken it out on, not her. She didn't understand what she was doing, she's a kid, and I should never have brought her into our life. But I did, and now I have to make amends.

'But you also threatened our Sean with a knife, and that worries

259

me. It scared him, Lorna, surely you can understand that? You are his mum, and you pulled a knife on your own child.'

Lorna knew better than to argue that Sean had been rude and disrespectful to her, that she had warned him on more than one occasion about arguing with her constantly, about anything and everything. That she had been in a bad place because of his father's fucking antics. Instead, she nodded her agreement and held her arms out in a gesture of supplication.

'I know that I need to take my meds, Angus. You know that I love you and those children with all my heart and soul.' She felt tearful suddenly. 'I just want to be the best I can be, as a mother and a wife, but it's difficult when you are out, night after night, and the kids are argumentative and disrespectful because you aren't there enough. It's so hard for me at times. I try, but they are like you, Angus. There's no talking to them, especially Angus Junior. Did you know he got into the safe? He saw the guns you keep there? He guessed the code was my birthday and he opened it.

'And, as for Sean – he attacked a boy at school, broke his nose in a fight over an item in the paper about you and one of the clubs. If you only knew the half of it, Angus, and what I have to put up with.'

Chapter Ninety-three

Angus knew that Lorna was over-egging the situation, but he didn't mind, because that was to be expected.

When she was like this, it was always the same. She justified everything, and with good reason, because he did believe that he was the cause of it all. As his old mum always said about his wife, if you went to Tenerife she went to Elevenerife. But this time, he couldn't just pretend that it wasn't really that fucking serious. Because this time, it was.

This time his Lorna had shown him what his mother had been trying to tell him for years, that she was a fucking Looney Tunes. He had always made excuses for her, and he had even kept everyone away – because Lorna didn't like too much company, unless she invited them – and he had happily gone along with that, because he loved her and he trusted her. It had also suited him; he had allowed her to be rude and controlling because it had made his life so much easier.

His mother had to practically beg Lorna to see her grandchildren, and those kids loved his mum and Gabriel. His mum had really had to swallow her natural inclinations – and he had known how hard that had been for her – but he saw that his mother had known that he would always take his wife's side, if challenged.

Now the kids were older, his wife couldn't control them any more, because they wouldn't allow her to. They resented her and her complete say over every part of their lives. They wanted to pursue their own lives, and that was healthy and normal. They were growing up, but as far as she was concerned, she would never let them be out of her orbit or out of her control. That was what he had to try and address before it was too late. He had to finally step in for his kids, so that they had a chance in life.

He looked at his wife, and he felt the usual love and affection that he had always felt for her. She was the love of his life, and she always would be, no matter what. She was the mother of his children. They had married in a church, and they would stay married, until one of them died. That was the contract they had made before God and, like his wife, he didn't take it lightly. She had always relied on him to look after her, and he had promised her that he would.

From now on, that was exactly what he was going to do.

Chapter Ninety-four

'So what are you going to do this time, Angus? Are you just going to overlook it like you usually do?'

Angus stared at his mother and knew that he could not lose his temper, no matter how embarrassed he was about his wife and her behaviour. His mother was more than aware of what he was thinking and feeling. He was tired out, and he really didn't want to discuss any of this now. But his mother would want to catch him off guard, because that was the only way she would get the truth.

Sometimes her knack of finding the exact right moment to demand answers to her questions could grate. But she was within her rights, because she had really helped him sort this whole fucking mess out, and he couldn't fault her on that. She had been straight in there with what she called 'damage limitation'; she had been the voice of reason, in more ways than one.

'No, I won't, Mum. And I have to hold my hand up, because I should have seen this coming.'

Diana shook her head in genuine despair. Lorna's reaction had been over the top in every way. What she had done to that girl was vicious and wicked, it was evil. Nothing could justify that kind of violence and hatred.

'Look, son, I get it. You love her. I love her, even though

she is two tea bags short of a box. But this time, you have to know that she needs proper policing.'

Angus poured himself a large whiskey and, after gulping it down, he replenished his glass once more. 'I know that, Mum, and I will make sure that it's sorted.'

Diana laughed nastily. 'No you won't, son. She will come home and everything will be back to normal, and you will do what you always do. You will all pretend that nothing happened. She will run herself into the ground again, and she will act like nothing untoward occurred, and you will let her, because it's easier than facing the truth. But that can't happen this time, Angus. She threatened your own son with a fucking knife! She was out of control, and you can't pretend that it's fucking normal any more.

'I've spent years keeping my mouth shut, because I didn't want us to fall out over her. She has goaded me, time and again, but I never gave her the chance to push me out of your life or the children's. I knew that you would choose her over me, which was what she wanted. So I didn't bite, even when I really wanted to. But she's gone too far with this latest debacle.'

Angus sank down heavily on the sofa that Lorna had bought and that no one had ever actually sat on. The house was a show home, and only the family rooms were actually used on a daily basis. The other rooms were only opened when they had visitors. He lay back on the comfortable sofa and closed his eyes for a few moments. That had been one of the things he had loved about being with Jenny. She wouldn't have given a fuck about keeping the cushions on a sofa straight – she would have been like him, lying on it and enjoying the experience.

'Look, Mum, I know you are right. But it's been a long few days . . .'

Diana laughed again hollowly, and he opened his eyes and looked at her properly. She was getting old, and that wasn't escaping any of them. But she had always had his best interests at heart, and that would never change.

'You're a fucking coward, Angus. You always have been where she's concerned. She's treated me like shit and you fucking let her, boy. I kept my trap shut for you, and now I am warning you that I won't be so fucking amenable in the future. I'm sorry that I didn't say my piece years ago, and be done with it. But you need to listen to me now, son. We need to all work together on this and stop pretending that she is the full fucking ten euros.'

Angus didn't answer his mother for long moments, and she shook her head wearily.

'I mean it, Angus, you have to listen to me this time. Or I will step away completely from both of you. But I tell you now, I will not walk away from my grandkids. So think on.'

The threat was there, and they both knew it. Angus was surprised – and also relieved, if he was honest – because he knew that he couldn't cope with Lorna by himself.

He looked at his mother and felt a wave of sadness at what she had endured because of him and his selfishness. She had been treated badly in so many ways, and she had still made a point of being his wife's advocate. No one else really gave Lorna the time of day; she wasn't a woman who made friends, not real friends anyway. She didn't know how to. The only people in her orbit were there because they could do something for her or get her something she wanted.

'I know that I have let you down, Mum, especially where the kids are concerned. I have always known that, but Lorna gave me the opportunity to have the best of both worlds, be a married man who could live the single life and dress it up as work. I am so sorry, because I know that Lorna always had an issue with you; she had one with any woman in my life. But I should have nipped it in the bud, I see that now. I should have nipped a lot of things in the bud, but I didn't.'

'Look, son, she's all right as long as she keeps on the medication. That is what needs to be sorted properly this time round. You know me, I have never seen the use of crying over spilt milk. It's happened, so get over it. But this time I am going to stick my nose in, and you and Lorna had better be prepared for that. I love those children and I know Lorna does too. But she needs watching, and I will personally make sure that happens this time. You need to stop deluding yourself where she is concerned.'

Angus nodded his agreement. 'I know you are right, Mum, and I promise that I'll work with you on this.'

Diana sighed. 'Do you know the worst of it all, son? She puts on a fabulous act. We will never know if she is really all right. We will always have to watch her like a fucking hawk.'

She sounded so sad and so resigned that Angus couldn't help but grab her hand and hold it tightly between his own.

'That's the problem, Mum, because I never knew the whole truth of it either.'

Diana sat down beside her son, and for the first time in years she held him in her arms tightly.

And when he laid his head on her breast, she knew that she had finally gotten through to him.

Chapter Ninety-five

'Oh, Dad, really?'

Angus Junior was laughing loudly. He had thrown his head back and was roaring, and his father was laughing with him. He had a really infectious laugh.

'Yes, fucking really! Come on, you and I both know that is true. But like most things in life, no one wants to admit to it.'

'I can just see Mr Allan admitting that he is a secret dope smoker! Dad, if he had a puff, he wouldn't be such a hard arse.'

'Well, I can only speculate, son. He's a maths teacher, and they have a different take on the world; he sees everything as numbers.'

Angus Junior laughed again. 'Well, he reckons I have an aptitude for them!'

Angus threw the end of his joint out of the window of the Range Rover. He didn't pretend any more where his kids were concerned, and it seemed to be working. He had finally listened to his mum's advice and he didn't lie to his kids about anything. They knew he had a puff, and they knew that he wasn't exactly kosher. He didn't explain his businesses or his life in too much detail, but he didn't deny them either.

His mum had always warned him that they would find it all out one day, and it would be so much better if the truth came from him and not from outside sources that he had no control over. The newspapers told them everything they needed to know and much more, but there wasn't much he could do about that. Plus he knew that it gave the kids a certain kudos that they enjoyed. He was glad that he had listened to her, because it had made his life so much easier to be his real self with them and it brought him so much joy. He was closer to his children than he had ever been now he was finally in a position to get to know them properly.

Lorna had kept them away from him, and he hadn't stopped her, because he had believed that she was absolutely within her rights. She had always pointed out that he was not a good role model, that the life he lived would taint them somehow. He didn't think he was a very good role model either, but he now knew that his kids needed him in their lives, no matter what.

He believed that Lorna had only had the children's best interests at heart, and he had forgiven her because now they both knew that she had been wrong. His children had not been allowed to understand, or be a part of, his world, until recently. Now they had chosen to be with him and experience his life and, like him, they were enjoying it.

He had not believed that his kids would ever want to know the truth about his life. Lorna had long ago convinced him that it would be catastrophic for them, and he had gone along with that. He had been more than willing to do whatever was needed to give his children the best start in life that he possibly could. Even if that had meant that he had to step away from them and not let them become part of his real life. And, given that they only had rare weekends together, it had become normal for him to keep himself at a distance.

Yet his mother had told him, time and time again, that he needed to take more of a central role where his kids were concerned. He had fought her over it and he had insulted her, because he had believed that his Lorna had all the answers.

Even when he was home, he had never been allowed to spend any real time with his children, because Lorna had made sure that every minute of their day was full up with everything she thought was important. She had done a marvellous job education-wise – he couldn't fault her where that was concerned – but she had made sure that he had never really been in a position to get to know them properly.

He had been amazed at just how great his children actually were when Lorna had been taken ill. He had also been made aware of his mother's closeness with her grandchildren, especially Eilish. They not only adored her but they relied on her to talk to when things got too much for them. His mother had made sure she had a relationship with them against all the odds.

When his children had finally been in his sole charge, he had not known what he was supposed to do. Lorna was in a psychiatric hospital, and he had been left to deal with the aftermath. Thank God for his mother and her patience.

His children had flourished under his tutelage and they clearly liked him too. He wanted more than ever for them to learn the businesses from him. Now that he had a bigger place in their lives, he could understand why they had rebelled against their mother so hard. Lorna had never given them a moment for themselves, and that grieved him. He should have made sure that they had been allowed to just enjoy being kids.

They had acres of land for his children to roam over, and they had not really had the chance. He saw now that his one weekend a month at home had been like a holiday for his kids. They had been allowed to act normal when he was there with them. How could he have not seen the truth?

Lorna now acted like she and Diana were the best of friends – not that she was fooling anyone. But, once again, they had all chosen to ignore that fact, because it made everybody's life that much easier.

'Come on, Dad, I can't wait to get to Soho. I love that we have clubs there – all my mates are so jealous. And when I tell them about Spain and Ibiza they are gutted!'

'Of course they are, son, you are the heir to all of this. One day, everything will be yours.'

Angus Junior laughed again. 'Well, Dad, hopefully that's not for a long, long time.'

Angus grinned that snide grin that told everyone within his orbit that he wasn't really joking. 'Oh, my boy, I don't think we have anything to worry about there.'

Chapter Ninety-six

Abad was more than ready for a night out. He loved coming to the UK, and he made the most of his visits.

He always had a good shop when he was here. He loved his clobber, and was willing to pay top dollar for it. He loved Angus like a brother; they had been friends for a long time, they were comfortable in each other's company, and always enjoyed a good night out together.

Abad had finally married a girl that his father had found for him, and he was very happy with her. He had been quite content with an arranged marriage – it worked for him, if he was really honest. Three sons and a daughter later, Aysha was still a good-looking girl, and she still had no real understanding of what he did or how he earned his crust. That suited him down to the ground, because he knew that he would never be exactly the faithful type, and he had never had any intention of even trying to be.

He loved his life as it was; he acted the perfect husband and father in his beautiful homes, and his wife loved and appreciated that. He treated her like she was the only woman in the world. When he was in her company, he made sure that she was happy and contented. She had no idea about the real world; she had been brought up to obey her husband and care for her children, both of which she did excellently. His father had chosen well for him.

His father-in-law was a man of means and a man of honour. He had family in Afghanistan and, along with Abad's father, they provided the best drugs on the market. Like most arranged marriages, it benefited everyone concerned. It ensured that wealth married wealth, and the men involved were now bonded by blood. All in all, Abad felt that he was a very lucky man. He had been given a wife who not only brought him wealth and kudos but who was also happy to let him dictate her every move, with a smile on her beautiful face.

But as much as he loved Aysha, he was champing at the bit for a night out with Angus. She was a lot of things, but exciting in the sack would never be one of them and so he wasn't averse to having a dabble when the fancy took him.

Besides, they had a lot of business to discuss, and a lot of time to make up for.

When Roy came in and offered him another drink, Abad was more than happy to accept and get the festivities underway.

Chapter Ninety-seven

Lorna was tired, but she knew that was one of the downsides of her medication. She was used to it, though, and she wouldn't allow herself to stop taking it this time.

She knew better than anyone how that had turned out in the past – after all, she was reminded of it constantly. Not that she felt she had been in the wrong, no matter how many times they all repeated it. But she was aware that she was good at the moment and that, as a result, she was not seen as a danger by anyone any more.

Oh, how that rankled! When she thought about what her husband and his mother had done over the years, she couldn't believe that they had vilified her for one aberration. The hypocrisy alone was hard enough to stomach. She had to remember that they were watching her, and she couldn't do anything about that. She was bipolar, she couldn't help her actions, but what excuse did *they* have for their outrageous violence?

She forced her thoughts away, reminding herself that it was the negative voices that caused her trouble. She knew how to banish them. When they overwhelmed her, she pushed them away and reminded herself that she was the captain of her own ship and she could choose not to let the darkness overtake her.

The medication helped her to live a life that was full and

productive. She still ran though – they couldn't stop her from doing that. She treasured that time alone with only the sound of her own breath. It was what she lived for now, if she was honest. Running had always been her escape from everything, and that would never change.

She smiled at her mother-in-law, and Diana smiled back. There was something about Diana and her life that still made Lorna's skin crawl. She was a woman who had no moral compass for a start, and who had happily become a legend in her own lifetime. Diana genuinely cared about her – she actually appreciated that fact – but it didn't change what she was. She was a violent criminal who dressed well and who acted like she was better than everyone around her.

That her mother-in-law looked down on her, didn't sit well with Lorna Davis. She knew that she was the better woman and the better mother because, unlike this creature, she had always had her children's best interests at heart. Diana had brought her son into the family business without a thought for his welfare. She had just allowed him access to her world from an early age and schooled him in how best to survive it. But Lorna had to keep that opinion to herself because her husband, like his mother before him, was successful at what he did.

'Are you OK, Lorna? Can I get you anything?'

'I could murder a cup of tea, Di.'

Diana smiled happily. 'Of course, darling, I'll make one now.'

Diana looked at her daughter-in-law with concern, because she would never stop worrying about her, even though she knew that Lorna couldn't give a flying fuck if she dropped down dead in front of her. She looked around the state-of-the-art kitchen that Lorna had designed herself and wondered how someone could have so much and yet appreciate it so little. Because that was Lorna's real problem: she had never once had to work for anything – everything had always been given to her as soon as she had requested it. Her son had seen to that.

She knew that she wasn't without blame either. She had bought her way into her grandchildren's lives. She loved them, and she had wanted to see them.

What else could she do?

Chapter Ninety-eight

'Fucking hell, Angus, he is like your double!'

Angus was laughing along with Abad. What he was saying was the truth. Even he could see it; watching Angus Junior was like looking in a mirror.

Angus Junior always enjoyed being in Abad's company. He also loved being in Soho; he had always loved the vibe of London and the West End. Like his father, he felt the excitement of just being there, especially in the clubs that his father owned, and the knowledge that he was a part of it all was heady. He was his father's son and this was his legacy. His father had just told him that one day this would all be his.

His friends knew who his dad was. They knew that he was a Face and a businessman who owned clubs all over the place. He was proud to be a Davis, proud to be someone whose family was to be reckoned with, was respected, and whose name could instil fear into the hardest of men.

His granny was the same. She didn't suffer fools gladly, and he knew that she was the reason his father was where he was today. His granny was the real deal and she had given her know-how to her son, his father, and his father would one day give that know-how to him.

Angus Junior couldn't wait. It was what he lived for.

'Shall we let him have a drink, Abad?' his father was asking.

Abad raised his glass in salute. 'Of course! He will learn how to be a man with us.'

Angus Junior sipped his beer and listened intently to his father and Abad as they discussed business.

He knew that his father expected him to try to grasp the basics of the conversation.

He was more than happy to do as requested.

Chapter Ninety-nine

'Abad is one of my oldest friends and business associates. He is also a dangerous fucker and don't you ever forget that, son.'

Angus Junior wisely nodded, because he knew that his father was giving him sage advice. They were in the VIP suite of Angus's club in King's Cross. He had made sure that Abad had a continual line of young blondes with big tits and big arses to entertain him. He knew exactly what his friend liked, and what he was expecting – and they were all on the house, of course. He wouldn't dream of charging Abad.

He could see his son's interest in the girls, and he was pleased about that but he wanted him to understand that, in their world, these girls were just matter-of-fact. They were nothing more than a perk of the job. Women – well, certain women – would always be available to them, but as yet his boy, as good-looking as he was, wasn't immune to these girls' charms.

'See her, son? Beautiful, isn't she?'

Angus Junior's eyes were on stalks. The girl in question was all of nineteen, blonde and well stacked, with an expensive fake tan and good shoes. She knew exactly how to make the best of herself, and Angus could respect that. She was a nice kid and, unlike the majority of the girls who worked the poles, she was capable of having an actual conversation.

'She is still a working girl, though, son, never forget that.'

Angus Junior turned to his father. 'I do know the score, Dad, you have explained it to me on more than one occasion. We are in a world where good-looking young women are in abundance. So they might not be exactly kosher. I had rather worked that one out for myself, if I'm honest.'

Angus slung an arm around his son, pleased he was listening to him.

'Seriously, Dad, I get it, they are out for the main chance, the money. It's a lap-dancing club, they aren't here for anything else.'

Angus raised his eyebrows comically. 'Well, they are, if you are willing to pay for it!'

Angus Junior looked puzzled. 'Not from us, though, surely? I mean, why the fuck would we have to pay? They work for us, Dad.'

Angus shook his head and, looking at his son, he said seriously, 'Listen, these girls are here to earn a wage. I'm paying extra for them tonight so Abad can have a good time. But we don't own them, son, they are working for us, and we can't take advantage. Why would you think otherwise?'

Angus Junior shrugged nonchalantly. 'If you say so. But if they work for us then they should be available, surely?'

Angus shook his head. 'I don't pay them a wage to be here, like the bar staff or the cleaners. They pay me a percentage to work here, son. I suppose you could say we work for them, in a way. But don't ever forget that, without these girls, we haven't got a club or an earn.'

Angus Junior smiled his agreement, but in reality he still couldn't see any logic there. They were no more than a commodity, as far as he was concerned, and they were there for his gratification and the men that they catered for. It was a business transaction. They didn't deserve anything other than his disdain.

That was the truth, as far as he could see, because these girls were everywhere, like rats. Every day, they had new ones lining up to work the poles; most of them were over the hill by twenty-five. He didn't see them as anything other than whores. Unlike his father, he didn't feel the need to justify using these women to earn a crust. They were willing participants, and they all knew the score.

But he was shrewd enough to know when to keep his own counsel. His mother had taught him that much over the years, especially where his old man was concerned. His mum had always tried to hide his father's real businesses from her kids but, unlike her, he didn't have a problem with any of it – far from it. In fact, he thought his father was someone to aspire to.

Along with his Granny Diana, his father was a fucking legend, and that was something he not only admired but was proud of. This was his bloodline, this was what he wanted and what he was determined to become an important part of.

One day, this would all be his. And he would be more than ready, when the time came.

Chapter One Hundred

Julie James was not what could be called beautiful, but she was striking.

She was tall, slim, and she had a pair of breasts that wouldn't look out of place in a Titian painting. The big draw was that they were natural – they practically defied gravity – and she was very popular, especially with the older punters. Unlike the younger men who came to the clubs, the older men weren't as enamoured of the surgically enhanced ladies, they were more interested in the natural look.

Julie had natural auburn hair, and that included both collar and cuffs. She didn't remove all her pubic hair like most of the girls, who wanted to look like prepubescent teens – she was happy to just tidy hers up, and it really worked well for her. She also was in possession of a fantastic pair of legs that she made the most of with the addition of six-inch heels.

She was a serious earner, and the other girls liked her because she was a genuinely nice person. She was bringing up two young boys on her own – their father was doing a wedge in prison, and she wasn't known to put herself about other than for work. All in all, Julie was a real asset. Abad had always had a fancy for her, and Angus made sure that she was available whenever he was in town.

It was the private dances that really earned the girls the money, and it was the dream to be singled out for a private party. Julie appreciated Abad always treated her well and she had a good time with him. They had a rapport, and after the business was concluded they often talked for hours. That suited Julie – the longer she was there, the more she would earn; she suspected that Abad knew that, and kept her there for that reason only. He would also slip her a serious tip when the night was over, which was always welcome.

So tonight she was pleased to get herself ready and willing for her handsome Moroccan man. It would be an easy night, and a very lucrative one. What more could a girl in her position ask for? She was to work with two of the newer girls, Abigail and Milandra. Both were nice lasses and they would be the opening act. She would come into the private room after they had done their dances, and she would only dance for Abad.

She knew that most men had a fantasy that was often very different to what they wanted from their wives or girlfriends, and that was fine by her. Once they came into the clubs, it was down to women like herself to fulfil that fantasy.

It was what made the world go round. Julie understood that the men who she interacted with weren't really being unfaithful to the women they lived with or were married to. They were just scratching an itch, letting off steam, and the women that they used meant nothing to them.

Abad didn't want anything out of the ordinary, and she actually enjoyed herself sexually with him. They were like an old married couple in some respects, because they had a routine and it worked for both of them. Afterwards, they just talked and laughed together, and she had a feeling that was something he couldn't do with his wife – at least, not the way he did with her.

In a different life, they would probably have made a great couple. She had a feeling that Abad knew that too, which was why he always came back to her.

Chapter One Hundred and One

Abad was in the private room with Angus and his boy.

He liked Angus's kids, but he wondered at him letting his older boy be a part of something like this at still such a young age. It wasn't his business but his own father had dragged him into so much, so early, he knew he wouldn't do that to his kids. His children would get an education – a good education – and then he would decide what their futures held. But Morocco and London were two completely different cities, and Angus Junior had been exposed to so much because of the newspapers and television that he'd had access to.

That was for Angus to worry about. Abad was relaxed and ready to party. He always enjoyed his nights here with Angus, and the girls he provided. He accepted another large whiskey, and he sipped it with relish. These nights out together had become almost a ritual; they both looked forward to them, and they enjoyed their time together.

Abigail and Milandra were both a bit nervous, because they knew that these weren't the usual private-room punters – this was Angus, their boss, and one of his important business associates.

Milandra was pleased to see that Angus Junior was there. She knew that she could do a lot worse – he was a good-looking lad, and he was going places. She wouldn't be averse to going there with him, should that opportunity present itself. She concentrated all her voluptuous charms on him, and he didn't look like he was going to refuse them.

Abigail danced for both Abad and Angus. She had been told the score earlier, and she wasn't going to deviate in any way. Abigail just wanted to dance, get her cash and go home; this wasn't a career for her, this was a stopgap while she was at university. It paid the bills, and that was all she was interested in. She was studying Law, and she was not going to be left with huge debts when she finally graduated. She knew exactly what she was going to do with her life, and this job was just a stepping stone.

The VIP room was larger than the other private rooms, and it had mirrored walls and subdued lighting. It also had a bar, as well as two huge black leather sofas. There were three poles for the girls to use, and small glass tables that were placed strategically to hold not only the punters' drinks but also baby oils, KY Jelly and assorted condoms.

Milandra was dancing closer to Angus Junior, and when he beckoned her over to him, she was happy to oblige, and she was smiling as she lowered herself on to his lap.

When Julie came into the room, she looked absolutely amazing. Both the younger girls knew she was the star turn. There wasn't anything they could do to compete with her. Abad's eyes lit up when he saw her. Julie was a fucking one-off. He pulled himself up from his seat and, taking her hand, he kissed it and bowed like a gentleman. Julie smiled graciously and began to dance, slowly and provocatively.

Angus knew the score and he went over to the bar and poured them all fresh drinks, including a glass of sparkling wine in a champagne flute for Julie. She had earned her special treatment.

Julie was pulled on to Abad's lap gently. She happily complied, and then she accepted the glass of wine from Angus, smiling her thanks. It was an old routine now.

Angus Junior was watching the dance with disdain. He had drunk a lot of vodka and he had also had a few lines of cocaine. He knew better than to let his father know that, of course, even though he was a cokehead extraordinaire. His father was funny about that; he would let his son drink himself stupid but he frowned on him taking drugs. It was such fucking hypocrisy, and that annoyed him. He wasn't a child, he was being introduced to the business, so why did his father treat him like one?

He was watching Julie and Abad closely. They were kissing like lovers. The music had been changed at some point, from dance music to soul classics. The whole atmosphere of the room was suddenly different and, as Freddie Jackson was singing 'Rock Me Tonight', Angus Junior got up from his seat, leaving Milandra. Flopping down heavily on to the other sofa beside Abad and Julie, he tried to slip his hand between Julie's legs.

It took a few moments before his father realised what was going on. As Abad grabbed his son's arm and threw him angrily across the room, Angus knew that he had to do something – and quickly. It had all happened so fast, he couldn't believe it. When Abad gripped his boy by his shirt and dragged him up off the floor, he knew that he had to stop it. Abad could kill on a whim.

He knew that whatever had happened had to be his boy's fault. Abad wouldn't disrespect him like this without good reason.

'You little fucker, who the hell do you think you are?'

Angus Junior was frightened, and that was more than obvious to everyone in the room. He had crossed a line, and his father wasn't rushing to his defence. That alone told him all he needed to know.

Angus pulled his son away roughly and threw him on to the nearest sofa. 'Hey, Abad, what happened?'

Abad looked at his old friend and, pointing his finger at Angus Junior, he said angrily, 'He put his filthy hands on Julie. He put his hand between her legs. What kind of an animal thinks that is acceptable? What the fuck would make him think that I would not be offended by such disgusting behaviour?'

Angus looked at his son and he could see that, even though he was scared and knew that he had done something really wrong, he was still expecting his father to make it right for him. He still believed that he was untouchable. He could see the insolence in his son's eyes and he knew that he had to nip it in the bud. His boy needed to learn that he had to abide by certain rules, like everyone else, or he wouldn't last five fucking minutes in their world.

Angus held his hands up in a gesture of supplication, and he said to Abad apologetically, 'He's drunk, mate. He needs a lesson in etiquette – and believe me, he is going to get one.'

Angus Junior sat back on the black leather sofa and grinned arrogantly. Then, holding his arms out, he said mockingly, 'Come on, guys, it was a fucking joke. It's not like that's the first time a strange hand has slipped between her legs, is it?'

Abad looked at Angus and, before he could say a word, Angus was pulling his son up by his hair. Grasping him around the throat, he said menacingly, 'Do you know something, son? You just made a novice mistake, because you just talked yourself into serious fucking trouble.'

The beating he gave his son was long, brutal and painful.

It was something that neither of them would ever forget.

But it was also something that his son would never forgive.

Chapter One Hundred and Two

'Look, Lorna, before you start, he asked for everything he got. He is lucky he got off this lightly because – I tell you now – if he wasn't my son, he would be a dead man. If he had been anyone else, Abad would have fucking murdered him. And he would have been well within his rights, because that boy of ours completely disrespected him. It was like watching a fucking car crash when you know you can't do anything about it.'

Lorna looked at her son lying unconscious in the hospital bed, and she didn't say anything. In reality, she couldn't criticise her husband, because their son had committed such a monumental fuck-up.

How could anyone think that a man like Abad would countenance such abominable behaviour? Especially not her son, who had known that man all his life. Abad was not only a close friend, but he was also privy to everything of importance concerning any business they conducted. Angus and Abad used each other as foils, so that if anything should ever happen to either of them, the other would know what had gone down and how best to deal with it.

They were each other's insurance, and that was because of a true friendship where they trusted each other implicitly. Both knew that they needed someone on the outside – someone they could trust to look after their interests, should the worst happen. Because in their world, you never knew what might occur when you least expected it.

Roy had filled her in on the circumstances, and she couldn't really say anything in her son's defence. He should have known better, because she prided herself that she had not raised any fucking fools. Seems she had not been as clever as she had believed. But she had warned her husband about bringing Angus Junior into the business at such a young age, and giving him access to everything before he had earned that right. He was a clever dick, because he had been privately educated, and he thought he was the dog's knob. He had never once had to do a day's collar, or earn his keep for real.

She had made sure that, when her children were small, they didn't get away with anything. She had kept them close, and she had been hard on them. But now that his father had taken over from Diana, it seemed that he had not been able to keep the boy on the straight and narrow. She had told Angus that their son needed a firm hand and that he needed to understand that he couldn't just do whatever he wanted. He should have listened to her, and she said as much.

'I told you he was still a baby, for all his bravado. You brought him in against my advice – and your mother's, I might add. Even Diana said to ease him in gently.

'He is seventeen and he has no real knowledge of the world you inhabit, only what he has read in the papers. He thinks he's a film star, that he's famous. He thinks that he can get away with anything, because no one has ever told him any different. Except me. And I have no say over anything where he is concerned any more, as you know full well. So if you don't mind, Angus, when he's back on his feet, I hope you remember that.'

Angus had honestly believed that his son would have been far more on the ball, would have known instinctively that what he had done was not acceptable to anyone around him. He knew that the papers had glamorised him and his clubs, but that had been all part of the game. His real businesses were conducted with the minimum of fuss and without any fanfare whatsoever. His clubs and his properties and his restaurants were all a front for the real earn. That his son had thought that was all there was to his world really grieved him, because his son had to know that wasn't true.

His Angus wasn't a stupid lad. He had really thought that the boy was much like him. His Angus wasn't one of the sheep; he didn't live by the usual standards. He had hoped that his boy had inherited some of his natural aptitude for skulduggery. He had never thought for one second that the boy would turn out to be a fucking liability.

Angus put his arms around his wife, and she settled into his arms. Squeezing her into his chest, he said quietly, 'He was out of order, Lorna.'

Lorna nodded sadly. 'I know. But he was always a loose cannon, and you should have known that. He was a know-all – even as a little kid, he would argue the toss over anything. Remember the drama about the hamster and how it had died? We both knew he had killed it in a temper, but he wouldn't admit it. He argued that it had bitten him, and that was why he had thrown it against the wall.'

Lorna honestly couldn't feel any real sympathy for her son. He had been asking for this for a long while. She had lost her hold over him and so she had thought that his father could keep him in order, but she had been wrong.

Once children reached a certain age, there wasn't anything

you could do for them if they didn't want your input. That had been a hard lesson for her.

She had warned Angus Junior enough times that his attitude would one day lead him to his downfall. She had been proved right. Hopefully, he would listen to her in the future.

She knew, better than anyone, that in their world the sooner you learned the harsh realities of life, the better off you would be.

Book Five

2008

If you hate a person, you hate something in him that is part of yourself. What isn't part of ourselves doesn't disturb us.

Demian: The Story of Emil Sinclair's Youth,
Hermann Hesse (1877–1962)

Chapter One Hundred and Three

Gabriel and Diana were both laughing their heads off until they saw Lorna pulling up in the drive. Her presence seemed to suck the fun out of the atmosphere within seconds. Lorna had a knack of bringing a pall of overwhelming depression with her wherever she went. They looked at each other in exasperation and sighed simultaneously.

Diana opened the door with a huge smile plastered on her face. Not that it fooled either of them, but it was a game they had played for so long, neither knew how to put an end to the pretence.

Lorna had always been the barrier between Diana and her grandchildren, and thankfully that was all over. Now Lorna couldn't dictate if and when her children could see their grand-mother any more, because they were all old enough to decide for themselves who they wanted to see, and when they wanted to see them. Diana knew that had to hurt Lorna, and she could find it in her heart to feel sorry for her, because Lorna had lost out in more ways than one.

Oh, it was a difficult road they all had to travel these days, but they did it with a smile – and the hope that Lorna wouldn't feel the need to point out where everyone was going wrong.

Lorna looked good and Diana told her so because, in fairness, even with everything she had endured she had looked after herself and it had paid off. 'Lorna, lovely, you look fantastic. Where did you get that outfit?'

Lorna walked into the house smiling genially as she said, 'It's only from Karen Millen but I love the cut of her clothes, and the materials are always such excellent quality.'

Diana smiled her agreement and followed her daughter-in-law into her kitchen. She automatically opened the fridge and poured out two glasses of white wine. She handed one to Lorna, who sat at the breakfast bar and nodded her thanks.

Sitting opposite her, Diana sipped her drink and said quickly, 'So to what do I owe this pleasure?'

It was friendly and to the point, and it meant they didn't have to dance around each other for ages, because she really wasn't in the mood.

Lorna was still smiling amiably. 'I just wondered if you know where my boys are? Only I can't get them on the phone – or Angus, come to that – and it's been a few days.'

Lorna was acting as if she wasn't worried in the least, and this was just a friendly visit. But Diana knew exactly what it had taken for Lorna to come to her like this and ask her outright if she knew where her sons were. Lorna had so much pride, too much pride really, more than was good for her. It saddened Diana that Lorna was being treated so badly, even though she understood the logic behind it. As much as Lorna had grieved her over the years, she still believed that she was owed enough respect from her children for them at least to let her know where they were.

Gabriel came into the kitchen and, kissing Lorna on the cheek, he said jovially, 'How are you? You're looking well.'

Diana smiled again and said pointedly, 'Lorna was just asking after the boys.'

Gabriel immediately understood the situation and, shaking his head ruefully, he said, 'Oh, Lorna, that's my fault. I told the boys I would ring you, but it's been such a bloody mad time. They went to Spain with Angus. There's a new DJ at the club in Banús – that Lifer Pete – and they were mad to go. He's really making a name for himself, and they were determined to see him. There is also Rowetta from the Happy Mondays doing a set with Bez, so you can imagine that was just too good to miss.'

Lorna listened to Gabriel talking without any kind of expression on her face. Diana could see the distress in Gabriel's eyes, and she loved him all the more for his kindness. He knew that Lorna loathed him, even more than she loathed her mother-in-law. She needed Diana at times, and Diana made sure that she was always there for her. It had never been an easy relationship, but though she had regained her grandchildren she also still carried the guilt that Lorna engendered in her.

Lorna sipped her wine. She had always been very feminine and very elegant; she could wear an old rag and still look like she had stepped off a catwalk.

'Oh, I see. Thank you, Gabriel, for letting me know. It was just . . . I was a bit worried, as I hadn't heard from them. But I suppose they are too busy having a good time.'

The implication that he had deliberately kept this knowledge from her was more than evident to anyone within a five-mile radius. Once more, Diana was reminded how much she loved this man because he had taken the onus off her. Gabriel always ignored Lorna and her hysterics, they were water off a duck's back to him. She bored him, and she always had done, and Lorna was more than aware of that fact.

'So! I'm glad we got all that sorted out.' He walked out of the kitchen and shut the door behind him.

Lorna smiled once more and Diana refilled her wine glass, saying carefully, 'I know how you feel, Lorna, it's so fucking rude. That's kids for you. But in fairness, they aren't children any more, are they? So they don't think to tell you their movements. I used to want to string my Angus up! But, believe me, you do get used to it.'

Lorna just smiled vacantly, and Diana knew that she was wasting her time trying to soften the blow. Lorna knew, as well as she did, that her kids had not bothered to tell her what they were doing because they couldn't be arsed. They avoided Lorna like the fucking plague, because she still tried to control everything that they did.

She had driven her children away with her constant interference. Lorna had pushed them all to the limits of their patience, and even Angus couldn't talk them into making allowances for her any more. Especially where Eilish was concerned.

It was as if her daughter didn't exist. It was strange really. Lorna had longed so much for a girl and when she arrived she had barely given that child the time of day. It had always been about the boys – and mainly Angus Junior, because he had been the surrogate for her husband and his total neglect of her for weeks at a time. As a result, it had been Diana that Eilish had turned to for any kind of maternal comfort – when Diana was allowed to be around, of course. But the seeds were sown and, now that they were free to be a part of each other's lives, grandmother and granddaughter were thick as thieves. Eilish had a steeliness to her that Diana recognised and, she reckoned, more nous than her brothers put together. Though she kept that to herself.

Now the kids just dismissed their mother and treated her like a distant relative; there was no real closeness or affection there.

Sean and Eilish both still lived at home, but they acted like it was a lodging house, while Angus Junior had his own place.

Lorna had no standing with her kids any more. They were each happy living their own life, preferably without her in it.

It was sad but it was the truth.

Chapter One Hundred and Four

Eilish Davis was a good-looking woman. She also knew that, in comparison to the lap dancers that worked for her family, she could be seen by some as lacking.

But Eilish had what those girls would never have: she had confidence, she had her mother's natural dress sense, and her grandmother's sharp brain. Furthermore, she had the added bonus of being their boss. She liked the girls and they liked her because she was fair-minded and she always made sure that they were treated with respect. They were in awe of the way she carried herself, and how she could hold her own with any man she came into contact with. True, that she was Angus Davis's daughter was well known, but that didn't matter because the girls knew that she could more than fight her own corner.

Even her father had finally accepted that, and he was proud that she could take care of herself. She knew that if she wasn't up to scratch, he would have no problem replacing her. After what had happened with her brother and Abad, she knew that none of them were in for an easy ride. That was what appealed to her; she didn't want to achieve simply because she was a Davis, she wanted to achieve because she was good at what she did.

Her grandmother was her idol. Diana had been the original woman in a male world, and she had made such a success of herself. Eilish knew that, if it had not been for Diana, her father would not have had such a walk-in. She loved her granny more than anything. Even though Diana was taking a back seat these days, her name was synonymous with respect, and that was what Eilish wanted for herself. She spent as much time with her grandmother as possible and lapped up every bit of knowledge her grandmother shared with her. Now the opportunity to prove herself to her father was paying off because he knew what his mother was capable of. And he admitted to himself that Eilish had his mother's drive and ambition.

Davey Proctor was smiling as he approached her, and she felt the usual rush of excitement at being close to him. She couldn't help her feelings for this man, even though she knew that he wasn't worthy of her or her time. He was a womaniser and a flake but there was something about his blue eyes and thick dark hair that just rocked her boat; the man was beautiful and he knew it.

'I've sorted the private party, as you requested, and the bars are ready for opening. I've also told Janine and Marina that they are finishing tonight over the trouble yesterday. Fighting like squaddies in the fucking top bar! I've got their pay ready and, providing they don't fuck up today, I will give it to them.'

Eilish nodded.

Davey grinned at her. 'Anything else?'

Eilish looked into his handsome face. He was laughing at her, but she wouldn't rise to the bait.

Looking at him for long moments, Eilish finally said coolly, 'I'll let you know.'

Davey knew when he was being dismissed.

As he walked away, Eilish added loudly, 'One last thing, Davey. Could you make sure in future that you keep a change of clothes here? It really doesn't look good when you wear the same shirt two days on the trot. And have a shave – you look like one of the punters.' Eilish was pleased to see that she had irked him – when he turned to face her, the usual trademark grin was absent.

'I was just going home to change actually.'

Eilish shrugged nonchalantly. 'I'm glad to hear it. But, in future, I would appreciate it if you changed before coming to work.'

Davey Proctor looked into her eyes and, smiling once more now, he said seriously, 'Of course, if that's what you want. I only came in today because you asked me to take care of the private party. And I had to sort out the girls. But, believe me, I have been told.'

He was laughing at her again. Eilish was so glad that she could keep a lid on her emotions – she had inherited that from her grandmother – but she was well aware that Davey knew the effect he had on her. It irked her, but there wasn't anything she could do about it.

She walked towards the offices and didn't even bother to answer him, but she could sense him watching her every move. Inside the office, she leaned against the door and allowed herself a little smile. He was a fucker but she couldn't get him out of her mind. There was something about him. He was unreliable where women were concerned, he was dangerous, and he was funny and great company. He was everything her father was, and more – and she knew that she should keep as far away from him as physically possible. But she couldn't.

Davey was like a drug to her. She just couldn't get enough of him.

Eventually, they would collide. And, when they did, she hoped that she could cope with him and all he entailed.

It was only a matter of time.

Chapter One Hundred and Five

Angus Junior and Sean were both in their club in Banús watching the DJs setting up.

The club was huge – it could easily hold a thousand people – but when it was empty like this, it looked so different. It was a great venue and no expense had been spared, which was why it was so popular. There were three VIP bars on the upper floors, and nine bars around the main dance-floor areas. There were huge TV screens so the punters could see the DJs at work, and the cages that the scantily clad lads and lasses danced in were scattered around. No matter where you were, there was something to see, something to experience. A can of Coke was a fiver, as was a bottle of water, so even without the alcohol, they would have made a profit.

Sean was laughing at something one of the sound men said, and Angus pretended that he had heard it and laughed too. He couldn't bear to think that he had missed out on anything, and he wouldn't admit to it either. That he was generally stoned didn't help his situation, and the fact that his brother, Sean, rarely indulged annoyed him.

Sean was a natural entrepreneur with a knack for finding the right people to do the right jobs, which gave him an edge. Sean was quiet and well liked, and Angus knew that he deserved to be because he was a good guy. He also knew that he wasn't so well thought of himself. He had earned his reputation as a loose cannon, and he was proud of that – even though it didn't endear him to people. Well, he could live with that. After all, he was Angus Davis Junior, he didn't need people to fucking like him. Eilish was like Sean; they both seemed to have a gift for making the people around them like them, regardless of who they were.

Angus recognised that his personality wasn't geared to liking 'the help' – and that was how he saw the people who they worked with. He banged the dancers, he was rude to the bouncers – he basically did whatever suited him. And his name and family guaranteed him a swerve.

He went to the nearest bar and opened two bottles of Peroni. Walking back to his brother, he gave him one. 'Come on, bruv, have a brew with me. It's a big night tonight.'

Sean took the beer from him and grinned. 'I can't believe it, can you? The top DJ, and Rowetta and Bez from the Mondays. What an experience! The weather's fucking excellent, so the punters outside will be banging. I can't wait.'

Angus drank his beer straight down and, burping loudly, he said, 'Let's have another, bruv, and get this fucking party started.'

Sean laughed and handed his drink to Angus. 'You have it, mate, I'm not a drinker, you know that.'

Angus drank the second Peroni straight down too. He was ready to rock and roll, and he wished that his brother would let his hair down.

Just once.

Chapter One Hundred and Six

Sean watched as his brother swallowed down a couple of Es with another Peroni, and he turned away from him and concentrated on the stages.

Angus annoyed him when he was like this. He would be out of his nut before the doors opened, and he would be looking for a fight before the first fucking set. It was like he wanted aggravation from the old man and, when their dad turned up, he would know immediately that Angus was already rocking.

He was sick of being their go-between.

Angus grabbed his brother's arm and pulled him over to the bar. 'Come on, Sean, it's a fucking nightclub. Have another drink with your brother.'

The staff were arriving and getting on with their allotted jobs. Sean knew that the bartenders would not be too thrilled at Angus and his antics. All they wanted to do was get on with serving drinks, and make sure that the tills matched the sales. When Angus was like this, there was no chance of that happening.

Sean pulled his brother away from the bar and, dragging him towards the lifts, he said loudly, 'Come on, you, let's go to the VIP bar. This place will be packed out soon.'

Angus followed him happily.

Sean knew his brother didn't care where they went, as long as he had a drink.

Chapter One Hundred and Seven

Angus Davis Senior walked into The Banús just after midnight. Sean had said to name their nightclub after the area, and he had been right. As he had pointed out, when people came to the Banús they went to The Banús. It made sense really.

His Sean was a good lad, and he had shown he had great potential. The fact that he didn't really drink or take drugs was a big plus, especially when he measured him up against Angus Junior. Angus Junior, in all fairness, was a shrewd businessman, providing you caught him before he went on it for the night. Once he was on the chop, he was a waste of fucking time and effort.

Angus loved him, but he despaired of his eldest child ever having the nous to really move up in his business. The boy had a terrible habit of falling out with people for no good reason. If these people were fucking nobodies, Angus would have happily swallowed, because no real harm would be done, but his son could pick a fight with a Trappist monk when the mood was on him. Once he hit that stage, he didn't care who he was rowing with. Consequently, Angus didn't trust his eldest son with anything of importance any more.

Now that was seen to by Sean, who had stepped up to the plate and proved himself a man of his word. Sean was respected for who he was, not just because he was his father's son, and that pleased Angus. Sean could close a deal, and close it well – he had been a real asset to his father. But Angus Junior needed to be put in his place again, and he wasn't looking forward to it.

The club was packed out and the atmosphere was almost electric. Angus and Roy stood by the main dance floor and surveyed the club and its patrons gleefully. This place was where everyone wanted to be, and where everyone wanted to be seen. He followed Roy to his private lift. As they made their way up to the VIP bars, Angus was shaking hands and waving at people. The punters would dine out on the story of his attention for years. He always acted like each one was an old friend who he was so pleased to see, and they reacted with genuine happiness. Angus knew *exactly* how to play the game.

In the lift, Roy laughed, saying, 'Did you see that fucking wannabe trying to get a photo with you?'

Angus laughed with him. 'See the size of his head? Like fucking Shergar!'

They were still laughing as they exited the lift.

Chapter One Hundred and Eight

Roy saw Angus Junior before his father did, and he sighed in disappointment. The only thing he had wanted was a good night with no trouble. He was getting too old for this shit.

Roy pulled Angus away from a young actress who had waylaid him, and nodded in his son's direction. 'You go up to the private bar, and I'll bring fucking happy Harry up in a minute.'

Angus nodded. He was annoyed and it showed. He saw Sean trying to catch his eye, but he pretended not to see him. If he went over there and Angus Junior started his antics, he would not be able to contain himself.

His son had promised him faithfully that he would not drink or take drugs too early in the day, because that was his downfall. He never knew when to stop. He didn't have a fucking Off button.

He called his private lift, and it opened immediately, but he could still hear his eldest son's belligerent voice, even over the DJ's ranting. Inside the lift, Angus unclenched his fists and took a few deep breaths, furious with how easily his eldest son could ruin his night.

Sean watched his father disappear into the lift. He knew that his father had deliberately pretended not to see him and he couldn't blame him. He had been trying to keep Angus down, trying to stop him getting so out of it. What hadn't helped the situation was Benny Rafter's sons coming over to say hello. Sean liked them enormously, and so did Angus – when he wasn't out of his box – and it had been fine at first. The fact they were in the main VIP bar spoke volumes, it told everyone about their standing in the community. But that didn't deter Angus; he had decided ten minutes into the conversation that Ronald Rafter's wife was fair game.

Tania Rafter was a good-looking girl. She was tall, she had long dark hair, and she was slim enough to accentuate her breasts. She had the face of an angel, and Ronnie was crazy about her – and in fairness, she was crazy about him too. Angus had grabbed Tania Rafter's breasts and asked her if she did the business. Tania had been mortified, especially as Angus had been at her wedding not eight months previously.

Ronnie had, quite rightly, taken umbrage, and Angus had happily accepted his umbrage and raised that with another insult: 'Come on, Ronnie, you and I both know she isn't exactly a wilting violet.'

Sean closed his eyes in utter disbelief and shook his head slowly. He had already called over two of the security men that he trusted, and they waited patiently for his instructions. Danny Rafter was standing in front of his brother now, talking him down. Sean looked across at Roy; he needed help to get Angus over to the lift and out of the situation.

The broken bottle came out of nowhere. It was so quick and unexpected, no one had seen it coming. Tania Rafter grabbed a wine bottle from the black granite bar and smashed it into Angus's head in one quick movement. Even Ronnie Rafter was in shock at her retaliation. His Tania was a nice girl. She wasn't violent; it wasn't in her nature.

She pointed the bottle at Angus again as she screamed, 'No one touches me, Angus Davis. How dare you, you fucking piece of shit!'

Ronnie took the wine bottle away from her and she fell straight into his arms, crying hysterically. The security men had already cleared the bar of onlookers. Roy walked Angus to the private lift, and one of the barmaids brought out a few tea towels to stem the bleeding.

Sean stayed with Ronnie Rafter and his wife, and did his best to minimise the damage. 'What can I say, Ron? I'm so fucking sorry, mate.'

Ronnie was still holding his wife in his arms and trying to calm her down. He looked at Sean and, shaking his head, he said angrily, 'That bastard crossed a line tonight, and you know it as well as I do. He assaulted my wife, and he mugged me off like I am some kind of cunt. Well, this don't end here. And you can tell him that from me.'

Sean nodded in agreement. He couldn't believe the turn the night had taken. Angus and his drunken shenanigans were becoming a regular event, and Sean didn't like it. He couldn't control his brother when he was like this, and he couldn't second-guess him either, because Angus was so erratic he was capable of anything.

'He has a drug problem, Ron. You know that he won't even remember this tomorrow.'

Ronald Rafter was holding his wife tightly in his arms. She was still crying, and he could feel her shaking in shock.

He said nastily, 'We were celebrating the news that my Tania is pregnant, so that fucker ruined not just a night out, Sean, but something that we should have remembered all our lives with happiness.'

Sean wondered why he was even trying to defend his brother's actions and his lunacy. In all honesty, he would rather spend the evening with the Rafter brothers than Angus. Angus was becoming an arsehole whose drug-taking was getting the better of him. These outrageous acts were becoming more frequent and more unpredictable by the day.

Sean nodded to the barman, who looked terrified, saying, 'Open a decent bottle of brandy.' Then, looking at Ronald and Danny, he said honestly, 'Do you want to know the truth? I'd fucking take him out if he treated me or mine like that. Nothing I can say will make any difference to this situation. But personally, I'm fucking mortified by his behaviour.'

Tania was calmer now, and she accepted the brandy gratefully.

Sean walked them to the sofas and, as they settled down, he raised his own glass in a toast. 'Just ... I apologise for my brother, and I hope you won't hold this against me.'

The brothers were aware that he meant not just him but his family, and they knew that no one would be that fucking rash. Ronnie had right on his side where Angus Junior was concerned, but if he sought retribution on any other members of the family, Diana Davis would see him dead and buried within twenty-four hours. That was without allowing for Angus Senior, if he should choose to take offence.

The Rafters were a hard family, and well respected, but they knew they couldn't take on the Davises, even if Angus was fair game by anybody's standards.

Chapter One Hundred and Nine

Angus looked down at his son and wasn't surprised that he felt nothing. He had not liked his eldest son for many years. He had watched as they put twenty stitches in his son's head, and he had not batted an eyelid.

He saw his son open his eyes and he stood up, ready to go. 'So, you're back in the land of the living, are you?'

Angus Junior looked at his father, and he was suddenly remembering everything that had happened in stunning clarity.

'What is it with you, son, and touching other men's birds? It's like a fucking disease with you, ain't it? Oh, I have heard the stories about you and women – word on the street is that you won't take no for an answer. No one has gone as far as calling you a fucking rapist yet – at least, not to my face anyway. But you do have a reputation.'

The boy knew better than to get into a conversation like this with his father. He was suffering not just from the pain of his injuries but also from the realisation that he had fucked up big time by anyone's standards.

'It's like you deliberately go out of your way to cause mega aggravation – and not just for yourself, but for me as well. Roy is so disgusted with you, he wouldn't even come in here with me. Sean's been trying to talk the Rafters down. Though when young Ronnie eventually captures you, this time you can go it alone. You are out, son. I warned you before that if you ever fucked up again, I would out you.'

Angus Junior looked up at his father and saw the likeness that was so evident to everyone. He wondered if his father saw it too. Did that bother him? Was that why he was so quick to dump him out of his life?

He knew he was being a fool. His father had given him chance after chance, and he had just naused it away. That was his biggest fault. He could work a deal with the best of them, he could suss a score in seconds. But once he decided to go on the drink and the drugs, all his good intentions went out of the window.

He liked Ronny Rafter, and he liked his wife, Tania – she was a decent girl, from a good family. What had possessed him to treat her so badly?

'I like Ronnie Rafter, Dad. It was the fucking drugs again. I know I have a problem—'

Angus laughed grimly. 'Oh, fuck off, son! Do you really think you can bullshit me at my time of life?'

'No, Dad. But what I am saying is, this time I know that I need proper help.'

Angus was laughing again, as if he had just heard the funniest joke in the world. 'Look, son, that shit might work with your mother – or even my mother, at a push – but not with me. I will get Roy to book you a flight home, and then you and me are Finitosberg. Goodbyesville. You can start getting yourself an earn, because you won't be getting a fucking wage from me any more.'

Angus could see his son was nearly in tears, but that didn't affect him at all – he really didn't care.

'Look at you – all glistening tears and "poor old me"! Well, I'm off. I have to talk to Daddy Rafter and do some damage limitation, thanks to you and your utter cuntishness.' Angus looked down at his son and felt not a single pang of regret.

'Please, Dad, you know that I can beat this, you know that I can earn.'

Angus sighed sarcastically. 'But not for me, though, eh? You're out, and you have only yourself to blame. Roy will bring you a ticket and some dosh, and that's me doing my duty by you. And, to be fair, it's more than you deserve. My advice to you is, when you finally apologise to Ronnie Rafter and his old woman, you do a fucking cracking job of it.'

As he left the hospital room, he didn't even feel the urge to look back. If he was being totally honest, he was relieved, because his son was a liability, and that was something he could never forgive. Nothing he could do would ever change his son or his ways. His Angus, his namesake, was a fucking snide of the first water. He also knew that his son's antics would be discussed by his own peer group. If he had not broken all contact with the boy, Angus Senior would have been seen as weak, and that was something that he would *never* allow to happen.

He wondered how Roy had explained it to Diana. She had to know the score, because she dealt with the Rafters on a daily basis – after all, she owned half of their businesses. She had been the one who had put up the bulk of the money for the first of Benny Rafter's betting shops many years ago. His mother had put more fingers in more pies than Sweeney fucking Todd, and she had had the foresight to keep them there as a silent partner. There was hardly a business in the Smoke that she didn't have a stake in somehow. He couldn't fault her. And because of her largesse in the past, she also had the goodwill that went with it.

His big worry was how his wife would cope with her eldest son's latest escapade. He had a feeling this could be the one thing to cause actual trouble between them.

Chapter One Hundred and Ten

'What possessed you, for fuck's sake?'

Lorna was fuming at her son and the foolishness of his actions. For his part, he was frankly amazed at her attitude.

'Look what that mad bitch did to me, Mum. The doctors thought I had been in a fucking car crash, because that's what my injuries looked like. How can you come in here and act like I'm the fucking bad guy?'

Lorna Davis looked at her eldest son, who she had loved with all her heart, but who had proved to be such a disappointment. She had lost him the moment he had finally understood the family businesses and what they entailed. She had accepted that she couldn't compete with the lap dancing or the nightclubs and everything that went with them. If it had been left to her, none of her children would have been within a donkey's fart of Soho. She had tried to offer them a different life, a better life, but it had all been in vain. They were infected with the Davis genes, and she couldn't compete with them. She only had to look at Diana and her own husband to admit that, where they were concerned, blood will out.

She had tried to shelter her children, she had tried to do the best for them, and they had systematically kicked her in the teeth. Her husband had been so thrilled at the children finally knowing the real truth of his world and not vilifying him for it. They had embraced it as if they had been waiting all their lives to be welcomed into the family business. The only thing they had seen was the huge earn, and Lorna could understand that. But her eldest son, Angus, had embraced it and then he had abused it, and she couldn't let him get away with that.

To see her son exploit his father's generosity grieved her beyond measure, because she knew that Angus had given this fucker every opportunity to prove himself and, more importantly, to show him that he was worthy of being his successor.

No chance of that now. He had guaranteed that by his actions and his arrogance. And by believing that, because he was Angus's eldest son, he automatically had a free pass.

She looked at her handsome son and she could see the worry and the anger in his face. She knew, once and for all, that this son of hers was flawed, that he wasn't capable of achieving what his father had achieved, because he didn't want to work for it. He wanted it laid out on a plate.

Her son was weak and he was greedy and he was without loyalty. He didn't know when to stop, especially when he'd had a few drinks, and that would forever be his downfall. Lorna looked at her son, with his injuries that his own behaviour had inflicted on him, and she saw that he still possessed that arrogant demeanour that he had always had. Even with his stitches and his bruises, he still believed that he had a God-given right to do what he wanted.

'Do you know what, Angus? You're an embarrassment to this family. You wanted to go and work with your father – against my advice, I might add. But you broke your neck to get taken into the firm, and all you have done since then is show us all what a complete liability you really are.'

Angus was angry and upset at his mother's reaction to his plight, but he was too shrewd to say that. It amazed him that his mother could still defend her husband, knowing what he was capable of.

He took a few deep breaths, before saying quietly, 'Do you know what, Mum? I don't know whether to admire you or scorn you when you defend your husband, after what he has done to all of us. He's cheated on you countless times, he doesn't come home for days on end, and when he is home he acts like he's in a hotel. He treats you like shit, and yet you still defend him.'

Lorna smiled suddenly. She was still a beautiful woman, Angus Junior acknowledged.

'That is why you will never be able to step into your father's shoes. You think you know about my life or your father's life? You still don't understand what makes us work, even though you had a front-row seat. Your father is the love of my life, and I am his. Those girls mean nothing to either of us. He works in a world that places temptation in his way, every day of the week. I accepted that, and he knows I don't give a flying fuck. You are not a kid, you should have worked that one out long ago. Eilish has, not that she's said it out loud, and so has Sean. They get the big picture, which unfortunately seems to be something that has eluded you from day fucking one.

'Your father wanted desperately to hand everything over to you as his firstborn, as his namesake. What a disappointment you turned out to be. You are a liability, and you need to understand that, son. The people your father deals with on a daily basis are really bad bastards, and they don't take any shit from anyone. You are out now, you are a pariah, and you have no one to blame but yourself. I love you, son, and so does your dad. But where the businesses are concerned, you have forfeited the right to be involved.

'Even your granny had the right hump with you, and she is still top of the tree where the Davis name is concerned. You had every chance to learn and to grow by watching her and your father and understanding how to survive in the criminal world. But you couldn't be arsed, could you? You wanted to be carried through life depending on your name and your family connections. Well, you, my darling, were born into the wrong family, because we don't take any prisoners. You have fucked up once too often, and now you are on the outside looking in. Your father is adamant that you are finished, and I have to agree with him.'

Chapter One Hundred and Eleven

Angus Davis Junior was looking at his mother as if he had never seen her before in his life. She was the one person he had believed would fight his corner, and he finally understood the seriousness of the situation that he was in. He was badly hurt, in pain, and he was still of the opinion that he should be given the benefit of the doubt, because he was his father's son. It had just been a drunken misunderstanding, and he honestly believed that his father should have been of the same opinion.

All his father's talk about loyalty and the importance of family seemed to be a bit hypocritical, considering this latest stance. His own father had thrown him to the wolves and was acting like he was without merit or importance. He was more than willing to apologise or whatever, but it seemed that no one was interested in giving him another chance.

He was just left in a hospital bed without any kind of back-up. He was frightened of being outed. He had never been outside the family or without the protection that his name had guaranteed him. He was terrified of being open to attack, and also being without the monetary advantages that working in the family business entailed.

He could see that his mother had guessed exactly what he was thinking. Taking pity on him, she took his hand in hers and said calmly, 'Don't worry, son, you are still a Davis, and you will be offered an earn by someone. My advice to you is to make a success of it, and prove to your old man that you are capable of standing on your own two feet. That will go a long way to inching your way back into the firm. But you need to address your drinking and your behaviour first. Abad would have nutted you the first time round, if you had not been your father's son. Now you have offended the Rafters, who the family have dealt with for years without incident. Tania Rafter is pregnant – did you really think that it was OK to treat her like a fucking whore?

'You need to think about what you have done, and find a way to make amends. And, take it from me, you better keep looking over your shoulder, because the Rafter boys will not swallow your actions lightly. They have every right to pay you back. And your father will turn a blind eye, because he has no choice. You crossed a line, and no one in their right mind would try and pretend that what you did was anything other than a sheer piss-take.'

Angus was aware that it would be useless to even try and argue his case with his mother. He should have known that she would take his father's side. His parents' relationship had always perplexed him. His father had rarely been there when they were all children; it had been his mother who had been the mainstay of their lives. They loved her as their mother but, once they could think for themselves, they had never liked her or enjoyed her company.

Lorna sighed and, sitting on the hospital bed, she said seriously, 'You are back home with me. Your father says you can't use the flat any more. He has had all your stuff packed and it's in the garages waiting for you.'

Angus closed his eyes in distress. The thought of living back home was unbearable. He couldn't just allow this to happen, he couldn't just sit back and accept this shit. He had to plan and use his head, because he wouldn't be pushed out of the life that he loved. His father had brought him into his world and he had no right to try and force him out of it.

Sean was the golden boy, because he toed the company line, but he would not be overtaken by his younger brother – or his little sister, if it came to that. Eilish was a real shrewdie. There was no disputing that she had a brain like a trap just like their grandmother. But she would fight his corner for him, he was confident of that much.

Sean he wasn't so sure of now.

He needed to have a rethink and work out how he could get himself back into the fold.

Chapter One Hundred and Twelve

Roy was happy these days, and it was evident to anyone who cared to notice.

Angus knew that he had a little bird on the side who was a real Brahma. She didn't want anything from him, and she wouldn't cause him any aggravation. She was young, she had a killer body, and she was up for anything within reason – or at least, that was what Roy had said. She was just thrilled to have bagged herself a Face, and that seemed to be enough for her.

Roy didn't play away from home very often, and never for too long. He was a good man and he loved his wife with every fibre of his being. But in their game there was just too much temptation, and even Angus could understand Roy's interest in this one. She was gorgeous. Angus had considered banging her himself, but she had no real conversation to speak of and, even worse, she was a vegetarian and she hammered her love of animals home to anyone who would listen. He had asked her what would happen to all the dairy herds and sheep in the world if everyone suddenly became a vegetarian. Would they be nutted, because there were a lot of them? And she had looked at him with her big doe eyes, and he knew that she had never thought beyond what she had read in a pamphlet.

Roy, on the other hand, seemed to find every word she said a jewel of wisdom. Good luck to him and all.

Roy sat in the easy chair by the window and looked out over Soho. He loved people-watching; they both did. The whole gamut of society seemed to make their way there eventually, and they loved to discuss the people they saw. They would laugh as they wondered why they were in Soho and what their lives were like.

'So Angus Junior is truly out then?'

Roy was looking out the window and pretending that his question wasn't particularly important. Angus appreciated that, because he knew that Roy was giving him the opportunity to backtrack on his decision. Well, that wasn't going to happen.

'Yes, he's out, Roy. I can't trust him, can I? He is a good little earner until he has a drink, then all bets are off. Every fucking deal he closes – and every fucking pound he brings in – is nothing when he brings such trouble to my door. Benny Rafter has been dealing with us since the year fucking dot, and his sons are good kids. Both good earners and trustworthy and, more importantly, they know how to conduct themselves in public. No, Roy, this time my Angus went too far. I've got to teach him a lesson that he won't forget in a hurry.'

Angus poured them both a large Jameson's and, as he handed the glass to Roy, he sighed. 'I'm so fucking disappointed in him, Roy. He humiliated me without a second's thought about what he was doing. Sean had tried to calm him down, by all accounts, but you know as well as I do that Angus Junior loses all control once he's had a few drinks. He's a fucking liability but, worse than that, I am ashamed of him. I'm ashamed that he has my name. How do you think that makes me feel?'

Roy sipped his drink, savouring the peaty taste and enjoying the company of his old friend. 'You know, your mum brought me in to keep an eye on you, and I did, mate. But over the years, we became good friends – even though you have done a few things that I didn't agree with. But, by the same token, I knew that you did them without spite or malice. Your Angus's biggest fault is that he holds grudges, and he is a fucking bully – the worst kind, because he bullied people that he knew couldn't fight back.

'He hasn't got the right temperament for our life, and he never will. He was disliked by the staff under him and by the people he had to work alongside. His removal is being celebrated, and that tells me everything I need to know. You have to keep to your decision and teach that fucker a lesson that he won't forget. And maybe, just maybe, he might one day redeem himself.'

Angus swallowed his drink down and immediately poured himself another. 'Shall I tell you the truth, Roy? After the Abad incident, I gave him the benefit of the doubt. But you and I know that he's a fucking predator – a sexual predator. I've heard the stories about him, and I know that you have heard them too, and I know in my piss that they are true. I've had enough. I will give him a wedge to get started, and then he's on his fucking own. I can't protect him any more, and I don't want to. I just feel so sad that a child of mine has turned out so fucking wrong.'

Roy didn't say anything for a long while, and both men were aware of the silence between them. They could hear the sounds of Soho in the distance: the police car sirens and the music from the restaurants and bars. It was the soundtrack of their working lives. It was the norm, it was what they were used to.

Eventually, Roy said honestly, 'Don't beat yourself up over him, Angus. He is a one-off. My mother used to say that, every now and then, every family gets a throwback from another age. He is your living image, but there is nothing of you in him, he has no moral compass. We might be drug dealers, whatever, but we have a code that we adhere to. We are straight arrows, if you like, but that boy has a kink in his nature, and there is nothing anyone can do to change that.

'Now Sean and Eilish are a completely different breed. They are like us, and they are people who can be trusted. You have to promise me, Angus, that you will watch your back, because I don't trust your firstborn as far as I could throw him. He's a chancer and a liar, and he has not got one decent bone in his whole body. I have to say this to you, Angus, because I love you like a son, and I would lay down my life for you, as you know. That boy of yours has a dark streak running through him, and I think he got it from Lorna, because you know as well as I do that she is not the full five quid.'

Angus looked at his old friend and felt a huge sadness wash over him. He knew what it had taken for Roy to say what he had, and that he had said it because he cared about him and was worried about him.

'Roy, you are like a second father to me. I know what you are saying, and I know that it's true. Lorna has her problems, and I'm doing my best to make sure that she is taken care of when everything becomes too much for her. I can assure you, that if my Angus becomes too much of a problem, I will take care of him personally.'

Roy nodded, because that was exactly what he wanted to hear. Angus Junior needed to be neutered, sooner rather than later, because he was not someone that could be trusted – especially now, when he had been ejected from the family businesses. This latest development would just make him even more bitter than he already was, and that guaranteed trouble.

The one thing that he had learned over the years was that personalities like Angus Junior's didn't take rejection well.

Chapter One Hundred and Thirteen

Sean had rung Eilish and filled her in on the latest developments concerning Angus Junior. She couldn't say that she was surprised, but she was glad of the heads-up.

Benny Rafter was a frequent visitor to Lady P's Lap-Dancing Establishment, and he was a good spender. He had his beady eye on a young black girl with long legs, fake breasts and relaxed hair. The girl in question, Chantelle, was thrilled with the attention, the money and the kudos.

Eilish wondered how Angus Junior would fare now that he was finally on the out. She had no interest in seeing him though now he was back at her mother's. She wasn't at all shocked by his latest antics. Her brother wasn't exactly the most decent of men where females were concerned. In fact, she had brought that to her father's attention and demanded that he did something about it. Angus Junior didn't frequent her establishments any more, she had made sure of that.

She walked out to the main bar and ordered herself a large vodka and tonic. She automatically scanned the club to see what she might be missing.

She saw a table of women in the corner. She suppressed her smile, because it made her laugh how the city girls thought that coming to a lap-dancing club and being drunk, rowdy and obnoxious made them feminists who felt they were empowered. They could all fuck off, as far as she was concerned, because she knew that the girls on the poles were more empowered than they would ever be – and most of these girls were only there because they didn't have the opportunities those silly fuckers had been lucky enough to get. They always talked filth to the poor bouncers too, like they were also merchandise.

She nodded to Big Rick the Rasta to keep an eye on them, and she could see the disappointment on his face; he was generally on the receiving end of the bulk of the sexual comments, and she knew it annoyed him. He was too good-looking for his own good, and he had a body that most people only dreamed of. He also had a beautiful wife, with red hair and green eyes, who had produced two fine sons and had once been the main attraction in this club.

Davey Proctor walked over to the bar and smiled that lazy smile of his. 'Large vodka? That's not like you.'

Eilish drank her drink straight down and enjoyed the look of amazement on his face. She wasn't really a drinker while she was working, because she believed in keeping a clear head – especially in her game, where violence could erupt over the smallest thing, and frequently did. The men were usually drunk as skunks, and the girls were often drunk or drugged, or both, by the end of the night. So when the arguments erupted, she knew that it was best to be the sober, level-headed one.

She motioned with her hand for another drink, and young Peter James was quick to provide her with it. She poured in the tonic water and took a long sip once again.

Davey watched her with genuine interest. 'So it's true, then, that your fucking brother Angus caused World War Three when he was out in Spain.'

Eilish wasn't surprised that Davey had found out about Angus's latest faux pas – she knew that he had contacts all over.

She nodded her agreement. 'Fuck-up of Olympian standards, this time.'

They smiled together. They both knew that the moment had finally come when she would allow him to accompany her home.

If they were both really honest, it was not before time.

Chapter One Hundred and Fourteen

Angus and Roy were back in Spain in The Blue, a new club in Marbella.

Angus had picked it up cheap from a good mate with a serious gambling problem. Angus had only bought it to help get his friend out of trouble with the loan sharks, but it had turned out to be a really profitable enterprise, and he was more than happy with it. Once he had taken over, he had revamped the bar staff – especially the bar manager, a Ukrainian girl who was obviously robbing the place blind. In all honesty, Angus couldn't really blame her; he would have done the same in her position. She had known her days were numbered, and she was taking what she could before the axe dropped. Well, the axe had been well and truly dropped, and she had left with her fake Gucci handbag and language that a Tilbury docker would have been proud of.

Angus had left Sean in charge of the reopening, and the lad had done a great job. That had not surprised him; he knew that his boy had a knack for the clubs and what was needed. Now it was another real earner, as it was seen as one of *the* places to be when out in Marbs. A lot of the interest came down to the fact that he owned it, and people wanted to be seen in his establishments, but he also believed that Sean had done such a great job that it would have been a success, even without him on board.

The main bar was huge, and Angus looked around him as the place was beginning to fill up. It was what Sean had called 'a great space' and he had been absolutely right. There was a good-sized area out the back of the club that now had a cocktail bar and comfortable seating. Sean had said it would be worth the expense, and it was already paying for itself.

Angus was well pleased with his new venture and, smiling at Roy, he motioned for him to go behind the bar and pour them each a large Scotch. The bar staff were used to seeing the boss pouring his own drinks and didn't bat an eyelid. The staff that he had inherited had all been associates of the Ukrainian lunatic and had systematically picked all the tills clean. Like their manager, they had not taken being sacked with good grace. It was only when someone had told them exactly who they were dealing with that they decided to go without a fight.

Sean had laughed about it, but Angus knew that his boy could not believe that someone who had invested so much money and time into a business would be fool enough to employ thieves and liars. Angus had explained that the original owner's big mistake was taking his eye off the ball, because once that happened it was all downhill from there. Especially in the clubbing industry, because there were just too many ways to cream off money. It was a cash industry, and that was like an open invitation for certain people who would happily go on the rob and smile at you while they did it.

He had told Sean to tell the staff that anyone caught on the rob would be answerable to the owners, as the police wouldn't need to be brought into the equation. It was enough to ensure that the more light-fingered staff were frightened off. They also left, within days, to go to pastures new – where they could ply their trade without fear of losing a few teeth, at the very least.

Sean was walking across the dance floor, and Angus watched him proudly. He was impressed with this boy and his natural business acumen. He smiled at Roy, and they both watched Sean as he spoke to the staff and chatted to the customers and generally kept an eye on the smooth running of the place. He had a good kid with this one – and his Eilish too. They were both trustworthy and on the ball. What more could a man in his position ask for? He grinned at Roy, and they clinked glasses loudly.

There was a little bird with long blonde hair and real tits, who had been putting herself directly into his eyeline for the last few nights – no matter what club he was in, she had turned up – and he was tempted, because she was really his kind of girl. She was a bit on the young side, if he was honest, but he was confident that she would know exactly what she was letting herself in for and she wouldn't be looking for an engagement ring or a wedding date. She would just take it for what it was, and be happy with her short-lived notoriety as his bird in Marbella. It was an arrangement that would suit them both.

Roy pushed him gently and, laughing, he said, 'Fuck off, Angus – what, are you cradle-snatching now?'

Angus had the grace to look sheepish.

Roy leaned into him and said seriously, 'She is not sixteen yet, and she's already been through the West Ham football team. Her mother will be here soon, and they do a double. You keep as far away from them as possible.'

Angus was shocked at the information. 'Fucking hell! How do you know that?'

Roy grinned nonchalantly. 'Your Sean told me; I think so I would tell you and warn you off, so he didn't have to do it.

He also said that he won't let either of them near the VIP areas, because the mother uses the daughter as bait and then brings up the girl's age after the dirty deed is done. It's a good earner, by all accounts.'

Angus said honestly, 'Fucking hell, I would have put her at twenty at least.'

Roy nodded sagely. 'Jailbait, and the newspapers would make a meal out of it.'

Sean came up to them with his usual easy smile, and holding a bottle of water. He didn't drink while he was working, and Angus knew that was something he had learned from his older brother's disappointing example. He regretted that as a result of everything they weren't close. Never having had a sibling himself Angus had wanted a big family – he believed brothers should be there for each other, and together they should look out for their sister. Not that Eilish needed much looking after, she could more than take care of herself. In many ways, she was shrewder than both his sons put together, but he knew that he could never say that out loud.

Eilish was his mother all over again. She looked like her, she thought like her, and she could fight like her, as he had been told on the quiet by Roy. He was proud of her and how she had fitted into his business life so easily and without any dramas. She could really make something of herself and she was working towards that, each and every day. She spent as much time with her grandmother as she could, and they were really close.

Angus knew that Lorna had been sidelined by her children, but what could he do? They were grown and he couldn't tell them what to do, any more than Lorna could, but he knew that it broke her heart. She was lonely, and she missed her children's love more than she would ever admit.

He had approached Eilish one day and said that her mother had been asking after her and that she should go and see her.

She had looked at him for a few seconds, before she had said flatly, 'As long as she has Angus, she won't miss me.'

Angus had been nonplussed by her answer, and had not known what to say.

Eilish had smiled at him and hugged him tightly. 'Seriously, Dad, she doesn't really want to see us, she just misses being in control of our lives.'

Angus had hugged his beautiful daughter back but had still not said a word in answer. He refused to get into any conversation about Lorna, because he knew that she couldn't help the way she was. He still loved Lorna, and he always would.

'She loves you kids, Eilish.'

Eilish had smiled politely once more and walked away from him to end the conversation.

'You all right, Dad?' Sean's question brought him back to the present.

Angus laughed as if he didn't have a care in the world. 'I was miles away, son, sorry.'

The club was getting noisier now and the music was pounding through the speakers.

Sean leaned forward and whispered, 'Come up to the offices, I have something to tell you.'

Roy and Angus followed Sean upstairs happily, because secretly both were pleased that they would be getting out of the noise of the club. The music was far too loud for them lately – not that either of them would ever admit that, of course.

Chapter One Hundred and Fifteen

Davey Proctor and Eilish were comfortable together straight-away, which stunned Eilish.

She was more than aware of his reputation as a womaniser – that had been what had put her off in the past. But in his car on the way to his flat, listening to jazz, they were both relaxed and Davey had even grabbed her hand and squeezed it, as if they were teenagers on a first date. Davey was a good fifteen years older than her, and he had not been known to settle down with any woman. Even the woman who had produced two children for him had never managed to get him to actually move in with her, though Eilish knew that Davey had provided her with a house and a car and anything else that she needed, so that his sons were well taken care of.

Davey was aware that June still harboured dreams of him one day turning up and marrying her. But that would never happen. June was a lovely girl, and she was the nearest he had ever got to loving someone. When she had fallen pregnant, he had been surprised to find that he was pleased, and he had encouraged her to have the child. June was a wonderful mother, and he enjoyed being with her and his kids in a family environ-ment. But he would never be able to settle on a permanent basis with her.

He wasn't sure he could do that with any woman, because he genuinely treasured his bachelor life and couldn't imagine himself ever being part of a couple. He liked the chase and the romancing of women, and he liked all different types. He could find something to admire in most women who crossed his path, and he loved talking to them and listening to them tell him about their lives and their problems. He was a good listener – that was a big part of his charm. He was also good-looking, and that was a huge bonus when he was out on the pull.

But Eilish really interested him, and he assumed that was because she had not been an easy conquest. In fact, she had ignored him, as if he didn't exist, from day one – and so, of course, that had piqued his interest even more. Women were usually drawn to him like a magnet. He had been given the come-on by women of all ages since he was a young lad, and he had not only embraced that but he had also exploited it at every available opportunity.

Now he was finally sitting in a car with Eilish and wondering if he was going to regret this night because she was, after all, Angus Davis's daughter. He worked for the man and he wasn't too sure how he might take to finding out that his daughter was another of his nine-day wonders. Angus thought that Davey's sex life was a grown man's dream and expressed admiration for his prowess at every opportunity – they often shared war stories of their sexual exploits over drinks. But if he found out that now included his little girl, he might not be so generous or forgiving.

Davey Proctor was, for the first time in his life, having second thoughts about a woman, and the knowledge shocked him more than he had thought possible. He pulled up outside his flat in Canary Wharf and, turning off the ignition, he turned to Eilish

337

and smiled. In the dim street lights she looked so relaxed and young as she lay back against her seat, he wondered at how he could ever have had second thoughts about taking her.

She was ripe, and she was there, and she would be his. Fuck being sensible, he could smell her perfume and feel the heat emanating from her body. She was looking into his eyes and he knew that if he was really going to stop this, it would have to be now.

Eilish was aware that, even knowing what she did about him and his lifestyle, she wanted Davey – and it had been a long time since she had wanted anyone this much.

'Kiss me.'

It was more a question than a request and, laughing gently, Davey pulled her into his arms and kissed her.

There was no going back now for either of them, and they both knew it.

Chapter One Hundred and Sixteen

Angus poured drinks for himself, Roy and Sean, and then he settled himself behind the desk that he knew was by rights his son's.

'That fucking music was going right through my head. It was awful!'

Sean laughed loudly. 'It was good, Dad, and what the punters want – especially after a few Es.'

Roy took a large gulp of his whiskey, and then uttered a loud, exaggerated sigh. 'So, Sean, what's the big secret you want to tell?'

Sean looked candidly from Roy to his father. 'Well, it's not good news. But when it concerns Angus, these days, it rarely is.'

Angus and Roy were both straight-faced and listening intently.

'Come on, son. Spit it out, for fuck's sake.'

Sean took a sip of whiskey and then shuddered because, as they all knew, he wasn't much of a drinker.

'It's about Jamie Thomas and his daughter Carly.'

Jamie Thomas was a Face in his own right. He was a real Brixton boy and he had a reputation as a hard man, a broker and a serious dealer. Angus and Roy had known and had dealings with him for years; they considered him a mate.

'Is Jamie dead?' Angus sounded shocked at the thought, but he assumed he had been either shot or had wrapped his car round a lamp post. Either scenario would be seen as viable by anyone who knew the man intimately.

Sean shook his head. 'No, Dad, he is very much alive, unfortunately. But his daughter Carly, the youngest one, is pregnant.'

Roy and Angus looked at each other in bewilderment, wondering what that had to do with them.

'How is this news, Sean? I couldn't give a toss if his daughter's in the club.'

Getting up, Sean refilled the two men's glasses generously with the Jameson's before continuing.

'Well, she is saying that Angus is the father, and that she was raped by him. She's fifteen, Dad.'

Angus and Roy were both silent, trying to take in what Sean had said, and he watched them as they tried to make sense of his words.

Roy recovered first and, swallowing his drink down, he said with quiet fury, 'Who told you about this?'

Sean looked at Roy and said angrily, 'Fucking Pete the Post. He overheard Jamie talking about it with Graham Gardener. He said he couldn't believe it at first, but it's the truth. He was delivering the usual to them and, once he heard what they were saying, he slipped outside and didn't go back for a while, so they wouldn't know that he had heard them. But he reckons Jamie is like the Antichrist, and he is after blood and guts. To add insult to injury, the girl's already five months gone, because she was too frightened to tell anyone what had happened to her. If her mum hadn't caught her unawares in the shower, she would have carried on pretending she was OK until she had the baby.'

'Christ Almighty, this is a fucking nightmare!'

Roy was completely thrown by the revelation, and as he looked at Angus he said, 'This is like a fucking Hammer Horror. This is something that can't be settled easily, because she is saying that he raped her. God forgive me, but I believe her, mate. His Carly is a tiny little thing – she only looks about twelve – and, from what I've heard, she's a bit of a brain-box, a clever girl. He had great hopes for her. He won't swallow this, even knowing that he's your son, Angus. And who can blame him?'

Angus didn't answer his friend because he really didn't know what to say. Like Roy, he instinctively believed the girl's claim that his Angus had forced himself on her. It wouldn't be the first time his son had been accused of something like that. Look at his recent actions with Tania Rafter! He could feel the shame burning through him, and he wondered where his own son – his flesh and blood – could have got his deviance from.

He was a womaniser himself, he knew that, and he would hold his hand up if questioned. He had romanced them, he had happily talked bullshit to them, but he had never once forced any woman into sex against her will. It was the unwritten rule, because rape was up there with the nonces, the child molesters – and from what Roy had just told him, this girl was like a child, a fucking innocent.

'I'll kill him myself, the filthy cunt. I'll fucking stab him, the dirty piece of shite.'

Sean went to his father and, pulling him close, he said seriously, 'Let Jamie do it, Dad. We can deliver Angus to him and give the man the satisfaction of paying him back for what he did to his daughter. We owe him that much at least.'

Roy was nodding his agreement, and Angus knew that his son was speaking sense. It was the only way to save face in this situation.

He had to let Jamie have his revenge, because at least that

way he could regain some kind of respect from his peers. He would have to live this down until his dying day, and he could never forgive his son for that.

The humiliation was already burning inside him like the Olympic flame. Just knowing that he had produced a predator, a man who preyed on women and children, was like a knife through his heart. The shame was already taking root inside him – he didn't think he would ever be able to hold his head up again.

Roy put another drink into his hands, and Angus drank it gratefully.

Sean stood up saying, 'I'm going to go and arrange the flights. The sooner we are back in the UK, the sooner we can sort this shit out, once and for all.'

Chapter One Hundred and Seventeen

Gabriel and Diana were sitting with Jamie Thomas's long-term girlfriend, Jamilla. Although he called her his wife, they had never actually sealed the deal, because Jamilla had never bothered to formally divorce her actual husband, Clovis.

Jamilla and Jamie Thomas were a genuine love match, and everyone who knew them was aware of that fact. They fought like cat and dog but no one could get a fag paper between them, they were that close. Jamilla was small in every way, from her feet to her hands. She was so slim and petite whereas Jamie was built like the proverbial brick shithouse.

He was handsome and he was enormous, and his full head of dreads just added to his height. He was respected and liked in equal measures because he was a decent man who was known to be as straight in business dealings as he was in his home life.

His mother, Arbelle, lived with him and his family in a huge house in Blackheath. She had come over from Jamaica for the birth of her first grandchild and she had never gone back. It suited everyone concerned to have her there, especially Jamilla, who loved her mother-in-law with a passion. She was the mother that she had never had, and Jamilla was the daughter that Arbelle would have killed for. They were closer than close, and they both adored Jamie and the children.

Her sons were two huge, strapping young men who were quite happy to go into their father's business, as neither of them were the academic type. But her baby, her Carly, was just like her mother – pretty and tiny, like a little bird. But she had the brains of a scientist, she was reading by three, and she had begun writing soon after. She was a natural student and she soaked up knowledge like a sponge. Her nature was quiet, and she wasn't known to push herself forward. She was a good girl in every way. Now, at just fifteen years old, she was over five months pregnant, and she didn't know what she was supposed to do about it.

Jamilla looked at Diana and shook her head in despair. 'She's a baby, Diana, she hasn't really even developed yet. She takes after me, I was a late bloomer. She's still a child.' Her voice broke and she began weeping.

Arbelle took a long drag on her cigarette, before saying, 'I was fifteen when I had Jamie. His father was a local boy and he skedaddled when I told him the news. I thought my world had ended, but it hadn't. It had just changed its path, that's all. Whatever happens, we will cope with it, because the Lord makes the back to bear the burden.'

Normally, Arbelle got on Diana's tits and she avoided her and her Bible-thumping, if possible. But today she was grateful for the woman's determination to see some kind of light at the end of this dark and frightening tunnel.

Jamilla looked at her mother-in-law and said pointedly, 'But you weren't raped, were you? Carly was a virgin when he gave her a lift home from school. He talked her into going to the scrapyard with him, because he had some urgent business to attend to, and then he took her into the Portakabin and he raped her. She trusted him. She had believed that she would be safe with him because he was her dad's friend, she had known him all her life.'

Diana felt physically sick as she listened to her grandson's crime being discussed out loud. The worst thing was that she had never once doubted that he had done it, that he was capable of it, because she had always known that Angus Junior had a dark side to him.

Yes, he could be violent if the situation called for it; she understood that kind of controlled violence – it was what was needed in the world they inhabited. But the issue was that he was capable of being violent even if the situation *didn't* warrant it. He was a bully and full of exaggerated bravado. He had spent his whole life on his dignity, looking for slights where there weren't any, and he could find an excuse to fight with anyone he saw as a threat to him.

She had once heard that he had been rough with some of the girls that they employed, but she had not really wanted to believe it then. After all, these were girls who could more than look after themselves if the need arose. But as time went on it became clear that there was something radically wrong with that fucker, and she blamed Lorna. He had always been her blue-eyed boy, her baby, her firstborn. And he had been like an animal let out of a cage when he had finally broken away from her influence.

Those three children had grown up in a house where they were isolated and indoctrinated with Lorna's strange take on the world.

As Gabriel had once remarked to her, as they were driving home one New Year, 'That house is like visiting a fucking cult, Di.'

She had agreed with him, because it was so true – except, unlike Gabriel, she had not found it amusing. His description had depressed her because of its accuracy.

Gabriel got up and replenished their Bacardi and Cokes, and Arbelle accepted hers from him with a small smile.

'You know that my Jamie is going to kill him, don't you?'

Diana nodded, the shame of her grandson's crime enveloping her once more. 'I know that, and I don't blame him.'

Arbelle took a long draught of her drink, before saying conversationally, 'This is good, you know, all of us here, making sure that justice is served to the satisfaction of everyone concerned. Let's not forget we'll be welcoming a new baby into our families. It will be my first great-grandchild, and your first great-grandchild too, Diana.'

Gabriel closed his eyes at that, because he knew it was the last thing that Diana would need to be reminded about, on this day of all days.

Jamilla wiped her eyes and said resolutely, 'It'll be my first grandchild, and no matter how it came into this world, the child itself is an innocent.'

Diana understood that Jamilla was going to bring the child up, so her daughter could resume her studies and her life – though after what she had experienced, Diana had a feeling it wasn't going to be as easy as Jamilla seemed to think it would be. She wondered how she herself would feel about the child, knowing it had been born as the result of a violent act perpetrated by her grandson. She hoped she could be as forgiving as Jamilla and Arbelle, because the way she felt now, at this minute, she wouldn't care if she never laid eyes on it.

Carly came into the room and sat beside her mother; Jamilla automatically put her arm around her and pulled her close.

Diana looked at the young girl and saw the belly that appeared so swollen on her thin frame and the face that was haunted and frightened. She wished that the ground beneath her would open and just swallow her up.

Chapter One Hundred and Eighteen

'I swear to you, Mum, that I did not rape her, she fucking came on to *me*!'

Lorna knew that, no matter how many times he swore his innocence, she couldn't bring herself to believe her son, even though she wanted to so desperately.

Angus was watching his mother's reaction closely. He had to convince her of his innocence, so she, in turn, could convince his father. With his mother on his side, it would improve his chance of being believed.

'She wasn't the wilting virgin she is making out. I could bring ten lads she's slept with here, and you could ask them yourself. It's not my baby! I swear on my life that I used a condom. I'm not fucking stupid, Mum, I wouldn't have unprotected sex, especially not with a whore like her. Who knows what she might have picked up?'

Lorna looked at her son, and she felt a crushing sorrow in her chest. 'You swear to me, Angus, that it's not true, you swear on my life?'

Angus felt the urge to smile in victory, but he knew that it was too soon. So, instead, he walked to his mother and he gripped both of her hands in his. Looking into her eyes, he said passionately, 'I swear on your life, Mum – may you drop down dead this minute if I am lying – that I did not rape that girl, and you know that I wouldn't say that unless it was the truth.'

Lorna was well aware that this son of hers had got a lot of her in him, and where once that knowledge had pleased her, now it just depressed her. If it had been anyone other than little Carly Thomas, she would have been open to suspending her disbelief. But even she could see that Carly was just a little kid.

Now her own son had just stood there in front of her, bold as brass, and sworn her life away, without a second's thought. He had not even needed a few seconds to build himself up to the lie – it had come as naturally to him as breathing. He had been a bit too quick off the mark for her liking. She would have worked with him and helped him, but not now.

She forced a smile at him, and he smiled back.

'You pour us both a drink, son. I need to visit the little girl's room.'

As she rang her husband, to tell him where their son was, she wondered at her life.

It had not turned out in the least like she had planned.

Chapter One Hundred and Nineteen

Diana and Gabriel were sitting together on her sofa, and they were both quiet.

Gabriel took her hand in his and squeezed it gently.

'Look, Di, it will all be over soon, and all we can do is front it out.'

Diana nodded. She didn't trust herself to speak. She knew her grandson was going to suffer for what he had done, and she just wanted it over – for his sake as much as hers. Even after everything he was still her grandson.

Gabriel lit a joint, and he took a deep toke on it before handing it to Diana.

'I admire your Angus being there with Jamie Thomas, and I get why he did it. This story will come out and everyone will hear about it at some point. As we know, stories get stretched in the telling. So this way, your Angus being there at the last moment shows everyone that he was as disgusted as everyone else. It's great PR really, Di. I take my hat off to him.'

Diana didn't answer him.

She was picturing the beautiful grandchild that she had held as a baby and she was wondering how he had ended up dying like a dog in a lock-up garage in Southend.

Chapter One Hundred and Twenty

Eilish was drinking a vodka and tonic at the bar in her club and waiting for the last of the punters to go home, when she saw her father walking towards her.

She could see that he wasn't himself, and she understood why. She went behind the bar and told the last of the staff to get off home, and then she poured her father a large Jameson's because she had a feeling he would need it. She had felt like the sword of Damocles was hanging over her head all night, because she had been given a heads-up about what was going down with her eldest brother. Angus took the drink from her gratefully, drank it and placed the glass on the bar for an immediate refill. Eilish could see that he already had a load on, but she knew better than to point that out, tonight of all nights.

Her father sipped the next drink and, after sipping her own, Eilish eventually said softly, 'So it's over then?'

Angus nodded.

Eilish lit a cigarette and drew on it deeply. As she blew the smoke out, she laughed grimly. 'Well, he has been asking for it long enough, and he finally got it. Fuck him! He deserved everything he got, I just hope it was painful.'

Angus looked at his daughter as she carried on smoking her

cigarette and he wondered at how she could be so cavalier about her brother's death. 'You don't care at all, Eilish?'

She shrugged nonchalantly. 'No, Dad, why would I? He was a bully and a mummy's boy all his life, and poor Carly wasn't the first he had forced to have sex with him. He thought that the girls here didn't matter, because they were lap dancers, and I threw him out over it. He blacked one of my girls' eyes when she refused his advances. Well, I say "advances" loosely. He would push them up against the wall in the ladies' toilets and just go for it. I caught him in the act, and we had a hell of a fucking row over it. He said to me, "Why do you fucking care about this scum?" I think that pretty much summed up his attitude. What he did to that child – because she was a child, Dad – was fucking outrageous, and now that poor little mare will have a reminder of what he did to her around her, day and night, for ever.'

Angus could understand his daughter's anger and disgust, but it still grieved him. Neither Eilish nor Sean seemed to care that Angus had died a terrible death.

'It will be your niece or nephew, remember. The child will be a part of our family – your mum is already decorating a room for it.'

Eilish lit another cigarette, before saying sarcastically, 'Well, of course she is. Her golden boy's gone; his child will be the next best thing. Let's hope she does a better job with this one, eh?'

Angus sighed, took her cigarette from her and had a cheeky puff.

She laughed delightedly. 'Don't let Mum see you smoking, she will go fucking spare.'

Angus grinned at her, and she was reminded of just how good-looking her father was.

'Fuck that! Why do you think I only go home once or twice a month?'

They laughed together now, trying to behave as normally as possible, both pretending that Angus and his death didn't really matter to either of them. As her granny had always told her, if you act happy you will eventually feel happy. But the shame he had brought on them all would never really go away, and they both knew the truth of that.

When Angus saw Davey Proctor walk into the bar, he smiled his most benevolent smile and, waving him over, he said jovially, 'I hear you are courting my only daughter, Davey, so I hope you are treating her right, otherwise we will have to have words.'

Davey took it in good humour. But they were all more than aware that it was a threat, and not even a veiled one.

As Eilish poured Davey a drink, she wondered at how a day like this would ever be forgotten.

Chapter One Hundred and Twenty-one

Angus Davis Junior was still alive when Jamie Thomas finally tipped his body into his grave.

He had put him in the garden of a house he now owned in Essex. It was a beautiful cottage in Dunton, and it had over two acres of land with it. They had originally rented it for a holiday. Jamilla loved it, and he was going to surprise her with the news he had decided to keep it as a weekend getaway.

He could look at this spot and remember this night, over the years to come, knowing that his daughter's rapist would always be nearby.

He had revelled in seeing Angus panic when he had finally realised what was happening to him.

Jamie opened another beer and sat in a garden chair. As he rolled a joint, he relished hearing Angus as he tried to fight the inevitable.

He wasn't fucking going anywhere.

Chapter One Hundred and Twenty-two

Lorna was walking through her house, and she stopped to watch the sun come up.

Whereas she had once longed for quiet, now she hated the silence since the kids had grown up, and she wondered why she stayed on. But she had put her heart and soul into this property and she still loved it, because it was her home.

There were always security men around, so she wasn't completely by herself. But they were only employees, and she disregarded them because she couldn't be bothered to make boring small talk. She was Angus Davis's wife, and she had to be treated with the respect she deserved.

She pondered going for a long run, but she didn't want to get changed – and she didn't feel she was in the right place mentally for a long run anyway. She went through to the kitchen and poured herself another glass of wine. The bottle was empty, and she smiled. She had been going through the wine tonight; she had finished her second bottle.

She opened the doors that led out into the gardens and sat at the table she had found with Angus, many years ago, in Cornwall. They had paid a fortune to have it delivered, and the day it had arrived she had been beside herself with excitement. Angus had been working, as usual, but that had not bothered her. She had made sure that her Angus didn't impinge on her life too much.

She had prided herself that that was why they were still together, after all these years. She had allowed him his freedom, and he had left her with the children and the house, and she had been quite content. Now, of course, she had a grandchild to look forward to and, despite the circumstances, she was thrilled by the prospect.

She sipped her wine and tried to picture the new child. If it was a boy, she hoped it looked like her Angus, because he had been a beautiful child. Everyone had admired him, even strangers. He had been a good baby too; he had hardly cried, and she had enjoyed looking after him. She wished they had all stayed babies – her life would have been so much easier.

She walked through the kitchen and opened another bottle of Pinot and, after she had refilled her glass, she walked around her house again. She had removed every picture of her eldest son, along with anything that he had owned or contributed to the house, including childhood drawings and sports trophies. She was pleased to see that she had been very thorough and she hadn't missed anything.

She made her way back through the kitchen to her little private garden and she sat quietly and finished her glass of wine alone.

Book Six

2011

Better to be killed than frightened to death.

Mr Facey Romford's Hounds,
R. S. Surtees (1805–1864)

Chapter One Hundred and Twenty-three

Angus had to admit that his granddaughter, Alia, was a captivating child.

Her skin was coffee-coloured, and she possessed startling blue eyes, and she had long curly hair that was raven black. She was beautiful and bright as a button. And, even at three, she had already worked out who she could rely on to get what she wanted.

Angus found himself popping round to Jamie and Jamilla's as often as possible and, when Alia shouted out excitedly, 'It's my Granddad Angus!', he felt a rush of love so deep it had surprised him. He loved the feel of her plump little body on his lap as he listened delightedly to her chattering. She had such an engaging personality and he loved being in her company.

Lorna saw the child regularly too, but Jamilla had set boundaries from the off, and Lorna knew she had no choice but to follow them. She was getting a taste of her own medicine after what she had put Diana through years ago. Jamilla was shrewd enough to know that, where Lorna was concerned, she needed to make her understand that she wasn't the main carer, and she was never going to be. Lorna only saw the child because *she* allowed it.

Jamie, like Angus, was enchanted with the child, and Eilish had taken to her too. Carly, though, at eighteen now, played with her but treated her more like a little sister, and Angus knew that suited Jamilla perfectly. She adored the child, but she also wanted her daughter to have the freedom and the lack of responsibility that had been stolen from her.

Carly was getting ready to go to university, and she couldn't wait to get away. She didn't see herself as a mum, because Jamilla had taken over the child's welfare from day one. Carly had been relieved that she didn't have to do the backbreaking work that came with a young baby. She was still free to live her life, the same as her friends.

Alia called Jamilla 'Mum', and that suited everyone – especially Carly. As Jamilla said, there was plenty of time before they had to say anything to the child about her parentage, and that was when Angus would feel the anger towards his son bubbling up inside him all over again. That he had fathered a rapist – a fucking nonce – still rankled and, even though he had made good, it would always be there like a cancer eating away at him.

When Lorna had told him what Angus Junior had said about Carly he had been stunned that his son could have been so callous and so hateful, considering that he had forced himself on a young girl and left her to suffer the consequences alone. Seeing Carly smiling again had been a big relief. She had been such a tiny thing when it had happened, and now she had finally blossomed and was acting like a young girl should.

He found that she was on his mind a lot, and he still felt the burn of guilt about her situation. The beautiful child that had been created because of his son's violence was loved by them all, yet she would always be a reminder to him of what his son had done, had been capable of. He wasn't sure that he would ever be able to come to terms with that knowledge. Angus forced the dark thoughts from his mind, because he knew they wouldn't bring him anything of value, and one thing he had learned early on from his mother was that if something wasn't worth pursuing in the early stages, then let the fucker go. She had been right, as always. But he knew that she understood how he felt about this grandchild, because she felt the same.

He turned around from his desk and smiled at Roy, who was gleefully counting the money that had been delivered from one of their clubs. Roy, like him, loved the feel of the cash in his hands. They liked the plastic in the more upmarket clubs because they could pay the bills easily – without anyone noticing or caring, most of the time – but in the smaller, less salubrious places they still insisted on cash. As Eilish had once remarked, carelessly, the cash clubs were where the lap dancers went when their best days were over. He wouldn't argue with that.

In his upmarket clubs the girls rarely got past twenty-nine – and that was if they were lucky. The emphasis on youth, especially extreme youth, was so entrenched in the public psyche these days, it was now a requirement, and it didn't sit well with him or Roy. He had to cater for what his punters wanted – he was running a business, and the customer called the shots – but that didn't mean he had to like it.

Some of the girls looked so young, he felt bad employing them. But if he didn't, some other fucker would. Plus his clubs were where the girls wanted to work, because he brought in the punters with a good wedge – and that was the name of the game, because his girls weren't dancing up a fucking pole because they needed the exercise. He also guaranteed the girls' safety, not just inside the club but outside; he made sure they got home safely too.

He glanced at his watch and was surprised to see how late it was. Roy was just finishing counting the money and, as he balanced the books, Angus poured them both a whiskey. 'It's nearly eight o'clock and we ain't had a fucking drink!'

They laughed together, easy in each other's company as ever.

Roy sipped his whiskey and sighed contentedly. 'Just what the doctor ordered.'

Angus sat back at his desk and asked Roy seriously, 'Talking of doctors, what do you think about Abad's new walker? I'm not sure that I trust him. I get that Abad wants to retire, and good luck to him. But even though Abad is quite happy putting his whole operation in this geezer's hands, there's just something about him that I don't like. I just don't trust him, Roy, he feels like a snide fucker. I can't relax in his company.'

Roy sat back in his chair and nodded his agreement. He was more than pleased that it was Angus who had brought the subject up.

'I know exactly what you mean, Angus. He has what my old mum would have called bad juju. The more he smiles and smarms, the less I fucking like him. But I just assumed that someone as astute as Abad wouldn't be giving him houseroom if he didn't think he was up to the job.'

Angus agreed. 'I suppose so, and I know you can't like everyone you work with – or, in this case, deal with. But I really dislike this one – what's his name? See, I can't even keep his name in my bonce. That tells you what an impression he's left on me. I just remember thinking that he creeped me out.'

Roy knew exactly how Angus felt, because he had the same doubts himself. 'Hamid Fazilla, that was his name, he's another Arab. I have put out feelers on the quiet but no one seems to have heard of him or know anything about him. He's like a ghost, Angus. Even the Old Bill seem to be in a quandary where he is concerned. It seems that his name has come up nowhere at all.'

Angus sipped his whiskey quietly for a while as he digested that information. 'As I said to you and my mum, in all the years we have worked with Abad, this geezer's name has never been mentioned. I want to know his history before I agree to work with him. Abad should know better than to try and slip a fucking stranger by me.'

Roy knew that Angus was right in what he was saying. They should just wait until they had spoken to Abad, one to one. Meanwhile, young Sean had proved himself more than capable of providing the clubs with anything deemed necessary, with the least amount of fuss and with a very good profit margin. He said as much to Angus.

Angus just laughed. 'My Sean has a brain like a fucking computer, you know that as well as I do. He can work out an earn in seconds, down to the last fucking penny. If he can tip the scales in our favour with his supplier then I will happily tell Abad that we wish him a happy retirement but we will be taking our business elsewhere.'

Roy couldn't argue with that. 'Sean is dealing with the Colombians, as you know. They like him, and they trust him. He is a real asset because he is well respected. Not just because he's a clever fucker but because there's never once been a derogatory whisper about him. He only drinks occasionally, he never touches drugs and he is always there when needed.'

After the let-down of Angus Junior, Angus was relieved he had at least one son he could rely on to carry on the family name with pride. His second son was a fucking natural in their world and he had slipped into his role without any fanfare whatsoever and without the need to make his reputation in the public eye. Sean belonged to the new generation of villains and he was already a man to be reckoned with, should anyone be foolish enough to step on his toes.

If Sean had a beef with anyone, it was sorted out privately

and with the minimum of fuss, and the person or people concerned would just disappear without trace. Sean thought everything through, right down to the last detail. But he also always tried his hardest to come to an amicable arrangement with anyone who felt they had a grievance with him.

Sean believed that violence should be a last resort, but if he was pushed too far then, like his father and his grandmother Diana, he could take it to the extreme. He saw it as a necessary evil.

Angus was thrilled with this son of his and his aptitude for the businesses that he had inherited. Diana too had been impressed at how easily he had fitted into the dynamics. So Angus was quite happy to let his son take over where Abad had left off, especially if that meant that he didn't have to deal with that fucking Hamid and whoever he worked for. Angus knew that once Abad was off the scene, whoever took his place would immediately want to make their mark, and that was to be expected. But Angus wasn't about to be dictated to by anyone, he didn't give a fuck who they were.

'You know what, Roy? Sean said to me the other night that when Abad walks away, it will be the end of an era.'

Roy laughed gently. 'And he is right. Your Sean is an ultra-intelligent man, and everyone knows that about him. Tangiers is all but over now, thanks to the European fucking Union and their determination to stop the drug trade. So we are already in bed with the Colombians in London and the rest of the UK. Like Sean, I think it's the natural next step to deal with them exclusively in Europe too, and move away from the Moroccans and the Afghanis. There's too much heat with Afghanistan and what is going on with them, so I think it makes sense to give them all a swerve and let Sean broker a new deal.'

Angus listened to his friend's advice – he was right. Abad pulling out of the deal gave them the perfect excuse to walk away without any real animosity being generated.

'Yeah, I agree, Roy. As Sean has a great relationship with the Colombians, I think we should pursue that and wipe our hands of the Moroccan connection. Given that it's Abad's decision to walk away, that means that we can do the same.'

Roy lit a joint and took a deep toke on it before saying seriously, 'Well, let's see what Abad has to say about it all before we start blowing up any balloons and lighting up our sparklers.'

Chapter One Hundred and Twenty-four

Eilish was tired, but that went with the territory of working all hours, and she was used to it by now.

She was still seeing Davey Proctor and no one was more surprised about that than she was. He had a reputation as the most unreliable man in London – she had known that about him from the off – and she had gone into her relationship with him without any expectations whatsoever. But three years on, they were still together and she couldn't fault him.

Sometimes she wondered if that fact disappointed her, because he had proved her wrong. What she couldn't deny was that she wanted him as much as ever and she could not imagine her life without him. She believed that he cared for her and that he loved her in his own way, but then she also knew that his reputation still preceded him, and because of that she wasn't sure if she could ever really trust him. That her father and Sean had finally accepted him was something that she was grateful for, because it meant they had made sure that he wasn't doing the dirty on her. Her father and brother would have paid people to watch him so closely they would have been able to tell her what time he had a shit in the morning and what coffee he drank beforehand.

As she looked around her and watched the girls as they gyrated around the poles, she couldn't help wondering if her Davey still hankered after them. The club was quiet, it was early evening and there were only a few city boys in. The Canary Wharf spenders were regular faces early in the evening, as they tended to come in before catching their trains. They would drink heavily and spend heavily, and the early birds – the girls who came in before nine o'clock – would happily rinse them of whatever cash they had on them. They were all waiting for their chance to get the later slots, where the real money was. Eilish made sure that the new girls did the first shifts, so she could weed out the head bangers and the thieves. The last thing any club needed was a punter who had been ripped off.

Eilish couldn't help smiling as Niamh tottered towards her on impossibly high heels. She was nineteen, with the face of an angel and a body that could bring a grown man to his knees, and she was also the nicest girl you could ever wish to meet.

'Jesus, how do they walk in these fucking shoes!'

Eilish laughed delightedly because she couldn't help but like this girl, and she had taken her under her wing. 'Niamh, give the shoes back to whoever you borrowed them off, and wear a pair that you can walk in properly. I have put you on till twelve tonight, so you will be on with the earners. Don't let me down, OK?'

Niamh smiled gratefully. 'Thank fuck for that! I could barely keep myself upright. I just wanted to thank you, Eilish, because you have been really good to me.'

Eilish pushed her away gently. 'Just get up there and do what you're best at, and I will see you later.'

She watched as the girl tottered off precariously, balanced on shoes that were far too high and far too old for her image. Niamh would earn because she still looked like a kid, and unfortunately with a lot of their punters that was a big attraction.

Davey Proctor watched Niamh walk away and he was smiling too. 'She's like a kid wearing her mum's shoes.'

Eilish grinned because she could see that, like her, Davey knew instinctively that Niamh needed looking after. 'She isn't the sharpest knife in the drawer, but she's sensible enough to listen to reason.'

Davey nodded. 'She will be all right, we will look after her. I only wish the other girls were as easy to control. They're like fucking animals some of them.'

Eilish laughed. She really couldn't argue with that. But unlike Davey and Sean, she understood how cut-throat this business could be, and how the girls would quite happily push themselves into another girl's punter, even though they knew it was frowned upon. But, in fairness, they were all here for one reason and one reason only, and that was to earn money.

'Come on, Eilish, let's go and grab a bite to eat before this place gets too busy. I have a feeling it's going to be another mad night. Indian or Thai, darling? You choose.'

Eilish followed him out of the club, all the time wondering why she didn't just stop seeing him, because that would make her life so much easier.

He grabbed her hand and pulled her towards his car, and she felt the draw of him once again. She wondered if it would ever go away.

Chapter One Hundred and Twenty-five

Sean was settled in the offices in Soho and was waiting patiently when his dad and Roy walked in.

Sean had a way with him that Angus admired. The man was so self-contained and so calm that he could put the people around him on edge. Even now, in his own offices, he could feel the power of his Sean's presence, and he knew that Roy could feel it too. It was something that was a part of his make-up, and it automatically put the people he dealt with on their guard.

After they had helped themselves to drinks and were sitting down, Sean said quietly, 'I've invited Granny and Gabriel, because I think she needs to know what I am going to tell you.'

Angus didn't question him. If there was one thing he knew, it was that this son could be relied on to do whatever was necessary, and he would do it right. Sean reminded him of himself as a young man – albeit more educated and far more privileged.

Sean answered his mobile and Angus smiled, because he knew Sean still couldn't believe that he refused to have one. That was a sign of the times, of course, and Angus accepted that he had no interest in computers and all that went with them. He left that to Sean.

Roy had one, and so did most of the people he knew, and Angus now felt that his refusing one for so long gave him a certain cachet. Angus still didn't trust mobile phones; he was old school, and what he couldn't understand he wouldn't give houseroom. Even now, if he had to make a call that was about business, he would drive out of London and use a phone box in the middle of nowhere. That was how he had always conducted certain business, and he didn't see any reason to stop that now – though he had to admit it was getting harder to find them these days.

Sean was forever trying to convince him about the merits of burner phones. But, as he pointed out, he had left the majority of his businesses to him and Eilish, so he didn't need one. They laughed at him, and he took it in good part, but he had a feeling that, one day, his natural distrust of everything pertaining to computers and mobile phones would be proved right.

His thoughts were interrupted when he heard Sean say, 'Granny's on her way up.'

Chapter One Hundred and Twenty-six

Lorna was contemplating Alia's room and wondering what else she could do to make it better.

She resented Jamilla and the way she had relegated her to second best. Alia was still her son's child, no matter what the circumstances of her birth might have been. But she couldn't say anything, because Angus had warned her more than once that, if she kicked off, Jamilla would be well within her rights to stop all access. She knew he was talking sense, but she also felt that he should have fought for her and for her right to see her grandchild as and when she wanted to.

She only saw him when Alia was here now, and that hurt. It felt like he was policing her, because he made sure that she was never alone with the child. Her Eilish was just the same; she turned up like a bad smell and wouldn't leave unless her father was there, and that fucking rankled. Why didn't they trust her with her own grandchild?

She took her medication, and she made sure that they were all aware of that. She just wanted to see Alia and enjoy the child alone occasionally. She could see Angus Junior in her. She had his eyes, his beautiful blue eyes, and she had also inherited his stance. She walked like she owned the place, and she was so quick like him as well. She could talk your leg off and make everyone around her feel like they were the only person in her world that mattered. She was a gorgeous child, and Lorna hated that she couldn't see her on a daily basis and teach her properly.

If it was left to the Thomases, the child would be brought up like an animal. Look at the sons! They couldn't string a sentence together if they were given two days' notice. And as for that Carly, she was bright enough, but she ignored the child. Anyone would think that Jamilla was the mother. No, it was all unfair, and she had to do something about it. She just didn't know what.

She was well aware that her own children avoided her if they could. She yearned for the days when she had been everything to them, when she had kept them safely within her orbit and she had looked after them and made sure that they were protected.

She prowled the house once more, and reminisced about her children when they were all still at home with her.

She needed another child to fill up her time and energy.

She needed a drink.

Chapter One Hundred and Twenty-seven

Diana was happy to see her Angus and Sean, and she kissed them both heartily. They hugged her back, as she expected.

She was looking frail lately and Angus felt sad to see it, because she had always been such a force of nature. Even with her make-up and her expensive clothes, she looked like an old woman now, and Angus was surprised to notice that Gabriel looked a lot older too. He had always had time for Gabriel. He knew that the man genuinely loved his mum and that had been proved, time and time again throughout the years.

Diana sat down and settled herself in her chair with the maximum of fuss and then, sipping her drink, she said pointedly, 'I am assuming this is about Hamid Fazilla?'

Angus wasn't in the least surprised that his mother was, as always, one step ahead, but he could see that Sean was. He guessed that Sean had prepared a whole speech and now it wasn't needed. He had just found out why his granny was still in the game. Sean recovered his equilibrium quickly, and Angus and Roy both suppressed a smile.

'What do you know about him, Granny?'

Diana smiled that lazy smile of hers and, taking another big sip of her whiskey, she said easily, 'His father is Ali Fazilla. I knew him years ago, when he worked with Abad's father, and he was a good bloke. He was murdered in the late eighties, in Kabul, by what were assumed to be rival distributers. Personally, I never believed that. I think he was involved with certain political factions. Whatever happened, his body was found on the side of the road, riddled with bullets. One thing I do know is that that event terrified Abad's old man. I had never seen him so frightened – and, believe me, he wasn't a man who was easily intimidated.'

She sipped her drink again and waited for her words to sink in. She was pleased to see that she had everyone's undivided attention.

'I wouldn't touch that Hamid or his associates with a barge-pole, and I think Abad knows that, but he had to put him out there for propriety's sake. He knows that I wouldn't countenance anything to do with Hamid or his so-called associates. But, in fairness, Abad would not have had any choice in the matter. These are not people anyone with half a brain would willingly want as partners, and why Hamid is involved with them after what happened to his father, we can only guess. Anyway, bottom line is, we swerve the fuckers and do what Sean says: stick with the Colombians.'

Sean was so impressed with his grandmother and her acumen, he was speechless. Angus stood up and began replenishing everyone's drinks. Unlike his son, he wasn't surprised that his mother knew the score.

'I had a feeling he wasn't on the up, Mum. There was some-thing definitely off about him.' Angus sat back down heavily. 'But do you think that if we blank him, he might try and force us to go into business with him?'

It was a valid question, and everyone was interested to know the answer.

Diana shook her head. 'No, these people only targeted us

because we could give them an in immediately. They won't try and force it. But they will still be looking for someone they can use to get a foothold here. So keep your eye out, because they will eventually want what you have, and they will promise that to whoever is fool enough to go into partnership with them – and we all know someone will. My guess is it will be one of the big Pakistani outfits. One thing we have going for us is the Colombians, because they don't take any prisoners and they are formidable enemies. All they are interested in is the earn, nothing more. They are all good Catholics too.'

Everyone laughed, Diana the hardest. The man had not been born yet who could scare her. She had gone into a man's world after her husband's death, and she had out-thought the men she had dealt with and always made sure that she had a better deal to put on the table. She had learned very early on that if she was to survive, she needed to be as ruthless as the people she had to do business with.

Her acumen and her reputation for earning a crust had been why people had come to her if they had a business proposition. And if she thought it had legs, she had been more than happy to bankroll it, but always as a silent partner. That was why she had her finger in so many pies, and why she was so liked and respected by her peers. Most of the Faces were only where they were because of her, and they knew that as well as she did.

She watched as they talked among themselves, and she relaxed once more in her chair. She had no real interest in her businesses any more. It was strange, but ducking and diving had once been the reason she had got up in the morning, and now she just wanted to sit back and enjoy the fruits of her labours.

Angus would be a worthy successor – she had trained him well – and that pleased her. She had to admit that she enjoyed being the fountain of wisdom where Hamid Fazilla was concerned today though. She had given them the benefit of her experience but she had to acknowledge that she didn't miss this life at all.

Gabriel was watching her and she knew that he would be able to tell what she was thinking. Even after all their years together, he still loved her, and she loved him in her own way.

He caught her eye and winked at her, and she winked back.

Chapter One Hundred and Twenty-eight

Abad wasn't surprised when Angus politely declined the opportunity to work with Hamid Fazilla. In all honesty, he was relieved. He would not have relished having Fazilla and all he stood for dictating his life – because that is what would have happened.

Hamid was smiling amiably, and Abad wondered if he had guessed what the answer was going to be before he even got to this meeting. Angus and Sean had taken them for a meal in the West End, and there had been no expense spared. There was no way Hamid could feel insulted. Now they were in the private bar of Angus's main club, and Hamid was happy with his large brandy and the girls that were on offer.

Hamid was a good-looking man with thick dark hair and dark eyes. He had the requisite beard that most Arabs had, and it suited him. He was well dressed and he had a good disposition. He spoke excellent English and he was knowledgeable on many subjects. All in all, he was a great companion, and Angus found himself enjoying the night – especially as Hamid had taken the refusal with such good grace.

There was a young blonde dancer called Mariah who was slim and lithe. Angus was sure she had said that she had once been a ballet dancer. She had something about her, and she was popular. Hamid was very taken with her, and she was quite happy to be his partner for the evening, because she knew that it would earn her a big wedge – and that was what it was all about.

Hamid was sitting and chatting to her, and Abad was with one of his usual girls, so Angus and Sean were quite happy to excuse themselves and leave them to it. Eilish had made sure that they had everything they needed, and she was waiting for them in the main bar.

'Fucking hell, Eilish, this music is terrible.'

Eilish laughed at her father. 'It's what the girls want to dance to, Dad, and what the punters like.'

Angus picked up his drink and, raising his glass in a toast to them, he said jokingly, 'Fucking Bolero it ain't!'

Sean was laughing, and Angus recognised it was with relief at how easily the night had gone. After Diana had given them the full story, they had wondered what they might be dealing with. Eilish and Sean were talking shop, and Angus looked at them proudly. They were both good-looking, well dressed and at the top of their respective games. They were children any man would be proud of.

Angus saw Davey Proctor approaching and he smiled and held out his hand to shake. He liked Davey, though he still didn't relish him being with his daughter. But what could he do?

'All right, Davey?'

He watched as Davey kissed Eilish hello, and he had to admit they had lasted a lot longer than he had believed possible. Sean and Davey got on well, and soon they were all chatting easily. Davey did a good job at overseeing the club and Angus appreciated that. There was a lot more aggro than people realised in the lap-dancing clubs and, when it occurred, it needed to be contained and dealt with as quickly and as quietly as possible. Davey was good at doing just that. Alcohol, drugs and half-naked women could cause murders, and even the most passive men had been known to throw a wobbler if they thought they had been had over.

Angus looked at the stage and watched the girls as they energetically grappled with their poles. They were good dancers and he watched as the men slipped them money for a smile and a private flash. The place was busy, as always, and he was pleased to see that, because he knew that they would clear a good few grand this evening.

Sean leaned towards him and whispered in his ear, 'I'm glad that's over, Dad, aren't you?'

Angus grinned. 'Yeah, son, but it had to be done.'

Sean nodded. 'Did Eilish tell you about Mum?'

'No, what about Mum?' Angus was now on red alert.

Sean rolled his eyes with annoyance. 'She's threatening to go round the Thomases and take Alia. She's got it into her head that Jamilla and Jamie aren't fit to look after her.'

Angus could tell a manic episode was on its way. Lorna had been building up to it recently. She had too much time on her hands, and that was never a good thing. 'She's been taking her meds, though, I know she has.'

Sean shrugged with irritation. 'We all know she forgets to take her meds, Dad! She's a nut, so give her half a chance and she'll go on a rampage.'

His son was right, but Angus still didn't like him talking about his mother like that. 'Come on, Sean, you know she's not well. She can't help it.'

Sean shrugged again. 'Well, that is your opinion, and I beg to differ. It's about attention and getting what she wants – and that's mainly getting you home.'

Angus didn't answer him, because he knew there was an element of truth in what he said.

'Why don't you divorce her, Dad? She's never going to change, is she?'

Angus had wondered the same thing himself over the last few years. But he still loved her, and he still felt responsible for her, and he knew that he always would.

Angus picked up his drink and sipped it slowly. Sean was only looking out for him, and that made him feel even worse.

The first gunshot was loud, even with the noise of the club.

The second was loud enough for the customers and the girls to stop what they were doing and look around them, trying to work out the source of the bangs.

The third shot caused chaos.

Chapter One Hundred and Twenty-nine

'Fucking hell.'

Angus was in shock. They all were.

Hamid and Abad were both dead. Young Mariah, who had been shot in the chest, was still alive but lying on the floor in a pool of blood and trying to talk to them. The other dancers had done a runner, and Angus couldn't blame them. He would have done the same in their position.

Angus sat by Mariah and, holding her hand in his, he kept saying, 'Don't try and talk, just wait for the ambulance. You are going to be all right, you are going to be fine, I promise you.'

She looked so young lying there, bleeding everywhere, and he grabbed a towel that was on one of the sofas and held it tightly against her wound. Sean and Eilish were doing speedy damage limitation, and Davey was making sure that the CCTV cameras elsewhere in the club would show nothing. They would peruse them later and try to piece together what had happened. It was a fucking nightmare.

Sean had rung his grandmother so she would make sure that any police involved would be from her payroll and would say whatever they were paid to say. But this was a fucking disaster – especially where Hamid fucking Fazilla was concerned. Angus had a feeling that Fazilla was the real target tonight, and Abad and poor Mariah were just collateral damage.

He waited with her until the ambulance arrived. Once she had been taken away and was safe, he stood up and bellowed, 'What the actual fuck is going on here?'

He was seriously angry now, and Angus Davis and his temper were legendary. Even the police were subdued, and that suited him right down to the ground.

The last thing he needed was those fuckers interfering in his private business.

Chapter One Hundred and Thirty

Angus really appreciated that both Sean and Eilish had refused to leave him. They had moved to the offices of the club, still in shock at what had happened. When Roy arrived, Angus just looked at him in genuine bewilderment.

Roy poured himself a large drink before saying, 'This had to be planned. Who else knew about Hamid and Abad coming here?'

Angus didn't answer him. Instead, he looked at his son saying, 'Can you think of anything that has happened recently that you thought was a bit off? Anyone new suddenly coming in here, or someone hanging about?'

Sean shook his head. 'No, Dad. But I rarely come here, as you know. I'm normally in Spain.'

Eilish chipped in. 'I have been wondering the same thing, and, in all honesty, Dad, I can't think of anything that was out of the ordinary. Davey is going to bring the tapes up and we can look at them in a minute. I hope to fuck there's something on them that can explain this shit.'

There was a polite tap on the office door and then Detective Inspector Lionel Marks walked into the room. He looked at Angus and said sheepishly, 'Do you have any idea what happened here?'

Angus shook his head in abject disbelief at such a stupid

question. 'Do you honestly think that I would arrange two murders in my own fucking club?'

Lionel Marks shook his large bald head in denial. 'What I mean is, Angus, was this someone coming after you?'

Angus was weighing up whether he could be bothered to punch this moron in the face when Roy said quickly, 'Well, of course not, use your fucking loaf! Whoever did this was after the Arabs. They are the ones who got shot, or haven't you noticed?'

Lionel Marks took a deep breath before saying calmly, 'What I am asking you all is whether anyone here has any idea why this might have happened. Were the men targeted for a reason that you might be aware of? And, if so, what do you want me to do about it?'

Roy sighed and Angus bellowed once more, 'No, Lionel, we have no idea why this happened! This is as big a fucking surprise to us as it is to you!'

Lionel knew better than to antagonise Angus or his cohorts, so he said quietly, 'I am going downstairs as I am the lead detective, along with Bill Smith, and I need to show my face. If you have anything to tell me, you know where I am.' He left the room as quietly as he had entered it.

Sean laughed nastily. 'What a waste of space.'

Eilish lit a cigarette and, looking at her brother, she said, 'Well, be fair, that is what we are paying him for.'

Roy looked at Sean and Eilish and said gravely, 'Think long and hard about the last few days, if there was one thing that you think might have been a bit off, no matter how small or insignificant it seemed at the time. Was there anyone who came into the club who shouldn't have been there? A postman, someone delivering a parcel, a fucking salesman. Have you had a new punter who didn't sit well with you? This meeting was only arranged three days ago, so whoever did this didn't have much time. And from what I have seen, this was a well-planned execution, because both Abad and Hamid were taken out together. That means that this wasn't personal – it was purely business.'

Eilish shook her head. 'No one out of the ordinary has been in – I would have noticed – and no one has used that private room anyway. I would have known about it, because I book the private rooms. The punter has to weigh out serious money beforehand, and I make sure I know who they are and what they do before they can even cross the threshold.

'Whoever did this had to have been here before this meeting was arranged. It has to be someone who knows the club and knows the layout, because most of the regular punters don't even know that room exists. Famous people use that particular VIP room because they know we can spirit them in and out of the back door without anyone even knowing they were there.

'This has to be someone who knows this place and knows that there is no CCTV near that room. We guarantee privacy, don't we? My real worry is that whoever did this came in the back door and left the same way. So what we have to ask ourselves is, who do we think might have let the fucker in?'

The three men looked at each other in agreement, because what Eilish had said made perfect sense.

Sean dropped down on to the black leather sofa by the window and shook his handsome head in disbelief.

Angus and Roy were looking at each other as if they could read what was going through the other's mind.

Chapter One Hundred and Thirty-one

Jamilla Thomas was surprised to see Lorna on her doorstep, but she did her best to hide her dismay.

She knew that Alia loved this woman and she knew that Lorna loved Alia – there could be no disputing that – but that didn't take away from the fact that Jamilla couldn't stand her. God Himself knew she had tried to put aside her dislike but, no matter how hard she tried, she just couldn't do it.

Lorna was strange in so many ways. Not all the time, but enough to worry her where Alia was concerned, even though the child came back from her visits with nothing but happy stories and good memories. But if Angus wasn't there, she wouldn't let the child go anywhere with Lorna. Angus had sworn that when Alia was at his house he was there for the duration, and from what she had gleaned from Alia that was the truth. Even the woman's own husband didn't see fit to leave her alone with a child, and Jamilla could understand why.

Lorna was still a good-looking woman, with a great figure. She dressed to impress and she was always perfectly made-up and impeccably turned out. Yet Jamilla knew there was something decidedly wrong with Lorna, and she could never be left alone with her grandchild.

'Oh, Lorna, I wasn't expecting you,' Jamilla said pointedly.

It was lost on Lorna who smiled widely. 'I was in the neighbourhood and I thought, if you didn't mind, I would pop in for a coffee and a catch-up.'

Jamilla had been here before with her and, against her better judgement, she opened the door and let Lorna step inside. Alia was at playschool, so she wouldn't see her anyway.

The one thing in Lorna's favour was that she had given up her son to his father. And she had apparently removed every photo of him from her home, as if he had never existed, and Jamilla could understand that. After all, what mother could ever forgive a son who was a rapist?

'Alia isn't here, she's at playschool. She loves it there! She is ever so popular too.'

Lorna was still all smiles. 'I bet she is. She's such a friendly and engaging child. She is a credit to you, Jamilla, a real credit.'

Jamilla nodded her thanks as she put the kettle on. 'Tea or coffee, Lorna?'

'Whatever is easiest, I don't mind.'

As Jamilla watched Lorna roaming around her kitchen, getting more and more agitated by the minute, she wished there was someone else in the house with her.

'Are you OK, Lorna?'

Lorna stopped her pacing and, looking at her intently, she said, 'Of course I am. Why wouldn't I be?'

Jamilla smiled as best she could and busied herself making the tea.

'Why does everyone keep asking me that? As if there's something wrong with me, and I need looking after? I don't need looking after, and there's nothing wrong with me. So now you know, you don't need to ever question me again.'

Jamilla didn't answer her, because she didn't know what Lorna wanted to hear. Instead, she waited for Lorna to start a real conversation of some kind and she prayed that it would be something she could relate to.

Lorna pulled out a stool and sat down at the large breakfast bar. 'No one knows what it's like to be constantly questioned about how you are feeling. It's wearing, Jamilla. It's just so depressing, honestly. I know my son did something really terrible, and I hate him for it, but I did the best I could for my kids. I think that some people are just born bad, don't you?'

Jamilla didn't know what to say for the best, but she tried. 'Yeah, Lorna, I think you are probably right. Some people are just born with a badness in them, and nothing anyone can do will change that.'

Lorna smiled again at that. 'I knew you would understand. I had a feeling that you, of all people, would be on my side.'

As Jamilla heard Jamie's key turning in the door, she let out a sigh of relief that she wouldn't be alone with this woman any more. Lorna actually scared her, and she wasn't easily frightened. One thing she was now sure of, though, and that was that her little Alia would not be staying at this fucker's house any more, no matter what.

Lorna Davis was as mad as a box of frogs, and she could not let her within a donkey's fart of her grandchild. This weirdness today was the last straw.

Chapter One Hundred and Thirty-two

Roy and Angus had stayed up all night watching all the available CCTV footage and, as Eilish had predicted, there had not been anything on it that was even remotely suspect.

Whoever had murdered Abad and Hamid had to have been invited in through the back door and then escorted out afterwards. It was beyond comprehension that someone that worked for them would even dare to do something so heinous, no matter how much money they might have been offered. Whoever it was had to know that they would find them eventually. Everyone on the payroll, even the fucking cleaners, would be watched like a hawk until this situation had been resolved to Angus's satisfaction. None of it made any sense, and it was torturing Angus.

Sean and Eilish were still sorting out the club and dealing with the police and the press. Angus had courted the press for years, so a double shooting in his flagship lap-dancing club would be a big story and one that could run for weeks. The Sunday papers would rehash everything, from his clubs in Soho to his clubs in Spain and the stories that had been told over the years. He couldn't do anything about that.

He picked up the phone and rang Lionel, his tame Filth, again. Lionel answered on the first ring.

'Any news on Mariah yet? Is she OK?'

Lionel told him, once again, that she was critical but stable in hospital. As soon as he knew more, he would let him know.

'She is fighting her end though?'

Lionel sighed. 'There's a policewoman outside her door who is keeping her eye on her and who will be the first to know if anything changes, Angus. Once she knows anything of relevance, she will call me.'

Angus put the phone down. 'If that little girl dies, Roy, I will never forgive myself. She didn't even get the chance to run. The other girls couldn't tell us fuck-all about the shooter, except that he had a baseball hat and a dark-coloured scarf covering the lower part of his face.'

Roy could hear the anger in his friend's voice. 'Be fair, Angus, they were all shitting hot bricks. All anyone was interested in was getting out of the situation, and who can blame them? Whoever it was wasn't going to let anyone see his fucking boat-race, were they?'

Roy was right, but it didn't make Angus feel any better.

'Look, Angus, we have everyone on our payroll out there asking around and trying to put this lunacy into some kind of perspective. Someone somewhere has to know something, it stands to fucking reason.'

Angus nodded but he wasn't feeling too reassured, because there was something about this whole situation that didn't ring true. There wasn't one fucking Face in the whole of England or Spain that would have enough front to think that they could get away with it. He was Angus Davis, and he knew his fucking worth, and he wouldn't rest until he knew who the culprit was and had him within his grasp. And oh, that cunt would rue the day he had thought for one moment that he could get one over on him.

Roy poured them both a mug of strong black coffee and handed one to Angus, who accepted it gratefully.

'The thing is, Angus, once we find the shooter we will find out why they were both targeted, because that's what has been bothering me.'

Angus sipped his coffee again. 'Oh, I have worked out why, Roy. Think about it: Abad brought Hamid here as his replacement. We knocked him back and, in fairness, he took that well, so whoever did this already knew we were going to refuse his offer. That means that it can only be whoever he worked for. My mother is already on it. She's talking to Abad's father as they go back years, and she also has the Colombians on it. They will be as interested as we are to find out who ordered it. She also pointed out that it's not personal, because they could have taken me out and they didn't, so this is about them – about Abad and Hamid. I want to know who did it and I want to make sure that they know, for the future, that they can't use me or my fucking premises to settle their scores.'

Roy got up and poured a generous measure of brandy into his coffee. 'That makes sense. But what if this is a warning to you to show you that they mean business? With Hamid gone and poor Abad – a close friend and someone you have had dealings with for years – shot to death in your club, maybe this is their way of saying you can't refuse their offer.'

Angus didn't answer him. He had already worked that much out for himself.

Roy sighed wearily. 'These are heavy people, Angus. And more than that, they are determined.'

Angus snorted angrily. 'Fucking bring it on, that's what I say.'

Chapter One Hundred and Thirty-three

Diana spent the day working from Angus's house. She had sent Gabriel to remove Lorna from Jamilla and Jamie's house, as requested.

The news about the shooting at the club was on every news channel, so Jamie had got in touch with Gabriel to ask him what he should do with Lorna. It sounded like she was on the verge of one of her psychotic breaks.

She felt sorry for Lorna, she always had.

The first time she had been sectioned, Angus had been away, and she had been called in by the then housekeeper because she had been getting increasingly worried about Lorna's strange behaviour. When Diana had arrived, Lorna had been manic and, according to the housekeeper, she had been running around the grounds for nearly two days, on and off. Diana had found her, exhausted and talking nonsense about the children being possessed by devils and how she needed to run constantly to stop the bad thoughts from intruding. The doctor had come and, within minutes, he had decided that she had to be sectioned. So with his cooperation, Diana arranged for her to go to a private mental health facility where her problems wouldn't become common knowledge.

Diana had stayed with her grandchildren and she had really

cherished her time with them and getting to know them properly. She had hoped that Lorna being sectioned would be the wake-up call that her son needed, to see that his wife had serious problems, but she had been mistaken.

Once Lorna came back home, he acted like it was a one-off and wouldn't happen again, because she was all better and on her meds. And Lorna had been well, for a while – still odd and reclusive, but able to function – until she stopped taking her meds. Then it would start all over again, and that had become the pattern of their life for so long, she supposed it had eventually become the norm.

Diana decided to take a break from the phone for a while. She was tired out and too old for this shit. Whereas once she had lived for the adrenalin of her lifestyle, now she just wanted to relax and enjoy her grandchildren. She was waiting for Abad's father to call back and give her the names of the main people Abad had been dealing with the last few years. He was devastated about his son and, like her, he wanted those responsible to pay. She could hear in his voice that he was a broken man.

He had arranged for his daughter-in-law and his grandchildren to be brought to him so he could protect them, if needed. The news of his son's death had already hit the Moroccan news networks. It had been picked up from the British news sites, where it was front-page and the only item that seemed to be talked about on the networks, so the poor man couldn't even grieve in peace.

Diana sighed and stood up so she could stretch her body for a few moments. There were security men surrounding the property and they were there because of Lorna. Diana wondered where this would all end. Because one thing she was sure of was that someone within their circle had served up Hamid and Abad for a price. And it would have to have been a serious wedge for whoever was responsible to not only go against her Angus but to be willing to risk his retribution, should they get found out.

Angus would skin them alive and enjoy every second of it, because such treachery was something that could not be countenanced.

Chapter One Hundred and Thirty-four

Eilish got out of the shower and wrapped herself in a white bath sheet. She wiped the steam off the mirror with her hand and looked at herself. She was tired and drawn, but she supposed that was to be expected after the night they had all experienced. She glanced down at the slight swell in her stomach that wasn't detectable to the outside world yet. That was for dealing with another time.

She still couldn't believe that Abad and Hamid were dead, even though she had seen their bodies broken and smashed to pieces. Abad had been hit in the neck, and the bullet had left a huge hole that gaped open and left him looking like something from an abattoir. It had been such a shock, seeing him so alive and full of fun one moment, and then dead and mutilated the next.

They had known him all their lives. They had stayed with him and his family in Morocco, and they had wonderful memories of him taking them to a souk or to the beach. She remembered when they had holidayed in Marbella and how much fun they had had together. It didn't seem real somehow.

But as her father had explained, it was always different when people died violently, because it left a mark on everyone who knew them and loved them. Whereas if they had died of natural

395

causes, like a heart attack or even cancer, it was much easier to comprehend, because then it always felt more normal. It was something that happened to so many people; it was the natural order, and it was their time to die. But when someone was murdered, it meant that someone had cut their life short, deliberately and brutally, and the violent nature of their demise was hard to accept.

She realised now, of course, that he was preparing them for the worst. Because in the world he inhabited, the worst was always around the corner. It was the nature of the beast. Seeing those men dead like that was something that she would never forget as long as she lived.

She remembered poor Mariah lying there on the floor, with that huge gaping wound in her chest. She had looked so young and so vulnerable. She was what was termed 'collateral damage'. She knew that Mariah being shot had affected her father more even than Abad's death, who he had loved like a brother, because she was an innocent who had been caught up in something that had nothing to do with her. She had just been in the wrong place at the wrong time.

Eilish rinsed her face with cold water and then she cleaned her teeth. She went from her bathroom through to the bedroom, dropped the towel and pulled on a cream silk dressing gown.

She walked through her apartment into her lounge and she saw Davey lying on the sofa drinking a beer. Every time she looked at him, she felt the pull of him. There was something about Davey that affected her deep in her soul, and she was at a loss to know exactly what that was. Since they had been together, she knew that he had never once been unfaithful to her and, knowing his reputation, she was not only amazed, she was also flattered.

He told her constantly that he loved her and wanted her, and she relished the attention and the feeling that she had somehow tamed him. She loved looking at him sleeping, or just watching him eat. She loved everything about him.

He was patting the seat beside him and trying to pull her down to sit with him, but she pushed him away. Instead, she went and sat on an armchair alone, and she laughed at his disappointment.

She watched him as he smiled lazily and continued to drink his beer. 'Doesn't it bother you what happened at the club?'

Davey sat up suddenly, looking serious. 'Of course it does, for Christ's sake!'

Davey was on the defensive now; he clearly wasn't happy with her questioning him or his motives.

'Seeing Abad and Hamid dead, and that poor young Mariah fighting for her life, it was horrific. I don't think I will ever get over it.'

Davey slipped off the sofa and came to where she was sitting. Kneeling in front of her, he said sadly, 'I know, Eilish, it was shocking. I don't think any of us will ever really get over it.'

She nodded slowly, watching him as he gazed at her with that look he had, the one that made her feel like the only woman on the planet. She loved that look and loved the way it made her feel. He tried to open her dressing gown and pull her legs apart, and she wondered how many times he had done that to her and she had been receptive to him and enjoyed his attention.

But not now. She couldn't.

'Will you stop it, Davey, what's wrong with you? After what's happened, how can you even think about sex?'

Davey sat back on his hunkers and she saw that he was irritated with her, because he couldn't distract her from what was troubling her; he took her refusal as a rejection of him personally. He really had a big ego, and that had always made her laugh in the past. Now she pushed him away and went to pour herself a glass of wine, savouring the taste.

'Who do you think could have let the shooter in, Davey? That's what is bothering me. Who the fuck could have done that?'

He shrugged and she watched as he went back to the sofa and sat down.

'Anyone who had access to the back door keys, I suppose. And that means anyone who works there. You know as well as I do that most of the girls who work in the clubs would sell their own mothers for a fucking score.'

Eilish sighed sadly. 'I suppose so, Davey. Though, in fairness, most of the girls are only there to get a few quid for their families.'

Davey finished his beer. 'Exactly what I'm saying, darling. Imagine if one of them got offered a big payday. Imagine what they would do for that.'

Eilish nodded her agreement and watched as Davey went out to the kitchen to get another beer. She drank her wine down and refilled her glass from the bottle on the coffee table. She still felt so het up after last night's events, and she knew that this was probably due to shock. She had never really understood that expression, until now, when she was experiencing it for herself.

Davey came back and tapped his bottle against her glass in a cheers motion and then, sitting at her feet, he settled back against her legs. Grabbing her hand in his, he placed it on his head and she automatically started to caress his hair. She glanced at the clock and saw that it was nearly noon. She took another deep gulp of her wine and she tried to force herself to relax.

Davey knelt up again and, looking at Eilish with concern, he said, 'I promise you this will pass, darling. What happened was tragic and brutal, but you will get past this.'

Eilish heard the doorbell and, as Davey turned away from her to answer it, she smashed her wine glass into his face with all her strength. It was a large balloon glass and she had chosen it for maximum damage. Standing up, she kicked him away from her. As he lay on the floor, pumping blood everywhere, she stepped over him and went to let her father and Roy in.

She had worked out *exactly* who had opened the door for the shooter. Now she was looking forward to finding out who had paid him to betray, not just her, but everyone and everything that she cared about, past, present and future.

Chapter One Hundred and Thirty-five

Diana and Gabriel had finally got home, both relieved to be away from Lorna.

Diana had given her the meds she needed and settled her down enough to be able to leave her. Lorna just sucked the joy out of everything around her, and it was so difficult to be in her company for any length of time without it rubbing off somehow.

As Gabriel pulled on to their drive, he was yawning loudly. They were both shattered. The day had been a very long and stressful one, and they had both had no sleep the night before.

Diana had a bad feeling about the latest events and she couldn't shake it off. There was something she was missing, and she just could not put her finger on it. Lorna and her usual lunacy had not helped, but what else could they do? Someone had to mind the mad bitch.

As they got out of the car, Gabriel saw something glinting out of the corner of his eye and he instinctively threw himself on top of Diana to protect her, as he had always protected her.

They were both shot in the head at point-blank range.

They didn't stand a chance.

Chapter One Hundred and Thirty-six

Davey had bled to death in the boot of Roy's car and Angus was fuming about it.

Eilish had somehow managed to cut into his carotid artery, and he had bled out in no fucking time. If she had severed it immediately, it would have been evident by the blood pumping out and spraying everywhere, like a sprinkler system on a well-manicured lawn. So not only did he not have the satisfaction of torturing the treacherous cunt, he also couldn't ask him who had been behind the shootings.

His mother had given him a few ideas, and he had been looking forward to matching those up with the names that Davey would have provided, if his daughter had not seen fit to glass the ponce – the so-called love of her fucking life – at the last minute.

He shook his head in anger. 'Typical fucking woman, eh, Roy? She had to get her ten pence in first, and now we are no better off than we were before.'

They were on a smallholding in Essex, by the marshes, that had been abandoned years before. It stood in seven acres and it had no near neighbours anywhere, so it was the perfect site for what they wanted. There was a roughcast bungalow on the land and numerous outbuildings, all in different states of disrepair. It was owned by an old friend who was quite happy to let them use it, provided they cleaned up after themselves.

Angus began to punch the dead body of Davey Proctor, over and over again, in his anger and frustration.

Roy pulled him away from the body roughly. 'For fuck's sake, Angus, what are you doing?'

Angus pulled away from him, shouting angrily. 'What the fuck do you care? He's already dead.'

They both started to laugh then at the absurdity of it all, and they were still laughing heartily when the first bullet hit Angus in the face.

As Angus dropped to the floor, Roy turned and felt the impact as a bullet slammed into his face. Unlike Angus, he didn't die instantly and, as he lay on the filthy floor, he felt the cold steel of a gun being pushed against his temple.

He knew that it was finally all over for them.

His last thought was that they had had a fucking good run.

Chapter One Hundred and Thirty-seven

Eilish was devastated to learn from Sky News that her grand-mother and Gabriel had been shot down in cold blood by an unknown gunman.

She desperately tried to contact Roy, because she knew that he had a mobile – unlike her father, who didn't trust technology. She rang Sean, who was still at the lap-dancing club, trying to make sense of all the carnage.

He told her that he'd just heard the news and he would be with her as soon as possible. 'Have you spoken to Dad, Eilish?'

She started to cry again. 'I told you, I can't get hold of Roy. His phone just keeps ringing.'

Sean tried to reassure her. 'All right, darling, calm down. I will be with you as soon as I can, OK?'

He ended the call, and she wiped her eyes and wondered who could possibly want her granny dead. This had to be a part of what had happened earlier, a part of something much bigger. She should have seen it coming – in fact, they all should have. She hoped that her dad found out everything from Davey, so they would at least know who and what they were dealing with.

Eilish looked down at her beautiful hardwood floor, and she once again busied herself scrubbing away the blood left by Davey Proctor. She was glad that she had left her mark on him now, especially if he had been involved in her granny's murder too. The news had said that her grandmother and Gabriel had been killed, execution style, and they were calling it a gangland hit. They were also adding the murders in the club into the mix. Diana was, according to Sky News, 'The Mother of Gangland Boss and King of the Club Scene Angus Davis'.

Her father would be so angry about his mother's death being publicly disrespected like that. Her granny had been wonderful to her all her life and, even though she had heard all the stories about her, she didn't care, because she had always been just her granny, and she had loved her dearly. She knew that she was like her, and she loved it when people pointed that out. It pleased her to know that she shared so much with such a dynamic woman – a woman who had been ahead of her time, and who had broken down barriers by making herself a force to be reckoned with in a world where women had been seen as no more than wives or girlfriends or mistresses.

Her granny had been a ruthless enemy, and a respected businesswoman, in the days long before fucking feminists and women's lib. Eilish wanted to be like her in every way, and she had already started to make a name for herself in their world by emulating her and remembering everything her granny had taught her. She could be as ruthless as needed; she had proved that again today. She had served up Davey Proctor, the love of her life, the father of her unborn child, without a second's thought, once she had realised what a fucking snide he really was. She had told her father as soon as she had known the truth, and she had waited patiently for him to come and take the piece of shit away.

She was crying again because the Sky News reporters were still outside her grandmother's house, and she had such wonderful memories of being there. The camera was static and just showing the front of the property while the presenter talked complete bollocks. She knew that if her granny was here, she would be saying sarcastically, 'Fiver says they will have a picture of the fucking Krays up in a minute, because they've got fuck-all else to talk about.'

She had always known her worth, and she had earned it honestly.

Eilish was going to do exactly the same.

Chapter One Hundred and Thirty-eight

Sean pulled up outside his sister's flat, and the first thing he noticed was Davey Proctor's brand-new Mercedes Sport sitting there like a beacon.

He would have to get rid of that fucking thing, sooner rather than later. It was an eye-catching motor, which of course suited a cunt like Davey Proctor right down to the ground.

He made a quick call and arranged for the offending vehicle to be taken away and left in one of the long-stay car parks at Heathrow Airport. At least that way his sister would eventually get it back. He knew that it was registered to the club, so it wasn't as if the wanker had actually owned it.

He buzzed himself in and made his way up to his sister's flat.

All he kept thinking was, what a fucking mad few days. And if he knew anything, they weren't over yet.

Chapter One Hundred and Thirty-nine

A woman walking her two pugs found the bodies of Angus and Roy.

It turned out that she had driven out to the marshes, as she sometimes did, and had let the dogs off their leads. They had run off as usual, and she had been alerted that something was amiss by their incessant barking.

When she finally caught up with them she had understood the cause of their panic.

Two dead bodies.

Even as a lay person, she knew neither of them had come to what might be classed 'a natural end'. It had taken her mind a few seconds to process what she was actually seeing.

It was bloody carnage.

She had been forced to drive over a mile just to get a signal on her mobile phone so she could finally alert the authorities.

She had been shaking like a leaf the whole time. Seeing the blood all over her pugs' coats, because they had been investigating their find, made her feel physically sick.

The police had been wonderful though. But she regretted ever finding this place where she'd thought her dogs could run in peace and tranquillity and she could enjoy the solitude of the early morning, before she had to set out on her busy day.

Chapter One Hundred and Forty

Eilish was still in shock at the news of their father's death.

He had been executed, the same as his mother and Gabriel. Roy had been killed with him, and Davey had been found in the boot of the car, though it seemed that he had bled to death.

How could such a huge catastrophe have happened to them in such a short space of time? That they had all been executed so ruthlessly was bad enough, but knowing that whoever had been behind it had planned it down to the last detail frightened Eilish. She was convinced that she and Sean would be next. Whoever had been behind this was determined to make sure that the Davis family were completely wiped out.

Sean seemed to believe that his grandmother and his father had been taken out because of their strong ties to Abad and his businesses. As he kept trying to convince her, if anything was going to happen to them, it would have happened at the same time as it had to everyone else.

He argued that bringing in Hamid Fazilla had been the last straw for someone interested in their business, because the people concerned had obviously wanted Abad's contacts and access, and it had looked like he was giving them to someone else. Whoever these fuckers were – and he vowed to his sister that he would find them – they were just cleaning house. And in reality, Angus would have done exactly the same in their position.

Now that Diana and Angus Davis were out of the way, along with poor Abad and everyone else, they didn't need to come after anyone else in the family. Eilish could see his logic, but she still had a feeling that something didn't add up. As Diana always said to her, people only did to you what you let them.

The police had offered her a 'detail', as they called it, meaning two PCs in a panda car sitting outside her flat. She had refused it with the scorn it deserved. She had already engaged her own security, and she felt much safer knowing that they were watching her back as opposed to two fucking plods. She had more faith in the fucking journalists who were camped out like eco warriors and weren't half as well dressed.

She had to sit and wait and think things through, until everything started to make sense.

Chapter One Hundred and Forty-one

As she drove through the gates of her childhood home, Eilish felt the usual feeling of depression wash over her. But she had to see her mother, there was no excuse not to. At the end of the day, Lorna had been married to her father for a long time.

They still couldn't bury anyone because of the ongoing inquiries, and that annoyed her. She couldn't bear to think of her flesh and blood lying in a mortuary, like sides of fucking beef, until the police in their infinite wisdom allowed their carcasses to be released. The only ray of light right now was that it looked like Mariah might pull through, though she wasn't talking yet.

She couldn't help but see the irony of her mother's security men that her father had arranged, not just because he was a Face but because his wife was a fucking grade-A lunatic. If only they had understood, as kids, that the things she had told them and expected from them had been the ramblings of a deranged mind. She knew that her father and grandmother had always protected them when Lorna had been on her more manic episodes, and that was when they had been grateful for the company of their grandmother and the stability she had given them.

Lorna came out of the front door and waited on the drive for her daughter to walk over to her.

'Hi, Mum. How are you feeling?' Eilish attempted a smile but she felt heartbroken.

Lorna, though, grinned widely – that manic grin that told anyone who knew her well that she was teetering once more on the edges of madness.

'I'm good, Eilish, never felt better.'

Eilish closed her eyes and took a few deep breaths to stem her anger and the retort she wanted to give. She followed her mother into the house and, in the kitchen, she accepted a glass of white wine. She knew it was never a good sign when her mother drank. It meant she was off her exercise and diet regime, and that meant that she wasn't taking her meds. It was a vicious circle.

When she thought now of how Lorna had made them all run for hours around their land, or made them cram for exams until they were ready to drop, she felt such anger and resentment – and not just at her mother but also her father, because he should have done something about it, a lot sooner than he had. He should have listened to his mother, who had tried to be a constant in her grandchildren's lives. Even though she had been insulted and pushed away by Lorna, she had just kept in there, no matter what, so that she could still see them all.

She wondered why Diana hadn't just outed the fucker and been done with it. After all, no one could have blamed her. She knew that her father loved her mother, and that he loved them all too. Unfortunately, that had not been enough in the long run. The damage had been done, and he was as much to blame as her mother – if not more, if you listened to Sean.

Eilish sipped her wine elegantly. 'We need to start thinking about the funerals, Mum.'

Lorna nodded. 'If you say so, love.'

Eilish forced a smile she didn't think she had in her. 'Well, do you want to come with me and Sean to choose the coffins and plan the services?'

Lorna sipped her wine quickly. In reality, she was gulping it, and they both knew that. But like so much in this family, no one would say it out loud. Lorna was staring out over the gardens and Eilish could see she was already far away from her and reality.

'Mum, did you hear me?'

Lorna put her wine glass down. 'To be totally honest, Eilish, I think you and Sean should be in charge of that. Because, you know me, I'll get it all wrong.'

'It's your husband's funeral, Mum. Surely you must want to be a part of that? You were together for years, and you loved each other so much.'

Lorna looked at her daughter and she said honestly, 'Truthfully, Eilish, I don't know what you want from me. Angus is dead and that's sad, I know, but you also know that I'm not capable of arranging funerals and things like that. I really don't care, love. I don't care about anything any more. You do it with Sean and send a car, and I will go. I promise I will pay my final respects. But truth be told, I feel nothing, darling. There was a time when I would have killed for that man, but that was long ago.'

Eilish remembered how much her father had loved her mother, even when she was mad as the March Hare. He had stood by her, through thick and thin, no matter what she had done. It seemed that, now she knew he was gone, she had relegated him to the back of her mind, as she did with anything that she didn't like to think about or dwell on.

'And I certainly don't care about his mother's funeral. I am glad she's dead. She was a horrible woman. She never wanted my Angus to marry me, you know. But he did, and we showed her.'

Eilish sighed as her mother rewrote history and, picking up her handbag, she kissed her mum lightly on her cheek. She was aware of Lorna pulling away from her, as if she carried a disease of some kind.

'I have to go now, because I have an appointment, but I will let you know the details of Dad's funeral, OK?'

Lorna grinned again. 'Well, if you're sure.'

Eilish walked out of the house and she didn't look back, because she knew it would be a waste of her time.

Lorna was finally where she wanted to be, in a world of her own creation.

Chapter One Hundred and Forty-two

Eilish and Sean were standing together outside the church. The coffins had been there overnight, and the requiem mass would be well attended. Roy's and Gabriel's funerals had already been taken care of by their respective families.

Sean had made sure that the Filth had not been allowed inside the church, and he had also made sure that any would-be gangster who wasn't known personally to them had been forcibly refused entrance. So today all those who weren't friends or associates had the sense to stay outside. They could still be a part of it, but they would not be allowed to gate-crash the ceremony. This was a funeral, and it would be conducted with respect and with grace.

The security were all professionals, ex-army for the most part, and well dressed in appropriate dark suits. They had been warned to keep as low a profile as possible. Every real Face, from London to Glasgow, was already there and, like her brother Sean, Eilish was pleased to see them turn out to pay their respects. She knew that they were there for the right reasons, and they were grateful that they didn't have to deal with the plastic gangsters and hangers-on that these occasions seemed to attract.

Eilish was aware that the TV crews were even more pleased to see them, but she knew she mustn't allow herself to dwell on

414

that, because there was nothing that she could do about any of it. This was a fact of life and, as her father had courted certain newspapers to promote his image, she knew she couldn't object now. Plus her father would have loved it.

'She's cutting it fine.'

Eilish hooked her brother's arm in hers and squeezed it tightly. 'Come on, Sean, you know what she's like. I promise you, she will be here.' If it was left to her brother, her mother wouldn't be given houseroom.

Jamie Thomas and Jamilla came up to them both and shook their hands gently. 'This is a fucking sad day.' Jamie had never once blamed them for what Angus Junior had done to their daughter. Jamilla kissed and hugged them both tightly, before they walked into the church.

Through their brother Angus, they now shared blood, and that had meant a lot to their father and Jamie Thomas. Eilish wondered, at times, at the twisted logic of the world they all inhabited, even though she actually understood it.

Sean looked handsome in his bespoke suit, and she looked good too – she had made sure of that. They looked every inch the heads of a successful family. Everyone here believed that all these deaths had been because of Abad and his business dealings, and they were waiting to see how, and when, they would retaliate.

Lorna's limousine pulled up to the kerb, and one of the security men rushed to open the door for her. She emerged from the car in full funeral mode and she looked spectacular. After her mother's hysterical ramblings on the phone last night, Eilish had talked her through every aspect of her outfit, from her tailored black suit and high-heeled Jimmy Choos to her professionally applied make-up and hair; now she looked the epitome of a woman who would have been married to a man

415

like Angus Davis. She was also on her meds, and that was the main thing.

Eilish saw the relief in her brother's eyes and knew exactly how he felt.

'You all right, Mum?'

Lorna looked at her two children and smiled brokenly. 'To think we would live to see this day.' Then she put an arm around each of them and, walking them into the church, she said sadly, 'He was the love of my life, and I was the love of his, and nothing can ever change that.'

Sean took his mother's hand. 'You look beautiful. Dad would have been proud of you.'

Lorna basked in the compliment and, wiping a tear from her eye, they walked together down the aisle and, as they all genu-flected before the Cross of Christ, Eilish knew that these two burials were going to go off perfectly.

No one had told Lorna that her husband, Angus, and his mother, Diana, were to be laid together, side by side. Eilish decided she would cross that particular bridge when they came to it. But it was what her father and his mother had specifically requested in their wills.

What had amazed her was that they had been far more attached than any of them had ever realised. They had a bond that even her mother couldn't quite break, and God Himself knew she had tried.

She knelt down and prayed to God with everyone else in the church, and as the service progressed she knew that they had done her father and her grandmother proud. She couldn't take her eyes off one of the photographs of her father and his mother laughing together, when he had been just a teenager. They were holding each other tightly and looking at each other with such love and affection, it brought a lump to her throat. They both looked so young and so carefree, and she knew that there had always been a genuine love between them, no matter what.

The priest was talking about her father now, and reminiscing about him and his mother, and the times he had spent with them. He talked about her grandfather's funeral and how hard his death had hit not just Diana but also his only son, who had been far too young to lose a father. When her mother was called up to the altar to give her eulogy, Eilish followed with her brother Sean and, though it looked to everyone like a family sticking together on such a sad day, they knew they were there to police their mother, because she just couldn't be fucking trusted.

Lorna looked out over the packed church in Ilford, at the familiar faces that she had known all her life, in one way or another. She looked at the two coffins that were resting side by side, covered in flowers and photographs of the two people they held. She saw a photograph of Angus, Diana and herself. She was holding Angus Junior in her arms, and they all looked so happy, and she knew that was because, at that moment, they were. None of them had known what the future held for them. How could they? You live for the moment, because that is all you can do.

'Angus was a wonderful man – a wonderful father, husband and son. He lived for his family, and I was blessed to be his wife. He was a man who was loyal and trustworthy in everything he did, from his family life to his businesses, and his innate decency was such that he was sometimes forced to make decisions that a lesser man would have done everything in his power to avoid.'

She looked at Jamie and Jamilla Thomas as she spoke, and everyone knew what she was alluding to and admired her for her honesty, as they had all admired Angus for his actions.

'His mother, Diana, was of the same ilk. She was a woman to

aspire to, a woman who taught her son the decency and the loyalty that made him into the man he was. I will miss them both, especially my husband, Angus, the father of my children and the love of my life. In truth, he was my first and my only love.'

She walked back to her seat with dignity, and Eilish accompanied her, breathing a sigh of relief. She knew the next person to speak was her brother Sean. She was relaxed now, looking forward to hearing what he had to say because as quiet as he was, he was a natural raconteur, and he could be hilarious when the fancy took him. She watched as he opened his suit jacket and took out his speech, and she smiled. She had known that he would have come prepared and written down some stories and memories he could recount.

She wasn't disappointed. Sean talked about his father and grandmother with such reverence and love. He also told stories about them both. Some were the stuff of local legend – stories that had been circulating about the family for years and had no actual basis in fact – but he made everyone laugh as he had regaled everyone with his father's and grandmother's take on them. He then told a few true stories about them as a family, and he made everyone laugh again, and then he made them think as he reminded them all of the two special people they had come to mourn.

Eilish and Lorna held hands as they listened to Sean, and they both laughed in all the right places. When he came back to the pew, he sat down heavily and Eilish knew that he was relieved to have got his eulogy over with. She could understand that. It was why she had not stood up to say anything, or even do a reading.

She grabbed his hand and squeezed it tightly. 'That was beautiful.'

They took Communion with Lorna and prayed for the repose

of the souls of Diana and Angus. Everyone said it had been a beautiful service, and it had.

Sean was there to help carry his father's coffin to the graveside, and beside him was Jamie Thomas and other long-time friends, Tommy Becks, Geoffrey Pole and Jonny Coleman. Diana's coffin was carried out by men who had worked for her in the past and who had been friends with her for many years. Eilish had been surprised at how many had come forward to offer their services, but she knew that her grandmother had made friends with people whenever possible. She believed that friends were always of more value than enemies, and much easier to control.

Diana Davis had taught her well, and Eilish would always be thankful for that.

Chapter One Hundred and Forty-three

Eilish and Jamie Thomas were both tired as it had been a long week. But, on the plus side, it had been a very productive one.

Eilish poured them both a brandy and Jamie took his and swallowed it down in one gulp.

He laughed at her. 'You call that a brandy, girl?'

She refilled his glass, making sure it was a decent measure.

'You sure you're feeling OK?'

She nodded and grinned. 'I feel good. Stop worrying, will you?'

Jamie shrugged. He believed her; she had inherited the same attitude that Angus and Diana had both possessed. She was as cool as a cucumber, and he couldn't help but admire her for that. It took some doing, especially when you were in a dangerous situation like this.

'He's late.'

Eilish sipped her brandy. 'He'll be here, don't worry. He wants to know the score.'

Eilish looked around the office and remembered being here with her father. She had loved it. She had always felt the excitement of being in Soho, and she had never forgotten it. It was the first time in her life she had ever really felt alive.

'I can do this alone, you know? You don't have to be here.'

Eilish loved Jamie for looking out for her, but she didn't need him or anyone else to do that. She was more than capable of sorting things out for herself. 'You sound like Sean. He still thinks I can't hack it.'

Jamie Thomas knew when to let things lie. That was one of his better qualities, according to Jamilla. But both could feel the atmosphere thickening as the minutes ticked by. Eilish sipped her brandy and kept her breathing steady. This was a big night, and she wasn't going to blow it.

When the internal desk phone finally rang, they both jumped and that broke the spell.

Laughing nervously, Eilish answered it. 'They are here.'

Jamie Thomas swallowed down the remains of his brandy.

Eilish placed her own glass down on the desk. 'Let's get this fucking show on the road, shall we?'

Chapter One Hundred and Forty-four

Ricky Manners was one of Jamie Thomas's best workers. He was also his nephew and, as Jamie had known him since birth, he trusted him with his life. He was one of his Jamaican crew, so his face wasn't that well known in London, though he had been angling for a spot here for a few years – and, in all honesty, Jamie couldn't blame him.

Jamaica was too small, so once you hit the heights you had two options open to you. Either America – generally New York – or London. London was often the preferred option, for a variety of reasons. Mainly the prison sentences, because they were mostly much easier and lighter than the US courts dealt out, and also because London was the gateway to Europe, and that meant it was easier to get lost, should the need arise.

Ricky Manners was determined to prove himself to his uncle and get himself a place in London, and he knew that if he worked hard enough – and showed not just willing but acumen – he could go places. He had brought two of his most trusted workers with him, to make sure that this went down with the minimum of fuss. He wasn't taking any chances; he was going to see this through, or die fucking trying.

He was sitting on a black leather sofa in a private room inside the lap-dancing club, and his two friends were both positioned by the bar. He had thought this through to the last detail.

He stood up quickly when his uncle walked into the room with the woman that he was doing business with. She was a looker all right, and he had heard from more than one person that she wasn't to be taken lightly. He was willing to believe that, until someone told him different.

'You ready?'

Ricky nodded confidently.

Eilish went behind the bar and started pouring drinks. Jamie Thomas sat down on the sofa, and Ricky joined him. The two men at the bar accepted their drinks quietly and Eilish was impressed when they didn't touch them, just left them on the bar.

When Sean walked in with Jack Barker, he was all smiles and camaraderie. He was entertaining a business partner, and that was something that he did well, even though Eilish knew that he didn't really enjoy it. But it was part of the game. He smiled at his sister and then shook hands with Jamie Thomas before he introduced Jack Barker to everyone.

Jack Barker was a bad man, and everyone who had ever had any dealings with him knew that. He wasn't tall – he was only five feet eight – but he was strong and wiry, and he could fight like a pit bull on amphetamines. He always won, even against men twice his size, because Jack Barker loved a good fight. He instinctively knew how to, and that, coupled with his determination to win, no matter what, made him a very formidable opponent.

He was also as straight as the proverbial die, and he treasured his reputation as not just a fucking hard bastard but as a man who was known to be honest in business, a man who could be trusted. His word was his bond, and if he shook hands on a deal it was as good as a written contract. In Barlinnie he had earned the nickname the 'Scourge of Glasgow', and he was proud of it. He was the main dealer in Scotland as a whole, and no one shifted anything of any real weight without his express say-so.

Diana Davis had given him the money to bankroll his first proper deal, and she had continued to bankroll him until he had got on his feet. She had believed in him, and he would never forget that, because without her and her help he would never have got anywhere. She had been given seven per cent of everything he had ever shifted, and he had never begrudged her a fucking penny of it.

Sean was smiling and chatting with Ricky Manners and Jamie Thomas. He loved setting up deals, and he had a feeling that this deal would be a match made in heaven.

Jack Barker went to the bar and kissed Eilish on the cheek. 'You have a look of Diana, you know. She was a beautiful woman in her day.'

Eilish grinned. She had heard that all her life.

The door opened and Les Carter slipped into the room. Angus Davis had never let him get past running a few bookies or chasing up debts, but Sean seemed to think that he was worth nurturing, for some reason. Les Carter looked like what he was: a wide boy who looked out for the main chance and who couldn't work out a two-quid bet without taking his shoes and socks off. Sean welcomed him like the prodigal son and started to introduce him to everyone.

Eilish suddenly turned the music up.

Ricky Manners brought out a large knife from inside his jacket, and his two friends followed suit.

Sean looked at the three men and he was actually smiling. Eilish knew that he was assuming that Jack Barker had to be the recipient.

When Jack and Jamie went to the bar and picked up their drinks, Eilish saw the complete and utter shock-horror on her brother's face as he realised that he had been well and truly rumbled. He looked into her eyes, and she shrugged nonchalantly.

Then, walking over to him, she shook her head in disgust and disbelief. 'You honestly thought I wouldn't work out that it was you?'

Sean pulled himself up to full height as he bellowed, 'I can't believe you would even think that—'

Eilish laughed.

There was nowhere for him to run, and he knew it. He was finally finding out what it was like to be betrayed by your own, by the people who you should be able to trust.

'I worked out that there were only two people who could have been responsible for that night's fucking work. And I was one of them.'

She walked away from him, and Jamie nodded his head and watched as Ricky and his cohorts did what had been requested.

In fairness, Jamie had to admit that it was a quick and professional job.

Stabbed straight through the heart, with the minimum of fuss.

He was impressed.

Jack Barker, who had been brought in to add credibility to the meeting – so Sean would think that he was brokering a deal that he could earn off, hugged Eilish to him tightly. 'You are Diana's blood all right, she would have done exactly the same.'

425

Eilish hugged him back. 'I know.'

Jamie Thomas looked down at Sean, a lad he had known all his life, and wondered at how poor Angus could have sired two fucking pieces of shite. He looked at Eilish and was pleased to see that she wasn't regretting her brother's death.

'Why don't you and Jack go out and have a meal or a few drinks? Go to one of the other clubs and leave this mess, I will sort it.'

Jack Barker took her arm and walked her out of the room, where the music was still loud and her brother was lying dead, with a surprised expression on his face.

Epilogue

2019

Fortune assists the bold.

Aeneid,
Virgil (70–19BC)

Eilish poured herself a cup of coffee and took it outside into the sun. She sat down on the garden furniture and, lighting a cigarette, she gazed at the landscape, enjoying the peace and quiet.

She loved the early mornings, especially when the weather was good, because that was when this house really came to life. She was on her second cup of coffee when she heard Alia come into the kitchen, and she called out, 'Morning, lady.'

Alia poured herself a coffee and, lacing it liberally with sugar and milk, she came out to join her aunt in the garden, as she always did.

'What a beautiful morning again!'

Alia was nearly twelve now. She was a nice child, and she was also showing every sign of becoming a stunning-looking woman. Having lost her baby, Eilish loved her niece like her own child, and they were very close. She knew that Alia loved her dearly.

'I don't want to go home today. I know that sounds horrible, but I don't mean it to be. I prefer being with you.'

Eilish knew she meant what she was saying, and she wished she could grant her wish, but she couldn't. 'Oh, come on, you will be back here before you know it. Anyway, your Mammy Jamilla will be champing at the bit to see you.'

Alia didn't argue, because she knew what Eilish said was true. She loved her Mammy Jamilla and her Granddad Jamie. But if she could choose where she could live all the time, she would pick here.

'Auntie Eilish, can I tell you something?'

Eilish laughed delightedly. Alia was a real busybody.

'Of course you can, darling.'

Alia sat looking at her aunt for a few moments and Eilish was, as always, stunned by the child's blue eyes and jet-black hair. It was like a raven's wing and, coupled with her coffee-coloured skin, the girl wasn't just attractive, she was downright beautiful. She was unusual, and Eilish would lay out good money that there wasn't another child like her within ten thousand miles. She was absolutely gorgeous. She had her father's eyes. But then they all had the Irish Davis eyes, they had inherited them from Diana.

'I know that Carly is my real mum.'

Eilish didn't say anything, because she didn't want to put her foot in it. This was something that Carly and Jamilla should talk to her about, it just wasn't her place.

Alia carried on talking. 'My friend Brianna told me. She said that she heard her mum talking about it.'

Eilish was suddenly wondering where Brianna lived, and what her mum would do when she turned up on her doorstep. Fucking gossiping bitch, without a thought for what her prattle might cause!

'But before she said anything, I had sort of guessed.'

Eilish lit another cigarette, before saying, 'Explain.'

Alia sipped her coffee and sighed. 'Well, my Mammy Jamilla is with my Granddad Jamie. So that doesn't make sense, does it?'

Eilish could see her logic, but given that her brother had

been the villain of the piece, she couldn't discuss anything of importance before the Thomases had.

'You need to talk to Jamilla about this, darling. It's really not something I can help you with.'

Alia didn't say anything for a while so they sat together, as they had many times before, in companionable silence.

'Your brother was my father, wasn't he? That's why you are my aunt and your mum is my Nanny Lorna.'

Eilish felt sick at the thought of this wonderful child finding out the truth of her parentage and, even worse, hearing how she had been brought into the world.

'Like I say, you need to talk to Jamilla, it's really not my place to discuss any of this. I'm so sorry, darling.'

'OK, Auntie Eilish.'

Alia accepted her explanation, and Eilish could feel herself relaxing. She would just have to ring Jamilla and warn her that Alia had worked it all out.

'What do you want to do today, Alia?'

Alia smiled and Eilish knew what she wanted.

'In the swimming pool again! Well, I can cope with that.'

Alia looked at her with such happiness and honesty as she said, 'It must have been wonderful to grow up in this house. You were all so lucky.'

Eilish didn't answer her.

'Do you miss your brothers?'

Eilish stood up, saying chirpily, 'Come on, madam, go and grab a shower while I make us some breakfast. How do you fancy bacon and eggs?'

Alia jumped up excitedly. 'My favourite, thank you!'

Eilish watched her as she skipped through the kitchen, her only thought now being what she was having for breakfast.

Eilish looked around her and sighed. She had moved back here because she'd had to. Her mother had needed her, and she had felt she should be there for her, especially after Sean. Now, though, she actually liked spending time here, especially when Alia came.

Jamilla would not allow Alia to see Lorna unless Eilish was there, and that had pretty much started a pattern. Her mother was once more away, having treatment. As the time went on, her mother seemed to spend more and more time in hospital, and the meds she needed were having less and less of an effect.

Eilish wondered what life held for her in the future, because she had no one now really of her own, except Alia. She was her only blood relative, after her mother.

She ran the businesses with an iron hand and she knew that she was respected because of that. She also knew that she quite liked her solitary life. She took a flier occasionally with a good-looking bloke and that just added to her reputation as a ball breaker.

Her life wasn't for everyone, but she found that it suited her. She had discovered early on that you couldn't trust anyone really, because eventually everyone you thought you could trust let you down.

She went into the kitchen to start the breakfast. She felt happy enough with her life and what she had achieved. As long as she had Alia nearby, she knew she would be OK. She would spend her life making up to that child for what her brother had done, and she was quite happy to do that. She wondered, at times, how both of her brothers had been capable of such treachery and corruption and betrayal. Angus was a rapist, and then her brother Sean had been capable of murdering his father and his grandmother for his own gain.

She pushed the thoughts from her mind, because it was futile to dwell on them. She had had enough sleepless nights, trying to make sense of it, even after all these years. Instead, she would concentrate on Alia and she would make sure that child had every opportunity she could afford her. Alia would live a life that was not tainted by her past, as hers was. She would make sure that something good would finally come out of this.

It was the only thing she could do.

Eilish put on the radio and, as she cooked the breakfast, she found herself singing along to Madonna. And, by the time Alia came back downstairs, she was actually in a good mood.